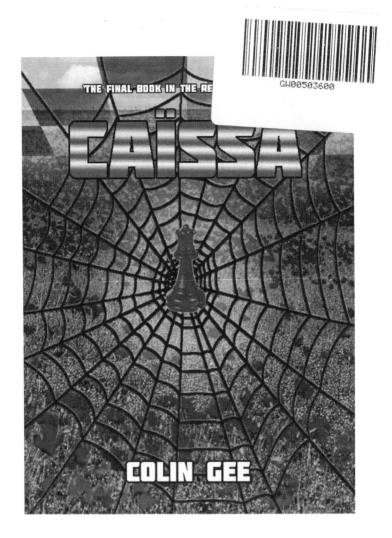

CAÏSSA

WRITTEN BY COLIN GEE

**The Eighth and last book in the 'Red Gambit' series.
5th April 1947 to 5th October 1947…
…and beyond.**

1

ISBN-13: 978-1974195039
ISBN-10: 1974195031

Front cover - Wiltshire Poppy field cover picture courtesy of Roo Cooper Photography.
https://www.roocooperphotography.com/
Thank you.

Rear Cover picture - German Military Cemetery in Krakow, Poland.
Own picture.

Series Dedication

The Red Gambit series of books is dedicated to my grandfather, the boss-fellah, Jack 'Chalky' White, Chief Petty Officer [Engine Room] RN, my de facto father until his untimely death from cancer in 1983, and a man who, along with many millions of others, participated in the epic of history that we know as World War Two.

Their efforts and sacrifices made it possible for us to read of it, in freedom, today.

Thank you, for everything.

Book dedication

Throughout this series, my dedications have, in the main, reflected my love of military history and my admiration for those who wear the uniform and discharge their duty for their national cause.

However, I could not complete the Red Gambit series without turning in and looking at my own past and service in uniform.

1 served as an operational firefighter for thirty-two years, all of them with Royal Berkshire Fire & Rescue Service, through a number of metamorphoses and name changes.

I retired as a watch commander, or as old school would more readily understand, a sub-officer.

During my service, I met some individuals best consigned to history, but I was privileged to work with many outstanding people.

I saw first-hand, in the most harrowing of circumstances, the British spirit that must have been present at Waterloo, the Somme, and the Blitz.

My career varied and, in truth, ended on less of a high than it should have.

Stress and other health issues took their toll towards the end, and I was less than I could, and should, have been, certainly much less than I promised to be in March 1991.

That month my life changed through circumstances beyond my control.

None the less, despite the numerous downs, the ups of my service will always triumph in my heart, and the memories of comradeship and laughter, togetherness in adversity, and the sharing of the very worst of times with the very best of men, will always be dear to me.

So, thank you to most of my former colleagues, and in general, to the firefighters of the world.

Oh, and yes… I'd do it all over again.

I encourage you to look at the Firefighters Charity, https://www.firefighterscharity.org.uk/ , which is a cause close to my heart. If you can find it in your heart to support the cause, I thank you in advance.

Foreword by author Colin Gee

If this is your first toe dipped in the waters of 'Red Gambit', then I can only advise you to read the previous books when you can.

If you have followed the characters and events of Red Gambit from its start to this point, then you are about to begin the final part of the journey that has recorded the events of World War Three.

This series has grown from the modest plan I first developed into a huge beast well in excess of a million words, and with hundreds of hand drawn illustrations.

It has demanded that I journey around Europe by car for thousands of miles at a time, from Denmark to Lithuania, Hungary to the Czech Republic, and many points in between.

My research allowed me to visit places such as the Wolfschanze and Wormhoudt, Nordhausen and the Chateau de Haute-Kœnigsbourg, the Baltic Islands of Denmark, and the wonderful Schönbrunn Palace in Vienna.

To stand by the river in Barnstorf was an incredible experience.

It is a simple place, with little of note in its history, but not for me.

Firstly, my mind's eye constructed overlays for every view and where I looked at a bridge or piece of ground, I tended also to see a trench, a burning tank, or the fallen.

But there was also the mound upon which I set the Black Watch's demise.

Barnstorf has no record of anything occurring on that spot but I sensed something as I walked over it, be it something historical now lost in the sands of time, or something imagined, as my thoughts galloped ahead to what I would set on its shallow slopes.

However, my deepest memory of the research trips will always be Auschwitz-Birkenau, and if you ever have the chance to go, take it.

It is not an experience to enjoy, but certainly one that you should have, for reasons that will become apparent as you absorb its sights and silence.

I also undertook another journey; the one of transition from someone who can write words to, hopefully, someone who can write books.

I have learned so much along the way and I expect, like many authors, would do things so differently were I to start on this series now but equipped with hindsight.

Simply put, I got some things wrong and had to correct along the way, such as the unit lists amongst other things.

Some things I got right.

For sure, the book covers were one, and my sincere and grateful thanks go to my brother Jason for his skill and expertise in putting my ideas into being.

I believe my concept of character was sound. I decided only to paint the picture to a minimum, or not at all in some cases.

That has meant that each reader has developed his or her own mental picture of the individuals concerned.

I will tell you now that I started this series with the view that I would have a handful of central characters, who would be followed from start to end. They were Crisp, Ramsey, Yarishlov, Stelmakh, Uhlmann, and Lavalle.

Yes, you read that right.

Initially, my plans did not include the two characters that have become the most loved and eagerly awaited in the series; namely Knocke and Nazarbayeva.

Both were to be bit-part players in the overall scheme, but both forced themselves forward to become central to everything I had planned.

It was a clear example of how flexible I needed to be in my writing, for the two quickly became firm favourites in reader's minds, and using them more and more was clearly the correct thing to do.

Finding the right balance has sometimes been difficult. The nature of the combat I write can, I accept, be wearing, and the intricacies of the behind-the-lines plots can sometimes be a little gritty, but I decided early on to stay with what I felt was right.

In short, be hung for my own ideas with no one else to blame.

I firmly believe that sticking to a chronological story line was correct. I think I only departed from that twice overall, and solely to keep the modest drama going.

Creating the maps by hand maintained a standard throughout, although I tweaked a little as I went.

Perhaps, on reflection, the chapter titles were a little too much, but once I was committed to the format, it was there to stay.

I shall learn from that in future books.

I have heard of the dreaded writer's block and don't think it visited itself upon me. I had periods when I simply wanted to step away, often after writing a particularly involved piece of combat. I remember such a week after completing Barnstorf. I remember the draining emotion I felt after finishing the Chateau scene with Haefali and Knocke tending to the Soviet dead.

Overall, I never lacked ideas or the urge to write, but sometimes I just needed to step back and recharge. That was something I was unprepared for; the physical and mental drain of the act of writing.

Red Gambit has been a fantastic journey for me and, when I finally write 'The End', it will be a moment of mixed emotions.

The success of the books has been fantastic, but I started the whole process just for me, and whilst I will be able to know that I have published something that has a certain value and is widely read, I will also be stepping away from a beloved friend with a finality that is unavoidable.

There can be no more Red Gambit.

However, my mind remains fertile and Red Gambit may have 'children' in one shape or another.

So, in ending, thanks to all those who have helped me along the way, in whatever shape or form, and thanks to those who took the step of investing a few of their hard earned pennies in purchasing some of my work.

In closing, I remember the communication I received from a US Army veteran who had just read a scene involving US troops fighting against Soviets. He queried how he could possibly have been cheering on the Red Army, given his previous military service.

Of all the communications I received over the course of writing Red Gambit, that one made me smile and feel content like no other.

A basic aim of my writing was to illustrate that bravery and honour dwell on both sides of the political divide and that *'There are no bad peoples, just some bad people'*.

It appeared I had succeeded in my goal.

Thank you and enjoy this final offering.

Colin Gee ☺

As I did the research for this alternate history series, I often wondered why it was that we, west and east, did not come to blows once more.

We must all give thanks it did not all go badly wrong in that hot summer of 1945, and that the events described in the Red Gambit series did not come to pass.

My profound thanks to all those who have contributed in whatever way to this project, as every little piece of help brought me closer to my goal.

[For additional information, progress reports, orders of battle, discussion, freebies, and interaction with the author please find time to visit and register at one of the following-
www.redgambitseries.com, www.redgambitseries.co.uk, www.redgambitseries.eu
Also, feel free to join Facebook Group 'Red Gambit'.
There is a Facebook page for 'Colin Gee', and other groups set up for each of the books.]
Thank you.

I have received a great deal of assistance in researching, translating, advice, and support during the years that this project has so far run.

In no particular order, I would like to record my thanks to all of the following for their contributions. Gary Wild, Jan Wild, Jason Litchfield, Peter Kellie, Jim Crail, Craig Dressman, Mario Wildenauer, Loren Weaver, Pat Walsh, Keith Lange, Mike Bauer, Philippe Vanhauwermeiren, Elena Schuster, Stilla Fendt, Luitpold Krieger, Mark Lambert, Simon Haines, Carl Jones, Greg Winton, Greg Percival, Robert Prideaux, Tyler Weaver, Giselle Janiszewski, Ella Murray, James Hanebury, Renata Loveridge, Jeffrey Durnford, Brian Proctor, Rosie Wolstenholme, Steve Bailey, Deborah Ratliff, Naomi Cowling, Paul Dryden, Steve Riordan, Bruce Towers, Gary Banner, Victoria Coling, Alexandra Coling, Heather Coling, Isabel Pierce Ward, Hany Hamouda, Ahmed Al-Obeidi, Sharon Shmueli, Danute Bartkiene, and finally BW-UK Gaming Clan.

It is with sadness that I must record the passing of Luitpold Krieger, who succumbed to cancer after a hard fight.

One name is missing on the request of the party involved, who perversely has given me more help and guidance in this project than most, but whose desire to remain in the background on all things means I have to observe his wish not to name him.

None the less, to you, my oldest friend, thank you.

Wikipedia is a wonderful thing and I have used it as my first port of call for much of the research for the series. Use it and support it.

My thanks to the US Army Center of Military History and Franklin D Roosevelt Presidential Library websites for providing the out of copyright images.

Thanks also go to the owners of www.thesubmarinesailor.com, from which site I obtained some of my quotes.

I have also liberally accessed the site www.combinedfleet.com, from where much of my Japanese naval information is sourced.

All map work is original.

The USMC badge was taken from the website http://www.hqmc.marines.mil , for which I thank the site owners.

Particular thanks go to Steen Ammentorp, who is responsible for the wonderful www.generals.dk site, which is a superb place to visit in search of details on generals of all nations. The site has proven invaluable in compiling many of the biographies dealing with the senior officers found in these books.

My thanks to the Helicopter Safety web site of the Flight Safety Foundation for the accident report on ZX-HJH, 4th June 2001.

Finally my thanks go to the members of my special reading group, namely Robert Clarke, James Hanebury, Hannah Richards, Rodger Raubach, Gary Banner, and Mike Bauer, for their support when my nerve failed.

If I have missed anyone or any agency I apologise and promise to rectify the omission at the earliest opportunity.

Author's note.

The correlation between the Allied and Soviet forces is difficult to assess for a number of reasons.

Neither side could claim that their units were all at full strength, and information on the relevant strengths over the period this book is set in is limited as far as the Allies are concerned and relatively non-existent for the Soviet forces.

I have had to use some licence regarding force strengths and I hope that the critics will not be too harsh with me if I get things wrong in that regard. A Soviet Rifle Division could vary in strength from the size of two thousand men to be as high as nine thousand men, and in some special cases could be even more.

Indeed, the very names used do not help the reader to understand unless they are already knowledgeable.

A prime example is the Corps. For the British and US forces, a Corps was a collection of Divisions and Brigades directly subservient to an Army. A Soviet Corps, such as the 2nd Guards Tank Corps, bore no relation to a unit such as British XXX Corps. The 2nd G.T.C. was a Tank Division by another name and this difference in 'naming' continues to the Soviet Army, which was more akin to the Allied Corps.

The Army Group was mirrored by the Soviet Front.

10

Going down from the Corps, the differences continue, where a Russian rifle division should probably be more looked at as the equivalent of a US Infantry regiment or British Infantry Brigade, although this was not always the case. The decision to leave the correct nomenclature in place was made early on. In that, I felt that those who already possess knowledge would not become disillusioned, and that those who were new to the concept could acquire knowledge that would stand them in good stead when reading factual accounts of WW2.

There are also some difficulties encountered with ranks. Some readers may feel that a certain battle would have been left in the command of a more senior rank, and the reverse case where seniors seem to have few forces under their authority. Casualties will have played their part but, particularly in the Soviet Army, seniority and rank was a complicated affair, sometimes with Colonels in charge of Divisions larger than those commanded by a General. It is easier for me to attach a chart to give the reader a rough guide of how the ranks equate.

Also, please remember, that by now attrition has downsized units in all armies.

Fig # 1[rev] - Table of comparative ranks.

	SOVIET UNION	WAFFEN-SS	WEHRMACHT	
1	KA - SOLDIER	SCHUTZE	SCHUTZE	1
2	YEFREYTOR	STURMANN	GEFREITER	2
3	MLADSHIY SERZHANT	ROTTENFUHRER	OBERGEFREITER	3
4	SERZHANT	UNTERSCHARFUHRER	UNTEROFFIZIER	4
5	STARSHIY SERZHANT	OBERSCHARFUHRER	FELDWEBEL	5
6	STARSHINA	STURMSCHARFUHRER	STABSFELDWEBEL	6
7	MLADSHIY LEYTENANT	UNTERSTURMFUHRER	LEUTNANT	7
8	LEYTENANT	OBERSTURMFUHRER	OBERLEUTNANT	8
9	STARSHIY LEYTENANT			9
10	KAPITAN	HAUPTSTURMFUHRER	HAUPTMANN	10
11	MAYOR	STURMBANNFUHRER	MAIOR	11
12	PODPOLKOVNIK	OBERSTURMBANNFUHRER	OBERSTLEUTNANT	12
13	POLKOVNIK	STANDARTENFUHRER	OBERST	13
14	GENERAL-MAYOR	BRIGADEFUHRER	GENERALMAIOR	14
15	GENERAL-LEYTENANT	GRUPPENFUHRER	GENERALLEUTNANT	15
16	GENERAL-POLKOVNIK	OBERGRUPPENFUHRER	GENERAL DER INFANTERIE'	16
17	GENERAL-ARMII	OBERSTGRUPPENFUHRER	GENERALOBERST	17
18	MARSHALL		GENERALFELDMARSCHALL	18
			' OR ARTILLERY, PANZERTRUPPEN ETC	

	UNITED STATES	UK/COMMONWEALTH	FRANCE	
1	PRIVATE	PRIVATE	SOLDAT DEUXIEME CLASSE	1
2	PRIVATE 1ST CLASS	LANCE-CORPORAL	CAPORAL	2
3	CORPORAL	CORPORAL	CAPORAL-CHEF	3
4	SERGEANT	SERGEANT	SERGENT-CHEF	4
5	SERGEANT 1ST CLASS	C.S.M.	ADJUDANT-CHEF	5
6	SERGEANT-MAJOR [WO/CWO]	R.S.M.	MAJOR	6
7	2ND LIEUTENANT	2ND LIEUTENANT	SOUS-LIEUTENANT	7
8	1ST LIEUTENANT	LIEUTENANT	LIEUTENANT	8
9				9
10	CAPTAIN	CAPTAIN	CAPITAINE	10
11	MAJOR	MAJOR	COMMANDANT 1	11
12	LIEUTENANT-COLONEL	LIEUTENANT-COLONEL	LIEUTENANT-COLONEL 2	12
13	COLONEL	COLONEL	COLONEL 3	13
14	BRIGADIER GENERAL	BRIGADIER	GENERAL DE BRIGADE	14
15	MAJOR GENERAL	MAJOR GENERAL	GENERAL DE DIVISION	15
16	LIEUTENANT GENERAL	LIEUTENANT GENERAL	GENERAL DE CORPS D'ARMEE	16
17	GENERAL	GENERAL	GENERAL DE ARMEE	17
18	GENERAL OF THE ARMY	FIELD-MARSHALL	MARECHAL DE FRANCE	18
	1 CAPITAINE de CORVETTE	2 CAPITAINE de FREGATE	3 CAPITAINE de VAISSEAU	

ROUGH GUIDE TO THE RANKS OF COMBATANT NATIONS.

Fig # 1a - List of Military map icons.

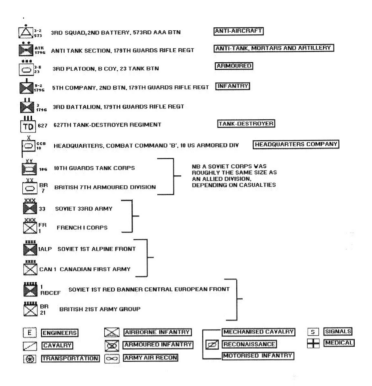

3RD SQUAD, 2ND BATTERY, 573RD AAA BTN   ANTI-AIRCRAFT

ANTI TANK SECTION, 179TH GUARDS RIFLE REGT   ANTI-TANK, MORTARS AND ARTILLERY

3RD PLATOON, B COY, 23 TANK BTN   ARMOURED

5TH COMPANY, 2ND BTN, 179TH GUARDS RIFLE REGT   INFANTRY

3RD BATTALION, 179TH GUARDS RIFLE REGT

627TH TANK-DESTROYER REGIMENT   TANK-DESTROYER

HEADQUARTERS, COMBAT COMMAND 'B', 10 US ARMORED DIV   HEADQUARTERS COMPANY

10TH GUARDS TANK CORPS

BRITISH 7TH ARMOURED DIVISION

NB A SOVIET CORPS WAS
ROUGHLY THE SAME SIZE AS
AN ALLIED DIVISION,
DEPENDING ON CASUALTIES

SOVIET 33RD ARMY

FRENCH I CORPS

1ALP   SOVIET 1ST ALPINE FRONT

CAN 1   CANADIAN FIRST ARMY

RBCEF   SOVIET 1ST RED BANNER CENTRAL EUROPEAN FRONT

BR 21   BRITISH 21ST ARMY GROUP

E   ENGINEERS   AIRBORNE INFANTRY   MECHANISED CAVALRY   S   SIGNALS

CAVALRY   ARMOURED INFANTRY   RECONAISSANCE   MEDICAL

TRANSPORTATION   ARMY AIR RECON   MOTORISED INFANTRY

Table of Contents

15

19

May I remind the reader that his book is written primarily in English, not American English. Therefore, please expect the unashamed use of 'U', such as in honour and armoured, unless I am using the American version to remain true to a character or situation.

By example, I will write the 11th Armoured Division and the 11th US Armored Division, as each is correct in national context.

Where using dialogue, the character uses the correct rank, such as Mayor instead of Major for the Soviet dialogue, or Maior for the German dialogue.

Otherwise, in non-dialogue circumstances, all ranks and units will be in English.

Fig #246 - Important European locations in Caïssa.

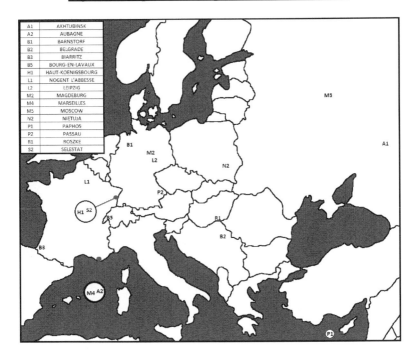

A1	AKHTUBINSK
A2	AUBAGNE
B1	BARNSTORF
B2	BELGRADE
B3	BIARRITZ
B5	BOURG-EN-LAVAUX
H1	HAUT-KOENIGSBOURG
L1	NOGENT L'ABBESSE
L2	LEIPZIG
M2	MAGDEBURG
M4	MARSEILLES
M5	MOSCOW
N2	NIETUJA
P1	PAPHOS
P2	PASSAU
R1	ROSZKE
S2	SELESTAT

Caïssa is a fictional Thracian dryad portrayed as the goddess of chess. [Wikipedia].
You may read into that what you wish.

I am Alpha and Omega, the beginning and the end, the first and the last.

The Book of Revelation - 22:13

CHAPTER 200 - THE CONVERGENCE

1424 hrs, Sunday 6th April 1947, Moscow City Zoo, Moscow, USSR.

It was a zoo of two halves, divided into old and new sections by the Bolshaya Gruzinskaya, a major Moscow thoroughfare.

The Allied contingent had the opportunity to look around and relax as best they could, albeit under the close attention and watchful eyes of a blizzard of uniformed and plain-clothes intelligence officers.

The throng of visitors opened up like a shoal of sardines before sharks as the organised party moved through them, the citizens keen not to get involved with whatever it was necessitated the presence of so many NKVD soldiers, and others besides.

On the road itself, street sellers peddled their wares, from souvenirs to hot food, the latter attracting the attention of a number of the hungrier members of the group.

With a savoury pastry in one hand and a hot sweet tea in the other, Ramsey could only just manage with his briefcase tucked up under his arm.

Helpfully, the closest Soviet observer offered to carry the case but her offer was declined and instead Ramsey offered up the tea and took a firm grip on his case.

It was to be expected, but it didn't stop the NKVD minder trying.

As was his way, Ramsey started to create a problem with his artificial legs, something he did to allow him to separate from the group on occasion, when other more clandestine duties called.

His personal minders remained close at hand, two men and two women, whilst the rest of the group, headed up by the irrepressible Horrocks, completed their journey across the Bolshaya Gruzinskaya and into the newest section of the City Zoo.

Ramsey was ushered to a green painted bench.

He sat down heavily and made a great show of rubbing his thighs.

One of the Allied group decided to stay with him and keep the British officer company.

"Playing up, John?"

"Too bloody right, Miguel. Very sore for some reason."

He continued to rub them as he and the US intelligence officer went through their pre-arranged routine.

"I need to sort the bloody strapping out."

Lieutenant Colonel Miguel de la Santos USMC looked around, seemingly in search of something, but already knowing just where to look.

He pointed dramatically.

"There's a head, John. That'll do, won't it?"

"Just the job, Miguel. Excuse me, Mayor... I need the toilet..."

He pointed to emphasise his words.

The impassive GRU officer simply nodded and moved aside to let Ramsey stand.

Ramsey offered Santos his briefcase for safekeeping.

It was an exquisite touch, designed to disarm the overseers.

Moving in apparent discomfort, Ramsey made his way across to the toilet and placed a few coins in the dish overseen by the fierce looking old woman who tended the spartan facility, and whose words of thanks sounded more like a diesel engine starting up on a cold morning.

The GRU Major stopped Ramsey from entering and sent in his number two, who turfed out the two men he found inside before checking the facility, and emerging to simply nod at his commander.

Ramsey was allowed to enter.

The cubicle's false wall swung open.

"Polkovnik... we meet in the strangest of places."

"General... that we do."

"It was necessary, I'm afraid, and thank you. No briefcase?"

"No... I don't need one."

"But..."

23

He reached down and unclipped his left leg.

Unscrewing the lower calf, he revealed a large cavity that could take a good size roll of A4-sized paper… similar to the large report file that was passed to him.

"What do I have here, General?"

"Vital information that you need to get to your commanders immediately. I vouch fully for its authenticity… and given what it is, you'll need to impress upon them that it's authentic and requires that they act immediately."

"I will tell them, General."

"I came here myself for that reason, and also to explain why… they'll ask you why, Polkovnik."

It was all too cryptic for Ramsey's tastes but he had to accept matters as they were.

"Go on, General."

"Because we don't wish this conflict to escalate to something that can no longer be stopped. There'll shortly be a change in the Motherland's leadership, and when it happens, you'll know that the new leadership are serious people who will do what's necessary to protect our Motherland."

Ramsey had just been handed a momentous piece of intelligence and was fleetingly thrown.

Gathering himself quickly, he reattached his leg.

"I will deliver that message, General."

"Good… now we must hurry or our people'll start to wonder what you are doing. Good luck, Comrade Polkovnik Ramsey."

"And to you, General Nazarbayeva."

The documents were passed through the channels and found themselves in the hands of senior men, who understood that Operation Viking was now more important than ever.

1500 hrs, Sunday, 6th April 1947, office of the Prime Minister, Belgrade, Federal People's Republic of Yugoslavia.

Molotov withdrew his hand, understanding that the handshake had held no warmth or friendship, and that the owner was nothing short of livid with him and his country.

The man opposite had been a Russian prisoner of war between 1915 and 1917, when he had learned to speak Molotov's language.

"Sit, Comrade Molotov."

The Soviet Foreign Minister made himself as comfortable as he could in a deeply upholstered chair that might as well have been lined with broken glass.

"Comrade Prime Minister, may I begin by saying that this present predicament is not of our making. We did no..."

The face opposite remained fixed in anger and resentment, throwing him off his predetermined delivery.

"The Allies attacked us. It was not us that attacked them, not even accidentally or..."

"Or one of your generals acting on his own initiative?"

"No, Comrade, of course not, that would never happen... it's unthinkab..."

"Like they did with the fucking nerve gas?"

Molotov cringed.

"No, Comrade Tito. That was regrettable, but you'll note that we accepted our part in that awful episode. In the matter of this latest round of hostilities, we categorically did not commence any military operations, planned or otherwise, against the Allied forces in Europe."

"Really?"

"Yes, Comrade Prime Minister. I'm here today to present to you our assurances... the personal assurance of Comrade General Secretary Stalin... that the Soviet Union is the victim of aggression in this instance. We did not start this!"

Tito looked to the man on his left, inviting a response.

Aleksandar Ranković, the Minister for Internal Affairs and head of the State Security Administration, passed the required folder without taking his eyes off the squirming Russian, all the time managing to look as malevolent as he could possibly be.

The furious Yugoslav leader opened the folder and read aloud.

25

"I'll just read from the summary… it'll save all of us some fucking time… following our investigations into a number of command levels in the Allied war apparatus, it is the informed opinion of the UDBA that the likelihood of the events of Saturday 15th March 1947 being precipitated by the Allies is virtually nil, the sole indications to the contrary being heightened readiness by Polish and German units, all of which is easily explained by scheduled exercises."

Tito paused and looked at Molotov, who wisely remained silent.

"It is inconceivable that, were the Allies to have planned for such an attack, that they would not have prepared the rest of their forces, that they would not have amassed considerable stocks of ammunition and other supplies, and that it would have been carried out in the wake of the loss of much of their hierarchy in the plane crash on 14th March 1947."

The Yugoslavian leader momentarily lost his place and ran his finger over the paper to help him locate the next piece.

"It is of note that the Allied evidence categorically supports incoming artillery fire and special operations on and behind Allied lines prior to ground action, but that no such evidence exists regarding similar events or units behind the Soviet side of the line."

"It is also noted that Polish and German forces made swift counter-attacks and gained ground. No such advances were made by Soviet units, which is considered remarkable although perhaps understandable, given the logistic situation experienced by the Red Army, as well as their reduced capability caused by serious losses in the last conflict."

Tito closed the folder and sat back, steepling his fingers as he spoke.

"So, not only did you attack the Allies, you did so without anything to show for it… no advances of note… nothing."

Molotov sprang up, bringing everyone in the room to their feet in postures varying from defensive to openly aggressive.

"Calm yourselves!"

Tito's words drew a few responses, but he backed it up with glares at those who seemed reluctant to remove hands from holsters.

He returned his stare to Molotov.

"Comrade Foreign Minister, I'll detain you no longer. You may relay this message to your leadership. On behalf of the Federal People's Republic of Yugoslavia, I officially withdraw our support for the Soviet Union and her allies indefinitely. Any of your forces within our boundaries have forty-eight hours to remove themselves. I will be ordering the volunteer units fighting with the Red Army to act solely defensively and withdraw safely by seventy-two hours from now. To that end, I'll be informing the Allies of the routes my men will take to avoid further loss of Yugoslavian life in this fucking fool's errand of Comrade Stalin's making. I suggest you make peace as quickly as possible… while they're prepared to listen. Good day."

Molotov's mouth hung open, the ability to speak gone in the face of such a monumental statement and dismissal.

Across the table, Prime Minister Tito cocked an eyebrow at him.

"I said good day, Comrade Molotov. You'll be escorted to the airfield."

The silent diplomat and his small entourage were shepherded out of the room, accompanied by a plethora of Yugoslavian security personnel.

Tito relaxed and lit a cigar, enjoying the rich smoke in silence as Ranković poured them both a drink.

"So, Aleksandar… it is done."

They raised their glasses to each other and knocked back the fiery liquid.

Ranković poured another rakija and it tumbled down their throats in an instant.

Tito picked up the phone and sought a connection to Jovanović, the Chief of the General Staff.

The conversation was brief.

"Hello Arso. Initiate the operation immediately… yes… all aspects… what?… really?… fine… make it twelve hours then. And you, Arso."

He replaced the receiver and answered Ranković's enquiring look.

"Arso thinks we need to wait to tell the Allies for twelve hours, not eight. A small point so no drama eh?"

Ranković answered with an inviting inclination of the bottle.

Tito's grin induced a refill.

"And our friends?"

"Friends… is that what they are?"

"Why else would you act on their request, Comrade Tito?"

"That's easy to answer. Because if they succeed we'll still have a socialist ally. If they don't, then we're all fucked."

Ranković laughed.

27

"I'll drink to that!"

The third shot disappeared as easily as those did previously.

"So, I'll tell them that it's all in hand."

"And if it all goes wrong, there's nothing to tie us in with future events in Moscow?"

"Nothing, Comrade... nothing at all. Everything is verbal, nothing is written. Nothing whatsoever."

"Just in case they fuck it all up and our man of steel hangs around."

Ranković nodded sagely.

"Pays to be careful, Comrade. I'll have the message sent immediately."

Belgrade was bathed in sunshine, drawing its citizens out to enjoy the unusually high temperature.

Outside of the Church of St Sava, the pigeons gathered to relieve visitors of the bread they had brought.

The benches contained old and young alike, each with its posse of voracious birds pecking away at the last crumbs, or waiting for a new handful to come their way.

Junior Secretary Kunesova allowed her children to throw their feed to the heaving mass around their feet, and was seemingly oblivious to the old woman who settled besides them.

She was anything but, and leaned across to the bag she had placed a little distance from her.

"Oh, where is the fourth bag of bread?"

"Perhaps you only imagined preparing it, my dear?"

"Perhaps I did, baka."

Code phrases successfully exchanged, the old lady started throwing her bread to the flock, keeping the birds around them now that the two children had exhausted their own supplies.

She lowered her voice and offered the bag to her younger contact, sharing a low laugh and a smile.

"The message is simple, my dear. Confirm to your master that it is done and all will be complete in seventy hours."

28

"I understand, baka."

A further rummage in the bag revealed another bag of bread and so the old woman rose up and moved on to another bench from where she fed a new gathering of hungry birds.

Within forty minutes, Kunesova was back in the Soviet embassy and her message was passed to her husband, the deputy rezident, for forwarding to his superior.

By nine that evening, Khrushchev and his co-conspirators were aware that Yugoslavia had adopted an openly negative stance to all things Soviet, and that Stalin's position was further weakened.

0512 hrs, Monday, 7th April 1947, Canadian coastguard station, Sable Island, Nova Scotia.

He hawked noisily and deposited the phlegm in the snow outside the window, all without removing the binoculars from his eyes.

"They're putting a boat ashore, Billy."

"Fat lot of good may it do 'em, Pierre."

The Quebec-born coastguard hummed his agreement.

Their role was the preservation and protection of life, not to provide spares and repairs for broken radios or engineering facilities for passing vessels.

The blinking lamp from the ship had told of radio difficulties and a problematic engine, or at least that was their understanding of the Morse code message, as transmitted by the operator on board the uninspiringly plain SS Adolf Bertil.

There were four coastguards stationed on Sable Island and they were all scanning the approaching boat with their binoculars, in reality just the light at its prow, which was all they could now see in the darkness that was just starting to lose its struggle against the approaching dawn.

"Best we go greet 'em. Find out a little more about them 'fore we report in. Johnny, don't worry about the official shit…get some coffee going for our guests, eh?"

William Craddock, the senior man, strode off towards the small landing stage, closely followed by the French-Canadian, leaving Johnny behind to contemplate a choice between the official shipping list and the coffee pot.

Had he chosen the former instead of the latter…

Fig # 247 - East coast of North America.

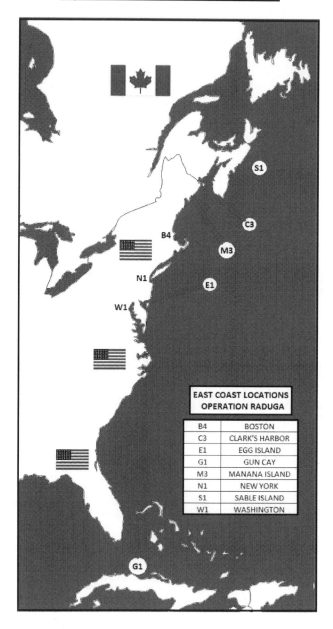

EAST COAST LOCATIONS OPERATION RADUGA	
B4	BOSTON
C3	CLARK'S HARBOR
E1	EGG ISLAND
G1	GUN CAY
M3	MANANA ISLAND
N1	NEW YORK
S1	SABLE ISLAND
W1	WASHINGTON

The coffee tasted good, the thirsty sailor had to concede.

He raised his mug in salute to the man who had made it, although the glassy eyes would never register anything ever again, frozen as they were in a combination of shock, pain, and fear.

Johnny Ballustock's blood still dripped onto the wooden floor, his neck gaping from where the blade had cut deep and ended his life.

In the chair opposite sat the corpse of the fourth member of the Coastguard group, still alive but not long for this world, his heart racing as it struggled to work harder, trying to overcome the blood loss from the gaping chest and throat wounds.

One of the ship's crew finished the task of destroying the radio, just in case they had missed anyone.

Coffee mug drained, the man in charge stood briskly and picked up his weapons and signal lamp.

He stood on the porch of the coastguard hut and directed a simple message towards the waiting ship.

An acknowledgement came and he set the lamp aside.

"You two wait here. Petty Officer… take two men and check the facility at the lake. The rest of you, come with me."

"Hai!"

"Chūsa-san. Signal from the shore party. Mission complete, radio destroyed, further search in progress."

"Thank you, Heisōchō. Carry on."

Commander Hashimata turned to the assembled officers of the Nachi Maru.

"Commence releasing the containers immediately."

"Hai!"

The officers scattered to get the parties organised ready to detach the two huge containers from their hull mounts.

Hashimata would be grateful to be rid of the encumbrances that had plagued the ship from its time in the Soviet port of Odessa all the way to the shores of Sable Island.

31

Not that it particularly mattered, for the rest of his mission required next to no seamanship.

The hull resonated with the blows of sledgehammers as the huge metal struts that held the pair of huge watertight containers in place were prepared for removal, the thick metal pins slowly but surely giving way to the constant blows.

Each container had five such anchor points down a length of just over one hundred feet, each with special mounts on the container itself, there to absorb the flexes and stresses of the voyage.

Trial and error had shown that the outer points should be released first, and they were successfully detached within a second of each other, whilst the upper deck team waited to attach their mooring lines to the special points on the fore, aft, and centre points.

The ship's first officer controlled everything, using the tannoy to issue his orders according to a special script that he followed precisely, ensuring everything was done correctly and in turn.

It took twenty-one minutes to detach the portside container; twenty-three for the starboard, as two of the metal pins were more reluctant to give up their hold.

It was difficult for Hashimata to wait, but wait he did, patiently allowing his men to do their jobs.

The phone shrilled its warning and Warrant Officer Nuiko answered.

"Hai!"

He replaced the phone and came to a stiff, formal attention.

"Daii Goima reports. Containers both at minus forty metres and maintaining horizontal trim. Ready for handover phase on your command."

Hashimata nodded his understanding and came to attention himself.

"Heisōchō Nuiko, initiate handover."

"Hai!"

The Warrant Officer picked up the phone and gave another order.

A below deck party rapped out a simple Morse message on the hull, sending sound waves out into the open sea that, under Hashimata's direct scrutiny, suddenly displayed all the hallmarks of a submarine's periscope.

'Good... the Russians are ready...'

During the planning stage, this had always been the time that had attracted most concern, and given that the vessels had negotiated the Dardanelles, Gibraltar, and the North Atlantic, that was saying something.

It was conducted as close to Sable Island as possible, despite the additional risks and potential interaction with those ashore, solely to derive every benefit from the shoreline's protection from the elements.

The operation to transfer the containers was relatively simple and required the submarine to take station ahead of the Nachi Maru, as the Adolf Bertil had once been known.

The disguised Japanese vessel would then reverse engines and leave the containers in place, whilst a boat's crew transferred the newly-attached hauling cables to the waiting submarine, which had special attachment points on her stern, well-positioned and designed, in order to prevent any possible fouling of the side-mounted propellers.

'Soviet Initsiativa' was exposed and helpless as she gently reversed towards the waiting launch, a state of affairs that Kalinin hated with a passion, but not quite as much as those below decks in the type-XXI, for whom any minute spent on the surface equalled a lifetime of worry and fear.

The manoeuvre had been well-rehearsed, although not with an Atlantic swell to contend with.

However, the operation went fantastically well, bringing cries of joy and relief from the bridge crew as the rear deck officer raised his arm to indicate that the containers' hauling lines were now successfully attached, and again when a second signal confirmed that the extremely important electrical control wires were joined into the hull mounting and made ready for submerging.

Kalinin spoke into the intercom.

"Initiate circuit check on both command systems."

Below one of the NCOs flicked a test switch and replied positively.

Despite the risk, Kalinin had insisted on a full check of both systems and, back on deck, his second in command stepped forward and examined both with studied care, even as the men around him cast their gaze into the sky, seeking out any risk, hoping not to find the tell-tale speck that would mark the end of their project, and themselves.

A second arm was raised.

"Initiate second circuit check on both command systems."

Again the results were satisfactory.

Kalinin joined with the vocal celebrations before issuing the welcome order.

"Clear decks! Standby to dive!"

As the men scurried for hatches or dropped down the conning tower, Kalinin turned towards the Nachi Maru, virtually unrecognisable since it had its facelift to resemble something it was not, and formally saluted her and her crew.

He fancied he could see Commander Hashimata return the honour, but spent little time focussing his eyes, preferring instead to drop down the ladder and into the control room below.

'Soviet Initsiativa' slid slowly beneath the waves, gently taking the heavy containers undertow, their five hundred tons offering little resistance because of the streamlining of the tubes.

Once the XXI was settled at forty metres, Kalinin initiated electrical commands to the on-board systems of the two containers, allowing both to sink further into the Atlantic waters, until his submarine and its charges were both at one hundred metres depth.

When everything was stabilised and normal, Kalinin went to the tiny wardroom to start a drill with the technicians who would be responsible for employing the contents of the containers. The watertight pods' origins lay in the German Kriegsmarine as the Prüfstand XII, although the deadly contents had normally been under the command authority of the Heer or the SS.

Up until the experiments with the towed missile delivery pod, the German Navy had nothing to do with V2 missiles…

… and certainly not V2 missiles carrying an atomic device.

0348 hrs, Tuesday, 8th April 1947, forty kilometres south of Clark's Harbour, Nova Scotia.

"… And … mark. Down periscope… take us down to 120."

Kalinin kept his voice low, as did all submariners in time of stress, as if a passing fish might overhear.

Their express orders had been to avoid any sort of contact on their journey across the Atlantic, and that had been successfully done, although passing up big and vulnerable targets was foreign to all, although clearly necessary to preserve the secrecy of the mission.

However, now, as the group of submarines neared the coast of the United States, it was proving more difficult to remain hidden as the waters grew heavy with the hulls of warships and merchantmen.

The 'mark' had recorded the angle of the enemy vessel and Kalinin leant on the map table with the navigator, examining the plot.

"Target, range five thousand, Comrade Leytenant."

The officer made a mark and together they apprised the tactical situation.

"Come to port... 247 degrees, Comrade Kapitan?"

"Agreed... Starshy Leytenant..."

His first officer was quickly at the table.

"Come to port, steer 247... keep us at this depth until our friend is off the hydrophone then back to normal. Understood?"

"Understood, Comrade Kapitan."

"Advise the others by Sheptat immediately."

He referred to the 'Gertrude' underwater communications system that had been stolen from the Americans.

The number one set about discharging his orders, leaving Kalinin a moment to look at the greater picture.

By now, Commander Nakamura Otoji's I-402 and the rest of his group, 'Soviet Vozmezdiye' and I-1, would be nearing the final staging point before they closed in to their pre-firing position off various of the Cays at the very north end of the Bahamas.

'... if they're on time... and if there's been no problems...'

Kalinin's attack group consisted of 'Soviet Initsiativa', I-401, and I-14, and the three of them, having rendezvoused off Newfoundland, were now moving gradually southwest, keen not to arrive in the heavily traversed waters ahead of schedule.

Their luck had not been overly tested during their voyage across the Atlantic, but it had certainly been given a full workout once they had arrived within range of land, with aircraft and naval patrol ships plaguing their every hour.

Once, I-1 had been subjected to an attack by a Canadian Liberator, but it had come to nothing.

The RCAF crew's after-action report was challenged and it was suggested that they had dropped on a pod of whales.

None the less, not knowing of the reprieve, the whole submarine group had taken a detour back out towards deep water, one that had used up valuable fuel, although I-353 still trailed the main force by some two hundred miles, ready to provide resources if needed.

Not that the Japanese boats would need them.

They had no plans to return home.

Kalinin handed over command to his first officer and returned to his quarters where, before he grabbed a few hours' sleep, he again reminded himself of the geography of his own target.

He dropped off to sleep and dreamt...

...of Jamaica...

...of Chelsea...

...of Charles...

...and of Harvard...

1122 hrs, Wednesday, 9th April 1947, Golitsyn Hospital, Moscow, USSR.

The infection that afflicted Yuri Nazarbayev was powerful but the doctors at the old hospital used every modern drug they had to hand to combat it, and they were winning.

The shoulder and heel injuries had been complicated but he had received outstanding care from the medical services, care that seemed to be all the more diligent once his identity, or rather, the identity of his wife became known.

The head wound was the simplest and least damaging of all those he sustained.

Yuri sat in his bed, his wounds much improved, save for the poisoning of his system caused by the infection in his calf, watching his wife receive a briefing from the senior doctor on duty.

She looked different, positively so.

The glint in her eye had returned, the weight she had gained seemed to have disappeared, but not enough to hide her decidedly curvy shape, and the colour in her cheeks spoke of a woman in the best of health... and state of mind.

Tatiana Nazarbayeva was a beautiful woman and he smiled, his internal struggle with the events in the Moscow dacha confined to the rubbish pile of history during his convalescence.

His wife and the doctor exchanged nods and handshakes and he watched her move towards his room, the almost imperceptible imperfection in her gait clear to him as ever, or perhaps, even more pronounced.

"Husband."

"Wife."

They kissed on the lips and both understood that things were different to the last time that they had met.

"The doctor tells me you're festering in clean sheets whilst better men labour. What have you to say for yourself, husband?"

"The absence of vodka is debilitating for sure!"

"Well I can't help you. I don't drink."

"Don't drink? Did we lose the war?"

"No, my darling, but I think I lost my mind."

"I think we both... well... whatever Tatiana... things are good again between us."

She held his hand tightly.

"Yes, my darling... they are."

"Good... so we can put it behind us and concentrate on getting me out of this place."

"Not quite."

"Not quite?"

"No. Not quite. Wait a while. You're about to be moved."

"But I like it here... with the rest of the boys..."

"We need privacy, Yuri... that's what I told the doctor... asked of the doctor... I think he misunderstood."

"What?"

"Doctor Tupolov probably thinks I'm going to jump your decrepit bones as soon as the curtains are drawn."

"Well, I confess that would be..."

"Forget it, you front-line ass! I'm a Leytenant General. I can't be seen holding hands with the likes of a Kapitan, let alone sleeping with one!"

She grinned as she held his hand tighter, although a sudden flurry of memories assaulted her, ones that contained the faces of sweaty men using her body.

Two nurses bustled into the ward and made a beeline for Yuri's bed and belongings.

"Come along, Comrade Kapitan, let's get you moved to a nice quiet spot where you two can... err... talk more freely."

The tone and looks both shot Nazarbayeva implied the hospital rumour machine already marked them down for a conjugal romp.

The other men in the room wanted to poke fun and offer lewd encouragements to their new friend, but the presence of the senior officer who was likely to be involved in any such proceedings kept them silent, all save a few carefully chosen words of farewell.

It took four minutes to move the wounded man into a side room, and two minutes more to get him settled in.

The younger nurse giggled as she left.

"Be gentle with our special hero, Comrade Leytenant General."

"Hero?"

Nazarbayeva raised an eyebrow at her husband, who looked coyly at her.

"What can I say? I'm a celebrity in my own right here."

"Yes, well don't get too carried away. You haven't got it yet! But well done... very well done, my darling."

She kissed him on the lips to congratulate him on the upcoming award of the Hero of the Soviet Union, earned in spades during the battle of Seirijai.

"Do that again."

She did, and this time the kiss was long and lingering, completing their rehabilitation.

"So, Tatiana. What's so important that we have to be in here and away from prying eyes?"

Yuri was nobody's fool.

She told him, and left nothing out.

It took a while, and was not all plain sailing, as the spectre of the dacha was raised again, but Yuri listened and understood perfectly.

Nazarbayeva only stopped when the young nurse came into the room unannounced holding a tray with the makings of tea, most likely hoping to add to her celebrity with a first-hand account of the famous Nazarbayeva in a sexual embrace.

The tea was accepted and Tatiana managed to convey, without using words, her opinion of people who burst into private rooms without warning.

The nurse departed feeling decidedly uncomfortable and Nazarbayeva finished the one-sided conversation with a question.

Yuri did not hesitate.

"Yes."

"But you haven't thought about it at all, husband. You need time to..."

"Yes. Yes. Yes. Why would I not say yes?"

"It'll be dangerous and..."

"Take a look at me, will you? I haven't been pressing wild flowers of late!"

She laughed and kissed his hand.

"I'm aware of that, Yuri. I've read the after-action report from Seirijai. General Obukov sang your praises, and Polkovnik Zvorykin wants to adopt you. I almost didn't recognise the man he was writing about."

Yuri shrugged, which action brought a grimace as a stabbing pain came from his recovering shoulder.

"When you're the husband of a state heroine, it brings pressures to measure up, you know!"

"You don't have to impress me, husband. I'd prefer you to stay safe. You were lucky this time."

Yuri could only nod at that statement, and the two lapsed into silence and sipped their tea.

"Anyway, yes is my answer. I'll do it... for the Motherland... and for the woman I love."

"Then you must get well, husband. Those bloody Poles have knocked you about and you'll need to be up and about."

"Mudaks! How could I forget! The Poles!"

Nazarbayeva went to ask but Yuri continued in a flurry of words.

"The Pole I spoke with... Czernin... he was injured... in a great deal of pain... but he was certain that his forces started the fighting."

Nazarbayeva slipped easily from the role of wife to that of GRU officer.

"What exactly did he say, Yuri?"

"I said to him that we didn't start the fighting. He said I know... we did."

"He said that... he said they started it?"

"Yes, most certainly... I was drifting into unconsciousness, but I remember it as clear as day."

"We thought so... actually, knew so. I shall speak with this Czernin."

Nazarbayeva stood up, as if to leave, which brought about a protest from her husband.

"You misunderstand, husband."

Moving the chair closer to his bed, she sat back down and grasped his hand, and, with her other hand, opened her tunic and guided his hand to her breast.

"Now my darling, this will have to keep you for a little while."

Her hand slipped under the sheets and found his manhood.

He moaned and after less than a minute's worth of labour, she was rewarded with his orgasm.

They kissed again and she straightened herself out, conscious of the missing shirt button which had flown off when he had slipped his hand inside her shirt at the moment of climax.

Her breast still ached from the tight grip heightened by his climax.

"Now sleep and get strong, my darling."

Yuri Nazarbayev was asleep before she left the room.

Czernin's evidence was added to the growing pile that clearly proved that the new violence had been brought about by the Poles and Germans, outside of other Allies' knowledge, purely for the purpose of furthering their own national aims.

Such evidence could possibly have brought Yugoslavia back onside, perhaps even fully into the combat.

But it was not in Stalin's or Beria's possession, and lay purely with the conspirators, and keeping it secret suited them better for now.

1255 hrs, Wednesday, 9th April 1947, NATO Headquarters, Leipzig, Germany.

The staff waited for the explosion, but it simply did not come.

It threatened and bubbled, but their commander held himself in check, a man now changed by his increased responsibilities, although not totally, as his reply to the bad news clearly illustrated.

"Goddamnit, General Clark, but you must push them harder. You're behind schedule... behind even the Brits!"

That was a lie as they all knew, a lie designed to spur national rivalry and get the US Fifth Army back on track. Less than an hour beforehand, Alexander had reported that the adjacent units of the British Fifteenth Army Group were failing and the casualties were mounting again as men, exhausted by the Soviet resistance, lack of preparations, and many years of war, lost their edge.

Patton had received the same messages from up and down the line. His units were running out of steam and his grand offensive was coming apart, and not because of the enemy, or at least not in the main.

Although the Soviet soldiers were performing remarkably in places, the Red Army was a failing force in so many ways.

The Allied forces should be making vast inroads, and yet it seemed that his soldiers had lost their fight too.

No amount of shouting at the likes of Mark Clark was going to change that.

The NATO forces had been unprepared for the latest abomination and it showed, in all but the Germans and Poles, who were the most successful at driving forward, their forces deeper into Soviet lines than any other units.

That in itself wound Patton up, for the Germans had been fighting longer and harder than the rest and were still full of fight.

The George Patton of the previous year would never have said the words that followed, but he was no longer that man, now burdened with the weight of supreme command, and in a position where he could no longer look to anyone else but himself.

"Right, General Clark. You will stop your attacks and hold your ground. I'm going to stop for forty-eight hours to allow you to consolidate, rest your men, and formulate a plan to discharge the mission you've been assigned. That will be a general order for the NATO forces. Use the time wisely, General Clark... yes, I'll confirm that order in writing soonest... yes, immediately... you betcha... use the time, Mark. And you."

The men around him had stiffened, ready to receive the instructions that were about to pour from his mouth, orders to halt the NATO offensive.

Von Vietinghoff protested that the German and Austrian forces were still capable of maintaining the attack, but understood the need to maintain an integral front line and removed his objection quickly, so quickly that Patton, and a few others, simply assumed his statement was nationalist bravado, a statement saying 'look at us, we're still game and full of fight'.

'Kraut bastard.'

Shortly afterwards, the orders were dispatched and within hours the offensive halted, save for the artillery who slung their ordnance into the sky, and for the airmen who battled to control it.

Whilst the guns fell silent, the Allied political leadership received the bad news.

Some not very well.

1802 hrs, Wednesday, 9th April 1947, the Oval Office, White House, Washington DC, USA.

The men sat around the low coffee table and drank in silence, each composing their thoughts on the news.

Truman led off, paraphrasing a Churchill statement from the Italian campaign.

"And I thought we were throwing a wildcat ashore when George took the job."

"Not totally fair, Mister President. He wasn't prepared for this... or the job for that matter."

"Hmm."

Truman grunted and finished his coffee.

"Well, whatever we thought we were getting, we now have a problem. The fightingest army we've ever had suddenly seems to have lost its stomach for a brawl... and not just us... the Brits and others too..."

"Not the Germans, Mister Pres..."

"No, not the Germans. I sorta reckon those boys'll be causing a ruckus in heaven or hell, wherever God puts 'em, long after their mortal remains have gone to dust."

The remark drew chuckles from the four others.

"Seriously though, gentlemen... forty-eight hours isn't long for George to get his boys back in the saddle... if he can do it, that is. What can we do here? Can we improve this situation?"

Stimson chimed in.

"Well. You were talking about visiting the front awhile back, Mister President. Admittedly, that was before the shooting war kicked off again, but there may be merit in a visit to remind the boys what they're fighting for, eh?"

"For sure… that's on the table. I'll get on scheduling something soon… but put your thinking caps on. What can we do now… as in now?"

The five talked at length, without finding the magic bullet they needed, not knowing that it would shortly be supplied by an unexpected source.

The enemy.

1130 hrs, Thursday, 10th April 1947, Timi Woods Camp, Paphos, Cyprus.

Crisp accepted the salutes of his leadership and watched as they sprinted away to get their men aboard the waiting aircraft.

He still had trouble thinking of it as an aircraft, so gigantic was the Spruce Goose that it promised to defy the very idea that gravity would ever relinquish its grip upon the airframe and permit it to rise into the air.

But, he reminded himself… fly it did.

The vast interior was soon to be crammed with his soldiers. It was already accommodating weapons, ammunition, food, and medical supplies, but the weights had all been calculated and the incredible aircraft gobbled up everything without batting a proverbial eye.

As he observed the loading of his soldiers, he caught sight of Hughes and his band of civilians, dressed in the same uniforms as his soldiers, gesticulating wildly as they argued over weight distribution, fuel consumption, and the plethora of things that seemed to exercise and amuse them on a regular basis.

They had dismissed the warnings about being captured and the likely outcome of having their identities discovered.

Their issue of the uniforms had been greeted with boyish howls, almost as if a dressing-up party was in the offing.

That the uniforms belonged to the Red Army would be enough to ensure that anyone captured wearing them would be shot, but they were simply essential to the plan to storm Camp 1001, otherwise Crisp would not be wearing one himself.

Crisp relaxed and decided on a cigarette before he took up his place on the Spruce Goose.

He sampled the calming smoke and revisited the minutiae of the plan.

Part of his force had gone on ahead, shoehorned into a number of Curtiss Commandos decked out in Soviet colours, their part in the operation to be discharged in a separate place, but just as vital as the main force's job in many ways.

Shandruk's force had also already departed, their crucial effort in 'Kingsbury' due to commence prior to the arrival of the main force.

The Ukrainians' role was vital, and could well mean the difference between success and failure in the ground plan.

Undoubtedly, the air plan would succeed, but in succeeding could well mean disaster for Crisp, his men, and those prisoners already on the ground.

On other bases, both on airfields or on slipways, aircraft with special roles to play were undoubtedly already being prepared.

The coordination required was incredible, and the original plan developed by Sam Rossiter and his team had been amplified and improved time after time.

Jenkins' fantastic model had proved to be invaluable in planning the operation, although the complicated structure had now been dismantled and its constituent parts destroyed and spread around so as to provide no clues as to its purpose.

Rossiter arrived on cue, to wish Crisp luck and shake his hand one more time.

"Can you do it, Colonel?"

"General... I can tell you this. We're ready and able, trained to perfection, and up for the mission. If it can be done, it'll be done... and if it can't be done... well, I guess the Air Force'll have to carry the ball."

Rossiter extended his right hand and grasped that of Crisp.

"The very best of luck to you and your men, Colonel Crisp."

"Thank you, Sir."

They saluted as RSM Sunday marched towards them, his bearing as perfect as if he were commanding a review on Horse Guards Parade.

"Sah! Mister Hughes reports that he's ready to take off. All men are aboard. All supplies aboard and secured."

"Thank you, Sergeant Major."

Ten minutes later, the green-painted Spruce Goose, decorated with the markings of an aircraft of Soviet naval aviation, rose slowly from the waters of the Mediterranean, destination Tabruz, on the Caspian Sea.

1207 hrs, Thursday, 10th April 1947, 7th Mechanised Cooperation Training School, Verkhiny Baskunchak, USSR.

The atmosphere was always relaxed, but today it was more so as the final exercises were almost complete. The units under training had performed superbly, the joint product of excellent leadership by the experienced commanders and of great teaching by the men in the room.

They had just briefed Colonel Bortanov on the exercise he was expected to undertake the following day, and had let him go to prepare his plans, along with the staff of 218th Tank Brigade.

Accompanying him was Lieutenant Colonel Tob of the 115th Naval Infantry Brigade, also training with Bortanov's unit prior to being attached to a newly forming Tank Corps, to be based around the 218th.

It was important for the successful final exercise that the staff of 7th Mechanised Cooperation Training School had no exposure to the home force's planning, as they were to participate as the enemy force.

In just a few weeks, Yarishlov had forged his experienced officers into a solid unit, and 218th Tanks and 115th Infantry would be the second group to pass out of the three-week training programme far better prepared than when they entered.

This exercise was also one of only two that did not suffer from the fuel restrictions that plagued the Red Army in the present times.

Despite new supplies and methods of production helping to improve the manoeuvrability of Soviet formations in the field, the problem still hampered the majority of front line forces in their attempts to hold back the Allied advances.

Far from the front line, they had not yet heard the rumours of the failures in fighting spirit such issues had caused.

As overall commander, Yarishlov had experienced men under him to oversee the various disciplines required for the advanced battle tactics and manoeuvre course that was his to design and deliver.

Colonel Nikolay Zorin, once commander of the veteran 39th Guards Tank Brigade, was his tank commander.

Although they had never served together during either war, Yarishlov held Zorin in high esteem.

He was still a thoroughly competent and innovative tank leader, despite the serious wounds he had suffered at Hamburg in the early days of August 1945.

45

Which was also another reason why Zorin held a special place in his heart; he had fought against his friend John Ramsey, and the pair of them often shared a vodka whilst Yarishlov listened to the stories of the incredible British resistance around the Rathaus and canals of the old Hanseatic League city, or he regaled his man with hushed stories of the horrors at Barnstorf.

Zorin and Kriks had become thick as thieves as a result, as had Colonel Zvorykin and Yarishlov's senior NCO, partially because of previous experiences together in and around Tostedt in August '45, and partially because Zvorykin and Kriks had a shared passion for chess and were well matched in ability.

Zvorykin's role with the training establishment was to command the infantry and anti-tank forces that opposed the units under training, a job in which he constantly outdid himself, much to the exasperation of Zorin and the tank training staff, although good-humouredly so.

Last of Yarishlov's unit commanders was Major Harazan, an engineer by trade and inclination, and a veteran of hard fighting against the SS Legion in the Alsace, where he had been badly wounded.

Subsequently, he fought with Chuikov's Alpine Front, where he sustained another wound, one serious enough that it removed him permanently from front line duties, although many observers failed to realise that he was not all present and accounted for, so spritely was he on the prosthetic limb that replaced his lower left leg.

The comradeship Yarishlov felt for his men greatly helped him overcome his daily personal struggle with pain and the after-effects of his horrendous injuries.

"Right… that's the guests sent on their way with their briefing. Any changes to the normal planning?"

Harazan raised his hand, as he always did, ever conscious of his lower rank and status amongst his fellow officers, and therefore always striving to achieve better and better results.

"Comrade General, I believe that we may profit from advancing our minefields. I've noticed that the opposing units tend to deploy into battle formation around here."

He leant over a detailed model table that covered all of the tank training grounds, from Bataevka on the Astrakhan-Akhtubinsk highway, across to the main base at Baskunchak, a distance of some thirty-five kilometres, and running north to south a mean distance of forty-two kilometres.

46

The Verkhiny Baskunchak facility was, at just under one thousand five hundred square kilometres, the second largest mock battlefield in the whole of the USSR.

Yarishlov examined the idea and found himself tightly flanked by his two colonels.

"I understand your suggestion, Comrade... but wouldn't that make getting around them easier?"

"Only if they know they're there, Comrade General. In the last three sessions run with this general scenario, this is the place where they shake out from march order to battle order... without fail."

Yarishlov looked at the men either side of him for input.

Both were clearly mulling over the issue.

Zorin spoke first.

"And if they shake out beforehand... and detect the minefields and go around them?"

"Hold on."

Everyone focussed on Zvorykin.

"If we advance the fields to this point, as young Harazan suggests... but we do so carelessly... so they can be seen... where would you deploy your tanks, Nikolay?"

Yarishlov had the answer already, but Zorin carefully considered his response.

"I'd be round the sides of it... both sides probably...yes, both sides... with a view to a two-pronged assault... actually, that would work better for me overall, so your idea's a non-starter I think."

Yarishlov laughed.

"I'm thinking that Edward Georgievich has something rather nasty up his sleeve. Tell him."

Zvorykin took the wooden blocks representing his rocket and gun anti-tank troops and moved them forward, carefully placing them in two crescent shapes either side of the minefield position and followed them up with a few of his infantry groups.

It was hideous to behold.

Zorin swore.

"Fucking hell. Remind me never to fight you for real. That's a bitch."

"Isn't it just? By moving up the mines... and moving up the AT screen, we disorganise them quicker and further out, take them in this more

47

favourable ground, and be back to our normal first line of defence long before they're back in condition to advance."

Both Zvorykin and Harazan beamed, until Zorin threw his bucket of water on the idea.

"They'll cry foul, of course. It's in advance of the agreed combat line, Comrades."

Their pink-skinned commander had a glint in his eye that no-one had noticed, not even Harazan, who had taken the idea to his general before the meeting.

Yarishlov had willingly participated in the little subterfuge to bolster the younger man's self-worth issues.

"There was an alteration to the written brief that our adversaries took with them. Did you not notice? And with your legendary attention to the smallest of matters too…"

Both colonels grabbed their copies and turned to the relevant page.

Zvorykin laughed and dropped his copy on the table.

"So, you two hashed this up between you, eh?"

"Not at all. I played a small part, of course, but it was young Harazan's idea from the start."

"Remind me never to piss off my commander, Edward. What a bastard!"

Zorin got a curt nod by way of reply, Zvorykin's rumble of laughter making him unable to speak effectively.

Yarishlov had altered the map work relative to the upcoming mock battle. It now reflected a different 'end of march' line, one that fitted in with Harazan's plans.

"Well, if nothing else, it'll teach the pair of them attention to detail!"

They all laughed, except Kriks, who adopted a face displaying mock anger and severity.

"Fucking officers picking on the poor front line soldiery again. Lying, deceitful lot! Just to make yourselves look good. I'm disgusted by the lot of you and I'll complain to Comrade Stalin first chance I get. He'll sort you out!"

"Now, now, you peasant. Calm yourself or the first chance you get will be when you get off the transport to Siberia."

The officers dissolved into laughter at Harazan's retort, as did Kriks, once he got over the shock of being harangued by the boy of the group.

"Fuck it. What do I care? Least we're all out of harm's way and the war's a million miles away. I need a drink."

He pulled out his flask and passed it round the cheerful group.

Whilst the war wasn't a million miles away, it was a long way off.

None of them has the slightest inkling that the war was coming to them, and that by the end of it all, more of them would be dead than remained alive.

2147 hrs, Thursday, 10th April 1947, RAF Shaibah, Kingdom of Iraq.

The smoke stung everyone's eyes but not a word was spoken, the air heavy with tension as well as the products of the cigars that were clamped between tense lips.

Banner drew on the fine cigar and remembered appropriating it and its friends from the personal supplies of a senior officer back in Europe.

The memory of it brought a smile to his face, as did the rantings of the army general when he realised his whisky and cigars were not all present and accounted for.

'Fun times... still... what's Mickey sitting on here... I'm gonna call...'

"Call."

The table broke into excited chatter.

The river hit the cloth and the chatter multiplied.

Jack.

The room fell silent again.

"Over to you, Crusher."

"I know how to play, son, so can it or you'll find yourself on latrines a-sap."

Banner slowly pulled a range of faces as he examined his hole cards in relation to the pair of queens and change that lay on the table.

It seemed that to the watchers that they had been waiting in silence for a lifetime, and no amount of wishing seemed to start to tease a word from the silent man.

49

The tension proved too much for one of the officers, the one still holding his cards.

"Goddamnit it, Crusher! Either you got the balls or you ain't? Which'll it be?"

Banner looked across at his opponent with eyes that reflected his amusement at the man's discomfort.

"Steady on there, old timer. Big decisions shouldn't be rushed. You know that. I'm thinking on it."

Banner looked again, as he had done a dozen times since the river card had hit the table.

It was the jack of hearts and it sat next to the two queens, one red, one black, diamond and spade respectively, plus the four and five of hearts.

His opponent was the ageing engineering officer, brought along to be in charge of the small group of highly qualified engineers that had accompanied the two B-29s to a godforsaken airfield in the middle of nowhere, surrounded by nothing of interest, with a camel for company.

What made RAF Shaibah vital was that it offered a runway far longer than most, the by-product of runway maintenance and laying training run by the Middle East command.

The whole site was also presently surrounded by the 26th Baluch Garrison Battalion of the Indian Army, accompanied by an ad-hoc unit of Sherman tanks and Humber armoured cars from the Chota Nagpur Regiment.

Whilst there were many aircraft swelling the normal numbers at the airbase, it was the six Silverbirds that were the focus of attention.

Them and the recently erected concrete bunker that was heavy with barbed wire and constantly overrun with US security personnel, in which dwelt the silent monsters that the aircraft would carry with them once 'Viking' was set in motion, or for other missions as yet unauthorised.

'Lady Paula Marie' and 'Tatanka' were rated to carry the bombs on the mission, and they lay the closest to the simple concrete structure that housed more destructive power than the world had ever seen before.

Not that the security arrangements bothered Lars Mikkelson, whose hand quietly sang to him, such was its strength, the ace of spades and queen of clubs almost caressing his fingertips rather than the other way round.

'Crusher' Banner, as he permitted his men to call him, but only during such events as this poker game in the mess hall, caressed his cards with all the finesse of a blind lumberjack.

"God's sake... hands like claws... will you ever not fuck the cards up, Colonel?"

Staring down Harold Keel, the pilot of 'Tatanka', with a mock look of disdain, Banner released his grip on the pair of cards and went with his plan.

"Pass."

The word carried all the fear and indecision that he could deliberately generate.

Mikkelson scented blood and pushed his stack forward.

"All in, Colonel. Let's see how big your balls are!"

The other players, long since out of the game, whooped and whistled at the bold move.

Mikkelson pulled deeply on his cigar and did his level best to fire the stream of smoke across the pot and into Banner's face.

The cards in Banner's fist were the same as the last time he looked, but he still checked and rechecked them, keen to stretch the moment as far as it would go.

Grabbing his chin in a mock display of doubt, Banner's face reflected his anguish and Captain Mikkelson grinned, content that he had read his commanding officer's special tell correctly.

His eyes started to understand the reality of the situation, as opposite him, Banner's own face metamorphosed into that of a cross between the Cheshire Cat and a vampire, the huge grin punctuated by the glowing cigar stuck between Banner's wide-open lips.

He affected his best 'southern gentleman' accent.

"Oh...pardonez-moi, y'all... think I'll call."

"Sonofabitch!"

Mikkelson, shouting in hopeful triumph, threw down his cards, queen of clubs and ace of spades, revealing the triple queens in all their glory.

"Gotcha."

His cry seemed tinged with a little despair as part of his brain warned him of what might be to come.

"Really? And I thought you ground crew were intelligent, sophisticated folk."

"Yeah... what you got... the other queen... you sure ain't got jacks in the hole? C'mon... throw down, Colonel, and let me have my mone..."

He stopped in full flow as Banner carefully set down a queen and king.

Mikkelson whooped with joy.

"Goddammit but I knew my ace was good!"

He laughed until the laughter stuck in his throat and he started coughing his stomach up.

Recovering from the short discomfort, he realised that Banner's eyes had never left him, and that there were others staring at him too.

Mikkelson crowed and then stopped crowing, all in the same breath.

He checked the cards and a part of him nearly died.

"How the... what the..."

Banner simply sat and puffed on his cigar, waiting for the Engineering officer to understand that his immediate celebration of his high ace was wholly devalued by the five hearts that made Banner's hand the winner.

"You... you... sonofabitch!"

"I've been called worse, Mickey."

Mikkelson watched as Banner scooped up the last pot of the night, representing the best part of one hundred and sixty dollars.

"Guess it's your lucky day, Colonel."

Banner bit back his comment.

"My lucky day. Sure, Mickey... sure."

He stood, bringing an end to the proceedings.

"Well, boys, let's get some shut-eye. Briefing room at 0500. The mission will be a go, of that I have no doubt. Sleep well. Mickey, a word."

They mumbled their pleasantries and went their separate ways.

Banner and Mikkelson engaged in conversation outside the hut, after which the pot changed hands again, leaving Banner penniless.

A few minutes later, he found himself sat in an uncomfortable chair with a glass of scotch in his hand.

He downed the fiery liquid swiftly and knocked back one of the Doc's pills.

In a second he stripped down and lay under the noisy fan, partially hoping that sleep would come and partially wanting it to stay away so that he could have a night with his thoughts and fears... a night to come to terms with the true horrors of the day ahead.

Some eight hours previously, Rossiter had sat quietly in Banner's office and told him the full details of the camp they were to bomb, and the possible cost of the mission they were about to undertake.

Rossiter offered to be the one to tell the men, but the gesture was turned aside.

That sort of duty fell to the man who led, leastways, it did in Colonel Garry Banner's mind.

In any case, he had already decided to bear that burden alone.

He visited the medical officer and made specific requests, both of which were denied in loud and indignant tones.

Banner, unusually for him, elected to reason with the man, and enlightened him as to his purpose and the stresses of what lay ahead.

Suddenly both horrified and sympathetic, the Doctor supplied his needs and promised not to speak of it.

Despite the sedative, Banner slept badly.

The night passed in turmoil, but the new dawn brought a calmness and resolution to his heart and mind.

At 0500, the briefing for their part in Operation Viking commenced.

At 0833, the four B-29s, two carrying Jasper atomic weapons, rose into the air, the force completed by four Cranefly observation and escort aircraft tasked from the RAF's Middle East Command.

Destination... Camp 1001, Uspenka.

Transport aircraft from a number of bases in Northern Iraq were already in the air, having risen into the early morning air over an hour earlier, carrying wholly different cargoes.

The 1st Special Service Force was already en route to Akhtubinsk and its rendezvous with a place in military history of mankind.

Shandruk's Ukrainians had left earlier still, their part in the mission requiring a much earlier arrival.

Adding in the bombers, fighter escorts, and reconnaissance forces used to mount diversions and distractions, the southern Soviet Union air space was crammed with over eight hundred Allied planes.

Operations Viking and Kingsbury were fully underway.

Can death be sleep, when life is but a dream,
And scenes of bliss pass as a phantom by?
The transient pleasures as a vision seem,
And yet we think the greatest pain's to die.

John Keats

CHAPTER 201 - THE UNDERTAKING

Friday, 11th April 1947, Operation Viking, Southern Russia

The Allied squadrons were up in force, hitting targets all over the southern USSR, some of reasonable importance, others not so much, but all designed to create confusion, draw a response, and to distract Soviet controllers from the relatively few aircraft that were undertaking the Kingsbury part of Operation Viking.

Allied planners had expected success, partially because of their superior numbers and partially because of their superior equipment, but they were unprepared for the destruction they wrought upon the Red Air Force.

Skilled and experienced Soviet pilots were few and far between now, and fuel quality issues robbed all but the very best regiments of top performance.

As midday approached, the Soviet response to the continued excursions had dropped away to a level that beggared belief, and suspicions started to grow.

They were quickly quashed as base intelligence officers started sending back figures that supported the possibility that the enemy's assets were bled out, the wild claims that fighter pilots so often posted initially refuted but subsequently borne out by the pitiful response to second and third wave attacks.

The boost for Kingsbury was obvious, and hopes rose amongst those who knew that Viking was more than just an all-out air and ground assault.

The Soviet hierarchy, relieved by the absence of pressure from the west, suddenly found themselves confronted with uncomfortable reports of fighter regiments immolated, and enemy soldiers crossing into Soviet territory in strength to the south.

Fig #248 - Bases for Operation Viking - Iran & Iraq.

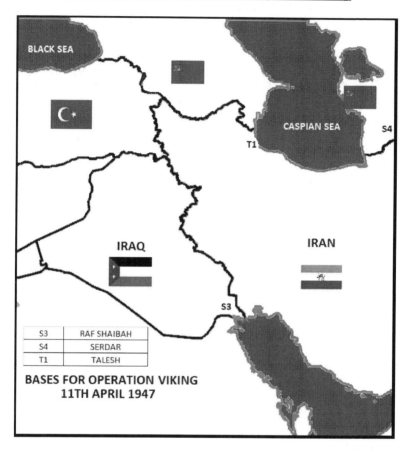

S3	RAF SHAIBAH
S4	SERDAR
T1	TALESH

**BASES FOR OPERATION VIKING
11TH APRIL 1947**

The Soviet base at Ashgabat had been off the air since the first word of a ground assault, and a garbled message from Serdar spoke of enemy, probably Australians, in the town, anouncing the severance of Highway 37.

Nowhere in the Soviet Union was the supply situation more critical than in the south.

Exasperated air force commanders spoke of regiments unable to fly for lack of fuel of any quality, and the same shortages affected the thinking of commanders on the ground, who had barely enough fuel to manoeuvre or retreat, let alone be constructive in defence or counter-attack.

All Soviet eyes swung south, as Allied aircraft controlled the skies over the shores of the Black and Caspian Seas, and as far north as Kharkov, Stalingrad, and Aralsk.

Squadrons from numerous Allied nations roamed over the skies of the southern Soviet Union from bases in Poland, Greece, Iran, Syria, and China, swamping the resistance of the defensive aircraft.

Any aircraft adorned with the red star had a very short lifespan...

...Except those that originated from the waters of the Caspian Sea off Talesh, or from the air bases in Iran that had been set aside for the clandestine forces of Kingsbury.

1040 hrs, Friday, 11th April 1947, Akhtubinsk-Astrakhan Highway, fifteen hundred metres northeast of Uspenka, USSR.

The first of the four transports dropped down onto the emergency strip that was nothing more than a normal road.

The men were out and assembling equipment before the second aircraft touched down.

Challenges from Soviet air controllers had been dealt with by way of garbled and unintelligible cries for help, and interceptions from Soviet aircraft had successfully been avoided, as those that had seen the gaggle of Lisunovs had quickly found more gainful employment in preserving their own skins as Allied long-range fighters bored in.

That the aircraft were actually original DC-3s and not Li-2s went unnoticed in the scramble for personal survival.

As Shandruk assembled his troops, those tasked with remaining behind and refuelling the beasts moved to the third and fourth aircraft to start manhandling the fuel drums.

The twenty-one men of Shandruk's force jogged off in a loose formation, heading for the main entrance of Camp 1001.

In the skies above, the remainder of the strike force descended, preparing to land on the airfield at Akhtubinsk-1 itself, escorted by specially modified Twin Mustangs, the extra fuel capacity extending their range enough for the trip and allowing for a little combat over the strip, should any of the resident aircraft escape the planned destruction.

Akhtubinsk-2 had long since been put out of action and was deserted. The more easterly of the two airfields was also considered more exposed to danger than the larger Akhtubinsk-1, which was nearer to the town but further from the soldiers of the training facility.

Fig # 249 - Important locations around Camp 1001, Southern Russia.

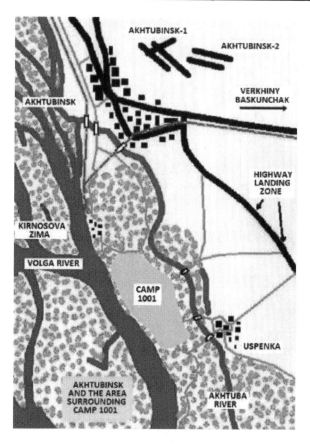

The disguised transport aircraft, long-range C-46 Curtiss Commandos, came in quickly as the fighters buzzed around them, occasionally firing a burst to convince the watchers of the mock air battle.

Quickly the transports taxied in all directions, seemingly in aimless and panicky fashion, but in reality with rehearsed precision, taking groups of men to various key points around the airfields.

Each transport held two Ukrainians in Soviet uniform, ready to bluff and talk their way through any immediate issues, and behind them were men from 1st SSF, who were to provide the muscle for the operation to negate the airfield's aircraft and communications.

Some of the transports contained the new British RCL Mk 1 weapon, a recoilless rifle of light weight and great portability that, when combined with the effective new HESH shell, made it ideal for dealing with any of the enemy tanks that might come from the tank training regiment that operated to the east.

Crisp had seen it as the perfect choice, but backed it up with a handful of the M20 Super Bazookas as well.

At 1052, the first transport stopped adjacent to the command buildings and control tower.

The two men who bailed out the door shouted angrily at the sky and fired their sub-machine guns speculatively in the direction of the circling USAAF fighters, or actually not in the direction of the fighters, had anyone observed the trajectories closely enough.

The American pilots had clearly noticed the lack of response from the Red Air Force, but amongst the ground assault group, it was Kuibida who first realised that the dispersed Soviet fighters were not responding.

They were not to know that the resident units had already been savaged that morning and that the survivors were now grounded for lack of fuel.

The plan was to use bluff and bravado for as long as possible, and other Ukrainians stepped out from transports, answering the first enquiries from ground staff.

It was inevitable that it would not last, and one encounter quickly turned to violence, as a group of Russians went for their pistols and were mercilessly chopped down.

That became the cue for each aircraft to disgorge its other contents, experienced men from 1st SSF, who fanned out and killed without mercy.

Two of the transports contained men from Trannel's 40th Transportstaffel, mainly to put together and operate the little 'ace up the sleeve' that Trannel had contributed to the covering operation, and so, as the killing spree gathered momentum, they set to work assembling their charges.

Kuibida and Gosling's men had the prime task; that of isolating and neutralising the control tower and its radios.

The Ukrainians were first into the main building and the battle was brief but intense, ending with the glass windows of the tower flying outwards as grenades ended the resistance of the control room staff.

The attackers spread out and suffered their first casualty.

Gosling's First Sergeant was put down hard by a burst of sub-machine gun fire as a group of mechanics rallied around a small tyre store.

The order to preserve AT ammunition was immediately ignored.

One of Crisp's old 101st troopers braced himself against a civilian cart and sent a bazooka rocket into the small wooden building, ending resistance in a spectacular fashion.

Screaming hideously, one wounded man half ran, half stumbled from the wreckage, clothes and hair alight, but a burst of fire found him and mercifully extinguished his life.

In less than ten minutes Akhtubinsk-1 was virtually secured and a coded transmission sent and received.

It was 1101.

Whilst the airfield assault team rounded up stragglers and Gosling's sergeant coughed out his last breath and became the SSF's first fatality, more C-46 Commandos were touching down on the emergency road strip, the heavy long-range transport aircraft bringing in more men and fuel.

The reduced Yankee Company, one platoon had been seconded to Zulu, deployed to secure the area as best they could, moving to both sides of the highway as the USAAF officer in charge tried his best to sort out the growing gaggle of aircraft that were moving around on the relatively level ground around the highway airstrip.

The last but one Curtiss C-46 made a poor landing and the port undercarriage buckled and swung the aircraft off the road.

It seemed that the pilots had wrestled back control but fate decided it had another card to play.

The bent undercarriage dropped into a small watercourse and the forward energy of the aircraft did the rest.

A graunching metal sound accompanied the sight of the eighteen-ton aircraft being flicked over like a paper toy.

A small fire quickly became a blaze that engulfed the whole airframe, leaving no reason for anyone to even consider attempting any rescue of the men who remained inside.

Explosives soon started cooking off and the aircraft slowly scattered itself in pieces around the surrounding area.

Captain Hanchard knew without looking at his documents that he had just lost one of the DRL special units.

He and a number of his fellow officers were not wholly convinced as to their worth. There had been precious little time to see them in action, but Crisp had agreed to take them anyway, as much to assuage his own concerns about the nearby training unit as to respond to Rossiter's forceful request.

After all, Crisp had reasoned, the equipment would not be coming home, and some extra firepower would always be welcome.

'...if the damn things worked!'

More important to the plan were the forty seats that had been lost by their inclusion.

The last Commando swept down and made a textbook landing, its tyres almost kissing the road surface.

Hanchard counted aircraft and even included the one burning in his peripheral vision.

'Fifteen'.

He took in the movement of the men of Yankee Company, who had moved out to surround the area as best as one hundred and ten men can surround something nearly four kilometres long.

He checked his watch and signalled his radioman to send the 'in position' message.

It was 1101.

1103 hrs, Friday, 11th April 1947, the Volga River, two kilometres southeast of Pshenichnyy, USSR.

Howard Hughes turned the huge aircraft to starboard and eased the beast closer to the water.

There was four kilometres of landing water to play with, but he wanted to get water on the Goose's hull as quickly as possible, in order to avoid having to turn back round to the landing area, and the risks that went with such a prolonged exposure on the water.

Behind him, long-range fighters buzzed around the sky, occasionally making a mock attack in order to fool the Soviet observers.

More than one Soviet anti-aircraft gun's barrels had followed the massive amphibian across the sky, but a combination of its green paint and red stars, and the belligerence of the Allied fighters had stayed hands, leaving the Spruce Goose unmolested and free to land.

So deep was Hughes' concentration that he failed to notice one of the Twin Mustangs disintegrate in mid-air as a Soviet 57mm AA shell exploded on its central wing.

The flight had not been without problems.

Some electrical systems had failed, meaning darkness in places, and a lack of announcements over the speakers.

At one stage, engine one had spluttered and thrown up some worrying oil pressure readings, but the 28-cylinder Pratt & Whitney had sorted itself out, leaving Joe Petrali none the wiser.

"Ode, give them the call!"

Odekirk shouted back towards the men in the seats behind him.

"Spread the word, Brace for landing! Brace for landing!"

The warning spread swiftly down to the lower levels and the men of 1st SSF prepared themselves for the worst.

The Goose had come in low so there was no great concern of speed of descent. It was a matter of judgement now, and a few practices plus the journey over from the States had provided the flight crew with extra valuable knowledge about speed and height in relation to a fully laden aircraft.

"Close cowl flaps to two-thirds."

"Roger."

"Throttling back... speed one-twenty..."

"Roger."

Too fast or too slow could spell disaster for the mighty aircraft.

Eyes anxiously swept the huge array of gauges for signs of any problem, but none was to be seen.

"Easy now... easy... easy..."

The Goose touched the water but was instantly airborne again.

"Shit."

Again the fuselage touched and Hughes struggled to keep her in contact with it.

"That's it!"

The fuselage stuck to the water on its next contact.

"Reverse thrust!"

Engines three to six, the four inboard mountings, could reverse thrust and Hughes called for this to help remove some of the Goose's forward momentum.

The first jetty had long since disappeared behind them, its barges and men quickly lost to sight.

The second larger jetty, where they intended to go ashore, swept past the left-hand window, although Hughes was too busy trying to slow his aircraft to notice, whereas Crisp was looking at the bank and groaned inwardly.

'Damn it... overshoot.'

The landing was surprisingly gentle, with little of the jarring they had experienced in either of the two fully laden practice flights they had found time for, a testament to the smoothness of the Volga as well as the skill of their pilot.

"Keep them buckled up, Sergeant Major."

"Yes, sir."

Crisp undid his belt and moved forward as Sunday looked around, keen to stop anyone following the colonel's example, but the handful of men from the headquarters platoon stayed firmly in their seats.

Those that were in the right positions were gaining visual information through the windows on the upper deck and relaying it to those who could see nothing.

1st SSF's commander made his way forward to the cockpit area.

"We've overshot the jetty."

"Can't help that but we're slowing up. I'll bring her round and back in. Just that the commies'll have more time to collect their wits."

They worked feverishly to slow the beast enough to start turning back upriver.

Durets ducked as a pair of Allied fighters swept overhead.

A triple Maxim mount sent a stream of bullets skywards, long after the air they passed through had been vacated by the strange aircraft.

In his mind, Durets half-considered screaming at the gunner to cease fire and stop attracting attention, but it was too late, so he turned his gaze back to the strange and simply huge flying boat.

"Whoever the poor bastards are, they're lucky to get down without a hammering."

"Indeed, Comrade Mayor."

The junior lieutenant would have preferred to be in his bunker while all the aircraft were moving overhead, but the arrival of Durets had forced him out into the open.

"Well... get a full guard turned out... politely deal with our guests as ever... but they don't get in here unless they've credentials from the General Secretary himself... even then Volga camp site only... and perhaps we can persuade them to remove that fucking monstrosity. It'll be like shit to flies for the capitalist aircraft."

The debate about what he should do next was ended by the sound of the camp siren, a moaning banshee-like sound that was taken up by sirens all over the large site.

"Right. Deal with that lot sensitively. Any senior officers that need ruffled feathers smoothed, handle it... or call our valiant leader to sort it."

They shared a stifled laugh, for Skryabin was an unpopular man at the best of times, and his recent antics with visiting dignitaries and the execution of a number of Allied officers for minor offences had earned him no marks from guards and prisoners alike.

The overall commander of security at the VNIIEF facility, one Major General Ivan Ivanovich Lunin, was absent yet again, his health still deteriorating, despite the friendlier climate.

This left Skryabin as de facto security head, something becoming more and more frequent.

"Call me if you need me, Comrade Mladshy Leytenant."

"As you order, Comrade Mayor."

Durets dropped into the passenger seat of the Soviet-made Gaz jeep and the driver immediately sped off towards the main entrance, which was his commander's duty station when the camp alarm was sounded.

As they picked their way through the checkpoints and enclosures of Camp 1001, Durets amused himself with nodding to prisoners he knew personally or examining the demeanour of the men who were lining up for the counts that followed the practice alarms.

Why Skryabin had chosen now to have such an exercise was beyond understanding. Not only did the fool know he was on the far side of the camp from his duty station, but also the air was full of enemy aircraft.

'Fucking idiot.'

For once, Durets' opinion was off, for the alarm had been sounded for all the right reasons, and much to the detriment of Operation Kingsbury.

The men jogged forward at a steady pace, the camp gates growing larger with each step.

They were fit, seriously fit, but Shandruk had pushed on at a stiff pace and more than one or two were blowing hard.

It didn't take twenty-twenty vision to spot that the camp guards were more numerous than expected, and most certainly on the alert.

The wind had carried much of the sound away from the sweating Ukrainians but Shandruk had thought he had heard sirens once or twice.

The alertness did not appear to be specifically aimed at the approaching Ukrainians, but unease spread through their ranks none the less.

A pair of Soviet fighters swept overhead, closely pursued by a gaggle of hunters eager for cheap kills.

They headed off towards a column of black smoke that rose from the highway landing ground, marking the demise of the Curtiss Commando and its load.

Shandruk and his men closed on the gate.

At his duty station by the Volga Gate, Junior Lieutenant Yashin cast his inexperienced eye over the approaching aircraft.

Its size was impressive, well beyond anything he had seen before, and he felt both strangely relieved and proud that it was the product of the Motherland.

The bullet holes in the aircraft's fuselage told of unsuccessful attacks by the enemy fighters.

Clearly, the leviathan had been lucky to escape.

Fig # 250 - Plan of Camp 1001, Uspenka, USSR.

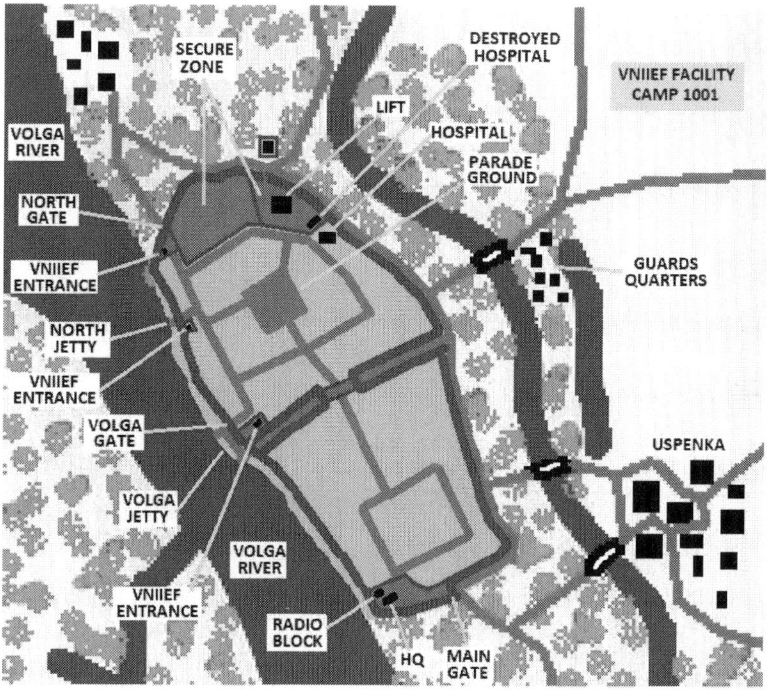

Of course, that is what they were supposed to portray, as part of the careful creation of an illusion to lull keen minds to sleep.

"Come with me, Serzhant. Get Sorolov to bring the guard to order."

He pointed at the junior sergeant to whom he was entrusting organising the parade of guards, should there be a dignitary aboard the visiting craft.

The sergeant shouted at his junior who shouted in turn at the group of men curiously examining the approaching seaplane.

They burst into life and formed two immaculate ranks at the end of the jetty.

Yashin strode forward, the senior sergeant and three men forming a line behind him.

A door opened on the port side of the aircraft's nose and a familiar uniform came into sight.

"Hmm... paratroopers."

Yashin aimed the comment at no one in particular.

Two of the base's guards caught the thrown line and, responding to the thrower's instructions, walked down the jetty to secure the nose as close to land as possible.

A pair of doors opened just in front of the port wing, and more Soviet uniforms came into view, one of which was clearly a paratrooper colonel, who saw Yashin and threw both a salute and smile in the direction of the NKVD officer.

The officer leapt ashore before the aircraft was secured at the rear.

"Comrade Leytenant. Sedov, 23rd Guards Assault Air Rifle Battalion. Perhaps we can save the rest of our introductions for later?"

"Yes, Comrade Polkovnik."

'Can't place that accent... Ukrainian possibly... I'll find out later...'

"I've wounded aboard and need to get the rest of my men off the Mamont immediately."

'Mammoth eh? A suitable name for the thing.'

"Of course, Comrade Polkovnik. Straight down the jetty and into the camp. There's a hospital available for your men. We're a prison camp so the Allies won't shoot."

'I hope!'

"Excellent!"

'I know they won't.'

Sedov slapped the NKVD officer on the shoulder and barked instructions to the men waiting in the shadows.

Stretchers appeared with men in the extremes of agony, their cries lending even more urgency to the situation.

"How many men, Comrade Polkovnik?"

"Two hundred and thirty."

"Blyad! Two hundred and thirty?"

"Room for three times that, Comrade Leytenant. Speed up, Comrades... move... move... move...!"

More and more men came piling out of the fuselage and headed off towards the camp.

And then it happened, or rather two things happened.

The first was an accident; a simple stumble.

One of Crisp's men stumbled and, despite the basic Russian each had been taught, cursed in his own tongue.

"Sonofabitch!"

The second could have been an accidental discharge but it simply didn't matter; the combination ended the subterfuge completely.

The curse in a foreign tongue combined with a sudden burst of firing from the other side of the camp.

It was enough for Yashin to grab for his pistol, a move that guaranteed his death.

Panasuk, stood slightly to one side from Colonel Sedov, or OSS Major Michel Wijers as most people knew him, brought up his SKS and put three rounds into Yashin, the impact of which threw his lifeless body into the Volga.

The Soviet paratroopers responded quickly, more quickly than the confused NKVD guards did, and bullets flew, ending more lives in a handful of seconds.

The firing from the main gate stopped as quickly as it started.

Yet more men flooded out of the fuselage, although the immediate NKVD guards were already dealt with.

Crisp emerged, resplendent in the uniform of a Soviet Guards paratrooper general, took a quick look round, and shouted back into the fuselage.

The doors suddenly disgorged more men, each pair carrying two long crates, each single man laden with smaller boxes, as many as each could usefully carry and still move at speed.

"Move, move, move!"

Crisp turned back to the shoreline and saw the men of Zebra Company already well into the camp, moving according to the plan, whilst the detached platoon from Yankee Company handled the boxes that were so crucial to their mission.

He quickly looked at his watch.

11:12.

'Shit!'

1105 hrs, Friday, 11th April 1947, Main Gate, Camp 1001, Uspenka, USSR.

The guard commander brought his men to readiness in order to challenge the approaching soldiers, although the NKVD uniforms were easily recognisable.

Skryabin's duty station was at the guard headquarters building adjacent to the main entrance, and he casually observed the approaching soldiers whilst receiving reports from all sectors, as commanders relayed their alert readiness status.

Skryabin had received the reports of the unexpected approach of a group exhibiting military bearing and gone straight to a full reaction in accordance with standing procedures, something he often decided not order, for reasons best known to himself.

He removed his sunglasses and dabbed cold water to his battered face, the result of a drunken tumble in Akhtubinsk two nights previously.

Under doctor's orders, he wore sunglasses to reduce the pain to his injured eyes, and bathed the swollen flesh regularly, convinced that small pieces of stone or glass were still present in the scuffed wounds that marred his features.

Complete with two of the blackest eyes and a puffy top lip, Skryabin looked a wreck.

The newcomers approached the gate and their commander called them to a halt, striding forward with a sheaf of papers in hand.

Something unrecognisable announced itself in the back of Skryabin's mind and he felt a sudden unease.

Leaving the command position to a junior officer, the battered and bruised NKVD detachment commander hurriedly grabbed his hat and belt before leaving the guard building and heading for the main gate.

The newly arrived officer and his guard commander were in discussion over documents that clearly illustrated the new arrivals were now attached to the camp guard force but, on the direct instructions of Colonel General Serov himself, autonomous and answerable only to him.

That the credentials of the new group were impeccable was beyond dispute.

But, the fact that they were missing from his extremely precise gate schedule meant that they could not enter without the specific permission of either Durets or Skryabin.

"Comrade Mayor, I do not have the authority to admit you. You're not on my schedule so..."

"Comrade Starshy Leytenant, you're holding passes and orders signed by Polkovnik General Serov himself, and you're saying you need more authority to act on them? Are you fucking stupid or what?"

"Comrade Mayor. This is an alpha site. You must know that I can't allow you entry without following procedures. That's an absolute. You must wait here."

"Very well, but quickly, please. My men will need to rest and there's much work to do."

Shandruk decided to wait on the man's 'procedures', knowing that the Serov paperwork would stand scrutiny and that they would be admitted.

It was the delay that worried him the most.

He took a moment to cast his eye over the target for his team; the camp's headquarters, or more importantly, the radio block slightly to one side.

The radio centre's destruction would be the signal for the rest of the Kingsbury plan to commence.

He fished out his water bottle, affecting a calmness that he did not feel, and indicated that his men should do the same.

The Ukrainians drank steadily, using the distraction to mark targets and check out the lie of the land, should matters get out of hand.

Skryabin advanced, his unease still present and unexplained.

The approaching guard commander saluted and handed over the documents that Shandruk had produced.

"Impressive... very impressive credentials indeed. Independent unit in my camp... don't fucking like that... don't like that at al..."

His brain jerked into action in the briefest of moments as the newly arrived officer turned back towards him.

"Comrade Spuransky, listen to me and listen carefully."

Shandruk watched the two men confer over waved papers.

The guard commander moved off towards the American halftrack that sat by the main entrance, whilst the senior officer advanced, clutching the papers.

Shandruk suppressed a grin at the battered visage, barely concealed by the larger than necessary sunglasses.

'Fucking hell... wonder what hit him?'

"Comrade Polkovnik."

Shandruk's salute was impeccable.

Skryabin's offering was less so.

"Mayor. Your orders seem clear and in order. Your purpose here is obviously less clear. Explain."

"I'm afraid I only answer to Comrade Polkovnik General Serov."

"And I answer to the Comrade General Secretary. This is an Alpha site, so no fucking posturing."

Skryabin took a moment to look around him and saw that the men under his command were more than alert.

Shandruk saw it too, and in that instant understood that he had failed.

His intended admonishment died before it reached his lips.

Skryabin sneered as he spoke.

"Comrade Stalin entrusted me with the safety of this facility, so do you think for one moment I'd let you inside, eh?"

Skryabin tossed the papers in the air and everything changed.

Shandruk fell for the oldest trick in the book, his eyes following the papers, not the moving hand, and he suddenly found himself looking down the barrel of a Tokarev.

All around his group, the camp guards were pointing their weapons at the new arrivals.

Removing the glasses, Skryabin savoured his moment.

"There's no way I'd let a fucking renegade Ukrainian and his men into the base... Shandrak or whatever your fucking name is. Surrender."

The face without the glasses seemed slightly familiar and then clarity arrived in all its awfulness.

"Skryabin!"

Reaching for his weapon, Shandruk took the first bullet straight in the chest and flew backwards.

It was the signal for a massacre, as the Ukrainians were mowed down from all angles, particularly by the 12.7mm machine-gun mounted on the halftrack, manned by Spuransky.

This was the firing that alerted Yashin at the Volga Gate.

The POWs were lined up ready for a count, one for which the start order was still outstanding, as the duty officer waited by the telephone to receive his instructions.

The senior NCO prisoners were gathered together as was their custom, ready to escort the Soviet counting officers as they assessed the groups under each man's command.

"Something's afoot, aye."

RSM Robertson, formerly of the 7th Battalion, The Black Watch, sniffed the air like an old soothsayer, convincing himself that he could sense portents.

"You ain't wrong, Murdo."

Julius Augustus Collins could only agree, but not because of any ancestral senses, just the vast amount of air traffic that had been and gone during the last few hours.

Between them, Robertson and Collins ran the camp like clockwork, all under the auspices of the officers who wisely let them have their head.

CSM Patrick Green, also captured with Robertson during the battle at Barnstorf, waited on instructions from the two men, as did his best friend, Randolph Black, a staff sergeant who served with Crisp's paratroopers at Sittard, where he was wounded and taken prisoner.

The Soviet duty officer stood staring at the telephone, almost willing it to ring and provide him with orders.

It was supposed to ring, so he waited, choosing not to seek orders or to issue any on his own authority.

He simply did nothing.

Robertson cast his eye over the assembled prisoners, proud of their military bearing despite their months in captivity, and proud of their fitness levels, partially sustained by an unexpectedly reasonable food allocation from their captors and partially from the physical regime he and his NCO sidekicks had enforced.

The few soldiers who had decided that Robertson and his team could go forth and multiply had 'rapid attitude adjustment therapy', which tended to be NCO-speak for a few hefty blows behind the shower block or even a beating at the hands of their hut mates.

72

Despite having been away from the front line for months, not one soldier on the assembly ground failed to recognise the sound of weapons, and those with keen ears caught the thump of a heavy machine gun mixed with the rattle of lighter automatic weapons, firstly from the direction of the main gate and then from the Volga dock side.

The Russian guards reacted swiftly and with shouts and rifle butts, herded the prisoners back towards their huts as the duty officer finally acted and yelled orders.

In the habit of prisoners the world over, some men moved slowly, too slowly for one of the younger guards, whose nerves were swiftly shredded by the shrill voice of his officer adding to the nearby shooting.

The SVT in his hands started into life, firing three bullets into the air before he brought it down to menace the surly POWs.

"Calm down, Ivan, you fucking tosser!"

Perhaps it was the lack of respect and the sneer in the voice, or the clear fright and confusion in the young NKVD soldier's mind, but whatever it was, the British corporal flew back as a bullet caught him in the upper chest.

There was no chance for a second shot as a British officer threw himself on the guard, smothering the man and weapon to preserve his soldiers.

Another NKVD solder stepped forward and brought the butt of his PPSh down on the officer's head, twice in quick succession.

Lieutenant Ames, once of the 53rd Welch Division, rolled away with a bleeding scalp and bell's ringing in his ears.

Green moved forward to help the artillery officer but found himself thrown to the ground by the impact of a body as he was rugby tackled without warning.

"Stay down!"

The firing erupted around the parade square, as men in Soviet uniforms emerged between the huts and started picking off the NKVD guards.

"What the goddamned fuck?"

"Stay down, Sarnt! Cavalry's here!"

From their prone position, Kearney and Green could see enough of the parade ground to observe the brief exchange.

A couple of the new arrivals went down hard as red blossomed and their uniforms. Here and there a slower POW also went down, hit by the crossfire.

Mainly it was the guard detail that suffered and both Kearney and Green watched as the guard commander, still shouting orders, took a burst of fire in the abdomen that dropped him to the ground, where he screamed for the briefest of moments before a passing 'paratrooper' put two bullets in the back of his head.

All over the parade area, men hugged the ground as bullets flew above them, although the lessening in firing was apparent to all.

Here and there, heads were raised, taking in the scene as more of the new arrivals moved through the area.

One man, wearing the uniform of a Soviet paratrooper officer, started shouting.

"We're Americans! We're Americans! Officers and NCOs to me!"

"Told you it was the fucking cavalry!"

Green could only nod as they both rose up.

"Check the boys, corp. Keep 'em together 'til we know what gives."

"On it."

Green headed towards the paratrooper officer, who was suddenly surrounded by men with many questions.

Galkin held out his hands to placate the assembly.

"There's no time for that. I'm Major Galkin, US Army. We're here to get you out, but we've another mission too and we need your help."

A Canadian Major stepped forward.

"I'm Roberts, senior officer on parade. What do you need from us?"

Galkin gestured towards the men handling crates and boxes.

"We brought weapons and need you to use 'em, Major."

Greedy eyes took in the boxes, now clearly identifiable as weapons and ammunition, which had been manhandled all the way from the Spruce Goose.

"How you organised?"

"Parade by hut, fifty plus under command of NCOs. Officers kept separate, but we're allocated to huts for responsibilities... welfare and command."

"Excellent. Can you organise into hut units… get armed up? No time to brief you so my men and I will guide you. We've a plan and need to stick to it. Once we're done, we fly out. Let's get moving!"

Many of the POWs were ahead of the game and 'helping' the weapon distribution process.

The planning had ensured that no weapons would be taken that would not be familiar to the prisoners, but many an American found himself with a Sten, and Brit held an unfamiliar Garand.

Grenades were not an issue, as they tended to have a universal language that was understood by all.

As the men sorted themselves out, the occasional swap occurred, but inevitably men ended up with unfamiliar kit, or in many cases, none at all.

Robertson, the camp's senior NCO, kept his liberated SVT-40 firmly in his grasp, the spare ammo filling trouser pockets.

He strode through the milling prisoners, shouting orders here and there, occasionally sorting a dispute, particularly when two men claimed the same gun.

Even the two dead paratroopers were stripped of their weapons and ammunition.

A number of other men had liberated the dead and wounded guards' weapons, further swelling the prisoner's firepower.

The troopers of X-Ray Company had already moved on, keen to relieve the Ukrainians who had been tasked with destroying the radio shack, a crucial element designed to keep the raid secret for as long as possible.

The lead element had no sooner spotted the pile of dead men at the main entrance than they walked into a wall of fire as Skryabin's men, alerted to their presence, put up a stubborn fight as the undamaged radio sent out the warning to anyone who would listen.

X Company reacted quickly, despite initial losses.

A bazooka was deployed, terminating the radio's existence as the first rocket flew true and entered the small aperture in the radio bunker's north wall, the resultant explosion destroying the apparatus and men in the briefest of moments.

The gunner took a bullet in the thigh but still managed to aim his weapon for a second shot.

The loader slapped his shoulder, marking the loading process as complete, and the rocket streaked across the open ground before exploding on the driver's vision slit of a halftrack whose machine-gun controlled the open ground.

Pieces of metal and flesh flew in all directions, one particularly large piece of a man wiping through two NKVD soldiers preparing a Maxim for action. Neither men nor machine gun were fit for purpose after the bloody torso's passage.

Despite the efforts of Jenkins and her talented interpreters, the nature of the main building had not been apparent until X-ray Company closed upon it.

For reasons best known to the builders, it was more of a bunker than a simple building, and now posed a formidable obstacle to 1st SSF's assault force, one that might be insurmountable in the limited time available.

Bud Tabot, X-Ray's commander, made a swift decision.

"Pete!"

The unit's air liaison officer who was supposed to set up in the main building once it was occupied, dropped in beside the bleeding officer, a wood splinter having opened up his left cheek allowing a steady flow of blood to demonise his features.

The same splinter or possibly another object had also struck the walkie-talkie which lay at his feet, bloodied and useless.

Fortunately, they had brought two.

"Pete, no way you're setting up in that fucker now. Use your radio to apprise the Colonel, will ya? Let him know we can't take the building as planned... tell him why too..."

Tabot indicated the clearly reinforced structure to emphasise his point.

The USAAF officer nodded his understanding and went to go.

An arm hauled him back in behind cover.

"Tell him I'm gonna bottle these fuckers up here with half my force. I'll open the wire up best as I can for the prisoners. Let the Colonel know that Shandruk and his boys didn't make it and chances are the word's out. Kapische?"

"I'm on it, Bud."

"When you're done, double back to the Colonel and find an alternate location. Stay safe, Pete."

"You too, Bud."

Peter George moved back to his air force contingent and held a brief radio conversation with Crisp before taking his men back to the Volga River entrance, where Crisp had decided the USAAF controller could set up in the highest tower.

Behind him, two platoons of Tabot's company encircled the main building and kept it under fire, whilst the rest spread out, rounding up errant POWs and, more importantly, cutting open areas of the camp's wire to permit swift exit.

The plan called for X-Ray to control the southern area and direct the prisoners there to escape towards the main road and the waiting DC-3 aircraft.

Armed prisoners arrived in rough groups, all under the command of officers and NCOs, and all wishing to spend time shooting up their recent captors.

Tabot kept one well-armed group under his command and sent the less well-armed ones off towards the main road, all with strict instructions to move like the devil was snapping at their heels.

The fitness regime and reasonable ration allocation stood the POWs in good stead, and they jogged off at a good pace towards the waiting transports and the safety they represented.

It took Tabot but a moment to understand that the places available would be insufficient and many men, likely himself as well, would be left behind.

Still, the plan did cater for that, provided they could get everyone out of the immediate area of harm's wa…

He looked at his watch.

'Oh fuck.'

What Crisp and his men were unaware of was that their mission was already, in most senses of the word, a failure.

The remaining completed atomic devices and many of the technicians had already departed.

Stalin's orders covered everything and left no room for delay or argument.

Only one device remained, and that was covered by Stalin's orders too.

Stripping down the centrifuges would take much longer than originally thought, and all but four were still on site, as were a handful of specialists from the centrifuge and enrichment teams.

The nearby infantry response force had been scaled down, its personnel used mainly to accompany the departed men and equipment as guards, but there was still a complete mechanised infantry company in the nearby barracks at Kirnosova Zima.

Under the command of a veteran Captain, the one hundred and ten men prepared to drive the kilometre from their camp to the north gate.

Crisp listened to the reports with some satisfaction, Jenkins' predictions seeming to be spot on.

Some of the huts that had appeared like regular prisoner accommodation were only ramshackle on the outside, the internal layout and facilities clearly designed for the comfort of the occupants.

Part of Zulu Company was already heading underground via one of the access points near the centre gateway, whereas the rest of the company swept forward through the buildings, trying to avoid shooting the few scientists they saw, and taking out the occasional guard who got in their way.

One of the buildings that the Red Cross report had stated was for bandage manufacture proved occupied by Russians who decided to offer firmer resistance, and three of Crisp's first platoon were already down and screaming in pain.

1st Lieutenant Fernetti had the situation under control and a base of fire was quickly established, followed by a rapid flanking assault that carried the southwestern end of the building in short order.

Crisp nodded to Fernetti and strode on, following close behind the giant frame of Bluebear, who pushed his men ahead as quickly as possible.

With Fernetti temporarily engaged, point duty fell to Second Platoon.

They surged ahead in three distinct groups, one on either flank, with the main body set in between but behind, ready to move up or support as required.

Rosenberg's group moved quickly up to the camp road and came under fire from their objective, the large building that had been the subject of Jenkins' aerial studies when the camp first drew attention; the one they believed held the main entrance to the underground complex.

Zorba, recently pushed up to Sergeant, took his group back into the left side, and moved further up under the cover of other buildings.

Lieutenant Blayne, Second Platoon's senior officer, brought his command group forward and moved up to Rosenberg's position to make his own assessment.

In the briefest of moments, he organised a .30cal into covering fire and dropped in behind his first sergeant.

"What we got, Rosie?"

The NCO pointed rapidly as he spoke.

"'Bout ten of the fuckers. Two positions either side of the main doors there and there... three men in each as far as I can make out. They were right about the flak post not being able to depress enough if you see, Lootenant."

Both men had the same thought.

'Thank fuck!'

"But the crew are shooting from up there. I reckon four of 'em."

Blayne took a look for himself.

"The .30 can occupy the guys on the roof some... hmm... no machine guns?"

"If they've got one, they ain't firing it, boss."

One of the enemy put some shots close to the mark and both men ducked as wood and paint splinters cascaded over them.

"Ben Zona! Mamzer!"

Rosenberg squealed as the sharp particles of paint made vision difficult.

"Canteen!"

79

Pfc White swiftly handed over his water and Blayne poured a healthy amount over his sergeant's face, washing the particles away.

"Thanks. You're a mensch, boss."

Blayne simply handed the bottle back to White and turned back to focus on the point of resistance, ignoring the burst of fire that could only come from Fourth Platoon's surge up the Volga riverbank towards the North Gate.

"No time for anything fancy, First Sergeant. Left and right, suppressive fire straight down the middle. You ok to lead?"

"Ready and rarin', boss."

"Take your men right. We'll suppress... go like blazes when you're set. Zorba will see what's happening and follow suit, no doubt about it. You got the right post and roof, 'kay?"

"Got it."

Rosenberg moved off and was followed by his men, all staying as low as possible in the distinctive crouching run of infantry under fire.

Blayne was halfway through his radio report when the assault went in.

One of Rosenberg's men went down in the silent and immediate drop that marked a man killed instantaneously, but the rest were on top of the door position before further casualties were sustained, half throwing themselves on top of the terrified NKVD soldiers, the other half taking the external stairs two at a time.

The lead man stopped to launch a grenade and Blayne watched as two of the Russians were thrown into the air and came to ground on the tarmac below.

Blayne grimaced, hoping that the explosion had not damaged anything vital on the roof, where it was suspected that lift machinery dwelt under innocuous square shapes.

Zorba had reacted as predicted and his own men leapt forward and overran the other door position, although the group took three casualties as a previously silent building burst into life on their left flank.

In their briefings, that building's purpose had not been identified, and so it was placed on the list of those that were not to be destroyed in an assault.

Whether he forgot or simply acted to preserve the lives of his men was unclear, but Zorba's bazooka team responded to orders and blew the small wooden structure to pieces with a single shot.

Blayne ordered part of his main group forward and they sprinted across the open road to the roller shutter doors that opened into what they suspected to be the main lift into the underground complex.

As he neared the doors he paused and turned to wave the second group across, which was enough time for an NKVD soldier to bring his rifle to bear and put a bullet into the platoon commander's back.

Blayne fell hard onto his face and knocked himself unconscious.

Some troopers from the second rush of men grabbed his senseless form and pulled it into the relative safety of the main entrance, slowly being opened by incredulous troopers.

They revealed a double lift and four sets of stairs leading downwards.

From the area below, a klaxon sounded its strident notes of warning.

Before he entered the building, Rosenberg used his position on the roof to eyeball the burnt-out building to the southeast.

It was exactly as he remembered from the photos and he crossed it off the threat list, the destroyed medical facility clearly abandoned and unmanned.

Elsewhere, men of the 1st SSF were moving through the buildings and leaving red chalk marks to signify those that had been visited.

Occasionally, a small team would emerge with bags or some other container holding the items of interest found in a quick search.

Ferdinand Sunday commanded the collection group, to whom the recovered items were handed.

It fell to the RSM and his small squad to organise the recovery and transfer of such items back to the Spruce Goose, ready for their departure.

Four of his men were already on their way back to the Hercules laden with intel or, equally as possible for all Sunday knew, someone's love letters.

Crisp entered the lift hall as Fourth Platoon reported occupying the north gate area.

Part of Hässler's heavy support group, held back under Crisp's command, was moved up quickly, as the enemy force stationed at Kirnosova Zima would be bound to be heading for the north gate by now.

Content that all was as it should be, or as close as he could expect it, Crisp followed his men underground.

1113 hrs, Friday, 11th April 1947, 7th Mechanised Cooperation Training School, Verkhiny Baskunchak, USSR.

Bailianov snorted at the radio report of an attack on the nearby POW camp.

"A security exercise surely?"

"I don't think so, Comrade Polkovnik."

Neither did Bailianov for that matter, but his mind rebelled against the possibility that enemy troops were on the ground nearby.

They had asked for confirmation of the worrying report but none was forthcoming.

Pulling a stint as duty officer, as did all the senior men in the 7th MCTS, he had never expected to be confronted with such a monstrous concept.

But he was, so he acted.

"All commands to alert status immediately. Level one, live ammunition loads. You... wake up the General immediately!"

Not that Yarishlov would be asleep, but the order sent a junior officer scurrying to the phone to alert the 7th's commander.

"Who's nearest out of our lot?"

It was wholly rhetorical as he knew exactly who was the closest to the camp facility.

As he swiftly consulted the situation map he mused on the undoubted blessing that the scheduled major exercise had been postponed until the following day.

Contaminated or sub-standard fuel, it had yet to be established which, had been used by many of the 218th's armoured vehicles, virtually immobilising the greater part of the attacking force.

On the minus side, the concept of advancing the exercise's defensive line against the 218th and 115th had, in one master stroke, placed valuable assets even further away from the possible enemy attack.

The first tank company was certainly the closest to the camp, centred around a parking area on the eastern outskirts of Akhtubinsk, just off the Ul. Kochubeya.

Slightly further east were his reserve infantry force and the supply train, where General Yarishlov always insisted that live rounds were kept to hand.

Not enough for full war loads for all men and vehicles, but enough to ensure that the experienced soldiers of the training unit's fighting group could give a good account of themselves.

"What's that?"

His subconscious caught part of a relaxed message from one of the school's recon units.

"3rd Platoon, 2nd Reconnaissance, Comrade Polkovnik."

"Where do they think the firing's coming from?"

"They think the airfield, Comrade Polkovnik."

"Akhtubinsk-1?"

"Yes, Comrade Polkovnik."

'Vlassov... a good soldier... he knows what he's doing...'

"Mudaks! Tell them I want immediate information on that firing. Check the airfield... report back immediately. I'm sending mechanised infantry to support."

The order was sent and reacted to with incredulity and barely concealed anger.

Bailianov understood the tone in the man's voice and could imagine the scene as Vlassov snatched the radio from his operator and sought to confirm that the man issuing the order understood that his unit had no live ammunition.

He interrupted the controlled tirade.

"Tell him we've no time. An enemy force has attacked the camp, possibly Akhtubinsk itself. I need information. Just go and look, not engage. I'll have ammunition sent to him as quickly as possible."

Regardless of the wording of his reply, it was clear that Vlassov was singularly unimpressed.

Another officer was quickly dispatched to ensure 3/2 Recon got some ammunition in short order.

He passed Yarishlov on the way into the command centre.

Bailianov quickly brought his commander up to speed on what he knew, what he believed, and what he had so far done.

Yarishlov reeked of the cream that he covered himself from head to foot in, a very necessary three-time daily process that kept his damaged skin supple and reduced his pain.

Interrupted half way through the application, he grimaced as a patch of untreated skin protested at his bending position.

"Good so far, Boris Ivanovich. So, the camp and the airfield?"

Neither man had any concept of the significance of the camp other than it held many Allied POWs.

"Camp and airfield... they mean to rescue and fly prisoners out?"

"Only thing I can think of, Comrade General."

"Then we'll stop them... fourth tanks... their status?"

"Closest to the ammunition train so they're already loading up, Comrade General."

"Excellent. Whichever of your infantry companies is ready to go first goes with them to the airfield. If we can reoccupy that, then they've already lost."

"Best to send Sixth Company. Fourth is nearer but they have the damned British carriers. Sixth will be quicker to arrive. I was about to give that order... the recon needs support there."

"Yes... good, good."

A major recorded the order and waited for more.

"Get that in motion immediately, Comrade Mayor."

Zorin and Harazan arrived together.

"No time for great explanation, Comrades. We have reports of firing and enemy soldiers at the camp... and at the airfield. This is what we've done so far."

Both men took in the map symbols and understood the tactical situation.

"I'm going to move Fourth Infantry Company up to Akhtubinsk... here... to babysit the road and rail bridges over the Akhtuba. Fifth Infantry will move to provide close support for First Tanks. I'll want your engineer group to follow-up in support."

Harazan nodded.

"My first company is already properly armed, Comrade General."

They all looked at the junior man.

"As the exercise was cancelled, I was intending some afternoon practice shooting proper bullets. This map isn't correct. They're actually positioned here."

He indicated a point a kilometre south of the first tank's laager position, just off the Astrakhan-Akhtubinsk highway.

"As soon as I heard that something was going on, I sent an order to my units to come to full alert... I made no contact with first company... I assumed... hoped... a radio problem."

84

"Get a motorcyclist off to them immediately... and provide a replacement radio just in case...first tanks can move to them and then use them as support... mission to close on the camp and isolate it. "

Yarishlov looked Zorin in the eye.

"Nikolay Terentievich... I want you to lead. Act as you see fit to prevent any movement towards Akhtubinsk. Obviously, we need to know what's happening at the camp ... just do what needs to be done, Comrade."

Zorin saluted and sped off as fast as his battered body would allow. His command jeep roared away as Yarishlov and Bailianov sent more orders out to the experienced soldiers of the 7th MCTS.

Not for the first time, Bailianov did a second take at the radio message, Vlassov's calm voice confirming an enemy presence at the airfield.

'Aircraft... at least a company of soldiers...'

"Tell them to pull back... await ammunition and the arrival of reinforcements!"

"That confirms it then, Boris Ivanovich... they're at the airfield in strength. They mean to fly out from there. We need more of our resources, I think."

The two pored over the map and started to bring more assets into play.

Their pupils, the 218th Tanks and 115th Marines, were ordered to secure the airstrips around the three Baskuntschaks: Verkhiny, Sredniy, and Nischni.

Both the 218th and 115th were also to form two mobile forces, the stronger one to head across country and cut the route south at Bataevka on the highway to Astrakhan.

The other force was to follow-up the training school's own troops heading towards Akhtubinsk.

Yarishlov understood that, with the fuel situation crippling the armour's mobility, the 218th could field fewer than twenty tanks in total, but they would be enough against whatever the Allies had sent to release the prisoners.

"Right, Comrades. I'll take over here myself. Boris Ivanovich, I want you at the airfield."

Bailianov saluted and sped away, calling men to him as he went.

"And you, Georgi Illyich... you I want on the Akhtuba crossings... here... and here. No one crosses. I want no surprises in Akhtubinsk, clear?"

"Yes, Comrade General."

Harazan saluted and departed in similar fashion, leaving Yarishlov alone with the situation map for the briefest of moments.

His thoughts were interrupted by the familiar voice at his elbow.

"I don't know what the world's coming to, I really don't. Can't go off fighting anymore so you bring the fighting to you!"

Yarishlov grinned but refused to acknowledge Kriks' presence, preferring to examine the map for flaws in his plans.

"Ha! I'm a senior NCO and refuse to be ignored, especially as I bring a pick-you-up for the officer."

Yarishlov laughed.

"Of course you have some illegal substance on your person. I should have you court-martialled and shot, you fucking scoundrel!"

"No one else would put up with your horrible ways, Comrade General."

Yarishlov accepted the flask, knowing better than to ask what it contained.

He took a cautious sip, all the time conscious of the grinning face of his senior NCO and friend.

"Donkey piss... mind you... not the worst donkey piss that you've served up."

Kriks leant forward so only his commander could hear his reply.

"The Comrade General's a fucking peasant if I might say so. That's Napoleon Brandy, I'll have you know! Next time I'll drain some rusting lorry's radiator for you."

Yarishlov choked on the deep slug he took, mock offence writ large on the Praporshchik's face.

"Later, I'll try some more... but for now, we've a problem to address."

The radio crackled into life as if to reinforce Yarishlov's words.

The General listened intently as the radio operator sought confirmation.

'Helicopters? Under attack by helicopters?'

Not that Yarishlov had seen such things in the flesh, but he had read the briefings and seen the pictures, as had his soldiers.

Those briefings never mentioned that they mounted weapons.

Actually, Vlassov had been a reliable officer, up to the moment one of Trannel's converted FL-282s set his M3 scout car ablaze, incinerating the reconnaissance troopers inside.

The Flettner Glühwürmchen involved shared similar characteristics with the B-2 version that had been a design modification of the original A-1, but Trannel's workshops had altered the majority of the B-2 modifications and traded the weight of the observer and his position in favour of a triple weapon mount on either side of the narrow fuselage.

A simple sight allowed the pilot to aim the six panzerschreck, which were fired individually.

Such a weapon had killed Vlassov and his men, and the FL-282, one of seven such aircraft assigned by the eager Trannel, returned to the Akhtubinsk airfield to rearm and top off its tanks.

The Glühwürmchen were the ace up the sleeve of the assault forces and the prime anti-tank capability of Crisp's unit.

The M3 died at 1118 hrs.

Racing away at just over one hundred miles an hour, the helicopter touched back down at Akhtubinsk two minutes later.

1120 hrs, Friday, 11th April 1947, VNIIEF facility, Uspenka, USSR.

The firefight had been brief but intense, leaving men lying on the concrete walkways as far as the eye could see.

Medics tended to the wounded and, quite naturally, to the American wounded first.

The defending NKVD troopers were mixed in with dead men in white coats or civilian garb.

The casualties amongst the scientists, he assumed that was what they were, were unfortunate, but his men had taken no risks to capture those who held weapons.

"Don't forget the scientists, boys. Patch 'em up as best you can now."

The NKVD wounded were another matter, one they had briefly touched on in the briefings. They would be left to fend for themselves, and everyone knew what that entailed.

Grimacing, Crisp strode forward as his lead squad pushed on.

This part of the operation was the riskiest, given the lack of any firm knowledge as to the layout and what the underground facility held in store for them.

However, the empty workstations, bays, and redundant tools left hanging on their racks gave life to the feeling that they had 'missed the bus'.

Many of the defenders had been gathered around a central core, a square building of two clear levels.

Taking it had cost Zulu Company seven dead. Ten more lay wounded and out of the operation, not counting those who bled but soldiered on.

The troopers continued to fan out, the whole movement undertaken in the strangest of silences, the men of 1st SSF having been trained to move as swiftly but as silently as possible.

Crisp halted to confer with Wijers and Garrimore, and all became conscious of the men moving around with the special detection equipment, or more precisely, the noise coming from each of the four Liebsen-modified Geiger counters.

Sveinsvold, placed in charge of the monitoring group, did not need to report as the sound of the counters was enough to warn of the presence of radiation, as the rattle of a diamondback warns those who approach of the thin thread on which their life might hang.

Watches were checked... 1121 hrs.

The group waited on their leader for further orders.

Crisp watched as the mapping team made their marks.

It had been an idea suggested by Holliday and Jenkins back in Germany, an idea seized upon immediately by an officer who could understand its worth.

The absence of any signage, even in Cyrillic text, made the decision an even stronger one.

The mapping team painted arrows to indicate the route out, drew maps on clipboards, and made marks on the floor every ten yards, adding a numeric to give the assault groups some idea of where they were.

Sveinsvold confirmed the latest mark and made a notation.

"Colonel, that's three-twenty to there."

Each man looked at his own map, a representation constructed from the aerial photographs, folded the tracing paper over the top, assessing the distance travelled and working out where they were.

Commanding the mapping team was a Captain from the Corps of Engineers, a late addition to the team, a man who had fought with the 291st Engineer Combat Battalion from the Bulge and the Rhine through to the unit's bloody and awful flaying at Vienna.

A few of his men were old 291st, the rest made up of a squad from Whiskey's attached platoon.

"Talk to me, Gus."

"Colonel, as we figured. Depth to this point Volga-side is less than a hundred... I figure eighty yards to the entranceway there. That's being formed up. Figure this hall as forty-five yards across. I think that means no closer to the river than one hundred, maybe down to eighty yards in places."

"Well, we always thought it was big. Any rhythm to the layout?"

"Sure seems to be... from this area so far we can see major causeways dividing it up into squares... occasional hiccup such as where we came in... probably just a security thing."

Crisp noticed Holliday waiting to speak but tactfully ignored him to let the Louisianian continue.

"This area seems to be a hub... which makes me think it could be that the other side there mirrors the one we've mapped... which would make the whole facility two hundred to two-twenty across, east to west. That could be horseshit of course."

"Reasonable call, Gus. Until we know how far this sucker goes north, we'll run with that ball. OK boys, listen in... sorry. Doc?"

Holliday spoke swiftly.

"Apologies, Colonel. Three of your men won't make it, five of the others need to be carried out... two walking wounded but out of the fight. Not every wounded man has reported in, but some of the troops are carrying injuries and I haven't time to hunt them out. I'm going to organise evacuation back to the Goose. Is that ok, Colonel?"

"Carry on, Doc."

The overhead gantry system drew comment from the RAF man.

"I'm no expert, but that has to be set to take a couple of tons."

Their eyes followed the tracks, the ceiling-mounted system providing a clear indication of the movements and processes on the floors beneath it.

The rooms that were either side of the main hall were assembly rooms, kept separate by distance and airtight doors, not that the watchers knew that.

What was apparent was the rails emerging from each room where they married with the two main systems, both of which led off towards as yet uncharted territory.

"Yep, my thinking too. OK, primary advance'll be down those two corridors. Follow the gantries. Let's hustle up. Time's not our friend today, boys."

1121 hrs, Friday, 11th April 1947, camp hospital, Camp 1001, Uspenka, USSR.

Momentarily undecided, the doctor decided to press on and ignore the ruckus outside.

'No matter. Time and medicine stop for no man!'

Dryden licked his lips in anticipation and made the cut, bringing forth squeals of protest.

The taut flesh on Murray's inner thigh yielded to the razor-sharp blade, one of three such scalpels that were allowed and constantly monitored by camp security.

"Jowww! Get ye tae fuck!"

Pus and abhorrence gushed from the now excised lump.

"And I thought you Scots were proper men."

"Och! Ye scabby bassa! Ye's relishing it… no fair with ye being a medical man!"

Lieutenant Murray, once of 7th Battalion the Seaforth Highlanders, a prisoner since the Battle of Lubeck in the early days of the renewed war, gritted his teeth through genuine pain as Dryden encouraged more of the foulness to flow, saving half an eye for the return of the senior orderly, who had been dispatched to discover the cause of the firing.

His half an eye failed to register the approach of armed men until they were through the door and into the rest area, from where De Villiers hailed him.

"Hey, Dryden man! We're leaving now! Our commandos are here and we're flying out. We're to help you with the sick. We move now, dokter!"

De Villiers had a way of speaking that always grated on Dryden, and his natural inclination was to bite back, but the insane words struck him temporarily dumb.

"Come on, rooinek. No time to lose now, man. You want a weapon?"

Dryden snorted and refused the pistol.

"What on earth would I do with that?"

"I'm yer man, Saffer. Give it ye 'ere."

The South African tossed the Soviet handgun to Murray and turned to the gaggle of men with him.

"Two to a man unless the dokter says otherwise. Carry them in the sheets... that ok for you, man?"

Dryden shook his senses awake.

"Right... yes, fine... except for our American friend. Four men... nice and easy... how far?"

"They've a bird on the river near the main dock gate. Won't take long in quick time."

Dryden debated leaving the dangerously-ill Schwartz behind for the briefest of moments.

"Carefully with him, blast you!"

He grabbed the Egyptian officer's arm.

"Hany... you go with Major Schwartz here... I'll organise the rest."

The Egyptian was as shocked as his senior, but also found enough understanding to drive himself on.

He oversaw the gentle lifting and carriage of the American officer.

In less than two minutes, the hospital resembled a ghost town, leaving Dryden and Murray alone.

"No time for niceties, Jock."

"Nay bother. I'm up forra wee stroll."

Murray went to rise.

"Wait. Quick dressing to keep the shit out."

Less than eighty seconds later, the two were moving fast towards the river, one with the precious bag of medical supplies that he had begged or borrowed from the camp guards, and a hobbling man in his underpants, trousers in one hand, Tokarev pistol in the other.

1122 hrs, Friday, 11th April 1947, Main gate, Camp 1001, Uspenka, USSR.

For some minutes now, groups of prisoners had been moving out through the holes cut in the wire and off down the road towards the promise of sanctuary offered by the waiting aircraft.

Encumbered solely by the occasional weapon, the men moved swiftly, again a testament to the fitness regime overseen by Robertson and his sidekicks.

None the less, Tabot knew it was a tall ask for the men.

As much as three kilometres to cover, embussing, taxi, take-off... all before the final part of Viking arrived to turn the whole place into a wasteland.

'Shit... hope they're gonna be late...'

Banner and his aircraft were already in the air, inexorably bearing down upon their target.

However, 9 Squadron RAF was not.

The lead aircraft had suffered a wheel strut failure during take-off and its pilot, desperate to save his aircraft, had tried to claw his way into the sky regardless, guaranteeing him and his crew a fiery pyre two-thirds of the distance down the runway and making the whole field inoperable for some time to come.

Even though fire crews struggled to extinguish the flames, and recovery crews waited to drag the wreckage clear, the fine time tolerances of the air plan in Operation Viking were tested, stretched, and exceeded.

9 Squadron was stood down, having done nothing but contribute eight dead men to the list of those who would die in Viking.

Sam Rossiter, in Shaibah for the mission and acting as operational commander, made the call without consultation or hesitation.

Technically, it might make the destruction of the facility less complete, but in reality, it gave those on the ground an extra twelve minutes before death descended from the skies.

The mission's secrecy ensured that the interested parties were not informed of progress or, as in the case of 9 Squadron RAF, failures of Operation Viking.

In places as far apart as the White House, Downing Street, Montgomery's headquarters in Tehran, the control room at RAF Shaibah, or in the briefing room in Leipzig, the great and powerful waited to hear the words that would signify the success or failure of the risky mission on which they had so willingly embarked.

Whether it was a risky mission or fool's errand was still to be seen, although the absence of 9 Squadron moved the possibility of the latter closer.

Not that Tabot knew that, or of the additional breathing space their absence had created.

All he knew was that the Russians were holed up in the main building, a veritable fortress, which was not part of the plan...

... and that the ex-POWs looked fit enough to cover the distance to the waiting aircraft in time to save themselves, which was a hope of the plan...

... and that the Ukrainians had failed to get through to the radio, meaning word had probably got out, which was a failure in the plan...

... and that good men had died already, which was an inevitability of the plan.

"Fuck it!"

"Major?"

Tabot took another look at the still shapes of the Ukrainian raiders who had fallen at the gate, mown down with little chance to defend themselves.

Three, including Shandruk, clung to life, but their hold was thin and fragile.

He had seen enough wounds to know that.

Tabot snorted back and spat a huge gobbet of phlegm to mark his decision.

"That fucker's going down now. I know what the Colonel said... I know what the ammunition issues are... but fuck it. Here's the plan."

He sketched his idea in mid-air with fast-moving hands, and the two officers nodded their understanding.

When it came to the application of brute force, there was little room for interpretation.

Two minutes later, Tabot's bazooka teams broached their restricted stock of rockets, not to be used under any circumstances except on enemy armoured vehicles, and levelled one end of the command building.

The assault went in and no quarter was given.

By the time that X-Ray and a hut group of POWs threw themselves into the ruined building, Skryabin and Durets, along with a security group, had left and were moving towards their objective.

The underground tunnel led from the command facility to an innocuous small room in the main complex and, once they had checked the coast was clear, the seven men emerged into its dim light.

The room suggested itself as a storeroom that had yet to be fully stacked out, the boxes and artefacts here and there intended to disarm the enquiring eye.

They had clearly done their job as the room had been thoroughly turned over by the Allied soldiers.

The door to the main corridor was open, more correctly hanging open by a single hinge, the other hinges shattered as the door had been expertly forced.

Skryabin drew close to Durets as two of his men checked the corridor outside, drawing their commander's attention to the red 'X' chalk mark on the threshold.

Durets beat him to it.

"Comrade Polkovnik. They did not come here for the prisoners... they're here for the weapons... scientists... information..."

Skryabin nodded, full understanding sweeping over him as the rattle of small arms from within the underground complex assaulted his ears.

"Comrade Mayor... our mission is clear. Our orders are clear. I'll remain and ensure the weapon does not fall into enemy hands. You must escape and contact the relief battalion and the training unit. They must not come close to us. I only hope you're senior enough to carry the weight of my orders."

They held eyes for the briefest of moments, but long enough for Durets to see the man's plan... and the man's fear.

"Maybe..."

Durets had been surprised when his commander took on the virtual death sentence mission, and was now comfortable that, with one word, Skryabin had so quickly declared his real decision.

'Senior... you're a fucking shit, Skryabin.'

"Yes... maybe you should, Comrade Polkovnik. Your seniority may be required and, after all, it doesn't require great skill to do what's needed now."

Making a great but brief show of reluctance, Skryabin acquiesced.

"Very well. Discharge standing orders, Comrade Mayor. The time is now... 1127. If immediately threatened then you must do what you must do. If you can secure it, then I suggest 1330, to give you and your men time to get clear. Agreed?"

Durets now had witnesses that his colonel had offered him the opportunity to save himself if circumstances were favourable.

He mumbled the name of some deity, thanking him for both the option and the witnesses.

There was no time to lose.

The intention had been to complete the improvement works, commencing in May. The original design had not linked all the security passageways, which was clearly madness, and that would have been remedied.

Durets route to the secure room was easy, as the entrance to the main security corridor was in the same plain little storeroom.

However, Skryabin and his men had further to travel and would be more exposed, moving for nearly eighty metres to where another small room held secret access to the longest of all corridors, whose design allowed two of the barracks to deploy men underground, and also permitted access to the motor pool.

It was to the latter that Skryabin intended to go, in order to seek transport to allow a swifter escape from the danger zone.

Things went wrong immediately.

Corporal Rideout's face and chest simply came apart as one of Skryabin's men let rip at close range, his finger pulling the PPD's trigger through a combination of reflex and sheer terror.

The lifeless fingers dropped the captured Soviet folders and Rideout fell to the concrete.

Shouts of warning reinforced the echoing sound of the submachine gun, all in voices speaking other than Russian.

The lead NKVD trooper stuck his head round the corner just in time to see an ankle and boot disappear around the next angle.

He pulled out a grenade and expertly threw it against the reverse wall, off which it bounced and disappeared after the owner of the ankle and boot.

Sounds of panic and shouting were quickly overcome by the resounding thud of the grenade.

A second man took up the lead and pushed around the corner.

A man in paratrooper uniform staggered out from the smoke and dust, clearly disoriented by the blast.

"Kill him!"

The man had hesitated, as the enemy soldier was clearly in no position to offer resistance, but orders were orders.

The bullets threw the man back into the corridor where two of his comrades lay badly wounded by the grenade's metal.

Warily, the NKVD group pushed forward a little more before halting, leaving Skryabin and the rear man with the two wounded soldiers.

The rear man acted on Skryabin's orders and set fire to the folders that lay strewn across the floor, and the flames quickly moved across paper, cloth, and flesh.

Whilst the lead men checked the way ahead, the NKVD colonel amused himself by grinding his heel into the throat of one of the casualties, gradually increasing his weight until vital soft tissue was irreparably damaged.

Leaving the man to die, Skryabin transferred his attention to the other wounded soldier.

A soft voice indicated that the point was advancing again, so he simply contented himself with a sharp kick to the man's temple before moving on, smiling at the delicious sound made when the man's skull had yielded to his blow.

More shouts indicated that enemies were closing in, and the small group increased the tempo to reach the safety offered by the secret corridor.

Behind them, the growing fire cooked off one of the grenades on Rideout's belt, sending flesh and burning embers in all directions.

"Anything?"

"Nothing... just three of our men dead... no sign of the leakers anywhere, Colonel."

Crisp could not afford to spend time hunting out whoever had suddenly appeared behind them.

A half platoon was already on the case, but the search for intelligence took precedence.

He turned to the man with the map.

"Gus?"

"We're now here, Colonel. The gantry system terminates at this entrance here... we didn't have it on our map... figure it for moving heavy equipment out of here and onto the docks, or vice versa."

"That the end wall?"

"Sure looks like it, Colonel. Two-seventeen by our count, so we can probably call it two-twenty. Still no figure on how far we run to the north."

A small party of unfamiliar men hastened past, driven by four of his troopers, two of which exhibited bloody dressings as signs of combat.

"Sergeant!"

"Sir?"

"What gives?"

"This lot was holed up in a restroom of sorts. No resistance, Colonel... just threw their hands up. Captain said to get them outta here pronto."

"Ok, Ray, roll 'em out."

Sergeant Barry followed on after his charges.

Crisp noticed that Sveinsvold was in deep conversation with 'Crazy' Gus Falloon.

He let them finish before letting his enquiring presence be known.

The ex-Navy man spoke up.

"Colonel, the readings definitely centre on the rooms off the main hall a'ways back. Then they move down the corridors where the gantries run. There's a coupla rooms off there where we have high readings too... both high-security rooms with special storage facilities... our pet scientist reckons they were both parts stores for the bombs... of which there's no sign... none... nix."

"What, none?"

"None, Colonel. We've moved away from the gantry but readings drop away. I've sent a recorder to gather readings at the river entrance... there...," he touched the map at the bunker exit that they rightly assumed led to the north quay, "... and he started getting good readings immediately."

Sveinsvold lowered his voice.

"The German reckons that the readings indicate the whole shooting match has disappeared up the rails and off down the Volga."

The German was a man to be reckoned with and was along as their expert on atomic weapons.

Crisp nodded, eyeing Diebner from a distance that he didn't wish to close, but knew he would have to.

He detested the man for no reason he could isolate from the general sense of disgust he had of being anywhere near a senior member of the Nazi's atomic weapons programme.

Some flashes made him blink as one of the cameras recorded something or other in an adjacent room.

"Then we continue the search... we've still got time."

Unconsciously, Crisp took a look up at the ceiling, his eyes seeking information on how things were going on the surface.

He could only trust Galkin and the rest of his men to be getting the house in order whilst he pursued the main mission.

One of Falloon's team came running up, ducking between soldiers moving in the opposite direction.

"Machines... lots of the fuckers... look sorta like the ones on the list... these ones, Cap'n."

The noncom fingered the picture of a centrifuge, an important part of the atomic weapon manufacturing process, which placed them very high on the list of things to locate.

"Plus... err..."

"Spit it out, man!"

"They've got Japanese markings."

There was a brief moment of silence as that was absorbed by all.

Falloon broke it.

"How many?"

"Least forty, Sir… didn't have time to count."

"Map it. Colonel?"

Not for the first time, Crisp looked at his watch before making a decision.

"Take Diebner with you. Let him have a look, but only a short one. Grab one if you can. Photograph 'em and smash 'em up. We're running out of time."

It was 1138.

Durets hesitated.

Clicking the switch over was no small matter, for it guaranteed the destruction of the entire facility and probably everyone for five miles in every direction.

'Orders are orders… but… blyad!'

That the device had only just been moved secretly to the small store number 17 was undoubtedly fortuitous as Durets saw it. That he had been shown how to time detonate the device only the previous morning was a decidedly welcome coincidence. He simply did not know that he was about to destroy the facility in advance of Stalin's orders to stage an accident.

His fingers caressed the immediate detonation circuit, and his blood ran cold.

They recoiled at the very thought of what it would initiate.

'Blyad!'

Checking the timer against his watch for the eighth time, he clicked the delayed firing circuit into place and activated the bomb.

From that moment, time was not his friend.

'1330… we must hurry!'

"Right, Comrades… to the Volga as quickly as we can… shoot our way through… get to the boat and get away from this place. Move!"

Behind them, Obiekt 907 counted down to the moment that it would self-detonate.

It was 1139.

It had taken Skryabin and his men longer to get to the vehicle park than he had anticipated.

Walking it in normal circumstances would be a matter of four minutes at a brisk pace, but with the enemy at hand, it had taken eleven.

The guard who was stationed on the inside of the entrance way challenged them nervously, aware that enemy soldiers were in and around the facility.

He reported having seen a number outside the entrance, but none recently.

Checking through the vision slot, the lead trooper gave the sign and the heavy door was unlocked and pushed open.

They swiftly moved outside and simply pushed the door shut behind them.

A Gaz-61 staff car drew their collective eye, and Skryabin nodded his agreement to the lead man, who moved quickly to the vehicle.

The five-seater struggled to accommodate them all, so two men clung to the running boards as the senior corporal started the engine.

Shots rang out almost immediately, although none came noticeably close to the vehicle, which leapt forward towards the north gate.

Skryabin checked his watch.

1140.

1141 hrs, Friday, 11th April 1947, North Gate, Camp 1001, Uspenka, USSR.

"Fire!"

A bazooka shell flew straight and true and the lead vehicle of the security battalion exploded in a fireball, claiming the life of the driver and front seat passenger in an instant.

The crew bailed out in various stages of distress, some alight, some bleeding, some both.

The lighter weapons of the defending 1st SSF opened up on cue and flayed the unfortunates as they sought cover.

A second bazooka shell hit the next vehicle's track as it was turning, immobilising it almost instantly.

Most of the crew chose to bail out on the sheltered side. The two men that chose poorly were shot down without mercy.

Behind them, the rest of the Soviet vehicles fanned out, seeking out the smallest of rises to shelter behind.

Two of them mounted DSHk machine guns, and these opened up, desperate to stem the incoming fire.

Here and there a deploying soldier was taken out but, in the main, they found some sort of cover and all started to return fire.

They were working independently without commands, without orders, and without real direction.

Their deputy commander was presently roasting in the lead vehicle, and their captain lay bleeding his last lifeblood in the sand, his shoulders ripped open by a burst from a .30cal.

The unit's senior NCO started to get a grip but the relief force had been stopped in its tracks.

Crisp received the report in silence, allowing for the man's gasps in between words.

"Here."

He handed the corporal his canteen, forcing a stop on him solely to give him a moment to recover.

"Thanks, Colonel."

"You'll be able to hold?"

"No problem, Colonel. We've... got some POWs there... as well... Them boys are tryin' to... make up for lost time. Terrible fierce souls they are too!"

That was a problem for Crisp, as not for the first time, the liberated POWs were where they should not be, all with the idea of helping their liberators.

The possibility of extra people trying to get aboard the Spruce Goose at the end made Crisp shudder.

He beckoned to Master Sergeant Hawkes who immediately stepped in closer.

Once again, he gave a blunt order.

"Master Sergeant, go back with the corporal. I need the POWs to get the hell outta there. Tell 'em to get back to the Goose. Don't take no for an answer. Can't have them fucking up the recovery."

"Sir, yessir!"

"Tell Lieutenant Al Habidi to get those POWs away and into the Goose. Tell him I may have to can the schedule. Sit tight on the radio but if not, stick to plan."

The two NCOs scuttled away, Hawkes allowing the corporal to lead for no other reason than he had no idea where he was going.

No sooner had the two disappeared around a corner than the inside of the bunker rang with the sound of firing once more.

A group of SSF troopers disappeared off in the direction of the sound without orders.

Crisp looked at the map.

"The dock entrance?"

Falloon nodded.

1148 hrs, Friday, 11th April 1947, North loading dock, Camp 1001, Uspenka, USSR.

Considering the number of bullets that had flown back and forth in a few seconds, Durets considered himself lucky to only have been struck three times, and none in a disabling way.

One of his men was screaming and trying to press the pain out of his shattered crotch, whilst another favoured a leg that dripped blood.

His own wounds seemed trivial in comparison.

A painful ear where one bullet had removed the lobe in surgical fashion, a clip on the left shoulder that had hardly broken the flesh by all he could feel, and his left hand.

Provided all the fingers stayed attached and he had timely medical assistance, he hoped it would one day resemble what it had once been, but for now it looked more like a piece of shredded meat with at least two of the digits more off than attached.

The soldiers they stumbled on had been working a piece of equipment, which distraction had allowed the NKVD soldiers the upper hand.

None the less, the enemy had reacted quicker than expected, hence the injuries sustained.

102

"Get Georgi up... let's move!"

He led his men forward, looking left, right, up, down, all the time gently winding a handkerchief around his ruined hand, an act made all the more tricky because he was holding his Tokarev pistol in the other.

Moving from cover to cover, the small group edged closer to one of the boat sheds, their chosen destination.

Assessing that the coast was clear, Durets sprinted the ten metres or so across the open area and threw himself through the half-open door, failing to work out that the door was already opening slightly.

His weight cannoned into a large man and both rolled on the ground.

Hampered by his wounded hand, Durets could find no way to break the grip of the man's hands around his throat.

His pistol had sprung from his grasp in the impact, so he balled his fist and lashed out at the man's face, ear, anywhere he could make contact.

The American paid no heed whatsoever and continued to throttle the life from the weakening NKVD officer.

One of Durets' men shot him, but still the grip held firm and a mist started to fill Durets' mind.

The soldier had no chance for a second shot as two more Americans grappled with him.

Eight men rolled, gouged, spat, snarled, and bit in an area no more than eight square metres, their thrashing fists and boots striking friend and foe alike as each man struggled to gain the upper hand in a confrontation that could only have one winner.

One NKVD corporal spotted Durets' Tokarev and grabbed it, finding the split-second he needed to fire into the snarling face of the American soldier on top of him.

The man's jaw flew off as the heavy bullet did awful work at short range.

The respite was enough, and the corporal turned the tide of battle, knocking the man off his officer with a single bullet in the side of the head, and then intervening in the other struggles.

The wounded man, dropped outside the door when his comrades rushed into the fray, yelled a warning, and accompanied it with a burst from his PPd.

"More of the bastards, Comrades!"

103

A pair of hands appeared and dragged him into the illusion of safety that the wooden building provided.

Durets, his mind gradually clearing, could not yet speak but managed an understandable gesture towards one of the two motor boats.

The corporal ordered the others to the boat and they quickly obeyed, guiding their stunned officer and dragging the wounded man with them.

Firing through the door, the corporal was rewarded with the sound of an enemy soldier screaming in pain.

The respite was grabbed with both hands, and he dashed for the waiting boat.

The engine coughed into life and the untethered craft leapt forward into the Volga and into a hard right turn.

A burst of fire kicked up water and the wheel went hard over as the steersman decided to avoid whatever it was that started to find the range.

Durets yelped as another bullet found his body, this time burrowing into the side of his right thigh.

The corporal simply fell overboard and disappeared under the water, his injuries obscured by the dark water.

The boat churned up the water, leaving the enemy behind as it headed southwards.

Towards the Volga dock…

Towards…

'Mudaks! What in the name of the fucking Motherland is that?'

Whatever it was, even the befuddled Durets understood it was not friendly, despite its familiar green paint and large red stars.

The POWs lining up to get aboard, the Soviet paratrooper uniforms that had now become a signature of the enemy raiders, and the shouts of alarm from the jetty were enough to convince them all.

The steersman pushed the boat wider towards the centre of the river, even as the first shots rang out.

Instinctively, they crouched lower, although nothing came close enough to score.

They were beyond submachine gun range, but the man with the SKS replied, although the bucking of the boat ensured he hit nothing but air or water.

The boat rounded the huge aircraft, widening the gap a few metres each second until fate took a hand.

A single bullet struck the steersman on the head, the glancing blow enough to knock him senseless instantly.

The throttle died and the boat immediately lost way.

It was then that a number of matters coincided to bring about the circumstances of the biggest risk to the Kingsbury mission.

As the boat lost way, the motion of the water died with its momentum, creating a more stable firing platform.

The boat lay almost perfectly in a dead zone, where SSF troopers had no line of sight, masked as they were by the bulk of the Hercules.

A face appeared at a cockpit window, drawn to expose itself in enquiry as to the source of the firing.

The SKS man saw the movement and, enjoying the newfound stability, put shots on target.

No sooner had he emptied the final rounds into the aircraft than Durets grabbed the controls and sent the boat surging out towards the centre of the river and away from danger, intent on reaching the military post on the River Gerasimovka, six kilometres south of Camp 1001.

Holliday, supervising the loading of wounded, heard the yelps of pain above him as his mind identified the sound of bullets striking wood and something softer.

Shouting for help, he moved up the ladders and onto the flight deck to find a charnel house.

The soldier posted by Crisp, Corporal Layder, had been killed by a single bullet, whose passage had barely disturbed the skin and brought death so quickly as to allow next to no blood to flow.

Layder's lifeless eyes recorded clear surprise and indignation.

Odekirk was balled up in his seat, clutching a shoulder that had been savaged by a single round.

The head wound was bleeding heavily, as head wounds did, but of no great concern in the first instance.

Holliday decided he could wait and turned to Petrali, who was out for the count, a combination of two bullets and wood splinters wounding him grievously.

As he tended to the wounded man, Holliday gave Hughes a look, seeing the eyes wide open but uncomprehending, the mouth working but no sound escaping.

One of the bullets that had struck Petrali had deflected off the man's rib and continued to strike Hughes in the right hip, actually jamming in the socket itself.

Another bullet had journeyed across the top of both knees, destroying bone and cartilage on its travels.

None of Hughes' wounds were life threatening, but Holliday knew instantly that the wounded man, actually the wounded men, would not be flying anytime soon.

The ramifications of that were not lost on him.

The medic with him started to work on Hughes, who suddenly became aware of the pain of his injuries and screamed with each gentle touch of the orderly's hands.

"Morphine."

"No!"

"What?"

Hughes gritted his teeth.

"No morphine... no fucking morphine!"

"But..."

"No fucking morphine. You put me to sleep and we're all fucked, y'understand me?"

He ended the lengthy statement with the most pained of moans as he inadvertently shifted a little in his seat and both knees and his hip vied for the position of most painful wound.

Doc Holliday made a quick decision.

"Mister Hughes. I'll give you enough to take the edge off, not enough to knock you out. But that's my final word."

Hughes didn't argue, or couldn't argue, as pain racked him once more.

The medic had already relaxed Odekirk with a dose of the painkiller and held out an ampoule to the RAF officer.

"You do it. A third... just a third. Keep it on hand so we can judge how much he's had."

Holliday turned back to Petrali, who was starting to deteriorate.

Two more men arrived on the flight deck.

One was given a simple brief.

"Find Colonel Crisp. Tell him the Goose won't be going anywhere unless he can magic up someone who can fly it. Tell him why... none life threatening," he made that statement in case the unconscious Petrali could hear him, believing that the man was not long for this world, "... tell him that the aircraft seems sound, no guarantees on that, but it's going nowhere with the three civvies all out of the fight."

He turned back to work on Petrali, the content of his words striking home in spades.

'We're fucked.'

'We're fucked.'

"Goddamnit!"

'1201.'

Crisp, busy finishing up business in the underground bunker and suddenly finding himself a minute behind schedule, was stunned at the news.

He wanted to know how it had happened... been allowed to happen... but the leader in him knew he had little time to waste on such luxuries; recriminations and blame would be sorted later.

Crisp surprised himself with the immediate thought.

"The prisoners... must be pilots there. Get that Canadian major... Roberts or whatever his name is... I want any pilots amongst his men... anyone at all. Move!"

His mind worked another problem and made an unpalatable decision.

"Lootenant!"

Hässler doubled over.

"Get topsides and fire the 'hold in place' signal... we gotta stay tight for an extra while."

"Colonel."

Within three minutes, Hässler had sent two red flares into the sky, a prearranged set that told the men of 1st SSF to hold position and await further signals.

Operation Kingsbury was starting to unravel.

1207 hrs, Friday, 11th April 1947, Akhtubinsk-1 Airfield, USSR.

The FL-282s had done extremely well, as the smashed and burning lead element of Yarishlov's tank training unit demonstrated.

Men experienced in the ways of war had been taken by surprise, despite the warnings from the survivors of the reconnaissance group that had already suffered at German hands.

One of the mini helicopters had been hacked down by nothing more than submachine gun fire, two mechanised infantrymen bringing the old but reliable PPShs to bear in converging streams at the low-level target, killing the pilot and causing the aircraft to fall from the sky.

Unfortunately for the defenders, it had just taken on board a full reload of HEAT for its panzerschrecks, all of which had now cooked off.

There were no more spare rockets, so the German pilots preserved their ammunition and made dummy runs to provoke a response or mistake from their attackers.

The British RCLs proved accurate and effective, their HESH shells devastatingly so, particularly as the Soviet's hurried antidote, internal chain mesh protection, was not fitted to the training vehicles.

Between the RCLs and Trannel's Glühwürmchen, the Fourth Tank Company had lost twelve of its vehicles, the remaining seven, remarkably including the bright orange official observer's vehicle, were still intact and using cover to preserve their lives.

Meltsov, the tank company commander, his eyes fixed on the burning metal shape that housed four men he had been with for two years, spoke in clipped tones over the radio.

"Uchitel-Alfa, Gurundov-shest'-sto, over!"

Back in the 7th MCTS headquarters, Yarishlov listened in as one of his radio operators took the details of the defeat of his airfield assault.

Kriks held out a lit cigarette as the duty officer made notations, reducing the figures for 4th Tanks and 6th Mechanised Rifle from nineteen and sixty plus mechanised soldiers out of action, nearly half permanently.

"Helicopters... anti-tank guns... machine-guns... mudaks!"

Kriks took a deep drag and exhaled as he considered his response.

"Throwing away men now, Comrade."

Yarishlov nodded stiffly, his skin tightening as the day wore on.

The breathless tank man detailed the loss of the mortar support before they could even deploy, yet in spite of everything, still requested permission to attack once more.

"No! No more... tell him to hold and await reinforcements... wait... ask can he prevent anything from taking off?"

The cigarette dropped ash across the map as the exchange went on.

"Give him that order. Keep the aircraft there but no further attacks."

Thrusting the handset back into the infantryman's grasp, Meltsov took a deep breath.

"You heard our commander, Comrade. We redeploy to cover the end of the airfield."

The two officers took a look at the terrain.

"Excellent... I think your men first... leave me a platoon for close support... my tanks will cover... when you're in position on that rise there... I'll bring my vehicles over and position behind the longer ridge... perfect position. Agreed?"

The hum was enough.

"Go when you're ready, Comrade, and keep your head down."

Kuibida and Gosling took stock of their situation.

The helicopters were more than proving their worth, although their combat time was now limited, as the surviving three craft had seven rockets between them.

They had refuelled the Glühwürmchens for one more flight each, and added the remaining 80-octane fuel to the greedy tanks of the C-46s.

The screams from a fighter pilot stopped them in mid conversation.

A Twin-Mustang had suffered a puncture on landing, probably due to some metal on the runway.

The aircraft flipped over twice before coming to rest upside down.

Two of Gosling's soldiers had braved the flames and pulled a man clear, but not before parts of him had been scalded by hot oil.

The crash had already severed his left foot at the ankle, but it was the awful scalds that gave him the most pain.

In the burning Mustang lay another body, unrecoverable and decidedly dead.

Running over from treating other casualties, one of the medics quickly plunged an ampoule of morphine into the wounded pilot's thigh, bringing both relief to his suffering and to the ears of those around him.

According to the schedule, Akhtubinsk-1 was to be evacuated on receipt of a signal from the highway group, one that indicated that the aircraft assigned there were preparing to depart with their fuselages stuffed with POWs.

Gosling and Kuibida's men had ravaged most everything of value on the airfield, and the few structures left standing were prepared ready for demolition, timed charges silently waiting to be armed by the final departees.

On receipt of the order, the charges would be primed and the helicopters dispatched to cover the withdrawal.

They would then fly south to the highway airstrip, only to be destroyed in place once their pilots were safely aboard one of the transports.

Yarishlov had unwittingly played into their hands by not continuing with the attacks, not that he or they knew that.

For now, Gosling had his own problems, as the radio remained stubbornly silent.

1210 hrs, Friday, 11th April 1947, 7th Mechanised Cooperation Training School, Verkhiny Baskunchak, USSR.

From the man's body language, the person on the other end of the phone was important, a view confirmed by the deferential reply and the rank employed.

'Polkovnik General?...... mudaks!'

Yarishlov accepted the phone from the white-faced operator.

110

"Yarishlov."

"This is Polkovnik General Serov speaking."

Yarishlov's fingers whitened on the handset, a reaction that was noticed by all watching.

"Comrade Polkovnik General. What can I do for you?"

Spurred into action by the stream of words that assaulted his ear, Yarishlov recited the orders and actions of his command in clipped tones; professional, controlled, and as briefly as possible.

Serov then issued his orders and explained the reasons behind them.

Yarishlov's eyes opened wide.

"I had no idea, Comra..."

The burst of fury down the phone was heard by those close by, as Serov exploded.

"Yes... yes... immediately... yes... none whatsoever as far as I am aware... no, our air force comrades are non-existent... yes... wher... Kiev... yes, Comrade Polkovnik Gener... I understand... ye..."

He took the silent handset away from his ear, staring at it as he digested what he had just been told.

'Fucking hell!'

Yarishlov bent over the map and started to rattle out instructions, concentrating his forces on the camp itself, or as he had just been informed, the secret facility of vital importance to the Motherland.

His orders from Serov were clear.

Reoccupy the camp, prevent damage and destruction, and destroy the attackers.

"Orders!"

Within minutes, the attention of 7th MCTS' forces were fully focussed on Camp 1001.

1215 hrs, Friday, 11th April 1947, Akhtubinsk-1, USSR.

The radio crackled into life, bringing the much-anticipated code word.

The radio operator, unnecessarily, repeated it at the top of his voice.

"Clothesline!

"That's it!"

111

Kuibida nodded and signalled to the small group of his men that waited to initiate the timed charges.

Gosling was already on the walkie-talkie pulling in his men, and the helicopters started up, ready to take off and cover their withdrawal.

Fig #251 - Codewords for Operation Kingsbury

CODE WORD	EXPLANATION
BACKSTOP	EVACUATION OF #2 THE HIGHWAY IN PROGRESS
BASERUNNER #1, #2, OR #3	ZONE EVACUATED, #1-AKHTUBINSK, #2 THE HIGHWAY, AND #3 CAMP 1001
CLOTHESLINE	ORDER TO COMMENCE WITHDRAWAL FROM AKHTUBINSK #1, ORIGINATING FROM THE HIGHWAY AIRSTRIP.
CURVEBALL	EVACUATION OF #1 AKHTUBINSK IN PROGRESS
DINGER	INITIATION OF WITHDRAWAL FROM HIGHWAY AIRSTRIP.
HOME RUN	ALL GROUND FORCES AIRBORNE AND RETURNING
PAYBACK	SERIES OF AIR STRIKES ACCORDING TO A PRE-DETERMINED PLAN, DESIGNED TO PROTECT #2 THE HIGHWAY AND #3 CAMP 1001 FORCES AS THEY ESCAPED.
SWEET SPOT	INITIATE THE EVACUATION OF #3 CAMP 1001.

Here and there, a group of troopers carried the body of a dead or wounded comrade, or assisted a limping man.

Casualties had been relatively light, and Gosling had to concede that the Luftwaffe helicopters had outperformed their expectations.

'One for the future there.'

The first Curtiss started to move, each aircraft relatively unburdened now that the spare fuel each carried was in the tanks rather than in the fuselage.

A brace of Twin Mustangs flew parallel to the airstrip and deposited a world of hurt on something out of sight.

He acted immediately.

"That'll do."

He spoke quickly into the radio.

"Whiskey-two-six, Whiskey-six."

Lieutenant Muggeridge of Second Platoon, the unit screening the airfield nearest to the enemy ground force, answered quickly.

"Whiskey-two-six receiving, over."

"Two-six, sitrep, over."

"Air just knocked out a nosey commie armoured car. Otherwise, the suckers have gone to ground, over."

The attack on the nearest Soviet forces provided Gosling with a golden opportunity to disengage, and he immediately grasped it.

"Two-six, saddle up, repeat, saddle up, over."

"Message received and understood six, two-six out."

Within thirty seconds, men from Second Platoon came into view, running for all they were worth towards their designated aircraft.

Gosling waited whilst a Commando accelerated up the runway and took to the air, almost immediately followed by another.

The Twin Mustangs swept back over the field, waggling their wings in salute.

'Don't celebrate too soon, flyboys!'

Second Platoon were closing on their aircraft, but the covering .50cal group held their ground, keen to make sure that nothing interfered with the evacuation.

"You're ready, Oleksandr Antonovich?"

"Charges set. I see nothing to keep us, Comrade Captain."

Kuibida's smile and attempted humour did not fool anyone, the strain set clear in his eyes.

"Roger that."

Gosling took one more look around, sweeping near and far with his binoculars, before giving the order.

"Olek, get it done and let's fuck off. Ok, boys! Rack 'em up and move 'em out! Let's get the hell outta Dodge!"

As the entire headquarters group surged towards their aircraft in something approaching a partially structured riot, Gosling talked as he jogged.

"Steel-six, Steel-six, Whiskey-six, over."

Crisp had his HQ radio group set up above ground, knowing full well that if they went underground the signal would not get through.

His signaller took the important message.

"Steel-six, Steel-six, curveball, repeat curveball, Whiskey-six over."

The unrecognisable voice acknowledged receipt of Gosling's message and the handset was passed back to the man running alongside him.

The men assembled in a semi-circle around the Commando, careful to avoid the whirling propellers.

One last check and Gosling gave the word.

"Move out!"

He and Kuibida stood either side of the door, half helping, half flinging men up the steps into the safety of the fuselage.

Over to the left, Gosling could see that the .50cal squad were now following hot on the heels of Second Platoon.

Elsewhere, the last men of 1st SSF were scuttling aboard the other waiting Commandos, as others commenced their jockeying for position on the runways.

The sound of heavy weapons drew the attention of every man, be they in the aircraft or outside.

A C-46, desperately clawing its way into the air for the short journey to the highway airstrip, shuddered as it was struck by heavy calibre bullets.

With all the grace of a block of concrete, the Commando tumbled from the air and pancaked behind a small ridge.

A fireball and smoke shot skywards from the crash site to mark the end of hope for those on board.

Gosling had no way of knowing if it was an empty aircraft, geared up to take more of the prisoners assembling at the highway strip, or one carrying his men.

He exchanged looks with Kuibida and followed the Ukrainian up the ladder and into the C-46.

Three Twin Mustangs were already diving to prosecute whatever had shot the Commando down, and the next aircraft in line was climbing into the sky and turning to port as hard as it could without stalling, clearly making sure it avoided the enemy gun.

The Mustangs enjoyed themselves with the few targets they could see, ensuring that the rest of the transports took off without incident.

Behind them, Akhtubinsk-1 and its aircraft lay in ruins.

Ahead of them lay another landing, this time on the highway, which was still packed with aircraft, troopers, and POWs, contrary to the Gosling's understanding of the 'Clothesline' code word.

It was 1224.

1219 hrs, Friday, 11th April 1947, Camp 1001, Uspenka, USSR.

Crisp had returned to the surface and was shielding his eyes from the sunlight.

Around him, troopers and prisoners were moving towards the Goose, none of them yet aware that the safety it offered might yet be an illusion.

He spotted Hässler moving swiftly towards him.

"Talk to me, lootenant."

"Colonel, sir... from Whiskey... curveball... one minute ago, Sir."

Their code words were derived from baseball, as devised by Galkin who was a lifelong Detroit Tigers fan and lived and breathed the 'game of games' as he called it.

Curveball indicated that the whole of the airfield force was evacuating.

"OK. Right. Get on the horn to Yankee, make sure they're advised. Get a sitrep. If they're ready to go, send 'em off."

Hässler moved back towards the radio and was quickly in touch with Yankee Company on the Akhtubinsk Highway.

Meanwhile, Crisp contacted the main gate party, speaking directly to Bud Tabot.

He was satisfied with Tabot's report.

"Roger that, X-Ray-six, standby for orders, Steel-six, out."

He called up the north gate party, from which direction firing again erupted, timed almost to the millisecond of his message.

The radio remained silent, but the sound of shooting increased.

He sought contact again but was unrewarded.

Charlie Bluebear emerged from the bunker entrance and Crisp seized the opportunity.

"Captain! Need you to get up to the North gate. Make sure you take a spare radio for them, just in case. I need a sitrep immediately. Waiting on that before I give the order to go. Clear?"

"Yes, Colonel."

Shouting orders to men nearby, the huge Indian ran off towards the sounds of battle.

'Where's the Canuck major?'

"Colonel, Yankee are initiating 'Dinger' but they're not full. Loading's been way slower than anticipated. Expect some crossover between their leaving and Whiskey arriving."

There was no point in Crisp interfering as Hanchard would have been all over the problem.

The prisoners had always been the unknown element in the evacuation equation.

He nodded as his mind chewed over the ever-increasing pressures of his command.

Speaking into the walkie-talkie, he sought contact with the air liaison officer.

"Alpha-one, Steel-six, confirm air situation, over."

There was a short delay as Peter George checked his facts.

He stared down at Crisp from his vantage point in the tower, gesticulating with his map as he spoke into the walkie-talkie.

"Most of the air's gone now, Colonel. I've two groups inbound for top cover over the Goose, another two over Whiskey but they're short on legs now. Tactical air's down to one squadron. FB-20 Craneflies. They're inbound to us in eight minutes, with twenty minutes loiter, 20 millimetre and rockets, over."

'Twenty-eight minutes... shit.'

"Alpha-one, roger. Out."

'C'mon, Bluebear...'

His eye caught the approach of the Canadian major as he passed the walkie-talkie back to his operator.

"Major Roberts. Tell me you've good news."

"Colonel, there's only two pilots amongst my lot...a South African jet fighter pilot, plus I've got a navy doctor who's also flown fighters. We never had more a handful of air crew."

116

The vast difference between the Spruce Goose and a sleek fighter was not wasted on either man.

The reason behind the lack of air force personnel amongst the prisoners would keep for less pressing times.

"They'll have to do."

"I already sent them off to the aircraft, Colonel. Felt you'd want them there as quickly as possible."

"Thank you, Major Roberts. Let's hope they're up to the task. Now, can you move your men along quickly? We've little time now."

The Canadian saluted and spun on his heel.

A roar of engines marked the nearby passage of a Soviet aircraft, a LaGG to Crisp's mind, smoking from some unseen damage.

The two Twin Mustangs following in hot pursuit both wisely decided not to fire whilst their quarry was anywhere near the camp.

They knew, as did the pilot of the damaged Soviet fighter, that the reprieve was temporary

Crisp wrenched his eyes away from the two Allied aircraft, quietly envying their freedom and lack of responsibility, and focussed his mind on the tactical problems.

Akhtubinsk was being evacuated.

The highway force was already taking POWs away, but behind schedule, meaning that the transports from the airfield with the extra capacity would be delayed.

The main gate resistance was crushed, but fighting continued at the north gate.

Out of sight, the lead Mustang hacked the wounded LaGG-3 from the sky and sent it plunging into the Volga.

'C'mon Bluebear!'

A single centrifuge had been rapidly removed from the site under Diebner's watchful eyes.

A mass of written intelligence had been recovered.

A number of men who looked like they could be scientists had been captured.

There were no atomic devices.

The flight crew of the Goose had been savaged.

'Fuck... who could've predicted that.'

The POWs were fit... a bonus... but slow to move for some reason... and evacuation was delayed.

Soviet reaction had been manageable so far...

117

'... so far...'

Air cover was still available... but...

As if to assuage his concerns, an Allied aircraft dropped its bomb load somewhere near the North gate, bringing hoots and whistles from his troopers, and cries of celebration and distress from nearby POWs, many of whom experienced the sight of napalm for the first time.

Two wounded on stretchers were carried past at high speed, the bearers keen to be away and into the safety of the Goose.

Crisp reminded himself of another fact.

Men had died.

"Steel-six, Zulu-six, over."

Crisp took the WT back and acknowledged Bluebear's call sign, although it was not Captain Bluebear doing the talking.

"Steel-six. Air just hit the Soviets with napalm. Zulu-six requests permission to disengage, over."

Crisp understood the situation. Bluebear was saying that the airstrike was on target and had bought them time whilst the Soviets recovered.

His decision process took less than two seconds.

"Zulu-six from Steel-six. Sweet spot... I say again... sweet spot, Steel-six over.

"Steel-six, Zulu-six. Sweet spot received and understood, over."

Crisp was already getting the word out to the other units.

Sweet spot was the order to cut and run.

Kingsbury had run its course and was now all about getting the boys home.

All over Camp 1001, the men withdrew towards the Spruce Goose.

1228 hrs, Friday, 11th April 1947, the Spruce Goose, Volga River, USSR.

The deposit of napalm on the enemy at the north gate had an impact on those POWs queueing to get aboard the huge amphibian.

With freedom just a few steps away, the huge wall of flame incited the majority to press forward, making the act of boarding more difficult and slowing up the process.

SSF and POW NCOs shouted and cajoled, but the surge of men proved difficult to control.

One of Crisp's troopers overused his rifle butt to keep the men in line and fists were thrown.

In an instant, men tantalised by the proximity of safety and charged by fear were brawling unashamedly.

A booming Scots voice rose above the melee as Robertson waded in, pulling men away, ably assisted by an equally vocal Julius Collins.

CSM Green and Staff Sergeant Black pushed and shoved men back into line and order was quickly restored, but not before Crisp's rifleman had been battered unconscious along with two of the POWs, somehow turned on by their own.

Understanding the situation, the two senior NCOs moved closer to the door, and partly helped, partly shoved men through the twin doors into the interior, where a pair of experienced USAAF loadmasters directed each man to their positions.

By the time that Crisp arrived, the embarkation was moving smoothly and there was no sign of the altercation ever having occurred.

He checked his watch.

'1233. Shit.'

"And that's all there is to it."

Hughes grinned through clenched teeth, his pain just kept at bay by Holliday's ministrations.

The area behind the flight deck was deserted, save for the inert form of Petrali, the groggy but conscious Odekirk, and the medic who tended them.

De Villiers and Dryden had volunteered immediately but what they were looking at, what they had just been given a brief on, bore scant resemblance to any sort of flying experience in their collective memories.

The wounded Hughes had quickly gone through the basics as best he could, and the fact that the two were pilots meant they had even understood some of what he said.

"So, Navy man, best you get acquainted with the controls there."

Dryden laughed nervously.

"Oh no, Saffer's much more experienced a pilot than I."

De Villiers shrugged in acknowledgement and went to move forward but Hughes held up a bloody hand.

"Experience isn't the problem. It's height. You're more my size, Navy. The seat adjustment's jammed... damaged when we took fire. You win the prize position, Captain."

Without further argument, Dryden slid himself into the seat, ignoring the wet and sticky residue, whilst De Villiers took position in the second seat, adjusting it to suit his smaller stature.

Odekirk, nursing the headache from hell, was in the engineer's seat, a job that would have been beyond anyone lacking a deep understanding of the aircraft.

Holliday had acquiesced and stopped administering the morphine to allow Hughes to concentrate fully on the job.

The wounded pilot propped himself up in the temporary seat and went through the controls with the two men, who absorbed as much as they could but were both clearly daunted and out of their depth.

Two of Crisp's troopers were rigging the chair in position using lines, securing it between the two pilots' seats and the small stair rails, something that Hughes had insisted on and which Holliday had not been able to deny him.

He needed to be able to see and advise and that was that.

The grand tour of the controls continued and the two POWs struggled to consume as much of the input as possible, all the time understanding that the moment of truth was rapidly approaching.

1239 hrs, Friday, 11th April 1947, the Volga Gate, Camp 1001, Uspenka, USSR.

Tabot saluted and quickly briefed his commander.

"No pursuit, Colonel. We used up our bazooka ammo on the headquarters building. They're either all dead or'll be nursing some serious fucking headaches for a week. All casualties recovered... dead and wounded... we've lost thirteen, plus most of the Ukrainian boys. Six of the POWs are dead too. Twenty-nine wounded all told. Wounded have gone on ahead... I've kept back our dead over there."

Tabot indicated a group of men who had taken a knee alongside the bodies they were responsible for transporting.

"I've a couple of squads screening our rear but the rest of my boys are on the way to the Goose."

"Shandruk?"

"Hit bad… very bad… can't say for sure, but my medic reckons he's not long for this world, Colonel."

Crisp turned to observe the Goose consume its human cargo, the more orderly lines slipping inside with greater ease, overseen by the severe POW NCOs.

Both men watched as some piece of machinery was prioritised, the eight men manhandling it swearing and sweating profusely. Only Crisp understood it was a centrifuge, and although he knew it was important, did not quite understand what it did in the greater scheme of atomic things.

"Have all the prisoners your side gone to the highway?"

"Yes, Sir. They've been kept fit, for sure. No doubts they'll make the hike."

"Great. Good job. OK, Bud. Get the rest of your men aboard. My boys'll handle rearguard."

They exchanged hasty salutes and Tabot moved off, calling his men to him and leading them away to the waiting amphibian.

Crisp silently watched as the bodies of men he commanded were carried past, some bearing grim damage, testament to the serious fighting in and around the main entrance.

The last men started to emerge from the underground facility, clutching more paperwork or, in one man's case, a bag containing all the typewriter ribbons he could find, a specific requirement ordered by Rossiter.

The cameras were already aboard and sealed in waterproof bags, the information they had recorded as safe as it could be.

Galkin made another mark against his list and showed it to Crisp.

"Getting there, Con, getting there."

He didn't need to look at his watch to know that the schedule had gone to shit, just as Galkin knew that he didn't need to remind his commander.

Gus Falloon, Garrimore, and Wijers led a few men out of the bunker entrance and counted them out before conferring.

The nods told their story but Crisp still waited for verbal confirmation.

1st Lieutenant Garrimore jogged over to his two seniors.

"Colonel, Sir. Everyone's out of the bunker. Captain Falloon's booby traps are set."

"Good work, Anderson. Get everyone away to the Goose. Quick as you can."

He acknowledged the salute and nodded at Falloon, who had been watching the exchange from distance.

The officers led their men away to the dock.

"Now just Bluebear."

"Yes indeedy, Colonel."

A look to the north revealed nothing, but at least there were no sounds of combat to warn of problems in the withdrawal.

Crisp made another decision and held out his hand for the WT.

"Alpha-One, Steel-Six, over."

Again, he looked at the air controller's position in the tower, seeking eye contact with the man on the radio.

"Steel-Six, Alpha-One, go ahead, over."

"Alpha-One, air mission... initiate payback, repeat initiate payback."

Crisp instigated the focussing of all air assets on protecting the highway airstrip and the Spruce Goose, the final pre-determined air mission before everyone was on the way home.

"Make sure your assets watch out for my aircraft. I want no mistakes, over."

"Steel-Six, Alpha-One. Payback... repeat payback. Will do, Steel-Six, Alpha-one, over."

"Alpha-One. Move out once complete. Over and out."

Crisp terminated the exchange quickly as men started to appear from the north, either staggering and in pain, or carrying a man too wounded to support himself.

"Con, stay here."

Crisp headed off towards the newcomers, a squad of the headquarters group in close company.

He met with Hawkes who was helping Lieutenant al Habidi to move back, supporting the wounded officer who had clearly lost a foot and sustained other wounds.

Crisp whistled up two of his own men to take over and the badly wounded man was moved away.

"Talk to me."

"When the napalm came down, Bluebear gave the order to fall back... the fuckers rushed us... guess they were keen to get close and out of the fire. Close quarter shit. They're all down but our boys and the POWs are stuck… too many wounded to move everyone out. Some more of the fuckers turned up at the end too. We need more men, Colonel."

"How many needed?"

"There's twenty, actually probably thirty men who need help. I left six fit men behind, including Captain Bluebear."

"OK, Hawkes. Get yourself back to the aircraft a-sap."

"Oh no, Colonel. I'm going back."

"No you're not! I'm telling …"

"No time for this horse-shit, Colonel! I can get you back there and out quickest, and you know it."

"Damnit."

There was no time for argument.

Crisp turned looking for assets.

'Galkin… no… needed where he is.'

The four POW NCOs were close by, having reported to Galkin on the loading of their men…

The air liaison team…

Falloon and his men heading to the dock…

A large group of men with Hässler…

'Falloon and Hässler!'

He resorted to a loud whistle, which attracted the attention of everyone in sight, and then hand signals to give instructions.

Gesticulating at the selected knots of men, he whirled his arm around his head, patted his helmet, and pointed back down the route that Hawkes had come.

The disparate groups converged on Crisp and his men, who moved off in the tracks of the rapidly disappearing Hawkes.

1241 hrs, Friday, 11th April 1947, North Gate, Camp 1001, Uspenka, USSR.

Crisp and his assorted men arrived gasping for air and flopped into the positions occupied by the remnants of the north force.

The dead were numerous; Russians, SSF troopers, and POWs intermixed in the scrapes and holes where hand to hand combat had been their end, or spread wide on the surrounding ground, cut down by bullet or high explosive, a tableau easily read by those experienced in the violence that war offers.

"Captain!"

Charley Bluebear had reacted to the unexpected arrival in his location with great speed and menace, so Crisp's warning was loud and clear, more than a little enhanced by fright at the towering Indian's apparent threat.

Bluebear relaxed when the recognition hit home.

"Colonel. Sorry, was not expecting you."

"No time now... we've got to get you out and back to the Goose. Are we safe to move?"

"No, Sir. Our enemy is coming. New men have arrived. We must stand."

The sound of engines carried from the Soviet positions, although partially muffled by the smoke from destroyed vehicles and other unspeakable things still burning after being bathed in napalm.

Crisp waved his men out into a firing line.

They responded quickly, even though most had already selected a wounded or dead man to carry back.

The engine sounds grew and, as the tell-tale clatter of T34 track pins became clearer and spoke of what was in the smoke, the enemy force burst through the black oily screen and into the assault.

Four tanks laden with infantry, accompanied by two armoured lorries.

On the right flank, Hässler snatched up a bazooka, noting that it was already loaded, the previous user having never got off a shot before taking a bullet in the head.

Confident that he could kill the nearest tank with a frontal shot, he waited on the order to fire.

One consequence of the circumstances was that each man could easily find a weapon of greater killing power somewhere near at hand, one no longer needed by its former owner.

The defenders marked their targets and waited on the order.

Crisp balanced the tactical issue; that of keeping the enemy at distance with the need to do maximum damage as quickly as possible in order to give his men a breathing space in which to successfully disengage.

The M20 Bazooka had an accurate range of about three hundred and fifty yards, so his decision-making was based on getting a good shot in with the two weapons that his men held ready.

He counted down the moments as the tanks drew closer, pushing forward in haste rather than caution, driven by the imperatives of Serov's command and Yarishlov's encouragement.

Crisp eased an AK-47 into his shoulder and relaxed his breathing, almost dispassionately selecting his target with one half of his brain as the other half wrestled with calculating the diminishing distance.

He shouted and pulled the trigger in unison.

The ad hoc force opened fire, sending a storm of bullets down range and into the advancing Soviet soldiers.

His own target flew off the side of the tank on which he had been perched as Crisp's burst crashed into him.

The lead tank disintegrated as Hässler's bazooka shell struck home, ruined metal and many of the men riding the vehicle cartwheeling in all directions in a fiery starburst of ruined metal and torn flesh.

The other target slewed as its nearside track and running gear was destroyed, its crew firing everything they had indiscriminately, in a desperate attempt to kill the threat to its existence.

Fortunately, the two SSF soldiers serving the weapon were experienced and the reload was done in record time.

Another rocket quickly struck home, catching the tank low on the turret.

As the Soviet tanks floundered, the mechanised infantry got to work, knowing that bloody times lay ahead.

One of the lorries had been flayed and its contents flung around in disarray.

The thin metal shields attached to the lorry for training purposes, purely to give it the look of a half-track, provided little extra protection against the machine guns at such close range.

Barely a man capable of fight escaped from the vehicle, and the few that staggered away were quickly chopped down.

Target selection by the light machine guns had let the gunners down and all three weapons concentrated on the lead vehicle, allowing the other vehicle to disgorge its contents relatively unscathed.

An 85mm HE shell sent pieces of Crisp's men flying in all directions, destroying one of the M20 bazookas in the process.

The two surviving tanks pressed on, their infantry grapes hanging on for all they were worth, or in one unfortunate's case, falling off and breaking both legs.

Their hull machine guns swept back and forth, causing more casualties amongst the defenders.

Hässler received a slap on the shoulder as the loader ducked away from the rear of the weapon, another rocket ready to go.

Stone and dirt stung his face as the nearest tank's gunner spotted the threat of the large calibre tube but the hull machine gun missed as the vehicle bounced over undulating ground, the driver jinking in response to the desperate instructions of the T34's commander.

The rocket flew true and struck the turret.

Inside the tank, the particle stream ruined flesh and equipment, killing the three men manning the turret instantly.

The driver altered direction away from the threat and bore down on the centre part of the defensive line.

Hässler and his loader were already relocating, as the second smoke trail had drawn more fire from the supporting machine guns.

In any case, he would not have been able to stop the T34 crashing into the defensive line, where it halted for the briefest of moments to allow the infantry grape to deploy straight into the Allied position.

Men went down on both sides as weapons spat bullets, but still the screams of the pair of wounded POWs underneath the tank reached all ears, even the two crewmembers who grinned mercilessly as the T34 spun on its tracks and ground them to a pulp.

Waiting Soviet soldiers saw their opportunity and rushed forward to support those already closely engaged.

The fighting became desperate as the Allied soldiers tried hard to disengage and the Soviets pressed close for revenge, both sides unaware that the clock was ticking on all their lives.

Overhead, a pair of Craneflies flew impotently, unable to decide who was friend and who was foe, their weapons silent for fear of killing their own side.

Experienced AA gunners on the ground wisely decided not to make the decision easier for the two marauding aircraft, and their weapons also stayed quiet.

In the defensive line, grenades, assault rifles, and submachine guns ruled.

Like a quality batsman, Robertson swatted a Soviet grenade with the butt of his weapon as Green sent one of his own back in return.

Yelps greeted their ears as shrapnel struck home, halting the Soviet push up on their portion of the line.

Some of Crisp's troopers were dragging wounded men away as more Russians arrived, the second lorry and its human cargo almost unscathed in its approach.

More grenades flew back and forth, bringing sounds of pain and injury.

The last tank allowed its grape of infantry to dismount, but stayed back from the line, preferring to use its weapons to pick off resistors as they became apparent.

Hässler and his loader had found a good angle on the tank and another rocket was readied.

Bazooka and machine gun fired together, and with equal accuracy.

The HEAT warhead struck the side of the angled turret in a perfect hit.

The hull machine gun hit both men in the same instant.

Hässler squealed in pain as a bullet smashed into his shoulder joint, the passage of a second bullet through his upper arm going totally unnoticed.

The loader dropped unconscious as a single round cracked his skull on its way into the earth beyond.

Seventy yards away, the T34 rolled gently onwards, inexorably moving forward with engine in gear and dead hands on the controls.

From his own position, Charley Bluebear witnessed the T34's death and the destruction being wrought upon Hässler and his loader and was up and running before thought occurred, intent on rescuing the wounded men.

Soviet soldiers saw the large, fast-moving object but simply couldn't get a decent shot on target as Bluebear covered the thirty yards in Olympic time.

As he rolled into the modest position, a rush of men caught his eye.

The Cherokee came up firing his Thompson, putting two or three bullets into the air at each target.

His natural skill at arms lay with other more earthy weapons, but still three of the attackers went down hard and out of the fight.

Other shots reached out and plucked more men from the surge, but five survivors reached the position.

The Soviet guardsmen very quickly wished it otherwise.

The first man to launch himself over the edge of the scrape had his face stove in by a swinging Thompson butt, and he lost interest in the fight in an instant. The blow was so hard that the wood shattered at the coupling with the weapon's body.

A bullet from an SKS grazed Bluebear's stomach, which served more to enrage him than inhibit him.

The Russian soldier loomed large, intent on driving his bayonet into the man, but suddenly realised his prey was not incapacitated and was filled with a malevolence he had never seen before.

"Tsuhnuhlahuhskim!"

The Russian screamed as the blade swung in from his right side, a scream that terminated in an instant as the battle knife passed through his throat, clipping his cervical spine as it went.

The body dropped, squirting blood from the terrible wound.

Another bullet hit Bluebear, causing him to bellow with pain. It struck him just to one side of the graze, penetrating and exiting without hitting bone, but damaging his intestine on its passage.

His stagger was interpreted as weakness and the man rushed forward, ready to swing his spade.

The blow would have decapitated Bluebear, but for the tomahawk that he thrust out to block the move.

The shock jarred both men but the Russian's momentum drove him forward and crashing into the Indian.

He recoiled, suddenly appreciating the physical presence of the American soldier, something masked by the fact that he had been stood in a hole.

The Soviet soldier swung his spade again but Bluebear ducked easily and drove his knife upwards, punching the long blade into the man's solar plexus and upwards into vital areas.

The enemy soldier fell away gurgling his last, but his roll away wrenched the knife from Bluebear's grasp.

A Soviet soldier pulled the trigger of his PPd but the burst went wide as four .30cal bullets simultaneously threw him backwards like a rag doll.

The environment outside of the position seemed more hostile than the inside, so the two remaining Soviets threw themselves forward.

One crashed into Hässler as he was trying to drag the insensible loader into an upright position.

All three men collapsed into a dishevelled heap, with the Soviet soldier recovering quickest.

His fists clenched and he smashed Hässler in the face with a left-right combination that would have made Joe Louis' manager wax lyrical with pride.

The effect was to stun Hässler and he fell back, allowing the man to commence throttling him with a powerful grip.

Bluebear took a rapid step to his right and swung the tomahawk with every ounce of strength he possessed.

"Tsuhnuhlahuhskim!"

The Indian battle-axe had never before been placed under such extreme forces and, as the blow went home, Bluebear felt the hickory handle shudder and protest as it sustained damage.

He couldn't hear it break, because the awful blow brought a sound of destruction all of its own; the loud obliteration of flesh, brain matter, and bone, blending into one precise but awful sound.

In his haste, he had delivered a backhand stroke, one that brought the hammer poll into contact with his enemy's head.

The tomahawk, driven by Bluebear's immense strength, and despite the blunt face presented to the target, moved through any resistance that the man's head offered, before sweeping out the other side, having trepanned the soldier in the briefest of moment's, the top of his head still attached by the smallest portion of skin and hair.

Despite his dazed state, Hässler was still horrified by the explosion of human matter in front of his eyes and he instantly doubled up and summoned up the contents of his stomach.

That involuntary move prevented Hässler's death, but it also left Bluebear open, and a Soviet guardsman took his chance.

Altering his thrust to pass over the vomiting man, he pushed hard at Bluebear.

The SKS' bayonet drove into the Indian's stomach, only two inches from where the bullet had struck him.

He went down, rocked backwards and knocked off balance by the ferocity of the blow.

The enemy soldier was clearly a veteran who knew his business, and he fired his weapon to make extraction of the blade an easier matter.

More damage and pain was heaped upon the Cherokee, but he still tried to get to his feet.

The SKS plunged forward again but stopped dead in an instant.

The Russian looked incredulously as the thrust was halted by a pair of bloody hands on the barrel.

The damaged tomahawk dangled from Bluebear's right wrist by its strap, but he could not use it as both his hands were needed to prevent the bayonet plunging home a second time.

For the first time in his life, Bluebear knew he was at a disadvantage, the enemy soldier being above him and pressing down, and his own strength failing second by second as the three wounds took their toll.

Charley Bluebear summoned his ancestors to the forefront of his mind and launched a huge effort, driving the SKS up and away from him.

The Russian staggered back, his heel catching on one of his unfortunate comrades, but he kept his balance and possession of the weapon.

As he contemplated the options of sticking the big bastard a few more times or simply shooting him, Marion Crisp intervened and ripped the man's chest and face open with his AK-47.

Quickly, the modest defensive position was filled with helpful hands, and the three wounded Americans were swept up and carried back, all under the cover of a veritable storm of protective fire.

Crisp himself covered the withdrawal, using the superb Soviet assault rifle to keep the enemy's head down, although no targets suggested themselves as the Russians exercised discretion and remained hidden.

He hobbled slightly as a bullet had clipped his ankle during the surge forward.

The obvious disinclination of the enemy to pursue, or even engage, convinced Crisp that they should move back to the Goose immediately.

The north gate defenders turned on their heels and ran.

It was 1252.

1250 hrs, Friday, 11th April 1947, junction of Ul. Astrakhanskaya and the Akhtubinsk-Baskunchak highway, USSR.

Skryabin railed at the tank officer, the spittle flying in his vehemence and near panic.

"Order your men forward, Mayor! I order you to order them forward!"

"But we've no munitions... no fuel, Comrade Polkovnik. We simply can't move against the camp without fuel... without bullets and shells... even you must be able to see that?"

"Even me? Even me! Listen... I don't give a fuck if you throw flowers at the bastards, just move your tanks now, you fucking coward!"

"No. I will not obey that order, Comrade Polkovnik."

The man was dead before he hit the ground, a single shot from Skryabin's pistol sending him to whatever the afterlife held for the veteran soldier.

"You! You're now in charge! Obey my orders!"

The female Senior Lieutenant looked at her dead commander and back at the undoubtedly unhinged NKVD colonel, clearly trying to make sense of the last two minutes of her life.

Herself a veteran of scores of battles, this was an all-new experience for her.

Her mind reminded her of another place; Wolomin in Poland.

It was there that she had earned her spurs.

In July 1944, it was on the outskirts of Wolomin, during the Battle of Radzymin, that she had earned the first of her two Red Stars and won the respect of those under her, although it cost her an ear and two fingers on her left hand, and 75% casualties in her tank company. The 3rd Tank Corps had been assailed by the 4th, 19th, Hermann Göring, and 5th SS Panzer Divisions.

Her courage had not failed her that day, or any day subsequently, and it did not fail her now.

Senior Lieutenant Alina Demkina stood erect and proud.

"Comrade Polkovnik. My unit's no live ammunition and low fuel stocks. To advance is suicidal and I'll not order it."

"That bastard said you had no fuel, and yet you say you do. Lies! Sabotage!"

"The Mayor was correct. We retained enough fuel for emergency manoeuvre and nothing more."

"Well, it's a fucking emergency, so manoeuvre your fucking tanks towards the camp!"

Skryabin brought the pistol up but hesitated, perhaps because it was a woman, or perhaps because of the radio that burst into life.

"Gurundov-Adin-Alfa, Gurundov-Adin-Alfa, Uchitel-Alfa, over."

The operator, clearly frightened beyond words, passed the handset to the newly-appointed commander of First Company like it was a scaldingly hot potato and then ensured he was not in the line of fire, should the clearly deranged NKVD officer start shooting again.

"Uchitel-Alfa, Gurundov-Adin-Tri, receiving, over."

Some miles away, Yarishlov frowned at the response, wondering where Major Udinov, the first company's commander was.

"Gurundov-Adin-Tri, report status and progress, over."

"Uchitel-Alfa, three platoons have advanced towards the camp with support from the mechanised infantry. Company headquarters and third platoon are halted with no fuel and ammunition, present location...," she grabbed the map and rattled off a reference.

She left out the bit where Major Udinov had drained his own vehicles and stripped them of all ammunition to give his lead elements the best possible chance of success.

"Gurundov-Adin-tri, report location of Adin-Alfa, over."

Demkina looked Skryabin straight in the eye as she spoke.

"Uchitel-Alfa, Adin-Alfa has been executed by the NKVD for refusing to obey an attack order that could not be carried out. A senior NKVD officer and his men are presently threatening me with the same."

"Poshol! Pizd..."

Yarishlov did not intend for his outburst to be broadcast, but none the less some of it reached Skryabin's ears.

He snatched the handset from Demkina's hand.

"This is NKVD Polkovnik Skryabin, acting under the direct authority of Polkovnik General Serov. Whoever you are, order these cretins to move to the camp immediately."

He tossed the handset back to the operator and returned to stand in front of Demkina, raising his pistol once again.

The radio remained silent and the tension increased with every passing second.

When the reply came, it came in angry and easy to understand terms.

It was also delivered in a slow voice, one that pronounced each word with great clarity, and with great venom.

"This is Mayor General of Tanks Arkady Yarishlov. I don't give a fuck what your authority is or whose ass you lick and massage in your spare time, you Chekist prick. Harm one more of my soldiers and I'll shoot you myself. Stand your men down immediately. You will remain at that position under close arrest until I arrive. If you step out of line by one fucking centimetre, I'll strap you to my engine grille and drive around until you're nicely roasted. If you attempt to leave, I authorise my soldiers to shoot you dead. Over and out."

The pistol wavered ever so slightly, but enough for those watching to understand that Skryabin appreciated that his world had suddenly changed dramatically, and decidedly not to his advantage.

Demkina extended her hand.

"Your weapon, Comrade Polkovnik."

Skryabin debated his options, but the deliberate easing of the strap on an AK-47 in the hands of a stony-faced Sergeant stood directly behind the woman gave him a moment's hesitation.

She seized the barrel and rolled the automatic out of his grasp.

Without consultation, and in the spirit of self-preservation, the other NKVD soldiers had already decided that as it wasn't obvious who to back, they would simply obey the higher rank's orders.

They lowered their own weapons and moved to one side.

Demkina nodded at the senior NKVD NCO.

"We'll not take your weapons, Comrades, but please place them by your vehicle."

They immediately responded, confirming their lack of support for their commander.

"Comrade Serzhant Frelov. This man is your prisoner."

The sergeant accepted the task readily, already willing the Chekist to make some move that would permit him to open him from throat to belly in revenge for the death of the valiant major.

Skryabin, deflated, collapsed onto a small campaign stool.

Frelov's leg swept it out from underneath him, sending him flying onto the earth.

It had been Udinov's stool.

"If you need to park your shitty ass, park it in the fucking dirt, Chekist!"

Two men carried the major's body away, an act that drew the gaze of those present, gazes that turned to stares aimed at Skryabin, stares that lacked any promise and warned of a very limited future.

1253 hrs, Friday, 11th April 1947, Akhtubinsk-Astrakhan Highway, fifteen hundred metres west of Uspenka, USSR.

Lucian T. Hanchard Jnr gritted his teeth as the dressing was wound around his head.

The Soviet attack had been swift and had arrived out of nowhere.

His helicopters had totally failed to see the approach, for they were oriented to the north and northwest.

The arrival of an enemy force from the southeast had immediately threatened the safe take-off of his force, and the landing of the airfield group too.

Smoke and fire marked the positions of the lead enemy vehicles, a mix of tanks and lorries.

The enemy had been knocked out by a combination of the RCLs and hastily summoned Glühwürmchens, not one of the Soviet vehicles getting close enough for his bazookas to bear.

Despite the surprise appearance and the disruption to the aircraft, the effect was not long-lived

218th Tanks and 115th Naval Marines southern prong was blunted and disorganised, as most of the leadership had died in the brief exchange.

Hanchard had nearly been claimed too, a single bullet clipping his forehead hard.

Fourteen of his men were down, their bodies already loaded aboard the nearest transport.

Conferring with his USAAF liaison officer, Hanchard ordered the air evacuation restarted.

The C-46s from Akhtubinsk-1 had been circling overhead since the appearance of the enemy force but, on receipt of his order. they now started to line up for their approach.

The business of loading the large number of POWs continued at an increased pace, the whole process given extra impetus by the near miss they had just experienced.

Hanchard was confident that he would achieve his task in a timely fashion and reported the same to Crisp, or whoever it was took his message.

1259 hrs, Friday, 11th April 1947, the Spruce Goose, Volga River, USSR.

Crisp, drawing heavily on the warm air after his desperate sprint back from the north gate, acknowledged his operator's words, thankful that the Soviet incursion at the highway had been bloodied and halted.

His own immediate problem was less easily resolved.

RSM Sunday waited on his decision.

The bottom line was weight.

In as much as there was too much of it, according to Sunday and the loadmasters, who had deferred to the RSM to confront Crisp with the news.

"Suggestions, Sergeant-Major?"

"Sah. Lose all the rest of the weapons... all the ammo... err..."

"Will that be enough?"

"No Sah, it'll help, but won't be enough by itself... not according to the loadmaster's calculations, bearing in mind it's the Goose and this is uncharted territory."

"Fittings in the Goose?"

Crisp knew the answer already but it just tumbled out of his mouth as his mind worked the problem.

"Already down to the bare bones, Sah."

Crisp paused for a moment and assessed the handful of men still waiting to board, plus the security screen he had left to guard the loading process.

'Another sixty or so bodies to shoehorn aboard...'

"Prisoners?"

"A dozen military, seven scientists, Sah."

"Get the military prisoners off her... they'll have to take their chances."

Which they both knew would be nil.

Crisp looked at Sunday, and understood that the man already knew what was needed, but couldn't bring himself to offer the resolution.

'Fifty or so bodies...'

"How many dead do we have onboard, Sergeant-Major?"

"Seventy-seven, Colonel."

It was a momentous decision, and one that would haunt Crisp until his dying day.

"No choice, Sergeant-Major. Ditch all the remaining weapons into the river... get our dead off the airplane quick as you can."

"Sah!"

Sunday threw up a tremendous salute, partially out of respect for the rank and partially in total respect of the difficult decision the officer had just made.

Within a minute, the sad sight of SSF and POW dead being unloaded gave Crisp a lump in his throat.

Galkin appeared but didn't question the sight; he didn't need to.

"Con, take over here. I'm going to find out if we can fly outta here."

Crisp climbed up onto the flight deck and was, much to his surprise, greeted with the sound of laughter.

Holliday met him at the head of the raking ladder.

"Colonel, sir. Seems like we're going to be fine. Petrali'll pull through I think."

Crisp slapped his shoulder in acknowledgement and slipped past the RAF officer to where the three pilots were deep in conversation.

"Gentlemen, Mister Hughes... are we good to go?"

Hughes' distress was obvious but he made light of it.

"Good as we're gonna be, Colonel Crisp. My boys here have soaked up the technical stuff like sponges, and I'm still awake enough to talk them through anything we encounter. Waiting on the loadmaster's report, but once that's in and I'm happy, we can be moving within two minutes of your say-so."

Crisp issued a silent thank you to his god, and then confirmed Hughes' suspicions.

"We were overweight, but we're sorting that out right now. I think we're real close to go. And you two... thank you."

De Villiers and Dryden grinned with a confidence neither felt.

"Wait for my word... and then get us the heck outta here!"

Hughes let out a yelp as Crisp inadvertently caught his leg as he turned.

"Damnit! Sorry... damnit!"

He placed his hand gently on Hughes' shoulder.

"OK, Mister Hughes?"

Hughes smiled through gritted teeth.

"Nowhere else I'd rather be, Colonel."

"Thank you, Mister Hughes. Me either."

Neither of them meant it.

"Thank you, Sergeant-Major."

He returned the NCO's salute, unable to wrench his eyes away from the sorry sight of the dead men laid out in neat order along the jetty.

"Shall I bring the rear-guard in, Sah?"

Crisp tore his eyes away from the site that made every essence of his officer's status rebel.

"Yes. Let's get them aboard as quickly as possible, Sergeant-Major."

Sunday nodded to the waiting radio team who sent out the word.

Galkin arrived silently by Crisp's side as he waved at the cockpit window, his signal returned by a waiting soldier.

The engines started turning and roaring into life.

Galkin raised his voice to counter the throaty roar of eight Wasp 4360s.

"Seems like Hughes is ready to roll."

"Loadmaster's report was obviously favourable."

Crisp's emotional tone revealed the heartache and pain that accompanied his decision.

Uncharacteristically, Galkin reached out and grasped his commander's shoulder.

"Hell of a thing, Colonel."

"Certainly is, Con. Has to be done."

"For what it's worth, I totally agree, Sir."

"Thanks, Con."

The sound of shouting and running feet grew, marking the approach of the last men on Soviet soil.

Crisp turned back to his fallen men for one last time.

"Atten-shun!"

Galkin, Sunday, and he came smartly to the attention position and gave their very best salutes, in honour of men with whom they had lived and breathed for what seemed like a lifetime.

"Right. Let's go."

The last soldiers threw their weapons into the water and piled aboard the Spruce Goose.

Crisp stepped inside and two of his troopers pulled on the door.

137

"How many, Sergeant-Major?"

"All told, eight hundred and ten, Sah."

"Thank you, Sergeant-Major. Keep 'em calm down here. Good luck."

"And to you, Sah."

As Crisp climbed the raking ladder once more, he offered up a prayer.

"Oh Lord, send your angels to carry us out of harm's way, to bring us home, and deliver us safely again to our loved ones. Amen."

"Amen to that, Colonel."

Without realising it, he had spoken aloud, and at least Galkin and Holliday had heard his plea.

"Mister Hughes, when you're ready... we're in your hands!"

"I hear that, Colonel"

It was 1310.

'Cutting it fine!'

The mooring lines were slipped and, under guidance, the two 'pilots' moved the huge amphibian away from the shoreline.

Hughes used words like 'thrust', 'hump', and 'drag', which the two concentrating men seemed to grasp but that might as well have been words spoken in Mandarin to the watching officers and men of 1st SSF.

The alternate take-off route had been selected for two reasons. It was the best for wind direction, but only just, and therefore required less manoeuvre by the inexperienced duo.

It also offered a take-off run of just short of eight kilometres.

The Hercules H-4 moved steadily down the Volga towards the point where the engines would be advanced and they would try to take-off.

Odekirk and Hughes had quickly examined the manifest from the loadmaster, and there was nothing more that could be done now that the last excess weight had been removed, so the manifest disappeared in favour of problems they could address.

The engines all seemed fine, and nothing but superficial damage had been found to the rest of the mighty aircraft, although they had been forced to rely on inexperienced eyes to look for it.

Despite its heavy loading, the Spruce Goose surged ahead, partially carried forward by the gentle flow of the great river.

1307 hrs, Friday, 11th April 1947, junction of Ul. Astrakhanskaya and the Akhtubinsk-Baskunchak highway, USSR.

Yarishlov's vehicle had hardly stopped before he propelled himself out and into the barn that held the object of his wrath.

His soldiers came to attention and, as he eyed the black-eyed NKVD officer, he listened to Demkina's report.

"Thank you, Comrade Starshy Leytenant. Did we do that to him?"

He pointed at Skryabin's battered features.

"We did not, Comrade Mayor General. The Polkovnik arrived looking like that."

Her tone informed everyone listening that she wished it were otherwise.

Yarishlov nodded and fixed the NKVD officer with a contemptuous stare, Skryabin's own look reflecting horror at the sight of the badly burned tank officer.

"Now, Comrade Starshy Leytenant... what exactly happened here?"

Skryabin went to speak but managed only the intake of breath before the tank general's voice filled the small barn.

"You shut your fucking mouth, Chekist. When I speak to you, you'll know. Starshy Leytenant?"

The violence of his words split a portion of his damaged skin, and a trickle of blood came from the edge of the Yarishlov's mouth.

Demkina briefly and faithfully outlined the events, starting with the stripping of some vehicles of all fuel and ammunition, to the final act of Skryabin's execution of Major Udinov.

"Thank you. You have conducted yourself well, Comrade Demkina. So, Skryabin... you executed one of my best officers for the reason that he could not move his vehicles for lack of fuel and had no ammunition to fight with, even had he been able to move. Is that a reasonable assessment?"

"Comrade Mayor General... the man reeked of defeatism... his cowardice was clear and..."

Yarishlov exploded.

139

"Cowardice? You fucking half-witted swine! Udinov had more courage in a fingernail than you'll ever manage to find in your miserable useless fucking life... fucking idiot... you fucking idiot... he was correct... and you shot him down because of your own fear!"

"I had orders fro..."

"Orders? Don't you dare hide behind orders, you fucking useless sadistic prick!"

Yarishlov stopped himself from going further by wiping the increasing flow of blood from his chin and turned back to Demkina.

"What is the resupply situation now, Comrade Demkina?"

"Twenty minutes out, Comrade Mayor General. The supply unit reported in just before you arrived."

"Good, now..."

Three vehicles pulled up outside, two of which Yarishlov caught a quick glimpse of and recognised as being from his own headquarters.

The doorway was filled with two shapes, Zvorykin leading, backed up by stony-faced Kriks.

"Comrade Mayor General."

Zvorykin walked off to one side, pulling Yarishlov into an urgent whispered conversation, which started with Yarishlov demanding to know why Zvorykin was not back at the command location and quickly moved to an explanation of a phone call from no less a person than Serov.

Their exchange was punctuated with looks at the NKVD officer, none of which was wasted on Skryabin, who felt a surge of optimism.

The look on Yarishlov's destroyed face made his hopes rise further.

The exchange finished and Zvorykin moved quickly to the radio truck, armed with a mission by his commander, who turned back to his prisoner.

"You have powerful friends, Chekist. For now, you're to be released."

A murmur sprung from the lips of the First Company soldiers in the barn, one of horror and incredulity.

Yarishlov explained, as much for their benefit as for Skryabin's ears.

"Polkovnik General Serov has ordered me to release you as your services are required during the present operations. When matters are concluded, you're to report to the Military area commander at Stalingrad,

140

where you'll be placed under arrest again, pending a full investigation of events. Give him his weapon back."

Demkina moved forward and extended the pistol, waiting until the last second to reverse it and pass it handle first.

How she wished things were otherwise, and in her mind's eye she could see the heavy bullets destroying the newly confident, almost smug face of the NKVD bastard.

"Understand this, Polkovnik Skryabin. I'll make sure that you'll stand accountable for this piggery, no matter who your uncle might be."

Serov had packed a lot of information into the short conversation.

"Until that time, get out of my fucking sight... the NKVD office in Akthubinsk's waiting for you...contact the Polkovnik General's office for your orders."

He took two quick steps closer to Skryabin, causing the NKVD officer to noticeably shrink back, "...And know this you piece of shit... touch one of my soldiers again... talk to one of my soldiers again... and Comrade Serov'll have to sweep up the fucking bits, regardless of orders. Ponimayu?"

Skryabin contented himself with thoughts of sweet revenge and the briefest of nods.

The NKVD colonel called his sheepish men to him and the Gaz-61 was soon disappearing towards Akhtubinsk.

"A dangerous man... with dangerous friends. But there will be a reckoning for that piece of..."

Yarishlov stopped himself.

"Right, Edward Georgievich... how are our forces?"

"Easy fellahs... that's the hump right there... feel it... go with it..."

Hughes, his pain almost forgotten, talked the two men through the take-off experience, one so different to that performed on a conventional hard field.

The hump he referred to was the point of maximum water resistance, just prior to the point where the resistance changes and the aircraft starts its attempt to break the water's grip and take off.

Although he had no hand on the controls, Hughes could sense the hump through his body and instinctively understood that the weight aboard was at the very top end of the Hercules' capacity.

"Power up... all together... steadily..."

The eight throttles were close together, but still difficult for the span of one hand.

On De Villiers' side was a mirror set, and Hughes had already told the South African that the important job would lie with him, leaving Dryden to keep both hands on the column and hold the Goose steady.

"Good, Air Force... good... a little more..."

Hughes felt the change.

"More right pedal, Navy."

The increased torque started to affect the amphibian's attitude as one wing dipped slightly, accompanied by a rise in the nose as the fuselage dug in at the rear.

"Excellent... ok, Air Force... ready on those throttles... Navy, watch that right pedal... keep the wings straight... feel the nose drop shortly, ok?"

Dryden, the sweat running off him like a waterfall, hummed a response as he chewed his tongue in concentration.

"OK, Air Force, advance the throttles again... gently..."

The nose stayed up but the increased power drove the Goose forward.

"A little more power... Navy, bring the nose down now... steady..."

The adjustments made the difference, and the nose attitude dropped as the giant aircraft started to skim across the surface, but not quite right.

"A little back stick, Navy... keep her ass in the water now..."

The gentle swells in the river started to bounce them, as weight was transferred from hull to wings.

This was one area where the Goose excelled above other amphibians; take-off.

"Full power, Air Force... keep that stick, Navy... good... good..."

The seats behind the flight crew were packed with troopers and officers from 1st SSF, none of whom was enjoying the experience.

"Stop the aircraft, I didn't sign up for this crap!"

The comment broke the moment, and Crisp's retort hit the spot.

"Go see the chaplain, Sergeant Hawkes!"

The laughter brought a little light relief in the taut situation.

"Blast it! Boat ahead!"

Dryden's warning brought all eyes to bear, and a small boat was seen directly in their path.

"Shit! No time... keep going!"

Hughes' reasoning was sound.

Any attempt to steer around could result in a crash.

There was no alternative but to keep going and if they hit the small craft, then so be it.

The contact, when it came, was almost imperceptible.

The huge amphibian simply swiped the boat aside.

Those on the flight deck ignored the fact that there were people in the boat.

The Goose kissed a larger swell and Dryden adjusted, too heavily and swiftly for Hughes' taste.

"Whoa there, Navy... treat her like a lady, not a two-bit whore! Careful now... she's up to the job... keep her straight and true now..."

He leaned forward to get closer to the sweating Navy man and to focus harder on the sensations that the Goose was bombarding him with and instantly regretted it.

Hughes' sudden movement reminded him of the state of his legs and he groaned inadvertently.

None the less, he sensed the change, the moment that take-off was possible.

"That's it. Navy... now... bring her up slowly... ease her up now... you too Air Force... slow and together..."

At the first attempt, the water's hold on the hull was broken and the Hercules rose slowly into the air.

Crisp opened his eyes and pulled himself back into the outside world. He had been entreating with his God, and his pleas had been rewarded.

Hughes oversaw the rise in altitude before he permitted Holliday to administer another modest dose of morphine.

143

As he settled back in his seat, enjoying the wave of relief that swept through his body, Crisp ordered a simple signal to be sent.

'Baserunner-Three.'

Brigadier General Rossiter was stood outside seeking shade and a cool breeze. Thus far he had found only the former. He drained the coffee mug and reinserted the cigar, more chewing than sucking on the fine tobacco.

'Damn but Shaibah's a hot place.'

It was a steady 38° and the absence of even the slightest breeze made life less than comfortable.

The door opened behind him and his communications officer passed a message slip into eager hands.

'Baserunner Two... hot damn... that's Yankee on the highway... just Whiskey and the main force to go now...'

He looked at his watch. The message was timed two minutes beforehand.

"Thank you, Major. I'll come back in."

In a number of buildings across the world, from the States to Germany, the messages were being followed with great interest, and not a little nervousness.

Rossiter handed his mug to the WRAF corporal and waited for the refill to appear before walking over to check all the message logs, as much to kill time as anything.

His mind wandered and immediately came back into line as Whiskey-Six broadcast a simple message.

"General, Sir..."

"Yeah, I heard, Major. Thank you."

In silence, Rossiter raised his mug to the men in the Hercules, willing them to get airborne and on the way home.

"Major."

"Contact Ostrich-six-three. Make sure they got that. It'll make things easier for them."

"Yessir."

Rossiter closed his eyes and listened.

"Ostrich-six-three, Ostrich-six-three, Mother-Goose over."

144

A tinny voice acknowledged.

"Ostrich-six-three, confirm receipt of baserunner-one and baserunner-two, over."

"Mother-Goose, Ostrich-six-three, baserunner-one and baserunner-two received. Hallelujah, over."

"Ostrich-six-three, roger. Good luck. Over and out."

Rossiter opened his eyes as he sensed the man's presence.

"They received the message, General."

"Thank you, Major."

Rossiter mentally shifted himself from the flight deck of the Spruce Goose to that of a Superfortress called Paula Marie, nose number six-three, rapidly approaching Uspenka at 15,000 feet.

He looked at the operation clock.

It was 1316.

'Only Steel-six to go now... come on Crisp... gimme baserunner three... gimme that home run and get your boys outta Dodge!'

1316 hrs, Friday, 11th April 1947, B-29D Paula Marie, airborne over Southern Russia.

He checked the speed for the thousandth time.

Three hundred miles per hour on the nose.

"They're just waiting on baserunner three now, Colonel."

Baserunner three would initiate the final signal of home run - a coded message sent by Rossiter's headquarters that would be the most welcomed of all, indicating that the entire assault force was clear of the target.

"Uh-huh."

Every essence of his being was screaming inside, but he knew what he had to do.

That didn't make Banner happy but it did make him determined, and also thankful that he had the foresight to ensure that he alone would take responsibility.

Events seemed to be headed down the route he feared, the route he had catered for in his dreams, and in his conversation with the USAAF Engineering officer, Mikkelson.

The man had tried to duck the matter, even with the lure of the poker pot dangled in front of him, but finally agreed to Banner's request and modified the bomber to the Colonel's specific requirements.

His number two had spotted the new switch as he settled himself in the seat.

"What's that, Colonel?"

"Fires up the ejector seat for any nosey co-pilots."

Hal chuckled.

"I hear that, Colonel... I hear that loud and clear."

Banner had nodded, grinning with a lack of sincerity and the matter had not come up again until now, as the time had come to address its purpose.

"Larry, come up to the flight deck will ya."

He summoned the bombardier as he mentally practised his lines.

"Take over, Hal."

The co-pilot acknowledged and took control of 'Paula Marie', immediately checking his station on 'Tatanka', which aircraft was leading the four-bird formation.

He then looked to either side, first to port and then to starboard, noting good distance between him and 'Tickertape Parade' and 'Moonshine' respectively.

"Colonel?"

"Larry, I've made a decision. I had Mikki fit an alternate release switch just in case. If we don't get 'home run' by time on target, I'll release the bomb on your command."

"Now hold on one cotton-pick..."

The co-pilot, Cheshire, and the mission commander all sat up in alarm.

"That's not negotiable, Larry. You aim it, you call it, but I drop it. What we're doing is necessary... we all know it... but dropping the Jasper on a load of our boys... well, that's a job that falls to me."

"Shitty deal, Colonel, but that's my job."

"No it ain't, Larry. I'm in charge here and..."

"Beg your pardon, Colonel, but no you fucking ain't!"

The naval officer had only just returned to his seat after completing the arming of the Jasper.

He was the mission commander and did not like what he heard.

He slipped off his belt again and moved closer to the discussion.

"You can't risk the mission, Colonel. It's not happening. You up for dropping the bomb, son? Despite knowing our boys might be down there?"

"Sure thing, Captain. Shitty as fuck but... it's my job."

146

Larry Delaney's eyes betrayed his inner conflict.

"That's that then. You drop it."

Banner turned and stared the sailor back into his seat.

"There's no risk to the mission. The bomb will be dropped on the aimer's command. I'll not have my man do this awful thing. If we don't get 'home run', I'll be dropping it. This ain't for discussion, Navy. Now, you can either shoot me or sit back in your goddamned seat and enjoy the ride. Which'll it be, Lieutenant Commander? The Wing Commander can drive if you decide on the former."

"Colonel?"

Banner looked at Cheshire, a man that he had come to greatly admire for his honesty, leadership, and capabilities as a pilot.

"Not negotiable, Wing Commander. It's a shitty deal, but it's my shitty deal. You understand."

In truth, Cheshire understood only too well. It was an issue he had wrestled with himself over the previous days, placing himself in the exact same position that had so weighed Banner down for more than one sleepless night.

Cheshire sighed and sat back in his seat without further comment, sparing a look for the naval officer who was debating his course of action.

The navigator's report broke the moment.

"Sixty-five miles to target."

The co-pilot acknowledged the requested heads-up.

Banner leant forward and spoke softly.

"I don't want this on your conscience, Larry. Just make sure I put it on the money. I'll take all the heat later, but this is my call. I'm asking you to do this for me... and for Joannie and Larry junior. Please."

Delaney's resolve broke in an instant, the picture of his wife and young son as plain as the hurt and pain in his pilot's eyes.

Banner won the day.

"You got it, Colonel. Drop it on my mark."

"Thanks, Larry. Everything goes as normal. Just give me the mark, and I'll drop the sucker."

Banner pulled back on his mask and addressed the crew.

"OK Boys. Listen up. We're on final approach for our bombing run. This is why you earn the big bucks. Keep it all tight and by the numbers. Good luck and it is a privilege to command you. Pilot out."

'Paula Marie' flew inexorably on.

147

"Well make it work!"

"It's not that simple, Colonel!"

Crisp never thought it would be, but the radio's refusal to play at such a crucial time strained his resilience to breaking point.

"Can we contact Whiskey or Yankee with the walkie-talkie? Maybe get a message to them?"

A single walkie-talkie had been brought along, part of the requirement for local communication when they landed.

"We can try, Colonel, but the range... well, we can try."

Crisp turned back and resumed his seat, helpless in the face of the failure of the Goose's radio.

His own radio was sat on the dockside by the Volga.

'Shit!'

He leaned in towards Galkin.

"The flyboys'll think we're still on the ground when they bomb... hell... if they bomb."

Galkin shook his head.

"They'll bomb, Colonel. They'll bomb regardless cos the stakes are so big. But we'll be able to tell 'em... imagine their little faces, Colonel."

"But if they don't bomb, Con... what if they don't bomb?"

More than one set of eyes took a glance at a wristwatch.

1328.

"Bomb doors open, Colonel."

"Roger."

Banner could not help himself.

"Radio Operator, Anything?"

"Nothing, Colonel. Just Mother Goose trying to get summat out of Steel. No response. Nix. Nada."

So there it was.

They were going to bomb their own men.

The time moved slowly, every second another heartbeat closer to the point of no return.

Banner knew that if they hadn't gone now, it was too late.

The blast would probably claim them, depending on how deep the Jasper burrowed.

'Paula Marie' was on the final approach now, the aircraft steady at 12,000 feet.

Delaney had slipped into professional mode, calling the stages as they came, calling out the minor adjustments, doing all the things that made missions go just right.

The navigator's voice cut into everyone's concentration.

"Colonel. Estimated time to target, ninety seconds."

"Roger."

"Colonel. Estimated time to target, sixty seconds."

"Roger."

'Where did that time go, for fuck's sake?'

"You got the aircraft, Hal?"

The co-pilot nodded and took a tighter grip on the controls, ready for the moment that 'Paula Marie' would surge upwards, the moment when the Jasper left her bomb bay.

"Steady… five…"

Banner's heart was pounding so hard he was convinced it superseded the roar of the Wright Cyclones either side of him.

"Three…"

'Fuck, where was four?'

"Two… one… mark."

Colonel Gary G. Banner pressed the switch and 'Paula Marie', suddenly 19,500 pounds lighter, surged upwards, towards the height that the three other B-29s had already retired to.

The Jasper fell away to earth, assuming a nose down position and spinning to increase accuracy.

By the time it struck the ground, just three yards to the side of the parade square it had been aimed at. The Jasper was moving in excess of one thousand feet per second.

The nose contacted the ground and immediately triggered a slightly delayed ignition sequence, only a matter of fractions, but long enough to ensure that the atomic payload detonated below ground and produced the maximum effect upon its target.

149

At 1330 precisely, the Jasper detonated roughly one hundred and forty-two feet below ground level.

1330 hrs, Friday, 11th April 1947, Secure Store 17, VNIIEF Factory, Uspenka, USSR.

The timing circuit on the bomb was faulty, so as far as Obiekt 907 was concerned, it was not yet its time, but the Soviet device didn't care.

The Jasper smashed through the ground and exploded underneath the factory level, and shock wave from the immense blast jarred the Soviet bomb into premature ignition.

For those watching from above, the results were unexpectedly spectacular.

The few people left in the camp knew very little. A handful of NKVD guards who had hidden themselves away at the first sign of a large number of armed men perished in the blink of an eye.

Twenty-seven of the prisoners had secreted themselves away, waiting to see who triumphed. They disappeared into the atomic maelstrom that developed with the detonation of two devices less than two seconds apart.

Around the perimeter and on the approaches, men and vehicles from Yarishlov's command were illuminated by a flash of incredible light as the Soviet device was raised above ground level by the subterranean blast of the Jasper before itself detonating.

In under three seconds, the area had been subjected to two explosions, the equivalent of forty thousand tons of TNT destroyed indiscriminately, as a pressure wave tore through the wooden huts as if they never existed, and demolished most of the more permanent structures in the camp and beyond.

The pressure wave killed many, certainly those in and just outside the facility; the incredible heat killed the rest.

Up to a range of over a mile and a half, men were incinerated in the blink of an eye.

The adjacent branch of the mighty Volga momentarily disappeared to nothing more than a soggy patch as its waters were turned to steam by the intense heat.

The work of the bombs would continue for many years to come, as those who escaped the immediate effects would die slowly of the side effects of radiation exposure.

The furthest immediate casualty was a soldier of the 115th Naval Marines, who was struck by a lump of concrete thrown from the site of the explosion.

Camp 1001 and the VNIIEF facility were obliterated.

The shockwave was expected but still disrupted the US aircraft, 'Tatanka' being affected the most.

The B-29 dropped a wing as the blast wave reached it and highlighted an age-old problem with the Wright Cyclone engine. Despite being fitted with the revised direct injection system, which improved reliability considerably, something in the engine decided to protest at the rough handling, and the blast brought about a major fuel leak which transformed into a fire even as Major Keel watched.

"Kill and feather number one! Fire extinguishers!"

The fire extinguishers were initiated and Keel watched and prayed as they struggled to overcome the burning fuel.

From his flight deck, Banner, once the shock wave had passed, watched in detached fascination as 'Tatanka' left a trail of smoke and flame in her wake.

He decided against using the radio, believing that Keel would have enough on his hands without his commander breathing down his neck.

As he moved his aircraft out of line, he grunted with satisfaction as the fire extinguishers won their battle and the risk to 'Tatanka' was removed.

"Tail gunner, report."

The mission dictated that 'Tickertape Parade' would radio back the message recording successful detonation, and 'Moonshine', with its array of photographic and recording systems, would be rearmost, in order to capture as much information as possible.

It was 'Tatanka' that carried the second Jasper, and would now be required to return with it, to land safe and sound.

151

Banner had little doubt that the weapons officer on board was already disassembling the system he would have armed in preparation for any issues on board 'Paula Marie'.

The four aircraft settled into a steady formation and flew southwards, friendly fighters already working to ensure they were not interfered with.

Sooner or later everyone sits down to a banquet of consequences.

Robert Louis Stevenson

CHAPTER 202 - THE AFTERMATH

1339 hrs, Friday, 11th April 1947, B-29D Paula Marie, airborne over Southern Russia.

Banner kept his own counsel, and let the crew work off their relief at a mission done by the numbers, as well as blowing off steam once they realised the enormity of what they had done.

It was the last point that particularly exercised Banner, and he called for silence on the intercom before proceeding with his rehearsed speech.

"Boys… we knew what this mission might entail… what we might have to do today… if things didn't go according to the plan."

He took a moment to swallow the rising saliva in his mouth as his men answered his words in their own individual ways, generally agreeing with the louder voice of the Flight Engineer.

"Fucking FUBAR, Colonel… fucking FUBAR!"

"Well, it sure as shit didn't go to plan… these things rarely do as we all know."

"Ain't that the fucking truth, Colonel!"

He smiled at his co-pilot's words, a smile without smiling, which was missed.

"I want y'all to know that you've done what needed to be done… and done it like the top guys you are."

The whoops down the intercom from the younger men made him both smile and shake his head.

"This is important, so listen carefully. The mission we've just carried out was of incredible importance… it's saved many thousands, perhaps millions of lives in Europe and in our homeland."

His eyes flicked across the gauges as he checked the aircraft's performance.

"Men have died today… fighter jocks have died to bring us here… and to take us home. Soldiers have died on the ground to try and steal the secrets of our enemy… and to try and liberate our prisoners."

153

The absence of whistles, whoops, and banter was marked.

"On that point, the mission was not a success. We all knew it was a possibility, of course. But I hoped... we all hoped... it would not come to that."

"What I want you all to understand... to come to terms with... is that you were under orders, my orders..."

Banner choked and leant forward to tap a gauge in order to mask his momentary weakness.

"If there is any blame here, it's mine to bear. The burden for what has just been done is mine alone."

The howls were genuine but Banner would have none of it.

"No. I could have called off the drop... I didn't... even though our boys were still on the ground... I didn't... the mission was the most important we've ever flown... and the stakes were high. It was my call."

Technically, it was the US Naval officer's call, as mission commander, but he wasn't going to split hairs with Banner at this time.

"The blame, when it is levelled... and it will be... is mine alone."

He waited for the howls of derision and denial to abate.

"Fellahs, it's been a privilege to fly with you. Now, let's make sure we get 'Paula Marie' home. Stay tight and alert. God bless you and good luck."

Making sure the co-pilot had the controls, he pulled off his headset and mask, massaging his face and ears back into life.

"I know why you did that. It was well done, Colonel."

Cheshire's hand gripped Banner's shoulder, and the USAAF colonel found the veteran's presence wholly reassuring.

"Still wanna fly a B-29, Leonard?"

"But of course!"

"I need to lie down. Got such a shitty headache. Here, have my seat."

Banner vacated the number one seat, and watched as Cheshire slipped his tall form in with relative ease.

"Try not to prang her, please."

"So says the junior buck!"

The two shared a genuine laugh, which tailed off as Cheshire took in the array in front of him.

Banner leant over Cheshire's shoulder and went through the basics, the older man absorbing everything like a sponge.

"All yours then."

Banner slipped away, confiding in the flight engineer as he moved past.

"Blair, I've got a hell of a headache, so I'm gonna lie down for a while. Call me if either of these two lamers fuck up my aircraft."

Blair Scranton stifled a giggle and reassured his commander that he'd keep a close eye on the two lesser mortals.

Banner made his way back through the communications tunnel to the rest station in the rear compartment.

After exchanging pleasantries with the men he came across on the way, Banner settled down on one of the crew bunks, citing his imaginary headache as a reason for taking some rest.

His thoughts were in turmoil at the enormity of his actions, the taking of friendly lives in a cold and calculated way... killing allies and fellow Americans for the greater good.

His mind had been made up many days beforehand, when he was handed the mission.

His decision was reinforced when he persuaded Mikkelson to provide a secondary bomb release button so that he alone could take responsibility.

It was further reinforced when there was no message from the force on the ground, meaning that the worst possible situation presented itself, and he would be killing his own.

No man could live with that... the life-long shame and anguish of it... that was how Gary George Banner saw it anyway.

He sat on the bunk and paused momentarily, studying the small rubber pellet.

Banner imagined harnessing the power of the L-pill, biting down upon it, breaking the glass inside and allowing the acrid contents to flow and fill his mouth with a burning sensation.

The potassium cyanide would do its work and start to close down his heart and nervous system.

Did his courage fail him, or was it some other reason that stayed his hand?

'Paula at home?'

'My kids?'

'Taking the coward's way out?'

"I'm not a fucking coward."

"What's that you say, Colonel?"

"Nothing, Elmer. Just thinking out loud, son. Wake me in an hour."

Slipping the capsule back into his jacket, Banner laid back on the crew bunk and fell into the deepest of sleeps.

His dreams brought him the faces of men he didn't know, the flight of a bomb, and the whiteness of an atomic explosion.

'Paula Marie' and her consorts flew steadily south, with Banner back at the controls.

The enormity of it all, the total futility of it all, ate away at him as he prepared to bring his aircraft and crew safely back to earth... until word came through that the Spruce Goose had been spotted by friendly fighters, which clearly meant that the 1st SSF and the majority of the POWs had escaped from Camp 1001 in time to avoid the effects of the bomb.

A real headache troubled Banner as the stress melted away.

The B-29s touched down safely and were immediately surrounded by ground crew and off-duty airmen, shouting and whistling in celebration.

The tired fliers were all whisked away and given thorough medical check-ups, psychiatric support, and pretty much anything their hearts desired.

As the base doctor conducted his examination, Banner silently returned the small capsule.

The matter was never discussed again.

There was a mood of quiet optimism throughout the command facility.

156

Sam Rossiter was finishing up the latest round of calls, passing on the latest information on the returning forces of Operations Viking and Kingsbury.

The news was pretty positive as far as he understood, so his calls were all upbeat on the matter of POW rescue, regretful regarding the known air force losses, and non-committal on the subject of Soviet Atomic weapons.

Such information would accompany the butcher's bill when he met the returning 1st SSF troopers and their liberated colleagues.

He kept his cigars in his pocket until the moment he could meet Crisp as he stepped out of the Hercules.

'Once I know what price we've paid for the mission, that is.'

"Your car's here, General."

"Thank you, Captain. Colonel Trannel?"

The DRL officer looked quite doleful, suspecting he had lost men and knowing that he had lost valuable equipment, no matter how the operation had progressed, as Kingsbury did not include the recovery of any of the Flettner helicopters.

With the USMC and DRL officers aboard, the vehicle sped the short distance to a waiting Avro York of the civilian BOAC group, which was rolling the moment they dropped into their seats, destination Rasht, where many of the transports were scheduled to touch down.

It was also forty-two miles southeast of Talesh, near where the Spruce Goose was expected to land.

1628 hrs, Friday, 11th April 1947, the Caspian Sea near Talesh, Iran.

"Look at those boats there, Navy... see how they're all riding the same way? That's the water flow... in our favour... that's swell... so we land parallel to the shore... which is perfect."

Hughes slapped Dryden and De Villiers in turn, happy with the good fortune presented to them, and still decided against telling them that the trickiest bit of all was about to present itself.

It was quite obvious that the two men were scared rigid by the prospect of bringing the huge plane down.

However, the Caspian Sea was in a benevolent mood, with next to no wind and waves, and the gentle current moving decidedly in their favour.

He went through the pre-landing list, getting the two men to trim the aircraft ready, having already decided that the power-on landing would be his choice, if only for the greater control it offered, were there to be a problem.

"Don't forget... the water's lower than you see it... you boys are sat high and proud here. A lot higher up than you think..."

Both men looked out of their side windows and immediately understood the truth in Hughes' words.

"Ok... you boys ready?"

"As I'll ever be, Mr Hughes."

De Villiers said nothing, as was his style.

Hughes twisted in his seat, aggravating his wounds to the point of yelping in pain.

Holliday, only just back from checking on some of the casualties below, was out of his seat in an instant.

"Not now, Doc... by all means, put me out the moment we moor, but for now... I gotta stay awake and alert."

"As soon as we moor, Mister Hughes."

"Pass the word to prepare for landing."

"Will do."

Holliday reluctantly returned to his seat as the wounded man made eye contact with Crisp.

"We'll be landing soon, Colonel. I've been in a few such landings so take it from me. You'll want to pass the word... it may bounce a few times."

Even though the grin was real, Marion Crisp saw through it to the real concern it was trying to mask.

"Ok, Mister Hughes. Good luck."

He took a deep breath, his thoughts tinged with the genuine fear of the nearness of the mission's end and the possibility of some late disaster befalling him and his men.

"Con, pass the word. Prepare for landing."

He looked back at Holliday.

"May be rough so make sure the boys all hang on tight."

"Yessir, Colonel."

More than one man occupied himself with silent appeals to a heavenly entity, seeking reassurance and hope for the future.

The Hercules dropped lower and lower, the two men gently adjusting the controls in line with Hughes' instructions.

"OK... extend the flaps... third setting... feel the click on the handle there."

De Villiers moved the flaps lever to the third setting, feeling the notch into which the lever settled.

Hughes saw no reason to change his landing method, even with the greater weight in the rear.

Partially extended flaps and low speed would bring the Goose down gently, with no chance of the nose digging in and, as he quaintly put it, 'sending the whole kit and caboodle ass over tit.'

It was necessary to bring the aircraft down with the tail slightly lower than the nose.

"Use the shore there... that'll help you judge the height... steady now... she's coming down nicely..."

From behind, Dryden and De Villiers looked calm and efficient, whereas it would have appeared a wholly different story had anyone been sat in front of them.

Dryden's face was distorted with concentration, his tongue half out of his mouth as he chewed on it.

De Villiers was almost boss-eyed, slipping his gaze from the shoreline, to the water slowly rising below his window, to the view ahead, and occasionally at the gauges in front of him, not that he understood many of them, even with Hughes' rapid schooling.

"Standby on the throttles."

Hughes waited, grinning to himself as someone in the seats behind him decided to noisily produce the contents of their stomach.

Someone else joined in out of sympathy, undoubtedly put over the edge by the sound of his fellow sufferer retching.

Not for the first time, Crisp wondered if pilots everywhere really did revel in the discomfort of their military passengers, as Hughes sniggered and shared a quiet joke with the naval man.

"OK, throttle back gently... watch the altimeter... watch the speed... gently now... ease her down a little, Navy."

Crisp handed Galkin a handkerchief to help clean the mess up, ignoring Hawkes' comments about 'lightweight officers'.

"Back on the throttle some more."

The object was to touchdown at the lowest possible speed, whilst still moving fast enough to retain control, but with a nose-up attitude.

"Steady... keep easing her down... you're on it, boys... on the money... easy now..."

The fuselage kissed the Caspian's warm waters momentarily.

Dryden inadvertently adjusted the aircraft and the contact was broken, the Spruce Goose rising imperceptibly.

"Ok, ok, ok... no problems... ease her back down again, Navy..."

Again, water and aircraft met comfortably, and this time appeared to remain in an embrace.

"Elevator... gently but firmly... great... that's swell, boys... fantastic..."

The speed bled away as water friction took hold.

The Spruce Goose levelled a little as the throttles were further reduced. Hughes had decided to keep the landing as uncomplicated as possible, so allowed for a long landing and taxi path.

"Whoa... not too much power off, Saffer... that's better."

The throttles were teased back up slightly, all the better to maintain a slightly nose-up angle.

"Outstanding! You two can fly with me any time, boys."

"Problem with number one again... losing revs..."

Hughes reacted quickly, clapping his hand on De Villiers' shoulder.

"Number one off now."

The misbehaving engine was soon closed down, the blade remaining unfeathered.

Hughes made a decision and spoke to Dryden.

"Right, Navy. We'll turn to port gradually...as we've overshot... nice and steady, pal... keep her level at all times... when you're ready."

The Spruce Goose turned out to sea, the lower power on the port wing encouraging a tighter turn.

Behind Galkin, Bud Tabot discovered that airsickness had been replaced by seasickness, and found more in his stomach to throw up.

160

Hawkes' ribbing was merciless and earned a disapproving look from Crisp.

His reply died on his lips as the Spruce Goose struck the extended mast of a sunken Soviet ship and tore a seventeen-foot hole in her lower fuselage.

The Hercules shuddered but drove on, further damaging herself below the waterline.

From downstairs came cries of concern and fear, and warnings of water in the aircraft.

Hughes' cool disappeared momentarily.

"Fuck it, we've no choice. Turn her towards the beach, nose on... drive her up the sand there."

To his credit, Dryden remained calm as he concentrated on the manoeuvre, although his tongue came in for further battering in his efforts to remain focussed.

Hughes turned to those behind, grimacing with pain from the manoeuvre.

"Get your boys ready... stay in the seats... hopefully we'll kiss the sand and just run up it... but we'll need to be off at the double. The rear'll settle if we're taking on that much water. Good luck. Colonel."

Hughes turned back to concentrate on advising the two pilots, leaving Crisp to get his men prepared.

Ashore, the celebrations at the sight of the huge amphibian had grown to fiesta proportions as she safely landed, and then died away when the Soviet markings became apparent, and then turned to horror as the obvious problem occurred.

Some people on the beach appreciated their own peril and ran as fast as they could. Others waited and watched, only understanding at the last moment that the Hercules was growing larger and larger, and aimed specifically at them.

Eventually, they joined the rapid rush for the safety of the tree line.

On the flight deck, the additional weight of water in the fuselage made the aircraft nose heavy, something that needed more elevator to control, making the whole process less manageable and decidedly more dangerous.

"Throttle up, Saffer... keep her speed up!"

The aircraft swung to the left as four engines on the right wing out powered the three on the left.

"Come back on eight... more... more..."

The Spruce Goose came back to something approaching straight as number eight was reduced back to offset the loss of number one engine.

"OK... that's fine, Navy... keep her like that."

It wasn't fine at all.

The increased forward motion was now driving more and more water inside the fuselage, increasing the weight towards the rear.

Odekirk grasped the issue.

"We need the nose out, Hal. Stop grabbing water. Nose out!"

"Yeah, yeah, yeah... Navy... more back elevator. Bring the nose up more."

Hughes pushed himself upwards in the seat, ignoring the pain, keen to maintain his best possible view of the approaching shoreline.

"Ok boys... this is gonna take some careful timing... ready on the throttles, Saffer... ready now... ready..."

Hughes sought visual information from the front and to the side, estimating the distance to the sand and the point that he could cut power and allow his aircraft to slide into the beach.

Too soon and he could stop her in the water, sink her, and men would die.

Too late and the landing would become a crash, and men would die.

"Ready..."

Below, voices were raised in command, keeping order amongst men who were frightened, contained in a habitat they were unused to, threatened by a situation beyond their control, with their fate was in the hands of people they didn't know.

"Ready..."

None the less, discipline amongst the 1st SSF troopers and the POWs was first class.

"Ready..."

A moment of self-doubt robbed Hughes of his speech, and then the moment was gone.

"NOW!"

The engines died away and Dryden adjusted the elevators.

The nose dropped and started scooping up the water once more.

The nose down attitude was more pronounced now, made worse as the water in the fuselage flowed back to meet the new surge coming in.

"Shit... keep the power up, Saffer."

162

It was a balancing act now, forward momentum brought onboard greater quantities of water, but also took them closer to safety.

The chances of bringing the nose up now were non-existent, so all Dryden could do was keep the Spruce Goose travelling on the shortest path to safety.

"Drop the left wing into the water!"

Dryden followed the instructions blindly.

The wing float bit and started to slew the Spruce Goose, bringing, as Hughes intended, the starboard side doors above the waterline.

The float broke away from the wing in a squeal of yielding metal and the wing itself sliced into the Caspian's waters.

Shouts and screams echoed around the interior of the Hercules, as the sudden pitch threw men around.

The forward momentum bled off totally as the wing tip found the sandy bottom.

"Starboard side doors! Starboard side only! Evacuate the aircraft!"

The shout rang through the aircraft.

"Starboard side doors! Everybody out!"

The manoeuvre had not been without risk, but without it, both sides would have been below the waterline, and getting out would have been difficult.

With Hughes' decision, life was granted to many men who would otherwise have died.

As an extra, two of the starboard engines also provided power to the aircraft internal systems, and lighting was maintained throughout the stricken aircraft.

Hughes and Odekirk killed the engines but left the two power providers idling for the moment.

It was a risk, but one that needed to be taken.

Water continued to rush in, and men struggled towards for the prized places on the surface, rather than sputtering in the mass below.

That being said, the discipline was incredible, as the wounded were passed to waiting hands.

Many had been placed in the wing voids, where the sheer size of the Spruce Goose allowed for stretchers to be accommodated.

These casualties were recovered, although the angle the aircraft had come to rest at presented some interesting issues for the men who worked to get their comrades out.

Men already out the doors slid down the hull and into the water, or remained on the fuselage and wing.

On the shoreline, military and civilian personnel alike reacted to the sight, and numerous craft were pushed into the Caspian's waters in a huge lifesaving effort, in spite of the obvious Soviet markings on the giant aircraft.

Some officers called men to them, organising the off-duty soldiers as best they could, in case the landing was by military design, rather than by accident, even though the Allied fighters that buzzed overhead seemed unconcerned.

The sight of Soviet paratrooper uniforms reinforced their decision, and more than one weapon was turned towards the floundering Hercules.

However, man's instinct to save life was the primary force, and many of the Australian onlookers had spent their young lives amongst the surf of the Pacific and Indian Oceans, so they plunged into the waters without a care, strong strokes bringing them to the Hercules before most of the boats had covered half the distance.

Men had already died in the fuselage, knocked unconscious in the landing and drowned unnoticed in submerged seats.

But most of the troopers and POWs emerged into the light, hundreds of them, each choosing between the water and the wing.

The confident ones grabbed a hesitant comrade and struck out for shore. Many simply waited for rescue to arrive, assured that the aircraft had come to rest and had no intention of sinking

Holliday, his head running red from a cut on his right temple, oversaw the move of his stretcher cases.

Crisp and Galkin, the latter's sickness now a distant memory, stood inside the great amphibian, overseeing the egress, their presence ensuring relative calm amongst the escapees.

The occasional man lost his nerve and jostled for priority position, but each was put in his place by those around him, occasionally with a friendly blow to bring sense to a panicking mind.

The large twin doors helped the evacuation immensely, even though the floor was not level, following the wing-dip manoeuvre.

More and more of the surface of the Hercules became cluttered with men, although the boats soon started to arrive.

Maintaining discipline, the stretcher cases and wounded were handed down first, that itself a difficult job as the height difference between the proud wing and the rescuing boats was often extreme.

Even with bringing the boats closer to the wing root, it was still a considerable drop from there to the water's surface, or to the deck of a rescuing boat.

Two men slid off the wing and onto a small rowing boat, their landings marked with the sharp crack of yielding bone as both broke legs on landing.

It served as a warning to others, and those that followed either slid off the wing into the water next to a rescuer or found other ways to lessen the impact.

One enterprising Iranian fisherman conned his boat right up to the wing, allowing men to scramble down the mast in relative safety, with nothing more than a splinter or two to show for their escape.

It was a testament to the swiftness of the rescuers and comradeship of the survivors that only one man drowned once outside the Spruce Goose, a POW who simply slipped under the water unseen.

Inside, Crisp and Galkin remained at their posts, helping their men through the doors, noting with grim satisfaction that the line of escapees was dwindling away, and with great pride that their troopers were ceding their place in line to the POWs.

Finally, after what seemed like an age, the last men passed out into the light.

Unspoken agreement drove both officers back into the depths of the aircraft in search of any remaining survivors.

Some interior lights fused out as the waters made themselves known, but sufficient illumination remained for the two to see that no one else was coming out under their own steam.

Moving through the surprisingly cool water, they moved towards the first tragic sight.

Two bodies floated side-by-side, top and tailing each other like children in a shared bed.

They took hold of one each and dragged the drowned POWs across the surface of the water until they could get good enough footing to grab them and drag them up to the exits.

Wijers, Hawkes, and Timmins had now appointed themselves as door guardians, and quickly plunged back into the fuselage to help with the recovery.

Passing their burdens off, Crisp and Galkin went back again, quickly finding one more unfortunate, totally submerged and held down by his straps, which had become entangled with a damaged wooden strut.

Ducking beneath the surface, Galkin used his knife to cut the strap and Sveinsvold's body came away in Crisp's hands.

Hawkes and Timmins had moved closer, and they took the burden from their commander.

There was one more shape in the half-light, and Crisp moved towards it, swimming the last few yards to the side of the fuselage before ducking under the water.

Again, the body was caught by its straps, a slightly dislodged bench seat ensnaring the drowned man, who had also clearly taken some sort of impact.

Crisp recognised him as the body came away from its restraint.

"Goddamnit!"

"You OK, Colonel?"

Con Galkin pushed himself across the water.

"It's Andy Garrimore, Con. Think his neck's broken too."

Galkin took his share of the load and the two swum back to hand the dead officer into Wijers' waiting hands.

There were no more casualties apparent, the other dead being further down the fuselage, well beneath the water level and beyond rescue by men not equipped for the purpose.

They returned to the exits and Crisp, as was his right, allowed Galkin to step out first.

Although he did not know for sure, he sensed that the depths of the Spruce Goose held more death, and he stopped for a moment of silence and sent a salute into the slowly rising water before being the last man to leave the stricken amphibian.

Twenty-two lives were lost as a result of the crash.

Some of the wounded found the experience too much and succumbed to their injuries.

The last two to die were a pair of severely wounded men who lay side by side on stretchers, neither conscious nor lucid enough to acknowledge the other, or to realise that either knew the other from a dark August some twenty-one bloody months previously.

On the night of 6th August 1945, the two had walked together down a street in Enns, to seek out General Mark Clark and warn him of the imminent Soviet attack.

John Schwartz and Ostap Shandruk, despite the best efforts of Hamouda and an SSF medic, lay under the burning sun on the crowded right wing of the Spruce Goose and died before they could reach the shore.

[Author's note - The mast that ripped the fuselage of the Spruce Goose belonged to the Soviet gunboat, Krasnyy Azerbaydzhan.

Its presence was unknown to the Allies, its loss being down to accident rather than positive action.

It is doubtful that, had it been marked on the maps, the impact would have been avoided anyway.

Howard Hughes' book on the whole Kingsbury Operation states that he acted on impulse, his main reason for turning to port being the higher power on the starboard side because of the loss of a port engine.

None the less, whilst Krasnyy Azerbaydzhan claimed more Allied lives in death than in her lifetime, the feat of bringing the Hercules home with such a small loss of life is still incredible, and a testament to Hughes and the two inexperienced men who flew her on her last flight.

Twelve more Hercules were built and saw mixed service, the last one being withdrawn from frontline duties in 1957.

One incomplete example is presently preserved at the Evergreen Space and Aviation Museum in McMinnville, Oregon.

The original Spruce Goose languished in Caspian waters for four months before efforts were made to recover her, although local fishermen and souvenir hunters had already removed most things of value, despite a constant armed guard.

On the night of 15th September 1947, she mysteriously caught fire and burned down to the waterline.]

Earlier - 1553 hrs, Friday, 11th April 1947, NKVD regional office, Akhtubinsk, USSR.

Serov listened intently as Skryabin spoke at length, understandably desperate to show himself in a good light and passing blame in all directions.

His story, for that was what Serov considered it to be, unusually praised the second in command, Durets, who clearly discharged his duty

167

properly by initiating the device. Major General Lunin, the overall head of VNIIEF security, came in for a scathing evaluation, and an insinuation that it was Skryabin who had to manage his commander's constant absences, absences that had clearly contributed to the enemy's success. By example, he had ignored Lunin's standing instructions and had managed to escape and raise the alarm. It also highlighted the deficits of the 7th Training Unit and its commander, specifically in hindering him in discharging his duties and not responding to his direct orders, orders made under the Colonel General's own authority.

A swift conversation with Beria had already illuminated Serov, who now knew, and wondered if Skryabin also knew, that the NKVD Colonel was untouchable.

Serov simply understood that the family link to Molotov, and the clear forbearance of the man's shortcomings, would ensure that Beria had plenty of leverage over the Foreign Minister in time to come.

The conversation became one-sided, as Beria had rapped out a series of orders, many of which were designed to distance the NKVD from responsibility, or more to the point, clearly lay the blame at the door of others.

Serov understood his master's needs, as they mirrored his own.

As Beria issued his final orders, two more reports came in.

He completed the call, acknowledging his new orders, and connected to the Dzerzhinsky Street secure typing pool, to whom he dictated his first official report.

It was typed and copied as fast as any document has ever been, and quickly taken to the Kremlin, for the scrutiny of the GKO.

Once Serov completed his report, and sampled a stiffening pepper vodka, he was back on the telephone to his secretary, summoning the man who lived a charmed life.

After a few minutes, there was a knock, and his secretary ushered Skryabin in.

"Right, Comrade Polkovnik, for some reason Comrade Marshal Beria still finds you useful. I have orders for you, and you better not fuck them up or not even he'll save you this time."

1609 hrs, Friday, 11th April 1947, the Kremlin, Moscow, USSR.

Stalin listened without a single show of emotion, his face emotionless, despite whatever must have been churning inside him.

The details were still incomplete, but Serov's initial telephone report made bad enough reading.

The whole of the VNIIEF facility had been transformed into a radioactive wasteland.

Whilst the GKO's collective horror was slightly less, given that all but one of their devices had already been moved away, the loss of most of the hi-speed centrifuges was a major blow, even though Japanese engineers were already assisting in the production of faithful copies of the original design.

Some critically important staff had clearly been lost, but most had already been moved to the larger facilities at Novouralsk, Ozyorsk, and Lesnoy.

In private before the meeting, Stalin and Beria had already had a heated discussion about the wiseness of a protocol that ordered the camp commander to blow the facility up with an atomic device if threatened, but both had decided that the issue was for another time, understanding that they had both signed off on the order when it had seemed like a good idea.

Reports from survivors in the area indicated a delayed, almost rolling explosion, a double effect that had excited the scientists beyond measure, sending them to check and recheck calculations that had been checked and rechecked a thousand times already.

There was absolutely no indication that the Allies had dropped their own device, and that the double effect was precisely that; two atomic bombs exploding within a few hundred yards of each in near synchronicity.

The reports, the investigators already on scene, and the intelligence information, all failed to even suggest that the Allies had launched the mission against the facility itself, rather than on the prison camp and as a rescue mission.

Skryabin had, for reasons best known to himself but probably based around self-preservation, decided not to mention the clear excursions of the attacking force into the secret facility, so Serov and the Soviet leadership were unaware that their secret was out.

The only note of discord was a section in Serov's initial submission, where he questioned the raid's motivation, as easier prisoner-based targets were well within range of the Allies.

Why Camp 1001 would be selected troubled the Colonel General greatly and he had already ordered a review of the prisoner files, in case some important person worthy of rescue had been unwittingly incarcerated.

Vasilevsky, out of his depth on the matter of the Army's involvement in the area, could not directly object to the investigation of the local commander and the possible failures of his unit. He was familiar with the scapegoat process that was so beloved of the leadership.

He was already sure that the NKVD would escape smelling of apple blossom as usual, and that some unfortunate middleman would absorb the blame in the normal way, either by execution or...

The Red Army commander checked himself.

'Get real, man!'

This one would cost a number of people their lives for sure, and probably none of them would be in the slightest bit guilty, as those truly culpable hid behind the organised bloodletting and finger pointing that accompanied such events.

Beria waited in silence as Stalin arranged his thoughts, sipping his tea whilst he determined his own stance on what he considered likely to spring from his master's lips.

"So... we proceed. This simply plays into our hands. We state to the world that the Allies have used a bomb on our territory. They'll deny it. We then initiate the second phase. Even that shit Tito will be baying for Truman's fucking blood after that. The Finns will crow like crazy... even the Swedes will agitate. This all works to our advantage... except for the loss of the equipment at Uspenka."

Halfway through Stalin's words, Beria had set down the cup and saucer and taken to polishing his glasses.

"I agree, Comrade General Secretary. We have an opportunity here."

Stalin puffed contentedly on his pipe.

"Then let's get the thing started, Lavrentiy. TASS and Pravda of course... but also let's be subtle."

Beria raised his eyebrows at the out-of-character suggestion, failing to hide his reaction from the man opposite.

"Yes, I can do subtle, Lavrentiy. We have an opportunity here and if we play this right we can restore our own status amongst our allies, and damage this NATO and the Allies for many years to come."

Angry that his reaction had not been controlled, Beria resorted to being efficient to cover his pain.

"We have contacts in many press agencies, of course. Sweden would be good, in view of phase two. England naturally, and France. Belgrade and Madrid most certainly... India?"

Stalin warmed to the idea immediately.

"Why not? The trouble is already brewing there. An excellent idea, Lavrentiy."

Beria reset his glasses and steepled his fingertips before posing the really important question.

"When?"

Stalin nodded his acceptance of the burden of command and grabbed his chin in thought.

"I say... be ready, but it'll be the Allies that set the agenda. We'll go with phase two as soon as they provide us with the opportunity."

Beria nodded in agreement.

"I'll ensure that everything is ready to go on your command, Comrade General Secretary."

"Excellent."

He relit his pipe and the two sat in what passed for comfortable silence between them.

"So, what of Kaganovich?"

"The game continues, Comrade General Secretary."

"Soon?"

"He's unsure, but very possibly. We must be wary that this latest matter doesn't tip the conspirators hands."

"Does he know them all yet?"

"No, not yet... another good reason for holding back and not rounding the bastards up. They're all watched, of course, even those that we haven't yet confirmed one way or the other."

"Are we satisfied that the names we have are the main conspirators?"

"Kaganovich is, Comrade General Secretary. He plays a dangerous game, of course. But I'm confident in his loyalty. He can definitely identify Khrushchev, Gorbachev, Gurundov, and Voznesensky ... and Kuznetsov... fucking GRU bastard..."

Beria made sure he reminded his master of the shortcomings of the rival intelligence service, something he intended to exploit when the bloodletting started.

"Bulganin remains unconfirmed, but Kaganovich is sure that there is at least one high-powered figure still behind the scenes, if not more."

"Khrushchev... who'd have thought it possible, eh?"

"Anything is possible it seems, Comrade General Secretary."

"So who's the military man behind this? Those two are small fry. Who is it?"

"Kaganovich is unsure..."

"But he suspects, of course?"

"Of course, Comrade General Secretary."

"Well?"

Stalin puffed more rapidly on his pipe to mark his excitement at hearing a name.

"Vasilevsky."

"Blyad... Vasilevsky? Blyad!"

"Suspicion only, but it has to be someone of status, or the army won't follow."

"Vasilevsky... I trusted him above all others..."

Beria looked sharply at his leader, who noted the reaction and unusually took immediate steps to defuse the moment.

"I meant in the military, Lavrentiy, in the military."

Beria nodded but still smarted inside.

Stalin shook his head, sucked on a pipe long since gone out, and tapped the bowl loudly, spilling ash and unburnt tobacco into his hand and across the desktop.

"And what of the woman?"

Beria so wanted to condemn her, and drag her into the shady and seedy world of the plotters, but Kaganovich was adamant on his facts.

"No, comrade... she's not involved. He believes she is loyal... rather surprising really, isn't it?"

He was imagining much more than was forming in Stalin's mind.

"No... not at all. She's a loyal member of the party and a true patriot... a lover of the Motherland. Despite her losses, she remains loyal. Excellent... excellent."

Beria wished it were otherwise.

"Kaganovich is on top of this? Truly?"

"Yes, Comrade General Secretary. The pressure on him must be enormous, but he is coping well... and he's a loyal communist. The venom

172

in him when he speaks with me about their plans... their conniving... truly he hates them."

"When this is done and the bastards are liquidated, we must give him the Hero Award, Lavrentiy."

"But of course, Comrade General Secretary."

Inside, Beria added, *'and a 7.62mm headache for the ambitious bastard who's after my job!'*

The mud bath was as good as he had expected, and Lunin's aching body relaxed and enjoyed its embrace and warmth.

Gelendzhik was a resort on the Black Sea, twenty-five kilometres southeast of Novorossiysk, a place where the hierarchy of the Motherland would go and while away their time recuperating in the mud, drinking from the mineral springs, or simply relaxing by the water's edge or on a forest walk.

Of late, Lunin had been almost a permanent resident here, taking more time away from his duties, often without informing his superiors.

The treatment centre was a quiet and relaxing place, but it was suddenly transformed into anything but as the sound of heavy boots bounced off every wall, bringing with them the promise of nothing but pain and heartache.

Even through the mud, Lunin could feel the vibrations as the body of men approached, the increasingly strong rhythmic steps marking the progress of an official, unchallengeable, and inexorable force.

He pushed himself up in the bath and cleared his ears in time to witness five armed men burst through the double doors immediately opposite him.

"Mayor General Lunin?"

"Yes."

"By order of the GKO, you are under arrest for cowardice and dereliction of duty. Dress yourself immediately."

The Major nodded at the man by his side, who moved forward and picked up the robe, holding it out to the stunned Lunin.

"What for? What have I done? What's happening here?"

"The prison camp... the responsibility from which you have absented yourself without permission... was attacked and destroyed by the Allies."

The NKVD Major was not privy to the real purpose of Camp 1001.

"Attacked and destroyed?"

"Yes. And where were you? Languishing in fucking mud when you should have been at your duty post, you traitor."

"Destroyed? All of it?"

"Totally. The prisoners escaped with the attackers... all of it with the camp under your command!"

"But..."

"Silence. Save it for the trial, Lunin. You're under arrest."

"And if I resist arrest?"

"You'll not be shot, if that's what you want."

His orders were very specific.

No offer of a quick death for this one, no escape by his own hand.

Lunin was to be the public face of failure for the trial to come, one where the problem would be laid at the feet of an individual and his shortcomings, not be part of a system problem, or even worse, the fault of higher authority.

Lunin understood this instinctively.

"May I shower?"

He considered the request.

The general was clearly unwell and would not cause any problems.

"Yes, of course... under supervision."

"Thank you."

Nine minutes later, the NKVD Major was screaming for medical aid as his men dragged Lunin from the shower, the robe's tie cord around his neck but his attempt to take his own life ultimately unsuccessful.

That task would fall to others, after a staged trial which would establish his guilt beyond any doubt, and see his body riddled with bullets and dumped in a rubbish pit.

The training school forces and to a lesser extent their visitors, had taken some desperate casualties.

The final assessment was not yet complete, as stragglers were still reporting in to the advance headquarters outside of Akhtubinsk, but the explosion of the huge explosion had almost certainly wiped out the entire 5th Infantry Company and the greater part of 1st Tanks.

2nd and 4th infantry had both taken heavy hits too.

Zorin was nowhere to be found and Yarishlov feared the worst, as the man would have been up front, leading his soldiers forward.

Harazan had been located and the reports caused him great pain, as the young engineer officer was found hideously burned and surrounded by the dead and wounded of his command, all caught in the post-explosion fireball.

His own skin rebelled at the images his brain threw up, the doctor's initial report stating that the engineer officer was not long for this world.

An entire recon platoon, the First, had certainly been lost, as they had been reporting in from the main entrance as the explosion occurred.

All told, including the encounters with the enemy force at the airfield and on the highway, his command had probably lost upwards of four hundred men, with surprisingly few wounded as opposed to dead.

His need was to be out amongst his men, helping to heal their wounds and to pin their morale and spirit in place.

However, Yarishlov's responsibilities and orders made him sit in his office, with nothing but runners and Kriks for company, as his officers went out to do the jobs he yearned to do.

The wounded Bailianov was still working out in the darkness, his shredded left arm in a sling, an injury sustained during an attack by one of the devil flying machines that had chewed up so many of his forces around the airfield.

Raised voices penetrated his consciousness as he read the latest report from the commander of 115th Naval Infantry, one that placed losses amongst the marine infantry at thirty-two dead and ninety-seven wounded, most around the Astrakhan Highway, where they had encountered the unexpected use of the road as an airstrip, defended by competent infantry,

175

and where yet more of the little German helicopters had proven so effective.

He had seen the remains of one that had been brought down, complete with its partially burned pilot, the hated Luftwaffe uniform resplendent with the medals of a successful military career, one abruptly cut short by impact with the ground and the resulting fire.

A shot focussed his mind on the growing scuffle outside.

The door flew open as four NKVD soldiers bustled in, holding weapons that were directly pointed at the tank general.

"What's is the meaning of this?"

As if he could not suspect.

Another figure stepped into the room, still wearing the smug look from the last time that Yarishlov had seen him.

"Skryabin!"

"Polkovnik Skryabin to you, you fucking traitor."

"What?"

"I'm here to arrest you for your failures."

"What?"

Skryabin paused, relishing the moment and Yarishlov's clear confusion.

"You're being held accountable for the loss of the prison camp and the secret facility. Your unit's failures to implement my requirements directly contributed to the destruction of valuable state property and the destruction of your command. So... Mayor General Arkady Yarishlov... under the joint orders of the General Secretary and NKVD Marshal Beria, I arrest you for dereliction of duty and cowardice in the face of the enemy."

"What?"

"Surrender your pistol immediately."

One of the NKVD soldiers moved forward and manhandled Yarishlov as he tried to get at his holster.

Pushing the man's hands away, Yarishlov received a backhanded slap across the face, one that drew blood from where the force of the blow split his already damaged skin.

Skryabin moved closer and spat in Yarishlov's face.

"Touch one of my soldiers again, and I'll shoot you out of hand myself, you bastard."

The NKVD soldier redoubled his efforts to extract Yarishlov's pistol, exercising even less care than before.

He looked the tank officer in the eye, taunting him with his contemptuous look, but suddenly melted inside as the eyes that stared back frightened him more than he could ever imagine possible.

He passed the Tokarev to Skryabin and sought safety behind his officer.

Kriks burst into the room, blood dripping from his side where a single bullet, the shot that had shaken Yarishlov into awareness, had struck him.

Two of the NKVD guards that stayed outside the room covered him with their weapons.

"Comrade General, are you harmed?"

"No, thank you, Comrade Praporshchik. I am, however, under arrest."

Kriks looked at the NKVD soldiers one by one, his utter contempt dripping from every pore.

"Say the word, Comrade General, and we'll send these Chekist scum packing."

"Silence, you piece of shi..."

"Silence your fucking self, you Chekist fuck! There are seven of you... hundreds of us... do you really think that you'll walk out of here alive if I give the word? Eh? Your life..." he looked around the four other men in the room, "Their lives... are all in my General's fucking hands. Breathe quietly and pray, you fucking bastard!"

Much as Yarishlov was tempted to allow his rescue, he knew that the end would be the same for him, but simply mean that many of his men would die too.

"Stand down, Comrade Praporshchik. Stand down."

"But Comr..."

"No, Stefan. My time has come, but I'll not have any more of my men lost to this foolishness... not even you, you old rogue."

"But..."

"Enough I say! I thank you and the boys, but no... stand down. You'll not harm these men. No matter what. That is my last but one order to you, and you **will** obey me."

Kriks stood erect, proud, and in turmoil.

"Yes, Comrade Mayor General... it shall be as you order."

Yarishlov focussed on Skryabin.

"I've given my order, and it **will** be obeyed, Comrade Polkovnik. On that, I stake my honour. There'll be no repercussions for the... err... misplaced loyalty of my men, of course."

Skryabin nodded without a moment's pause, knowing that he and his men had been granted a reprieve by the man they had come to arrest... come to kill.

"And now, Comrade Kriks, my final order to you."

Yarishlov sat down at his desk and, locating paper and pen, hastily wrote a note.

He challenged Skryabin with a look but it was not responded to so he continued.

Yarishlov unpinned the second Hero Award from his upper chest, the one that he won so dearly at Naugard, wrapped it in the paper and sealed both in an envelope.

Yarishlov stood and handed the envelope to Kriks.

"Come and embrace me, Stefan."

The two old comrades hugged each other for one final time, a long hug between men who had shared the same mud and smoke for what seemed like a lifetime, a hug long enough for Yarishlov to whisper his final orders into the ear of the man he valued above all others.

Breaking the hold, Yarishlov stood back and away from Kriks.

"You understand your final order, Comrade Praporshchik?"

"Yes, Comrade Mayor General. It will be as you command."

"Thank you, my friend."

Yarishlov's voice crackled as the emotion hit him, but he still managed a salute worthy of the May Day parade, one that was returned with equal skill by a tearful Kriks.

"Now go, my friend. Good luck and goodbye."

"Comrade Gen... Arkady... I..."

"I know, Stefan... it's the same for me, old friend... now... away with you."

Kriks moved carefully past Skryabin, who had already resolved to relieve the NCO of the package and find out exactly what the prisoner had said.

Wisely, he decided that now was not the time.

"Leave us... but remain outside."

The four NKVD soldiers left quickly, leaving the two officers alone.

"So... comrade general... what are we to do here?"

178

"We both know what you intend, so get on with it."

Skryabin weighed Yarishlov's Tokarev automatic, chambered a round then slipped the magazine out and into his pocket.

He walked forward, placing the weapon on the desk between himself and his prisoner.

"It would be extremely embarrassing for the Motherland to arraign a double Hero of the Soviet Union on charges of cowardice, don't you think?"

They both looked at the weapon, which lay butt towards the NKVD man.

Skryabin smiled, reading his prisoner's mind, and produced his own weapon.

"Now, now, Comrade... I'm offering you a way out... one with honour and dignity, and you're thinking about shooting me. Hardly in the spirit of what I'm trying to offer you, is it?"

Yarishlov's eyes bored into the man, contempt, hate, and scorn flowing like a river.

"Fine. As you wish. Let's not fuck about then, you cowardly fuck. I will walk out of here and leave you with the pistol. One bullet remains. Use it wisely. I'll not come back in until I hear the shot. If you don't use it within five minutes, you'll be dragged out and humiliated in front of your men before I have you hung."

"You wouldn't dare."

"But I would. I've clear orders... orders from the top... the very top. You're going to die... but due to your previous heroic service, you can choose the manner by which you depart this earth. More than fucking generous in my view... personally, I'd have hung you by your balls on the Kremlin walls."

Still holding his pistol on Yarishlov, Skryabin pushed the Tokarev across the desktop.

"You have five minutes. After that, whatever you had or whatever you were, will be lost in a world of humiliation and pain. Make the sensible choice, Yarishlov."

Skryabin moved back to the door.

"My money's on you lacking the balls to do the right thing... and personally, I'm fine with that. I'll enjoy myself. See you soon, coward."

He closed the door and left Yarishlov alone.

Skryabin enjoyed a cigarette amongst his men as the personnel of Yarishlov's staff sat around in confusion, some continuing with the work, most stunned and unable to understand what exactly was going on.

Kriks had already informed them of Yarishlov's order, something that the NKVD NCO had confirmed to Skryabin as soon as he emerged from the office.

The NKVD colonel relaxed into his cigarette.

A single shot rang out and he continued to draw down on the rich tobacco, feeling calm and satisfied, despite the overt emotion sweeping through the assembled staff, expressed in the many tears shed for those who knew their commander well.

Kriks, despite being junior in rank to most present, gathered his wits and ordered the staff to leave the building.

It was a testament to his popularity and status that the group, up to and including Majors, simply moved on instantly at his command.

In seconds, the whole headquarters belonged to Skryabin and his eight men.

He stubbed out his cigarette and tugged his tunic into place.

Two of his men opened the door for him and the three of them trooped in.

Skryabin was confronted with a scene unlike that which he expected to encounter.

Yarishlov was sat at his desk holding the still smoking Tokarev in a firm hand, his eyes burning deeply into those of the NKVD officer, who in an instant understood the true meaning of fear.

On the desk were three magazines, clearly full.

'How could I have been so fucking stupid?'

"How could you have been so stupid, Chekist?"

One of the soldiers raised his AK-47 and immediately flew back against the doorframe as a bullet took him in the upper chest.

The other soldier was slower but chose to move as well, so the bullet aimed at him hit his shoulder; messy but not life threatening.

Skryabin suddenly displayed more courage than he had ever done in his previous years and grabbed for his own weapon.

Yarishlov put three bullets into the NKVD officer, none of them as aimed as he would have liked, but already there were more soldiers coming through the door and they distracted him.

Skryabin went down screaming, leaking fluid from two serious wounds and a graze.

Yarishlov, his skin protesting with the contact against the wooden desk, ducked down as the next man in fired a burst from his AK.

He caught the sling on the door handle and it pulled the weapon off target. From under the desk, Yarishlov took his opportunity and put two bullets into the soldier, propelling him back through the door and into the man trying to back him up.

A single bullet had clipped Yarishlov's left arm, but nothing vital was inhibited and he used the lull to slide a fresh clip home.

Outside the room, the NKVD NCO decided on how best to proceed and quickly came up with a plan.

One of his men went off in search of the means.

It seemed that no one else existed in the world, so quiet had the building become.

The laboured breath of wounded men was all that Yarishlov could hear.

The soldier with the shoulder wound moaned in pain, a soft moan almost like the wind passing through treetops.

The other wounded man whimpered and breathed in a laboured fashion.

Skryabin's wounds would be sufficient to kill if he didn't receive immediate medical attention, which seemed less likely as the moments passed.

A combination of pain and malevolence was writ large on his face.

Yarishlov moved across to the wounded soldier and pressed some soft paper to the wound.

181

"Here, soldier. That should stop you leaking. Beware who you follow in future. Drag yourself out the door now."

The man nodded, seeing the tank officer in a new light.

He recoiled as blood and flesh flew over his face as Skryabin's bullet caught Yarishlov in the neck, dropping him onto the floor beside the wounded man.

Yarishlov bled profusely and he knew his time was limited.

He tried to tighten his grip on his Tokarev but his hands simply refused to follow his instructions.

Any attempt to raise his weapon was too much effort, although he persevered.

Skryabin's face twisted in pain and hate and he brought his pistol again, intent on inflicting more pain on the burned officer.

Resting his hand on the dead body next to him, he aimed at the tank officer's torso but instead shot the Tokarev out of Yarishlov's grasp, his bullet wrecking the wrist as it travelled through, shattering bone on its path.

His target whimpered but did not scream, something that enraged him as his own pain was becoming unbearable.

His next shot missed but was close enough to cover Yarishlov with bits of plaster as the bullet struck the wall by his side.

The struggle in front of his eyes amused him, and he delayed his next shot as he enjoyed the sight of Yarishlov trying to bring up his pistol, whilst knowing that he couldn't, and enjoying the fact that Yarishlov knew he couldn't too.

"You chekist bastard."

Another shot crashed into Yarishlov's shoulder, sending a spray of crimson blood up the wall.

Yarishlov hissed impotently through clenched teeth as his body started to concede the struggle for life.

"I hope my bullets are enough for you, chekist."

"I'll live... and I'll piss on your grave... and that of your men."

Yarishlov renewed the effort to reach his pistol, and succeeded for the briefest of moments before his ruined arm gave up the struggle.

"I'll have the last laugh on you, you fucking coward. Your men will die... know that... they'll all die!"

Whatever it was that landed on Skryabin's leg, bounced away, struck the desk, came back at him and found a resting place against his thigh.

He looked down and saw death in all its glory.

The last thing he heard was Yarishlov's laughter.

A laughter of a man that understood that he would not die alone.

The grenade exploded and brought a swift death to them both.

Bailianov returned and, after a rapid conversation with Kriks, took command of the scene and ensured that the NKVD survivors were properly treated and kept safe, as per Yarishlov's instructions.

As had been hoped, the act saved the 7th MCTS from further ignominy and retribution.

The eye of the inquisitors moved elsewhere and the survivors were left to lick their wounds and mourn their dead.

Yarishlov's body was taken by the NKVD and never seen again.

He was not afforded military honours, and the location of his burial, if he ever had one, was apparently not recorded.

As far as the public and history were concerned, he simply ceased to exist, except in the hearts of those with whom he served.

The USSR spread the word across the world, knowing it to be a lie, but knowing that the Allied denial would serve little purpose in the end.

No one important would believe that the Allies had not dropped an atomic device.

Observers were already being courted to attend the area once safety zones were in place, in order to view the dastardly crime in its full glory.

Others would work amongst the entourages, making simple observations about the outcry when a small rogue group used Tabun Gas, comparing matters to the clearly organised and sanctioned attack conducted by a group of nations, an attack that was so badly organised that it simply obliterated a large prisoner of war camp.

The Soviet propaganda machine would swing into full speed and wavering Allies and concerned neutrals would be courted and made amenable to the needs of the Motherland.

A by-product of the events of Friday 13th April was to knock the conspirators off-balance and their plans to act on the afternoon of Saturday 14th April were postponed, a delay that proved to be of huge significance.

1419 hrs, Saturday, 12th April 1947, Nikolskoye on the Volga River, USSR.

Their lovemaking had been frantic, so long had they been apart.

He, an infantry officer home on leave to recuperate from wounds sustained in combat.

She, a doctor who had experienced a psychiatric breakdown following seventy-two hours of non-stop operations on desperately wounded men.

Both had returned independent of each other, only to find themselves back home and with their childhood sweetheart close at hand, and both of them in need of consolation.

The sort of consolation that can easily be found in the act of love.

She groaned her way through his attentions, enjoying his presence and proximity as much as the feel of him inside her.

He gasped and moaned as his orgasm approached.

He came noisily and collapsed panting, his heart pounding so hard she could hear it in his mouth.

"Fucking hell, Annushka!"

"Darling."

She sniggered and planted a huge kiss on him as he rolled off to one side.

"You can stop moaning now, Ilya."

He passed her a cigarette.

"I'm not moaning, Anna."

He looked at her and dramatically sealed his lips tight to demonstrate the truth of his words.

She accepted the light and drew deeply on the tobacco.

"So who is?"

Ilya the lover suddenly became Ilya the soldier as his senses transferred themselves from his loins to his ears and then to his survival instincts.

His pistol was out in an instant and he moved swiftly, despite the protest from his healing wounds.

She, contrary to standing orders, had not worn her uniform so her pistol was still in the drawer in their modest riverside isba, some two hundred metres away.

"Fucking hell! Anna! Come quickly!"

The sounds of splashing, moaning, and cursing assailed her ears as she rushed forward.

Ilya was pulling something barely recognisable from the water's edge.

"Blyad!"

Her escape from the terrors of front-line medical work was over.

Before her lay a man so hideously wounded as to defy real description.

She was incredulous that the man even lived.

"Fetch help, Ilya... quickly... there's a phone at old man Horgan's place. Then bring my medical bag back with you."

As a Lieutenant Colonel in the Red Army Medical branch, she was used to instant obedience, plus she outranked her lover.

He sprang away, leaving her to comfort and tend to the poor wretch in her arms.

As she made a deeper appraisal of his wounds, she started to take in other details.

"Calm now, Comrade... I'm a doctor..."

'Officer's tunic... what's left of it anyway...'

The quality of the man's boots had already suggested he was a man of rank, but the tunic was a confirmation. She gently pulled some of the fabric away, careful not to provoke pain where the injuries were combined with the destroyed clothing.

'A wallet?'

She teased the damaged object out of the pocket and placed it to one side as she continued her examination.

Whoever it was had lapsed into unconsciousness, so she conducted her examination with only the lapping sounds of the Volga as a backdrop.

Annushka Gorievna tended his wounds as best she could as she waited.

She ripped the arms off her shirt to use as bindings, the bones poking through the unfortunate man's skin telling of incredible injuries underneath.

She made a swift cut with her penknife and tore the material into strips.

A huge wooden splinter in the man's side received particular attention.

Lastly she separated the dangling fingers from the mangled hand, simply by a flick of the penknife, and wrapped the stumps in more of her shirt.

She finished doing what she could and settled down to monitor her charge.

Gorievna lit a cigarette and examined the object.

The pouch was torn and part of its contents damaged.

However, the soldier's identification was intact enough for her to understand that the man was important.

'A major... NKVD no less.'

Within the hour, the information had reached ears that suspected the importance of the man concerned, and a full medical squad was en route from the large Army medical facility at Kharabali.

On arrival they took over a whole function room in the nearby hotel and turned it into a facility that would give their casualty the very best chance of life.

So far, he was the sole known survivor from those who served at Camp 1001 and he was guarded well.

Other men quietly watched and waited for the moment the casualty would be able to answer a few simple questions.

Every hour, their commander phoned through to Akhtubinsk to report on Durets' progress.

1420 hrs, Saturday, 12th April 1947, Embassy of Sweden, 60 Mosfilmovskaya, Moscow, USSR.

The Swedish embassy was their home whilst they were in Moscow, and in recent times it had become their castle.

The Allied contingent had sought sanctuary there as matters on the front line affected their status in the Soviet capital.

Outside, the blatant presence of armed men looking in reminded them that their liberty hung by a small thread.

Horrocks stood at the window, drinking tea and chatting with Ramsey, both men casually observing the men observing them.

A car pulled up at the Soviet roadblock and the occupants dismounted as the vehicle was thoroughly searched.

The driver seemed unconcerned by affairs, smoking a cheroot and rubbing his fingers over his bald pate as if waiting on his superiors to get their act together, whereas the two men in the back, wearing the expensive clothes that marked them as senior diplomats, argued loudly and gesticulated over briefcases and a large wooden box dragged from the boot by the inquisitive inspectors.

"Diplomatic pouch... blah, blah, blah... every time the blighters do this to our Swedish cousins..."

Ramsey grunted as something stirred in his memory.

A cloudy image surfaced at the back of his mind but refused to identify itself.

'Hair... bald...'

"Mind you, Sir, the Swedes are being very dramatic today. New boys too. None of the regular crowd."

"I thought that too, Ramsey. All seems very... well... very theatrical, I must say."

Ramsey's mind was searching for the answer.

'Bald... hair... theatrical...'

One of the Swedes clearly moved too close and received a shove from one of the NKVD guards.

This resulted in shouts and posturing from the Swedish soldiers guarding the embassy gate and tensions rocketed in an instant.

"Oh dear... watch out... things could get out of hand here..."

A Swedish captain stepped forward and controlled his men with calming words, their rifles dropping as they relaxed.

On the other side of the barrier a senior Soviet officer stepped out of a nearby building, his voice reaching those stood inside the Swedish Embassy some sixty yards away.

On the trestle table lay the items in dispute, which were clearly diplomatic in nature, and therefore beyond interference and inspection.

At least, that was how the theory went.

The Soviet officer, a full colonel by Ramsey's estimation, held up his hand to interrupt the flow from the NKVD team commander and spoke to both Swedish diplomats in a more controlled fashion, so much as that the observers could see the two men relax instantly.

Within a moment, two of the NKVD guards were handling the unopened box back into the car, against a backdrop of hand shaking and salutes.

'Hair... bald... theatrical... is it... yes!'

"Bingo!"

"I'm sorry, old chap?"

Horrocks surveyed the source of the outburst.

Ramsey weighed up the pros and cons and decided that he had to share his discovery.

"You were right, Sir... what we just witnessed was a piece of theatre, enacted purely for the benefit of our Russian hosts, and all to permit entry of something extremely valuable."

"I say. The box, you think?"

"No, Sir... I didn't mean the box. Who knows what's in that. Probably nothing. Part of the distraction. I mean the man."

"They're new. Didn't recognise either of them."

"No, General, I mean the driver. He's known to us."

"Good Lord. Espionage is such a strange business. Who is he? One of ours?"

"No, Sir. He's a Swede and his coming here himself means something important is up. The man's name is Per Tørget and he's head of Swedish Intelligence."

"Spying royalty, eh?"

"Yes, Sir... and his presence here means nothing good... and on that, I'll stake my other leg."

"You don't have any legs, Colonel."

"Quite so, Sir. I meant the third one."

Horrocks snorted at the crudity.

Ramsey's 'leg' proved to be safe, for Tørget brought news and orders.

Across Europe, and then across the world, the news of the Allied atomic strike gathered momentum, accelerated by the Soviet propaganda apparatus.

The story gained credence amongst former allies of the Soviet Union, and caused further division in the Allied ranks, alienating some members of NATO from others who felt that atomic weapons were the spawn of the devil, and those also objected to the use of such weapons in their name but without consultation, which was pretty much everyone.

Stalin and Beria could not understand the lack of Allied denials, but welcomed the absence with both hands, seeing it as weakness and immaturity in the statesmanship game, not realising that the Allies would not deny dropping a bomb… could not deny dropping a bomb.

The one man who would have told them otherwise lay in a room in a hotel adjacent to the Volga, hideously injured and clinging to life.

Truman and Churchill spent time dealing with those Allies who were more than cross not to have been informed about the planned bombing, using the need for secrecy as the major excuse for not sharing the vital information.

The information that a Soviet bomb facility had been destroyed in the raid did not always assuage them, particularly the South American contingent, the tenuously neutral Yugoslavs and Italians, and most surprisingly, the Australians.

The proximity of their forces to the blast was of no real consequence, but they **were** the nearest, and the scenario played into the hands of those who wanted to leave the European war to the Europeans.

All in all, the whole affair could not have gone much better for those in Moscow, whereas it could not have been seen in much worse a light as far as the Allies were concerned, even with an excellent intelligence take from the mission and the rescue of many POWs.

The scientists were already excited about the Japanese centrifuge, and some of the captured documents were proving similarly stimulating.

However, the greatest piece of intelligence came from the lips of one of those 'men in white coats' who had been taken from the site.

The USSR had a total of eight fully operational devices.

In the Oval office, the Cabinet office, and a number of other important political places, the briefers briefed, giving a moment's pause to those who controlled the Allies' own weapons.

Intelligence services were put into overdrive to discover where the Soviets had stored their weapons and, as importantly, what were their intentions.

In the Kremlin, unaware of the advantage unwittingly placed in their hands, Stalin and Beria contrived decisions that would turn the world upside down.

Orders went out to a special NKVD unit in Vilnius, Lithuania.

Orders went out to two special NKVD units in Kiev and Odessa, both in the troublesome Ukraine.

Orders also reached out across the Atlantic to brave men whose resilience was being tested on a daily basis.

Orders that could ignite the world.

Our scientific power has outrun our spiritual power. We have guided missiles and misguided men.

Martin Luther King, Jr.

CHAPTER 203 - THE REACTION

The mist cleared slowly as his mind gained control and asserted itself over the sleep that had been so rudely interrupted.

"Goddamnit, man!"

Colonel Charles Codman shook his commander again, knowing that the act would earn him more rebukes.

"I'm awake, goddamnit, Charles! Where's the goddamn fire?"

"Sir, we're receiving reports of a huge explosion at around oh-seven-hundred near the Lithuanian capital, Vilnius. General McCreery's headquarters has issued a Waterfall-green warning."

"What the fuck!"

Waterfall was the codeword to be used for a Soviet atomic strike, green was added to clarify that it was purely suspected... at this time.

"Wake 'em all up! Everybody up and in now. I want information. I want that codeword re-sent to all commands immediately. Has it gone to the President?"

"No, Sir."

Codman, as duty officer, had followed the correct procedures from the moment the 'Waterfall-green' was received, and they did not involve the President of the United States at this time.

Patton saw it differently.

"Right. I'll be down directly. I want McCreery on the line with more information. Then I want a line to the White House. Move it, soldier!"

Patton dressed quickly and stood for a moment in front of the mirror, taking in both the reflection and the enormity of the possibilities the day held.

"Fuck."

The discussion with McCreery was brief but full of portents.

Reports from the air and ground talked about the unique after-effect of the huge blast. The mushroom cloud was there, as described in the briefing documents.

The reports from units closest to the explosion described the pressure wave and incredible burst of light.

The specialist officers attached to McCreery's command examined the reports and gave their opinion.

McCreery passed it on with his endorsement.

'Waterfall-red.'

Patton, for all his bravado and offensive spirit, quailed inside.

His discussion with McCreery had not ended before sounds of frantic activity reached his ears and a harried staff officer approached bearing a report that seemed, from the way the man was holding it, to be red-hot.

"One moment please, Sir Richard... spit it out, man."

Colonel Hood read the brief message.

"Sir, from the DRL liaison officer. Air reconnaissance noted a massive explosion in the area of Kiev in the Ukraine at approximately oh-seven-thirty hours. Initial intelligence assessment's Waterfall-green."

"Eh?"

Patton snatched the report from Hood's fingertips and read the damning words for himself.

"Get that firmed up, Colonel... Sir Richard..."

He repeated the report down the phone to the British officer and they shared a moment's silence.

"I think that changes everything then, Sir."

"You're goddamned right it does, Sir Richard. Wind your boys up. Press in hard and stay close to the bastards, come what may. Push the bastards wherever they'll go, but always stay tight. Remember the area avoidance requirements of these weapons. I'll get Air Force onto attacking likely sites. Scatter our supplies and rear-echelon as per Plan Starburst. Keep me informed of any more details. Same goes for me... I'll keep you informed. Questions?"

There were none.

"Goodbye."

Patton pressed the cradle down and released it, all in one decisive movement.

"Get me Washington."

The colonel stood waiting.

"All commands. Immediate and most urgent. Initiate Starburst."

Hood moved off at a speed that belied his years.

Given the time difference, Patton was quite surprised at finding himself speaking to his commander-in-chief within two minutes.

"Mister President."

"George. What can I do for you at this late hour?"

"Sir, I must report that it is extremely likely that there have been two Soviet atomic detonations in Europe in the last hour."

"What?"

"Firstly, I received reports from the British of a huge explosion around Vilnius, Lithuania. This was categorised as Waterfall-green, but has since moved to Waterfall-red."

"I see."

"The second report is from the German air force. Their recon force spotted a large explosion in the vicinity of Kiev in the Ukraine. That was also classified Waterfall-green. In the light of Vilnius, I would expect that to go red. I have initiated two actions, Mister President. Firstly, I have ordered Plan Starburst as a defensive measure, and secondly I am in the process of ordering all NATO forces to press home attacks on a general front, intending them to stay as close to the enemy as possible, which will negate the likelihood of tactical use, as per the scenarios discussed in Washington, and the general orders issued by General Marshall last month."

"Very good, George. These explosions... they're both inside Soviet-held territory. Am I correct in thinking that?"

"Yes, sir, you are."

"And you are content that Waterfall is appropriate for both incidents?"

"On the information I've received, and following a discussion with Field Marshal McCreery, I agree with the assessment."

"OK, George. We'll be burning the midnight oil here, so keep us informed, no matter what the hour. Anything you need from us right now?"

Patton had the inkling of an idea and he ran with it.

"Sir... our weapons... are they available... in case an opportunity presents itself?"

The silence lasted for a few seconds and then Truman was back speaking, a hard and final edge to his voice."

"General, I will not release the weapons to you. However, I'll issue orders that our atomic forces are to prepare themselves, ready for my order. If a target of opportunity presents itself, I'll authorise a strike if I am convinced that the use is militarily and politically justified."

He waited for Patton to respond, not knowing that another piece of paper had arrived for the general's immediate attention.

"Sir... err... I've just been handed a transcript of a Soviet radio broadcast... in which the Soviet Union states that the NATO Alliance has, without justification, dropped more atomic devices on the Soviet Union and her allies, namely the Lithuanian capital, and Kiev and Odessa in the Ukraine, causing hundreds of thousands of casualties They are calling upon the free world to condemn the actions of the aggress..."

"Three... there's another one?"

"Yes sir, Mister President."

"We didn't do it."

"I know, sir, which means..."

"Which means... good god, George... you can't be serious..."

Two brains worked hard but only managed one solution.

"That's monstrous. Not even Premier Stalin could conceive of such a thing!"

"Sir, nothing would surprise me. They'll point their fingers... we'll deny... no one'll believe that they've done this to themselves... no one, but no one'll believe it..."

"I need more information, George. I'm going to order the atomic force to prepare for missions against priority political targets. If that changes, if new information comes to light, I will act accordingly. Now, get me more information, George!"

A barely discernible voice reached Patton's ear as someone spoke to the president.

"Right. I must go, George. Winston's on the line. Get me more information. I must understand what's going on here."

The call terminated and Patton stared at the silent handset, searching for more answers.

He replaced the receiver with studied care and looked up at the waiting entourage.

"I want a full briefing in twenty minutes. I want confirmations from every command... every command... of the orders I've issued so far. I want everything the intelligence services have on Soviet atomic capability. Ensure this information goes out to all other commands immediately... including MacArthur in the Pacific."

By the time that the full briefing was ready, the transcript of the latest Soviet communiqué took centre stage.

"On the morning of Sunday, 15th April 1947, the fascist and capitalist forces, without warning or justifiable cause, attacked and destroyed the friendly nation Lithuania's capital city of Vilnius, and the Soviet cities of Kiev and Odessa. The weapons employed were the new and terrible atomic bombs, also recently employed by the fascist-capitalist faction against a non-military target near the Volga, and also without warning or justifiable cause. Casualties have been enormous and valiant rescue teams are struggling through the wreckage to locate and tend the numerous wounded."

"The people of the Soviet Union and her allies condemn this escalation in the war, which stands now as a very real obstruction to the ongoing peace talks."

Codman, reading it to the gathered staff, cleared his throat and carried on.

"These renewed hostilities were not sought by the Soviet Union, and we would still offer to find a route by which the fighting can be brought to a swift and just end."

He looked directly at Patton as he completed the statement.

"None the less, this abomination cannot go unanswered, and will not go unanswered. The people of the Soviet Union will respond in kind, and in decisive fashion, to strike back at those who threaten our world. It cannot be otherwise, and no one would expect us to simply permit this heinous assault on our Motherland, and the land of an ally, to go unpunished. We will strike back soon. We will strike back hard. Our retribution will be absolute, so that the aggressors will understand that the use of such weapons will never be tolerated, and will never be without immense cost to themselves. When the Soviet Union has completed its reprisals, we will return to the negotiating table in Sweden and do everything in our power to bring about a lasting peace, for the benefit of all the world's citizens."

Codman ended his reading of the document to a few gasps, toothy whistles, and more than one mumbled prayer.

195

Patton leant closer to Harold Bull, the assistant CoS, and Arthur Tedder, the deputy commander of NATO forces.

"Fascist-Capitalist faction. New rhetoric."

Tedder replied with typical dryness and no little irony.

"New situation, General Patton. Warfare has taken a great leap forward this day."

"Why have the bastards done this to themselves, eh? What purpose does this serve?"

"Makes us the bad guys to the world?"

"At the cost of thousands of their own people?"

"Technically not, Sir."

Both Tedder and Patton looked at Bull seeking clarification of the statement.

"Lithuania and the Ukraine… both have a history of rebellion… neither is truly Soviet in will or inclination."

Patton baulked at the very idea.

"So… thousands of people could be sacrificed for some grandiose political gambit… because they're not Russians?"

"Well… yes, Sir."

Tedder rolled his eyes in disbelief.

Patton stood up, sending his chair flying backwards.

"Goddamnit, but this is all gonna get out of hand. If those commie bastards are prepared to kill their own for leverage, then God help us all!"

Bull removed his spectacles and pinched his nose in thought.

Tedder pursed his lips before replying.

"We'll put everything up we have. Nothing will get through in the air. They have to know that we can stop any incursion."

"Does that sound like the rhetoric of people who think we can prevent them, Arthur? Harold?"

Their silence confirmed his thoughts.

"No… these bastards think they've got us already."

1132 hrs, Sunday 13th April 1947, Sanduny Banya, Moscow, USSR.

As with all such facilities, the steam rooms of the Sanduny were awash with NKVD informants, but Kaganovich was their boss and so the four men were able to find themselves alone for long enough to reach a decision.

"Regardless of what happens now, we must proceed quickly. This whole situation could get out of hand."

Khrushchev carried them along with his words.

Zhukov spoke for the army.

"We stand ready to do our duty. Give me a definite date and all will be done."

Kaganovich vouched for his part of the operation.

"I can also be ready. My assets can be in place as soon as I know our decision here."

Gorbachev's views were crystal clear as ever. If he had his way, the group would march on the Kremlin now and gun Stalin down themselves.

However, his approach was more coy than normal.

"We'll do our part, but what of our colleague? The part to be played there is of vital importance."

All eyes turned to Kaganovich.

"She'll be ready to play her part when the time comes. No question of that... and with this new furore... the opportunities have increased."

"So?"

"So... I say our best opportunity would seem to be Friday afternoon. I think fifteen hundred hours would be right?"

Kaganovich looked around the assembly, seeing both agreement and resolve in their eyes.

Khrushchev made the decision.

"Then fifteen-hundred on Friday it is. We must go through with the matter, come what may. The Rodina stands in peril the longer the rabid pair rule over us. There's no turning back. It must be done this time, regardless. No more delays! Are we agreed?"

Glasses were swept up into their hands and clinked together to seal their agreement.

The coup to remove Stalin from his position would take place less than one hundred and twenty-four hours from the moment the vodka bit their throats.

[Author's note - I feel obliged to inform readers that the Prüfstand XII is no figment of my imagination, and that three were manufactured in whole or part, with one ready for use in May 1945. They were quite huge items but, in my opinion, their intended use was perfectly feasible, given the enhanced capabilities of the Type XXI and German engineering. They were designed precisely for the purpose in which I employ them. In a time of all-out war, they might not have made the journey I have described as they would have been extremely vulnerable. However, in this war, where the Soviet Navy has all but ceased to exist and Allied eyes are turned elsewhere... well... read on...]

0644 hrs, Monday, 14th April 1947, the eastern seaboard of the USA.

"Read it again."

The signals officer carefully recited the order.

"Thank you."

Kalinin immediately disappeared off into his small cabin and extracted a sealed envelope from his safe.

Returning to the control room, he made a great show of opening the envelope and comparing the codes on the message form with those cited in the most secret document.

He had opened the envelope at the first opportunity he had and sealed it back up afterwards. The experienced captain in him was not prepared to go in harm's way without a lot of planning, which is why the name 'Boston' was no surprise to him.

"Navigator. How long to get to this location?"

Kalinin showed the coordinates of Mañana Island, a modest blob of land off the coast of Maine, dominated by its neighbour, Monhegan Island.

"Five hours twenty minutes, Comrade Kapitan. Come right to course 310, speed six knots."

"I think not, Comrade Leytenant. Four knots only please."

A quick mental calculation brought the revised timing.

"Eight hours, Comrade Kapitan."

Kalinin did his own maths and was satisfied.

Kalinin slapped the navigator on the shoulder and gave his orders.

"Helmsman, come right to course 310, speed four knots. Comrade Starshy Leytenant, if you please."

His second in command drew closer.

"Bazili... warn the diving team... I want their equipment tested and retested before we arrive on location. Prepare our tech... no... I'll speak with the technicians myself. We'll let the rest of the men have some rest. Minimum sea watch, I think."

Bazili Urstan acknowledged the order and went to move away but Kalinin grabbed him by the sleeve.

"We'll have a good hot meal too. Tell the cook to spare nothing... prepare the best meal he can for... five hours from now."

"Yes, Comrade Kapitan. I understand."

Urstan and Kalinin had discussed the attack on a number of occasions and, whilst upbeat for the benefit of their men, neither of them expected the submarine to survive the pursuit that would inevitably be prosecuted with an understandable wrath and extreme prejudice, if they even survived the process of preparing and actually delivering their attack.

As word spread throughout the crew, and the divers commenced rechecking their diving equipment, 'Soviet Initsiativa' and her precious cargo slipped through the cold North Atlantic waters towards her designated launch point.

The other two ships of the northern group, I-14 and I-401, were assigned to targets on the northern coastline.

However, I-14 had struck a mine five days beforehand, her loss unknown to her consorts and not even suspected by the patrolling Americans.

The origin of the large oil slick drifting off Delaware was unknown but such things were commonplace and the authorities were unconcerned, as fuel oil was often released from the wrecks of vessels sunk during the U-Boat's 1942 Paukenschlag offensive off America's coast.

The loss of I-14 spared the residents of Philadelphia from unspeakable harm.

I-401 had been given the prize target; New York. The Japanese prime vessel had also been allocated one of the three atomic warhead equipped rockets available. The others were with 'Soviet Initsiativa' and her sister vessel.

Elsewhere, 'Soviet Vozmezdiye' and I-402, also in receipt of firing orders, closed in on their own firing locations on the eastern seaboard of the USA, off Miami and Charleston respectively.

The other AM class, the I-1 was suffering radio problems and did not receive her orders for another three hours, orders that sent her away to her firing position some 175 miles from Savannah.

Finding himself behind schedule, the I-1's captain pushed his vessel hard.

Too hard.

The I-1 drove straight at the USCGC Taney (WPG-37), a Treasury-class cutter of the US Coastguard, manned by veterans of the Atlantic War against the U-Boats.

By the time that I-1 knew of the threat, the depth charges were already in the water.

Lifted by one proximity burst, I-1 briefly broached the surface, earning her the attention of 5", 40mm, and 20mm guns.

She dived down again as the Taney turned her bows for a front-on attack.

The hedgehog launcher coughed its explosives into the air, and each fell to the surface ahead of the slowly advancing cutter.

At least two struck the Japanese submarine, condemning it to the depths of the North Atlantic.

The Coastguard's report was, at best, treated with a degree of scepticism by the 'real' navy men to whom it eventually made its way.

Taney was a veteran vessel with a veteran crew, from its first combat at Pearl Harbor through to the Battle of the Atlantic, and back to serve in the Pacific again, where she served on one of the legendary picquets off Okinawa in the summer of 1945. None the less the report was, depending on the receiver, ignored, derided, dismissed, and undoubtedly universally disbelieved.

Her captain spoke bitterly at the third request for confirmation and more details.

"Ye fucking gods! What don't they understand here? Tell them it's big and it's dead! Belay that... just confirm the sinking of a large unknown submarine operating in restricted waters... possibly Japanese AM-class... repeat the coordinates for our hard-of-hearing friends... if those fuckers ask for confirmation one more fucking time, I'll turn the ship's guns on their office when we get back to port."

The yeoman scurried away, half laughing, half-anxious to get away from his captain's wrath.

Back ashore, the report ended up on the desk of a USN Captain from 10th Fleet, who found himself having to juggle a number of balls that day.

Some of his superiors were away dealing with family issues following the tornadoes that had hammered Oklahoma, Kansas, and Texas the previous week.

His immediate superior was immersed in dealing with the problems raised by the reports of a huge explosion in Texas City just after 9 am.

The Rear Admiral was increasingly harassed and called for more help.

It was an easy decision for the Captain, who shelved the coastguard's clearly exaggerated report in favour of gaining kudos with the struggling senior officer.

The opportunity was missed.

Something that the Rear-Admiral and Captain would regret for the rest of their days, the latter's cut short when he took his own life, unable to bear the burden of his error.

1239 hrs, Monday, 14th April 1947, off Mañana Island, Maine, USA.

The diving team were exhausted but successful, and the rocket pods were now levelled off and poking above the surface, ready for use.

Kalinin had had the systems checked constantly throughout the unhitching, levelling, and rehitching process, and there was one nervous moment when one of the pods' electrical circuits failed completely.

The divers raised the Prüfstand XII rocket pod slightly higher in the water and replaced the connector mount, which remedied the problem but cost an additional thirty-two minutes of time, placing 'Soviet Initsiativa' behind schedule.

The technicians were in the pods, either in the control rooms or working from access platforms within the Prüfstand's main body, performing the fuelling top off, checking the propulsion unit, setting the gyroscopes, or fitting the altimeter, barometric, and contact initiators. They would not open the pod doors until the firing sequence was ready to be initiated.

Although Kalinin hated being so close to shore on the surface, he understood the need for a stable navigational point of reference to allow accurate aiming of the two rockets.

It did not stop him wanting to scream down the intercom to the technicians but he held himself in check, knowing that they would be as keen as he to complete their task and that his interference could only make that task more difficult.

The chief technician had been one of Klaus Riedel's protégés and knew his business, that much was clear.

But this was the Atlantic and the swell was growing... enemy territory... aircraft... prying eyes on the shoreline...

'Come on, you bastards! Come on!'

Kalinin eyed the sky nervously but there was nothing, not even a bird.

In the submerged rocket pods the work continued, the technicians becoming almost unhinged as their own nerves started to take a toll on their work rate and efficiency.

Once their work was complete, they would check in on the intercom and then climb the ladder.

The minutes ticked by and 'Soviet Initsiativa's' schedule was slowly reduced to ashes.

'Yob tvoyu mat! Come on!'

1239 hrs, Monday, 14th April 1947, Egg Island, Delaware Bay, USA.

In selecting the firing point for I-401, Nobukiyo had taken a great risk, but one that he considered reasonable in the circumstances.

For one thing, no one would possibly expect an enemy submarine to penetrate Delaware Bay.

The need to have a fixed point of reference was a given, but the officially designated firing point off Block Island had been quickly rejected, sitting as it did on a major thoroughfare for shipping.

By moving into Delaware Bay and sitting close to Egg Island, the I-401 had an excellent chance of remaining unobserved, as the island offered a number of acceptable inlets and was, for the most part, uninhabited.

Disaster had nearly overtaken I-401 when a USN training group practising inshore operations suddenly appeared, forcing the huge submarine to drop quietly to the floor of the bay and remain silent and unmoving whilst the group ran exercises for two hours in the waters above their heads.

202

The Americans eventually moved off to another area and I-401 continued her move towards the selected small bay adjacent to King Pond on Egg Island.

1241 hrs, Monday, 14th April 1947, off Gun Cay, The Bahamas.

The 'Soviet Vozmiezdiye' lay as similarly exposed and vulnerable as her sister ship, but worse off as the Atlantic was being less kind, the movement much more marked and undoubtedly hindering the technicians in their pods.

The Grumman G-44 Widgeon was a small seaplane that was wholly suited to the role of maritime reconnaissance, in which role it was employed by the US Navy, US Coastguard, and the Royal Navy.

A few were also used by the Civil Air Patrol, an organisation that harnessed the enthusiasm of civilian flyers to a wagon with military purpose.

The G-44 that flew lazily off North Cat Cay was such a craft.

Piloted by a husband and wife team, the Widgeon was on a registered patrol off the Bahamas, flying out of its base at Key Largo.

"Well, if you're going off to play golf with Larry, then I'm having Margot and the boys over for the weekend."

"Sounds like a plan, honey."

"Will you be taking the car?"

"Actually no. Larry's gonna have his driver pick me up, so it's all yours, honey."

"Oh goody. We can go to the Coral Castle… and drop in on Grace too… and maybe some shopping… stay the night at Kendale Lakes… all weekend you say, George?"

"What the fuck?"

"Language, sweetheart! You going for the whole weekend?"

"What the fuck?"

"George! Will yo… oh Lordy. What the hell?"

The shape grew larger.

And then… *'what the fuck is that?'*

203

Immediately, there had been problems. The radar simply refused to function. It was quickly discovered that a seal had been ruptured in some way, permitting seawater to enter the electric connectors.

The repair would take much longer than he intended to remain on the surface, but the Soviet Commander ordered it started in any case.

The first V-2 soared into the air leaving a dense smoky trail and an incinerated Prüfstand behind it, the whole inside of the pod turned to a mush by the powerful rocket motors.

On board 'Vozmiezdiye', the bridge crew scuttled back up, having been withdrawn just in case there were issues with the rocket launch.

The second lookout up ran his eyes through his assigned air space and immediately shouted a warning.

"Aircraft! Bearing 165 low!"

Binoculars flew to eyes as the bridge crew sought the potential threat.

"Gun crews, standby!"

The Captain did not recognise the type but could see enough to know it was a floatplane and looked like it was probably civilian.

"Hold your fire!"

He confirmed his assessment with a more studied examination.

"Hold your fire… just track it for now."

The rear-facing twin 20mm gun mount followed the aircraft as it flew steadily towards them. The forward mount's crew waited their opportunity.

Inside the Widgeon, both pairs of eyes were firmly on the smoke trail of the long-since disappeared rocket.

"Honey… we gotta call this in. Get on the radio quickly. Just tell 'em what we've seen."

Barbara grabbed the handset and checked the map.

The radio was already set to Port Royal's frequency, as they had recently checked in with the station at the small South Bimini township.

"Port Royal-one, Port Royal-one, this is Air Patrol one-niner, over."

"Go ahead, one-niner, over."

"Port Royal-one, observed large smoke trail heading into the sky off Gun Cay, west beach, coordinates..."

"What the fuck! That's a fucking U-Boat!"

She looked up at her husband and followed his gaze, and they both looked at the profile sheet, and then back at the growing shape.

It was unmistakably a type XXI U-Boat, the silhouette matching the illustration taped to the ceiling above George's head.

"Port Royal-one. German submarine on the surface off Gun Cay, west beach... Jesus! It's huge."

"One-niner, say again, over."

"Tell 'em it's a twenty-one... a goddamned twenty-one!"

"Port Royal-one, I say again, German twenty-one on the surface off the west beach, Gun Cay... steady, George!"

Her husband finally reacted and put the Widgeon into a sharp turn, causing Barbara to spill the map onto the floor.

The manoeuvre initiated a response from the 'Vozmezdiye'.

A nervous gunner pulled his triggers and the rear AA mount spat shells into the air.

"Goddamned thing's fired at us!"

Barbara, feeling both scared and exhilarated spoke quickly.

"The goddamned thing's fired at us! Port Royal-one, I repeat, the submarine had fired at us..."

'Calm down, girl... calm down... get it right...'

She searched her memory for the correct words and, surprising herself, found them and spoke them with ease.

"Port Royal-one, identified and engaging large enemy submarine of the German type twenty-one class off the west beach, Gun Cay, Air-Patrol one-niner, over."

There was no reply as the man at Port Royal was writing down her words. His companion was already on the telephone to the US naval air base at Great Exuma, a social call that suddenly turned into an urgent plea for help.

The phone then connected to a number on the US mainland.

"Camp J. Clifford R. Foster. Duty officer speaking."

The young Lieutenant j.g. received the wake-up call to beat all wake-up calls and shortly afterwards began waking up the rest of America's east coast.

The arrival of the Soviet Vozmezdiye's missile did the rest.

The modified V-2 missed its intended target, the Miami-Dade County Courthouse, which had been selected from a travel advertisement purely on the basis of it being one of the oldest buildings in the city.

Instead, the rocket came to ground at a speed approaching three thousand miles per hour, overshooting its intended target by nearly three miles.

The errant rocket struck the roof of the main hall and obliterated itself and those inside in the blink of an eye.

The initiation process should have been started by a combination altimeter/barometer detonator, which failed, as did a great deal else, not that many of the staff and pupils of Miami Senior High School would ever care.

Those in the hall were killed instantly, without warning, without knowing.

In the surrounding area, casualties were caused by flying debris and the modest explosion and fire caused by the small warhead and remaining fuel and oils, added to by the combustible nature of their surroundings.

The atomic device failed completely, which was always a possibility, so rapidly had it and its sisters been produced.

Untested and, in theoretical and engineering terms, on the extreme edge of Soviet ingenuity and capability, it still spat out uranium in all directions, a deadly substance that would claim the lives of a number of the survivors and rescuers in the years to come.

Someone in the Naval Command received the reports of the rocket off Bermuda and of the submarine, married it to the explosion in Miami and all hell broke loose, initially along the eastern seaboard of the United States, and then the world over.

"Shoot it down! Now!"

The 20mms hammered away, sending their explosive shells in the direction of the small seaplane.

"How long?"

"The engineer says eight minutes, maybe more, Comrade Commander!"

"Too long! Tell him it's fired now or never. Get it in the air!"

Previously kept below, two 12.7mm heavy machine guns were brought to the bridge and quickly got to work.

The civilian aircraft, moving incredibly slowly, seemed to live the proverbial charmed life until one of the 20mm's shells struck the port float and exploded, tossing the Widgeon over on its starboard wing.

Inside, George Cazavedes, took a piece of metal in the hip, causing him to yelp, more in surprise than pain.

He had once been known as Captain George L. Cazavedes DSC of the 8th Aero Squadron of the US Army Air Service, until a crash at Saizerais in France in 1918 had robbed him of his left foot and his continued participation in the Great War. He had experienced direct fire many times before.

However, Barbara had not and her screams of terror burned into his mind and spoilt his concentration.

"Will you pipe down, Honey. Let's get in and out now. Just stop screaming, Honey… please stop screaming…"

She did, for no other reason than a 12.7mm neatly took her head from her shoulders, leaving little recognisable as the woman he had been with for forty-two years.

"God! You fucking bastards! You fucking fucking bastards! I'll kill you all, you fuckers!"

The small amphibian side-slipped, avoiding two streams of tracer intent on coming together in a whirl of metal.

Cazavedes gripped the stick tighter with one hand and held the simple toggle that would release the two depth charges attached to the aircraft's wings.

He felt the impact as more 12.7mm chewed up the fuselage, and understood that his legs no longer worked properly.

The pain washed over him when his right thigh came apart as two heavy bullets transited it from knee to hip.

He screamed in agony.

He screamed again as the body of his wife, released from her seat by a bullet that severed her belt, fell across his extended arm and into the fresh wound. The weight of her body caused him to pull the release and the two charges dropped away before he intended.

In an instant, Cazavedes decided on a singular course of action, and aimed for the conning tower.

"For my Barbara, you fucking bast…"

The 20mm got its aim right and the Widgeon exploded in mid-air, sending pieces, both large and small, metal and flesh, in all directions.

One piece of whirling metal smashed into the submarine commander's sternum, killing him in the fraction of a heartbeat.

Another hit the nearest 12.7mm, blinding the gunner and dislodging the weapon from its mount, causing the breech to smash into the loader's temple.

The bridge was suddenly awash with blood and all interest in the igniting rocket was lost.

The V-2 was exiting the pod as a depth charge exploded underneath it, tilting it violently and fatally.

Unable to take the stresses of the explosion and the twisting of the pod, the rocket simply split apart, allowing fuel to spill and ignite in dramatic fashion.

Those on the bridge tending to the wounded were consumed in the fireball that swept over 'Soviet Vozmezdiye', reducing each man to nothing more than a pygmy-sized piece of charcoal.

Even though relatively safe down in the XXI's control room, the two men nearest the hatch still received burns, and no one failed to feel the heatwave that swept through the submarine.

The deadly cargo carried by the second rocket was mostly consumed in the intense heat.

Mostly, but not all.

The sight that greeted those who rushed onto the conning tower was beyond description.

The Third Officer took command and quickly dropped the wounded submarine below the surface.

The second pod had already lost its mooring to 'Soviet Vozmezdiye', the first pod stubbornly refused all instructions to let go, so the new commander was forced to flee the area with the encumbrance still attached.

Unwittingly, the rescuers had carried sufficient Bubonic Plague below with them to ensure that the submarine would never see home again.

I-402 put both her missiles into the air and they fell on Charleston or thereabouts, neither even close to being accurate.

One carried Bubonic Plague and Anthrax and detonated in the sky over Mount Pleasant, some five miles of its aiming point.

Lewisite and Cholera were gifted to the residents of Goose Creek, over ten miles off its aiming point.

In I-401, Nobukiyo replaced the handset, the sounds of the triple 'Banzai' still ringing in everyone's ears.

That the eyes of the Emperor were upon them all was undoubtedly true.

That the eyes of the people of the sacred islands were upon them was also most certainly true.

That the eyes of the survivors of the atomic atrocities inflicted by the American bombers were upon them was unequivocally true, and probably the source of their greatest motivation.

His words had reflected those three truths, and his expectations for their work in the coming moments.

He had not bothered to reflect upon what would come afterwards, as he expected that they would all die this day.

'But not before we have done our duty!'

"Everything is ready, Commander-san."

"Thank you, Jinyo. Surface."

"Hai!"

Orders rang through the submarine's control room and I-401 started the journey to the surface.

As soon as the submarine broached, the well-trained teams swung into action.

One of the lookouts shouted a warning.

"Surface vessel, bearing 170, range five thousand plus, confirmed warship."

The sonar had been accurate, but even so, Nobukiyo had hoped, no... prayed, committed as he was to surfacing and firing his missiles, that being concealed in the small bay would stand to his advantage.

His assessment seemed correct and he did not expect the enemy vessel to see him.

The 401's gentle rise to the surface had been controlled to ensure the minimum of surface disturbance to help keep their presence secret.

Nobukiyo quickly checked to see if the warning had affected Jinyo's deck parties. There was no visible reaction, earning a grunt of praise from their commander.

The warning shout had reached the deck party, but they pressed on with disciplined application, knowing that time might not be on their side.

"Torpedo sight to the bridge! Hold your fire but plot a torpedo attack for the target bearing 170. Prepare tubes four and eight."

The Sen Tokus had no rear tubes, but two of their front-facing array contained updated Type 96 torpedoes equipped with homing mechanisms copied from the German Kriegsmarine's Wren acoustic torpedo, fit for the purpose of hunting down the enemy craft if it so much as twitched in their direction.

Use of such a weapon was not without its own issues, and at least two U-Boats had been sunk by their own Wren during WW2.

Nobukiyo shelved that problem to the back of his mind.

"Lookout, report."

"Commander-san, vessel is steady on course, bearing now... 178."

"Good."

The small ship, USS Annapolis, a Tacoma class frigate, leisurely continued on its course, not seeing the large submarine against the green backdrop of Egg Island.

Nobukiyo knew that would change soon enough.

'Turn the submarine before firing the rocket, fool!'

'No! Don't listen to old Ito. Turn while the second rocket is being readied!'

He smiled at the suggestions from his ancestors and thanked them silently for their advice and protection.

"Lookout, report."

"Commander-san, vessel is steady on course, bearing now 181, about to disappear behind the headland... now."

"Good."

The deck crew were almost done, Jinyo's fussing over the details apparent as the majority of the men sprinted back to the hangar.

The preparatory signal came and suddenly the deck was occupied solely by the erect V2 rocket bearing the proud Rising Sun and the many messages scrawled in chalk by the men who had tended the giant rocket during its passage across the ocean.

The hangar door started to swing shut, its warning buzzer initiating the clearing of the bridge and weapons stations.

Nobukiyo himself was last down, taking a good look around the whole 360° to satisfy himself that there was no immediate threat.

The hatches were pinned and he arrived in the control room to a strange mixed atmosphere of excitement and fear. It was against every instinct of the submariners to sit on the surface with no one to keep watch.

Jinyo observed the launch platform through the solid glass port in the hangar door.

"Missile control to Commander. Request permission to initiate."

"Initiate."

Nobukiyo, seemingly unconcerned, contented himself with establishing the draught of a Tacoma-class frigate, for that is what he thought the tiny warship was.

'Four metres... shall we say six then... what say you, Sosen?'

The ancestors bowed to his greater knowledge of naval tactics and remained silent.

The submarine shook as the V2's engine fired up and soon raised it into the sky, destination New York.

Nobukiyo gave orders to turn the ship and prepared his torpedo firing team for action, with revised depth settings for six metres.

The V-2 rose into the air with a roar, a fiery tail and smoky trail marking its progress.

Already the bucket crew were throwing sea water over the deck, removing the residual heat as the rocket crew emerged from the hanger, ready to bring the second device to the launch pad.

'Now we shall see!'

The first rocket had taken an age to get into place, or so it seemed to the watching Nobukiyo, although the stopwatch had indicated eleven minutes and three seconds, beating their best time ever by a comfortable seventeen seconds.

The second V-2 was already trundling down the rails when the dreaded warning came, although it was not the warning he had anticipated.

"Disturbance in the water, bearing 165, range four thousand!"

Nobukiyo's heart pounded and before he could locate the source of the man's panic, the lookout screamed again.

"Submarine surfacing, enemy submarine surfacing! Bearing 166, still four thousand!"

"Calm down! Report properly!"

He spoke into the intercom to designate the new target.

The torpedo officer acquired the new target with the sight, the details automatically reflected in the firing station below.

The repeated orders and updated information flowed back to him, demonstrating that his fire control party were on the job, changing target values, updating angles, with the sonar adding its own information to the plot.

"Jinyo! Jinyo!"

The voice travelled well and attracted his second's attention despite the frantic activity on deck.

"Firing torpedoes! Stay alert!"

They had never fired weapons and erected a missile at the same time so a warning was more than appropriate, even though Nobukiyo felt that there would be no problem.

None the less, he also added a warning to the diving officer to ensure the boat's trim was kept perfect at the moment the torpedoes were fired.

He checked out the American submarine.

'A Gato.'

He knew her vital statistics off by heart. She was deeper in draught than the frigate.

"Set torpedo depth on tubes four and eight at eight metres."

The order was repeated back. Something he was only vaguely aware of as he assessed the work on the foredeck.

"Standby to fire torpedoes four and eight!"

The officer on the torpedo sight made his adjustments, which automatically updated information on the firing board.

Nobukiyo's binoculars brought stark images into focus.

The Gato class submarine had men on its conning tower... and more moving to man the 3" gun.

The American now had the edge in firepower, with 40mm and 20mm weapons at either end of the large conning tower.

His own heavy weapon, a 140mm, could not bear now that he had turned his boat; neither could the majority of his 25mms, and he could not turn back as the rocket's aiming was already in progress as to do so would mean delay.

There was no choice.

'There is no choice, Sosen.'

"Fore gun mount... standby to engage submarine target on my order. Be careful of our rocket!"

The V2 was now being raised into the vertical, far too slowly in Nobukiyo's view.

'What will be, will be, Sosen.'

'Hai!'

"Torpedo ready?"

"Hai, Captain-san."

"Engines off."

"Hai, Captain-san."

A small time without steerage way was a small price to pay to avoid the Wren coming back home.

"Standby... sonar, check bearing to target."

'172?'

Nobukiyo rechecked and the report tallied with his own observations.

"Bearing 172, Captain-san."

"Standby, on bearing 172, on my mark... tube four... fire four... tube eight... fire eight..."

Despite its size, the submarine still shuddered as the two deadly weapons were discharged, although the trim was maintained superbly and there was no effect on the V2's movement.

He watched the trails and assessed the distance, leaving five hundred metres of clear water before getting the engines back on.

There had been surprisingly little movement and I-401 was soon back in perfect position.

Still the Gato stayed silent, although I-401 was undoubtedly filling their gunsights.

The Type 96s ate up the distance between the two submarines at just over forty-six knots, the slightly lower speed considered a fair trade for the extra weight of the acoustic detection.

Another lookout shouted a warning.

"Enemy warship, bearing 181, range two thousand five hundred metres!"

The frigate had returned, its engines thrashing the water to get it in a position to observe where whatever it was that had screamed into the sky had come from.

Nobukiyo was wrong about the submarine. It was in fact the SS-435 Corsair, a Tench-class vessel, and a more modern proposition than a Gato.

Corsair's Captain made a decision.

The Annapolis' Captain made a decision.

Type 96 torpedo serial number 96-399291911 made a decision.

Events made Nobukiyo's decision for him.

The Corsair's 5" deck gun fired and threw up a huge spout of water some sixty yards off the I-401's starboard beam.

Annapolis added shells from her own 3" weapons, and the two crashed down closer still.

96-399291911 turned to starboard.

The Sen Toku's 25mm hammered out at the submarine, churning up the water next to the ballast tank before the gunner walked the shells into the rear deck gun crew.

Two pieces of metal closed on each other at breakneck speed, with a combined speed approaching seventy knots.

Set to detonate at eight metre depth, 96-399291911 was 3.8 metres beneath the keel of the USS Annapolis when the magnetic detonator executed its simple task.

Five hundred and fifty kilos of Type 97 explosive detonated in the fraction of a moment, producing a catastrophic effect upon the frigate and her crew.

Annapolis rose up out of the water, leaving her bow and stern wet but her centre with daylight underneath.

She broke in half almost immediately, her crew of one hundred and eighty-two men almost equally split between the two pieces.

Nobukiyo turned his attention to the enemy submarine.

The teller talked down the time to impact and then past it, indicating a clean miss.

His fist hurt as he punched the unyielding metal.

On deck, men were dead and dying, as shrapnel and cannon shells flayed the open area.

The V2 was erect and, incredibly, unaffected by the storm around it.

Jinyo screamed at his men, and screamed at the stump where his left hand used to be.

"Clear the deck!"

"Fire it, Jinyo! Fire it!"

Jinyo ran towards the open hangar door as his men fell around him.

A shell burst at the top edge of the hangar door, scattering pieces of the gun crew into the sea and over the conning tower.

It was a telling shot in a number of ways.

The obvious damage to the hangar door meant that it would never close again.

Some of the shrapnel smashed into Nobukiyo's face and destroyed his eyes as completely as could a surgeon with a scalpel.

Yet more struck Jinyo and dropped him panting to a deck soaked with seawater and blood.

Two other pieces struck the V2.

They were not the first, and both Nobukiyo and Jinyo had simply missed the damage sustained on the side away from their gaze.

However, one or both of these fragments provided a spark that ignited the leaking rocket fuel, turning I-401's upper works into a spectacular life-consuming fireball.

Not one man on the deck or in the conning tower survived the blast as the V2 simply disintegrated.

The warhead was consumed by the heat, preventing the Sarin nerve agent from affecting anything of note.

The open hangar door invited the fireball inside, and a secondary explosion amazed the onlooking crew of the Corsair as the large superstructure simply opened up like a bursting bag.

In the control room, the survivors tried to dive the I-401, but the integrity of her watertight doors had been compromised in too many places so, rather than the controlled descent they hoped for in water just sufficient to cover the boat, the wounded leviathan simply dropped onto the floor of the bay with as much control as a house brick.

Corsair fired two torpedoes and turned to port, desperate to help the handful of men struggling in the water around the sinking pieces of Annapolis.

The shock wave of the torpedo exploding underneath the frigate had broken many legs and hips, as metal was driven upwards with great force and human bone and tissue gave way under the strain.

Injured men who had survived the explosion now drowned in sight of their homeland, as the struggle to stay afloat defeated them.

The rescuers aboard the Corsair barely spared a look for the roiling water as one of their torpedoes found its mark on the submerged Japanese submarine.

1249 hrs, Monday, 14th April 1947, off Mañana Island, Maine, USA.

"Fire missile one!"

The Prüfstand discharged a single V2 into the air with relative ease and the missile soared high into the sky at ever-increasing speed.

Kalinin had remained on deck, contrary to protocol, and was fascinated to see the deadly object's speed.

He snatched himself away from his wonderment and issued a quick order.

"Prepare to fire missile two!"

The two pods were some distance apart, separated by the modest current, which permitted Kalinin to contemplate a rapid second release.

He examined the sea's movement and the position of the charred Prüfstand and worked out his next decision.

"Time to second missile launch, Starshy Leytenant?"

Urstan interrogated the technician through the intercom link.

"Four minutes, Comrade Kapitan."

"Excellent. Cast off pod one."

The used pod was let free and, as was the standing order, the electronics opened up two valves that dropped the now useless lump of metal into the depths.

The four minutes lasted two lifetimes to those on deck, possibly three such spans to Kalinin and Urstan.

The message came through and was universally welcomed.

"Standby missile two."

Everything was ready.

"Fire missile two!"

216

Nothing.

Urstan took the hasty report.

"Electrical malfunction, Comrade Kapitan!"

"Get it sorted!"

Kalinin stood impotently on the bridge, using his binoculars to sweep the sky as a distraction whilst others tried hard to rectify the problem.

"Problem resolved, Comrade Kapitan. Simple fuse. On your order."

"Fire missile two!"

Nothing.

"Electrical malfunction, Comrade Kapitan!"

"Get it repaired immediately! You have the bridge, Comrade Starshy Leytenant. Make way there!"

Kalinin disappeared down the hatch in search of heads to roll.

"Talk to me, Comrade Technician."

The man was calm, which reassured Kalinin immediately.

"Comrade Kapitan, the circuit tests fine. When the firing command is initiated, there's a problem which causes the fuse to blow. In my estimation, this could be an issue in the control room on the pod, on the external coupling on the pod, or the one on our stern. I suggest the stern coupling is checked first."

Kalinin was impressed with the technician's report and recommendation and placed a reassuring hand on the sweating man's shoulder.

"Get it done then please, Comrade Technician. How long will it take?"

"Once we locate the issue, it'll depend on what it is. I can't say, Comrade Kapitan."

The man was being reasonable, but Kalinin still wanted to fly off the handle and, unusually for him, actually struggled not to.

'Our lives depend on you! Get it fucking done and... he's doing the very best he can, Mikhail!... you're right... '

Instead, he encouraged the man to get the issue sorted and took his seat in the control room.

217

The tones of the 1812 Overture were soon heard, as Kalinin hummed his standard piece while he waited, the gentle sound calming all who could hear, including Kalinin himself.

The technician pressed the headset to his ears, better to listen to the report. He suddenly grew excited and jabbered some instructions into the intercom.

Another of the technical party soon appeared, holding a replacement part.

This was checked and the senior technician was quickly satisfied, dispatching the man and part to the stern.

"Comrade Kapitan, the issue has been located. A seawater leak on the stern connector, nothing more. Short circuit knocked out the firing system. Less than five minutes to fix."

"Excellent, Comrade Technician. I'll return to the bridge."

Kalinin moved through the control room and climbed the ladder to the conning tower, the humming growing in intensity as he approached 'La Marseillaise' with renewed vigour.

He turned his attention to the stern and was rewarded by the sight of three men working furiously.

"I have the deck."

"Kapitan has the deck."

Kalinin explained the problem to a curious Urstan.

The sound of running feet ended their discussion as the repair party scurried back to the rear hatch and disappeared below deck.

"Missile two repaired. Ready for launch on your order, Comrade Kapitan."

He checked around automatically and issued the firing order.

The second V2 rose into the air, incinerating the pod that gave it life.

"Cast off pod two."

The second Prüftstand disappeared beneath the water on its journey to the seabed.

"Now, let's see if we can live through this day. Diving stations!"

Within minutes, 'Soviet Initisiativa' was underwater and heading away from her enemies.

NEW YORK

During the Blitz of '44, the V2 had given no warning of its approach, little of its arrival, and simply engulfed its point of impact in a huge explosion.

The double crack of something moving through the sound barrier caused concern, but few knew it for what it was.

There was no counter to it at that time, so the British went after the launch sites, and used subterfuge to persuade the Germans that their missiles were off target. False information was fed back to the Germans, making them think that the rockets were falling short, which led the missiles to overshoot London as the V2s were 'corrected'.

No such ploy was available to the residents of New York, and few of those that heard the double crack understood what it was.

In any case, within a heartbeat, the V2's atomic warhead exploded at four hundred and ninety-eight feet above the ground.

Aimed at Manhattan and the iconic target of the Empire State Building, the missile was off target by some considerable distance.

It exploded over Independence Park in the Ironbound area of Newark.

For a thousand yards in every direction, people died in the briefest of moments as the pressure wave killed indiscriminately, destroying buildings and throwing cars around like toys.

The intense light and heat wave followed on closely, using the ruptured buildings as ready sources of fuel for the fires that sprang up everywhere in the wake of the blast.

The pressure wave moved out further from the centre, waning in power as it progressed, but still claiming lives and buildings.

Ruptured gas pipes added their own contents to the inferno that consumed hundreds of structures and thousands of people.

It was later estimated that over thirty-five thousand people died in the first three seconds alone and that number grew over time, as radiation and wounds took its toll.

The atomic explosion smashed so much but, as in Japan, seemed to be selective in what it consumed. Very near the centre of the blast, on Pulaski Street, stood the relatively undamaged Saint Casimir's Roman Catholic Church.

Its roof was broken but the structure stood proud and tall, the slightly displaced spire the most noticeable mark of the explosion.

Those inside did not survive the experience but the church did not burn, unlike most of the piles of rubble around it.

Within seconds, the phones were ringing in Washington.

BOSTON

The delay experienced by Kalinin counted for very little in the greater run of things.

A few telephones had rung around Boston; the Mayor, head of the fire department, the police commissioner, the local army commander, all had heard the words but had no comprehension of their meaning.

The bright light that consumed a number of those whilst they were still on the telephone marked the arrival of the 'Soviet Initsiativa's' own atomic warhead.

Again, the target had been selected for political reasons.

Harvard.

Again, for technical reasons, the missile was off target.

It exploded just over four miles to the east, almost directly above the USS Constitution.

Kalinin's missile detonated perfectly, although the altimeter detonation still could not cope with the speed of descent and detonated late, this time at a height of three hundred and twenty-eight feet.

The venerable old frigate and symbol of American freedom disappeared into ashes, along with thousands upon thousands of Bostonians.

The rivers proved no obstacle and the blast and firestorm spread out, hitting Chelsea, Eagle Hill, Jefferies Point, old Boston, and into Cambridge.

A large group of people marking the anniversary of the Titanic striking the iceberg had taken to a pleasure boat in the Mystic River. They and it disappeared in a moment, and only seven identifiable pieces of human remains were ever located.

All around the centre of the explosion, fire consumed old and new buildings equally.

In Boston, in the initial blast and subsequent destruction, later estimates put the loss of life at approaching fifty thousand.

It was only in later months and years that the true horror of the strike on Boston was fully appreciated.

The second V2 arrived almost unnoticed, such was its speed.

No one recalled hearing the double crack of the second missile.

It smashed into the bank of the Charles River adjacent to the Harvard Bridge and disappeared from sight.

Some saw it land, but by that time, there was no telephone network worth a damn, and scant few people in authority to report it to.

MOSCOW

"Comrades! To the men and women of the Red Army, Red Air Force, and Red Navy... to the commanders and political instructors... to the working men and working women... to the collective farmers... to the workers in the intellectual professions... to all the peoples of our great Soviet Motherland... and to all our Allies in friendly states...I have news of great importance!"

Across the Soviet Union, indeed the world, ears pressed close to radios to listen to what the Soviet Dictator had to say, although some people many thousands of miles away already knew, and were already planning their response.

"On behalf of the Soviet Government and our Bolshevik Party, I am greeting you and congratulating you on your incredible efforts in the face of the renewed aggression by our enemies, led by the arch enemy in chief, the United States of America."

Applause broke out from the assembled audience in the Bolshoi Theatre.

"Comrades, we find ourselves operating in strenuous circumstances as we approach the thirtieth anniversary of the October Revolution. The perfidious renewed attack on us by our enemies, and the war which has now been forced upon us, have created an unprecedented threat to our country. We have experienced temporary setbacks but the forces of the Motherland have been strong and stand resilient and steadfast."

"I believe that our enemy believed... no... hoped that after the very first blows our army would be dispersed, and our country would be forced to her knees. But the enemy has gravely miscalculated. In spite of these temporary reverses, our forces are heroically repulsing the enemy's attacks along the entire front and inflicting heavy losses upon him, while our country... our entire country... has yet again organized itself into one fighting camp in order to encompass the rout of the Allied invaders."

"We have been in this position before, when the Germans were at the gates of Moscow, and we triumphed then, and will do again. There were other times when our country was in a still more difficult position. I, of course, refer to 1918 and the birth of our nation."

"To-day the position of our country is far better than six years ago, or indeed thirty years ago. We now have a splendid Army and a splendid Navy, who are defending, with their lives, the liberty and independence of our country. We experience no serious shortage of either food, or armaments, or army clothing."

That drew many murmured responses from listeners far away, none of them complimentary about Stalin's reflection of the truth, but understanding that the speech was mainly for other ears.

"Can there be any doubt that we can, and are bound to, defeat the Allied aggressors?"

There was a great deal of doubt, though the vast majority of it went unspoken, if only to preserve the life of the doubter.

"The enemy is not so strong as some frightened little intellectuals picture them, despite the events on the Volga last week, in Kiev and Odessa, and in our ally's capital, Vilnius."

"The Allied nations, unheralded, brought unspeakable force to bear on three places full of innocents, places of little or no present military value, and in contravention of their own treaties on the conduct of war!"

222

"We have had such weapons for many months, but have not used them, considering them both unsuitable for the modern battlefield, and morally wrong in their employment."

Stalin played to his listeners in neutral and unaligned states.

"However, these atrocities... these outrages have not gone unanswered, and I have replied in kind."

Stalin took a deep breath and plunged ahead.

"Forces of the Red Navy, in conjunction with Allied nations, supported by technicians from our scientific departments, have delivered a stunning attack on our enemy in chief, the United States of America. Even as I speak, the fires still rage in New York, Philadelphia, Boston, Savannah, Charleston, and Miami."

Applause rang out in the great building as those listening showed their appreciation for the claimed capabilities of the forces of the Motherland.

Across the world, the reactions were different, depending on where the listener was, and on the individual's grasp on the new realities of war.

"We have inflicted grave casualties and huge damage upon them, but we will now draw back. Yes, even now, we show restraint. I have ordered our forces to disengage and await further orders."

The implication that the capability to inflict further strikes upon the USA was left hanging.

"I will not expand this war further. I could, but I will not permit these weapons to become commonplace. I have simply responded to the incredible aggression offered by the enemy forces."

More applause interrupted the Secretary-General, and he used the break to moisten his lips from the glass of water at hand.

"The American devil is not as terrible as he is painted; they have few of their devices left, this we know. But the devil that is atomic warfare is more horrible than we can imagine, and our enemies should know that we possess many more such weapons, and also the will to use them if we are further provoked."

More applause echoed through the theatre and through the villages, towns, and cities of the Soviet Union, as peasant and professor alike finally grasped that their country possessed so much more power than their enemies.

In Belgrade, Rome, and a few score of other capital cities, listening politicians saw things a little differently to how they had been perceived that morning.

"We are a peace loving nation, but we are capable of bringing war against our aggressors in ways that they can only imagine, and cannot resist!"

The applause was almost frenzied in nature now, and Stalin needed to wave his audience back into their seats before he could continue.

"None the less, we will desist from further use, and invite our enemies to discussions with a view to negotiating an honourable end to the hostilities, bringing about a lasting peace, and obtaining suitable reparations for the losses sustained by ourselves and our allies."

The assembly burst into further adulation but remained seated this time and Stalin again took the opportunity to moisten his mouth before bringing them back to a frenzy with the culmination of his delivery.

"And if they do not come... if they decide to continue this war, then I will deliver to you a victory that will cost the Allies everything they possess. Anything less would be unacceptable to me, and to the soldiers, airmen, sailors, and workers of our great country!"

"Long live our glorious Motherland, her liberty and her independence!"

"Under the banner of Lenin, let us move forward together!"

Stalin's closing words were lost in cheers and applause as the audience went deliriously wild, inspired by his words as much as the watching NKVD soldiery.

In Washington and London, his words were received much less favourably.

WASHINGTON

"For the record, gentlemen, I'm not making these decisions whilst I am angry... although I am angered by the words that man has spouted... lies... more lies. Again, he blames us for Kiev, Odessa, and Vilnius, and most independents seem to believe him over us... and why wouldn't they, eh? Who could imagine that he could be so monstrous as to destroy thousands of his own people... even now... with his track record... and yet he did. We know it."

He left unsaid the cold receptions that US ambassadors had already experienced, their denials of Allied involvement met with anything from stunned silence to derision by leaders across the globe.

Truman could not speak openly of the coming change of political leadership in Russia, as not all of those present were privy to the information gleaned from Nazarbayeva's file.

"Mister President, I can only advise again. We must consider this escalation very carefully."

Everyone understood that he was only talking about one portion of the agreed response, but still they stared at him, willing him to withdraw his objections.

Stimson knew he was casting his seed on stony ground but, none the less, felt the need to restate his views.

Governor Dewey's call had been decisive in that regard. The sound of a man such as he crying as he related the story of the suffering in his city, not to mention his own, his face, neck, and hands almost certainly permanently scarred by the burns he had received. It was a testament to the man that he remained in charge as his city was still leaking from its wounds and commenced the process of burying its dead.

Now, everyone in the room, in the country, wanted to see blood; Soviet blood.

After all, it would be the first time they had employed atomic weapons, Camp 1001 aside, against mainland Russia, not that the world saw it that way, as both Stimson and Steelman had cautioned.

Byrnes, Forrestal, and Marshall had already made up their minds before Dewey's emotion call, but now only Stimson's voice spoke of caution.

Conversations with J.Edgar Hoover, Leslie Groves, and Robert Oppenheimer had all brought encouragement, as had the intelligence reports from OSS and all the other agencies actively seeking out news of the enemy's plans and resources.

It fell to Truman to announce the decision that had probably been made the moment the bombs went off on mainland USA.

"We cannot and will not let these acts go unpunished. Our diplomats must push that message, and we must find unequivocal proof that this destruction in the Ukraine and Lithuania was not our doing. But," he conceded,"... we will offer the Soviet Union a chance to come to the negotiating table and end this conflict. The British plan is our way forward."

It was something that British Intelligence had devised months previously, in cooperation with the FBI and OSS, and for which select people were already equipped. They simply needed the go-ahead and some extra information with which to impress their audience.

Truman allowed Churchill his glory by calling the operation what he did.

Blenheim.

"So, again for the record, I authorise the use of Atomic weapons against the stated targets, in coordination with the British plan. Exact timings will be decided by those in Moscow."

He did not mean Stalin and the Soviet leadership.

"Now, thank you, gentlemen. I pray for success in all departments of our endeavours in the coming days. Good luck and God speed to you all."

"Mister President."

They all chorused the words as they trooped out, leaving only John Steelman behind.

"Mister President, the press… I thought the East Room?"

"I'll leave that to you, Jack."

Ahead of Truman lay his address to the American people, followed by an unprecedented appearance in front of the full array of press hacks, hence the use of the largest room in the White House.

Today the American people, and subsequently the world, would hear the truth and what was to follow in the wake of the Soviet attack upon their nation.

"Thank you, Jack, Now, Winston first."

He picked up the phone and sought a connection to the man waiting in Downing Street.

His second call was to Douglas MacArthur.

LONDON

Churchill took a moment to light his cigar and puff thoughtfully.

226

There was no other way to proceed in his eyes.

Retaliation would probably happen, but at least with the plan devised by Menzies and his gang there was a chance to switch off the bloody thing before the world disappeared in flames.

He sought the required connection and waited patiently as his secretary fight his way through the people on the other end of the line, who would pass the call through only when Sir Stuart Menzies of MI-6 was on the phone.

"Prime Minister, Sir Stuart Menzies…"

The connection was made.

"Prime Minister, how may I help?"

"Sir Stuart, I have just had a conversation with my cousin and he would like to proceed with the matter we discussed."

"I see. When, Sir?"

"We would need to have a sense of timing from our party, but as soon as is practicable would be the order of the day."

"Right-ho, Prime Minister. I will set the wheels in motion and keep you informed directly. Anything else you need, Sir?"

"Not for now, Sir Stuart. Good luck."

The connection was broken.

Before Churchill could take another puff on his cigar, Menzies was arranging for a message to be sent to Ernest Fenton, a low-level civil servant in the British Embassy to the Court of Bernadotte, and MI-6's top man in Sweden.

He would ensure that the Swedes passed the precise instructions to their own embassy… in Moscow.

MOSCOW

"Sir, a secure message for you."

Horrocks rose from his seat in the window where he and Ramsey had been sat observing the comings and goings in the street outside.

There were few, except Soviet security personnel patrolling with a view more to keep people inside the cordon that intruders out.

They had again singularly failed to identify Tørget as he left, disguised as something indescribable but decidedly Russian.

After a while Horrocks returned, his normally rosy complexion decidedly blanched by the orders he had just read.

Ramsey chose to remain silent, allowing the senior man to recover his composure.

Whilst he was sure that the Swedes had chosen not to bug their every conversation, Horrocks instinctively kept his voice down and leant forward, drawing Ramsey closer.

"Seems our special mission is on, old chap. Stuff arriving in the Swedish diplomatic pouch from Fenton. We've to arrange a meeting with Uncle Joe himself... tomorrow. They'll be waiting on our confirmation of timing for another matter crucial to the war effort."

"Good lord!"

"Quite."

"Can we do that, Sir? Is there time?"

"Not through the normal channels, I would say. No, definitely not. Surprised our leaders didn't reflect on that one a teensy bit. No, but... perhaps we can use our contacts, eh?"

"I'm due to see the timber merchant later. I'll put out the sign and see if we can get our friends to meet. Get them to pass a message on to our...err... friend?"

"My thinking exactly, Colonel. Use her whilst she's on our side. Have the big cheeses use their power to make sure we get our meeting, what?"

"Yes, Sir. What time?"

"Well, we've been given a window. Between twelve hundred and fifteen hundred hours, not a minute before, and not a minute later."

"What sort of effort, Sir?"

"Eh?"

"What sort of effort crucial to the war effort, Sir?"

Horrocks laughed.

"Buggered if I know, Colonel. Why should they tell me? I'm only the chap who has to stand in front of Uncle Joe with my trousers down."

That Ramsey would be stood next to him was left unspoken.

"Right then, Sir. No time to lose. If they get the message, what do I say to the contact?"

Ramsey took his seat in the back of the car, a trip to the prosthetic limb specialist providing the reason for his journey.

It had been a close-run thing but the acknowledgement sign was in place, the simple placing of a pile of rubbish on the kerb side opposite the embassy indicative of both understanding and a plan.

Ramsey never knew what it was, but he always found the GRU extremely imaginative in their casual interference in his prosthesis routine.

The 'timber merchant', as Ramsey called the Soviet prosthetic expert, was highly skilled and had improved on the original work quite considerably, but demanded twice weekly sessions with Ramsey to develop, record, and monitor his work.

Ramsey closed his eyes, his NKVD minders acting relaxed and comfortable with the routine.

The crash was a surprise to everyone.

As is the habit of Russians under pressure, voices were immediately raised and threats flew back and forth.

It was only a minor accident but observers would have been forgiven for thinking both vehicles had been written off from the vehemence of the argument and the brandishing of a weapon by the NKVD driver.

Another vehicle, a military lorry, came to a halt alongside and an armed party of soldiers emerged, immediately surrounding the scene.

A female Major wearing the patch of the Commandant's Service, the Red Army's de facto Military Police, silenced the unshaven civilian who displayed all the hallmarks of an excess of vodka, and spoke calmly to the man in uniform.

Her request for his papers was so softly and delicately put that he never thought to use his NKVD status to tell the woman to go and fuc…

"And who is that, Comrade Yefreytor? An enemy of the state, no less?"

He explained the situation and received nods of understanding.

None the less, the officer demanded to see Ramsey's identification and the NKVD authorisation, just to ensure a complete report.

That was something he could understand, and her ordering of the arrest of the drunken driver further relaxed him.

The NKVD Leytenant in charge emerged from the car to receive his report, listened intently, and nodded his understanding. He saw no reason to complicate matters and, as the woman was more than attractive, charming compliance was the order of the day.

He signalled to Ramsey and the other guard to alight and both men immediately did so, with Ramsey's uniform drawing excited comments from both the soldiers and the few civilians that had taken time out of their busy schedule to see what was going on.

The Major examined the NKVD paperwork first.

The final guard was answering her questions as an impatient driver, stuck behind the temporary roadblock of two cars, honked his horn.

"Shall I leave him to you, Comrade Leytenant?"

As she expected, the NKVD officer puffed out his chest and stepped away smartly to offer the intolerant taxi driver a choice between shutting the fuck up or a trip to Siberia.

As planned, the distraction gave her a chance to get close to Ramsey.

She extended her hand and accepted his paperwork, which she examined upside down.

"Polkovnik Ramsey V C…"

She pronounced his award with studied care, telling him all he needed to hear.

'Good grief! I'd never have recognised you! I'm impressed... what a charade!'

He had but a moment and took it with ease.

Coughing, he swept his hand to his mouth and deposited the small packet into his hand, the same hand with which he accepted his papers, and with which he passed on the brief message.

The NKVD officer returned, satisfied that he had impressed the woman with his extended tongue-lashing of the taxi driver.

"Everything's in order, Comrade Leytenant. I'll deal with the drunk… I assume you have frightened that impatient shit to death?"

"But of course, Comrade Mayor."

They shared an insider's laugh.

"For your own report, I'll be filing my paperwork with the office of 4th Security Company, Komendantskaya Sluzhba, Moscow Military District. Report number..." she waited as he extracted a pencil, "... 47-4-130-AT. Is that sufficient for you, Comrade?"

"Yes, thank you, Comrade Major. May I ask your name?"

He wanted to ask when she got off duty and whether she fucked on a first date, but that would wait as he was on a timescale with Ramsey and already behind the mark.

"Mayor Anastasia Tembaya, attached to the 4th Security Company."

"Thank you, Comrade Mayor."

They saluted formally and the two parties went their separate ways.

In the cab of the lorry, the small message was opened and the contents memorised.

Hana Rikardova lit a cigarette for herself and her driver, before applying the naked flame to the paper, removing all trace of her liaison with Ramsey.

Twenty-two minutes later, Khrushchev was informed.

1600 hrs, Monday, 14th April 1947, the Church of the Twelve Apostles, Moscow, USSR.

They listened in shocked silence.

Stunned beyond words.

Incredulous and disbelieving.

None the less, Kaganovich was adamant.

The attacks on Vilnius, Odessa, and Kiev were not the result of Allied bombs, but Soviet devices placed there by NKVD troops loyal to Beria.

The leadership had deliberately killed tens of thousands of people to gain a dubious political advantage and to excuse their own excesses.

The explosion at Camp 1001 was definitely Soviet made. New standing orders had required it if the camp was under threat, but the delirious mumblings of the one survivor so far located suggested something else might have occurred.

Perhaps the Allies might have dropped a bomb of their own... the NKVD officer was presently beyond interrogation, so the doctors said, his hold on life tenuous at best.

"Madness! Fucking madness!"

Gorbachev broke the silence and then they all joined in.

Kaganovich raised his hand, seeking an opportunity to speak.

"Our allies' missions in America are reporting huge numbers of dead and injured. There's nothing but the rhetoric of revenge over there, which is to be expected. The biological weapons employed seem not to have been successful, by the way. We can be sure their reply will be in kind. The complication is difficult to judge. To the world, Comrade Stalin ordered a retaliation, whereas we now know it was not. How will the Amerikanski view this?"

Khrushchev raised his hands, demanding silence, as the crypt rang with their suddenly raised voices.

"I can help there, as I have news too, Comrades. The Allies intend to retaliate tomorrow... I don't know where... but we can all guess, of course. Perhaps the only safe place in the Motherland will be right here in Moscow? The Horrocks party is securing an audience with the General Secretary for tomorrow. They'll be trying for a defined timeline... between midday and three o'clock... which is interesting in itself, eh?"

"They intend to strike tomorrow after three then."

A shrug conceded that Kaganovich's statement was most probably correct.

"However, again, circumstances play into our hands. The Allies are using their contact with Nazarbayeva to arrange the visit. They clearly think her special relationship with the General Secretary will ensure they get the audience they want at the time that they want."

They thought through that scenario individually, and each came to the same conclusion.

'Excellent!'

They each then arrived at another less palatable conclusion.

'Blyad!'

Kaganovich spoke first.

"I assume you've just realised that we have to advance our timetable?"

"Mudaks! Of course we do... no fucking choice!"

Khrushchev slammed his hand on the crate that supported their drinks, sending two cups rolling off and onto the stone floor.

232

"Are we ready? Can we advance our plans from Friday?"

Kaganovich contemplated the politician's words and followed up with an answer.

"I can... but the woman... yet again... it all depends on the woman. If we advance our plans and the audience is not granted then we ..."

Gorbachev nodded.

"My units are ready for my orders...but I agree with Ilya Borisevich... if the woman fails to secure the meeting... can we... I think I can... but should we encourage Comrade Stalin to accept her request... just to make sure?"

"That has difficulties."

They understood the wiseness of Kaganovich's words and fell into the sort of silence that marked brains at work.

They turned as a previously quiet voice entered the discussion.

"There is a way, one of betrayal, but which ultimately serves all our goals."

Zhukov's words were deliberately cold.

The other three failed to grasp his meaning, forcing him to expand.

"Curiosity killed the cat, Comrades."

"Stop talking in fucking riddles, Comrade Marshal!"

Khrushchev slipped back to his peasant roots in an instant.

He held up an apologetic hand to the senior army man, which Zhukov acknowledged with a simple nod as he expanded on his idea.

When he finished both he and Khrushchev looked at Kaganovich expectantly. Gorbachev could not bring himself to look at any of them and simply examined the floor.

"It can be done... it will be done. The woman'll understand and see the need for it... just to be sure."

Khrushchev voiced the unspoken fear.

"And they won't act precipitously? Arrest her at once?"

It was a fair question, and Kaganovich took a moment to consider his reply.

"If I know them in any way, they'll enjoy toying with her. Beria for sure will want his savoured moment. I think not."

"Then, Comrades, we must establish the time of this meeting quickly, so we can set our own timetable. What time do we wish this meeting to take place?"

Again, they ceded the floor to Kaganovich, who spoke his thoughts aloud.

"Between twelve and three for the allies' needs. Too early and we risk problems in our own plans... we've always looked at later in the day... but too late and we risk passing the Allied deadline... I'm trying to remember the diary... wait... tomorrow at two... I'm a fucking fool... tomorrow at two... it's perfect... fucking perfect... the Yugoslavian's Ambassador and military envoy are due to see our leadership... they'll play along... they cancel and a gap opens up."

"And the Marshal's proposal?"

"It'll ensure that the spare slot is given to the woman and the Allied delegation. We cannot risk pique from the General Secretary. Too much depends upon it, eh?"

Zhukov slapped his hands on his thighs and stood straight and with purpose.

"Two o'clock."

"Two o'clock", they chorused in agreement.

Kaganovich picked up his greatcoat and slipped into it with practised ease.

"The banya at ten tonight? I'll know for sure by then.

"Agreed."

The four men left independently of each other and by separate entrances, observed by the security cordon that Kaganovich had placed around the old church in order to keep their meeting secret, a small number of ten trusted men who kept watch from the shadows.

A simple headcount would have revealed that there were eleven pairs of eyes keeping watch on the Church of the Twelve Apostles that day, one pair that reported directly to Marshal Lavrentiy Beria.

Within twenty minutes, Nadaraia was whispering in his master's ear.

Shortly after that, Beria's secretary opened the door to his office and a senior NKVD officer was ushered in.

He seated himself and waited until the secretary closed the door behind him.

"Comrade Marshal. I've important news on the traitors' plans and we don't have a moment to lose."

Kaganovich's words of betrayal flowed from his mouth and into the ears of an increasingly excited Beria.

The call from the Yugoslavians was not unexpected, neither was the one from the office of Lieutenant General Nazarbayeva.

Stalin's secretary played his part to perfection, openly allowing for the special relationship between his boss and the woman, and reluctantly found a spot at two pm.

News of the meeting arrived with Nazarbayeva and Horrocks, both of whom felt a huge attack of nerves for wholly different reasons.

In the Sanduny Banya, the news was greeted with a mix of excitement and trepidation.

None the less, the dice were cast.

As they were at RAF Shaibah in Iraq, and Karup in Denmark

In fact, all over the world, decisions had been made that ensured that Tuesday 15th April 1947 would be a day that would live in history.

We make war that we may live in peace.

Aristotle.

CHAPTER 204 - THE DAWN

0537 hrs, Tuesday, 15th April 1947, defensive positions of 363rd Rifle Division, 20 miles northeast of Chiya, Siberia.

The first light of the new day started to announce itself.

Amanin and Arganov enjoyed the early mornings, the pleasures of the crisp air and the cries of seagulls in pursuit of a meal or each other were far more agreeable than the harsh environment of the Shtrafbat from which they had miraculously escaped with their lives.

The horrendous casualties suffered by the Soviet officer corps had meant that their services were once more employed as regular commanders of men, in their case, as the OC and 2IC of 2nd Battalion, 404th Rifle Regiment, 363rd Rifle Division respectively.

The defensive responsibility allocated to their unit was an innocuous piece of coastline far from anything that resembled civilisation, from a beak headland some twenty miles northeast of the village of Chiya, extending along the coast to the southeast some ten miles, where the most distant unit butted up against the men of Third Battalion.

For two months now, 363rd Rifle Division had spread further and further along the coast, until the three active battalions covered a front of nearly one hundred miles.

The units they had relieved had long since disappeared towards the west.

The requirements of the active European front had been syphoning away the best men for months and months, and stocks of everything from food to ammunition were at record lows, with the few remaining tank units barely possessing enough fuel to manoeuvre for more than a few hours.

Most of their good weapons had also travelled west, and many of the tanks were of questionable reliability, already considered vintage when the Red Army conquered Berlin.

363rd was part of a huge maskirovka, partially aimed at persuading the Allies that the coast was still manned in strength, and partially to conceal the moves from east to west.

Worse still, each of the battalions had lost one man in four to form reserve units that moved around openly, all to fool the frequent Allied aerial reconnaissance flights.

The two officers occupied a well-constructed bunker position recently vacated by an anti-tank artillery unit, one that was so well appointed that they decided upon it as the battalion headquarters, even though it was not ideally placed.

Two mugs of tea arrived and they drank heartily, the hot sweet liquid easily dispelling the slight chill that had descended upon their bones.

"There he is!"

Atalin pointed and they swept their binoculars to their eyes immediately.

"So he is!"

"Told you!"

"True enough, Kon... hold on... look behind him!"

Atalin strained his eyes further.

"The hen! How did we not spot that nest!"

The two amateur ornithologists were excited beyond measure, the anticipation of being able to watch the Osprey family flourish almost too much to bear.

They clinked mugs in celebration and emptied them, extending them in expectation of a refill.

It was not immediately forthcoming.

The orderly was spellbound.

"Oi! Vassily! More tea!"

"Comrade Mayor... look!"

They turned back towards the sea.

"Mudaks!"

The greyness had revealed darker patches, patches that suddenly illuminated themselves in swathes of orange, yellow, and red.

"Yob tvoyu mat! Contact headquarters, Dmitri... tell them... tell them about that! Go!"

"Immediately, Comrade Mayor!"

Dmitri Arganov took precisely two paces before two six-inch shells from the USS Phoenix arrived roughly ten yards either side of him and Atalin.

237

The warning message died with them, although the simple truth of it was that the bombardment by ships of the USN Pacific fleet woke up everyone from Chiya to Moscow.

Fig #252 - The Sea of Okhotsk landing zones.

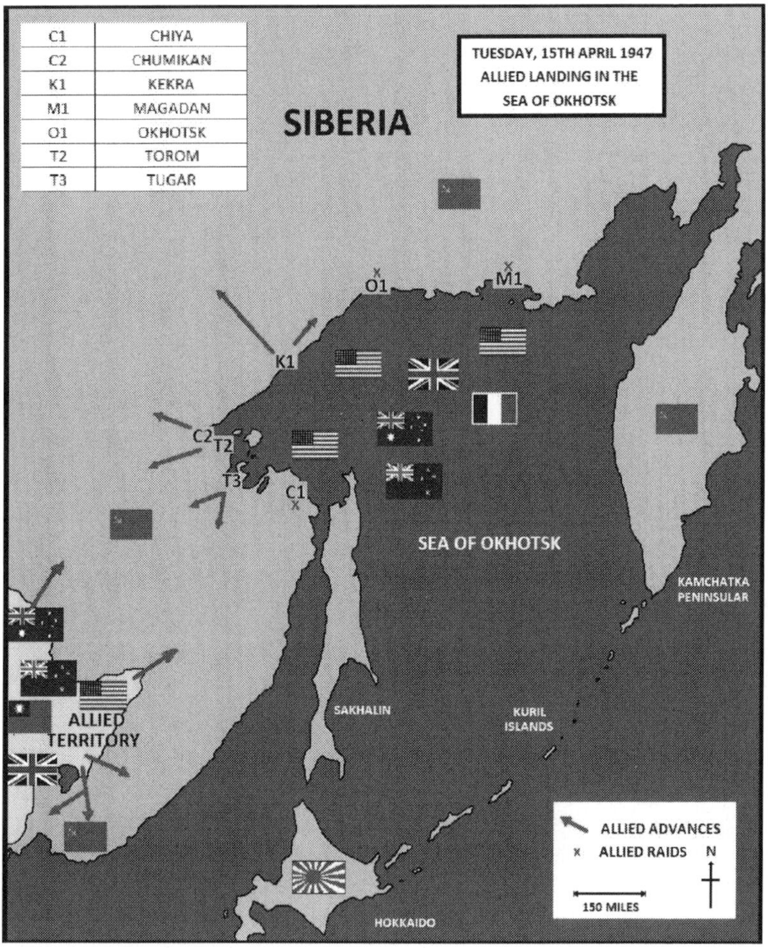

C1	CHIYA
C2	CHUMIKAN
K1	KEKRA
M1	MAGADAN
O1	OKHOTSK
T2	TOROM
T3	TUGAR

TUESDAY, 15TH APRIL 1947
ALLIED LANDING IN THE
SEA OF OKHOTSK

SIBERIA

SEA OF OKHOTSK

KAMCHATKA
PENINSULAR

ALLIED
TERRITORY

SAKHALIN

KURIL
ISLANDS

ALLIED ADVANCES
x   ALLIED RAIDS   N

150 MILES

HOKKAIDO

The Sea of Okhotsk was undisputedly owned by the Allied navies, and they sailed upon it with impunity.

Over the preceding weeks, the occasional aerial or waterborne challenge was met and defeated in short order, so much so that the Soviet commanders had long since stopped such excursions, and any meeting of forces was now most often accidental.

Coastal batteries and observation points had all been pummelled so that scarcely more than a handful of positions were still functioning.

Sakhalin had long since been reduced to a pile of ashes, and the garrison cowed by nothing more sophisticated than pure hunger and deprivation.

The Kurils, ceded by the Soviets to their Japanese allies, posed no barrier, each with strong American or Commonwealth garrisons in place, permitting the free flow of men, supplies, and ships in both directions.

Kamchatka had been visited on all but two days in the last month, as USN carrier aircraft and bombers flying out of Japan struck everything of value until everything of value was gone, and they then struck everything else.

By 5th April, there was not a single functioning Soviet aircraft on the peninsular, not that it mattered, as there was no runway from which it could have operated.

The huge armada committed by MacArthur had been at sea for eight days already and the soldiers were keen to get ashore, if for no other reason than to be rid of the motion of the sea and the confines of the ships that carried them.

Twice already, the move ashore had been called off at the last moment.

The might of the US Navy was concentrated in the seas off Southern Siberia, and in four specific places in the Sea of Okhotsk, had commenced putting ashore US marines and soldiers, supported by men from a number of Allied countries.

The shoreline was subjected to a furious bombardment, well in excess of that inflicted upon the coast of Normandy three years previously.

Above the landing zones and ranging inland, the naval aircraft of the huge US carrier forces and the accompanying Royal Naval carrier group held sway, shooting down all comers and falling upon anything that moved, be it civilian or military in nature.

Large-scale landings were conducted at Chumikan and Torom, and east of that at Tugur.

The landing at Chiya was mainly diversionary, hoping to pull Soviet reserves into a trap.

The more risky landing was conducted at Kekra, the issues being more of routes away from the beachhead than of expected resistance to the invading force.

The assault troops would require speed over all other things, in order to move beyond the mountains that embraced the area and into ground where their superior firepower could be brought to bear.

Okhotsk and Magadan were both struck by landing forces designed to resemble proper landings, but that were actually no more than raids to destroy naval facilities and anything else that might aid the Soviet resistance.

The operations had already been called off twice, as concerns over Soviet atomic weapons and their effect against a concentrated bridgehead overrode the necessity of opening another front.

MacArthur had used the time wisely and spent more time developing the plan, specifically the logistics element, which now saw the greatest efforts by the merchant marine forces of the Allied nations.

The landing forces would want for nothing in the long and difficult journey planned for them.

Striking up from China came more forces, an almost equal number of Commonwealth troops moving northwards with the US divisions.

Not to be left out, the Chinese had insisted on sending four of their own divisions along, despite the growing difficulties with the Communists in their own land.

Large paratrooper forces waited for their moment, MacArthur's plan of splitting Siberia down the Lena River probably still many days from realisation.

Whilst the British had husbanded their more advanced tanks to the European Front, the US armored force possessed a high number of the newer types, which gave it a huge technological edge over the depleted Soviet forces, most of whom still worked with WW2-era equipment.

At no point, on land or on a beachhead, was the Allied advance met with anything more than scant resistance and Allied casualties were mercifully few, whilst the prisoners were taken in their thousands. By the end of the day, MacArthur was able to report unprecedented success in all areas of endeavour.

The bigger losses were sustained at sea, where the CA-45 USS Wichita struck a mine and sank with the loss of three hundred and one men, CL-104 USS Atlanta took a torpedo hit from a Soviet attack craft off Okhotsk, forcing her captain to beach her rather than risk sinking.

As the night closed in, the HMNZS Black Prince, a light cruiser of the Dido class, accidentally rammed the HMNZS Sanda, an Isles class minesweeper. The smaller ship succumbed almost immediately and was lost with all hands.

Black Prince sustained relatively light damage and remained on station.

The final casualties at sea occurred when a USN Douglas BTD Destroyer crashed on landing on the USS Franklin D. Roosevelt, killing the pilot and seven deck crew.

As the 15th departed and the 16th arrived, MacArthur's generals drove their soldiers on.

Assassination has never changed the history of the world.

Benjamin Disraeli.

CHAPTER 205 - THE DAY

1352 hrs, Tuesday, 15th April 1947, the Kremlin, Moscow, USSR.

They were late.

Deliberately so.

Nazarbayeva allowed the Allied delegation to proceed ahead of her as she exchanged silent looks with Orlov and Rufin, both men with important parts to play in the hastily arranged plan.

The scrutiny of the guards was firmly focussed on the enemy soldiers and, despite the metal detector finding nothing of note, save the metal in the Englishman's false leg, they gave each man a thorough body search as well.

Nazarbayeva had a moment's hesitation as fear gripped her, but it passed as quickly as it came and she entered the detector.

As usual, the warning sounded and, as usual, the guard commander stepped forward.

"With regret, Comrade Leytenant General."

He indicated that she should step to one side and prepare to be searched thoroughly.

"You'll be late, Comrade Nazarbayeva. Won't do to keep the boss waiting!"

The NKVD officer sprang to attention as Kaganovich loomed up behind him.

"Quickly, Comrade Kapitan. The General Secretary doesn't like to be kept waiting."

"I have my orders, Comrade Polkovnik General."

"I know. I wrote them, you fool. It's her metal foot strap... it's always her metal foot strap... now hurry up and get it over with, man!"

The kapitan made a play of examining the foot and decided that he had enough on his plate already, with a drunk on duty charge from his Colonel possibly waiting for him after last night's celebrations, so he stepped back.

"All is in order, Comrade Leytenant General."

He handed back the briefcase that had been searched by one of his NCOs.

"Thank you, Comrade Kapitan."

Kaganovich looked smug, despite himself.

The threat of a 'drunk on duty' charge had been a nice touch, he thought.

The party and escort moved forward and headed towards the Military briefing room, where Kaganovich took his leave.

The two NKVD guards positioned at the door, part of Kaganovich's hastily introduced revised security measures, both carried the latest AK-47s, and they eyed the Allied contingent suspiciously, fingers loitering near triggers.

Stalin's secretary opened the double doors and they walked in, followed by Nazarbayeva, who attended at Stalin's direction.

Stalin, very deliberately, remained seated, whilst Beria sat back and to the right of his master, studiously polishing his glasses and seemingly oblivious to the presence of the two Allied officers.

"Good afternoon, General Horrocks. You were indeed fortunate that I had time in my busy schedule to receive a visit from my enemies. Were it not for my agreement with the Kingdom of Sweden, I'd have you and your cronies thrown out... or worse."

Beria deigned to notice the new arrivals as he replaced his glasses.

"Now, speak, and be quick about it."

"Premier Stalin, I bring a message to you and the Soviet people, from the leaders of the Allied nations, one that is serious and should be well heeded."

Stalin's hand slapped the huge, solid table.

It was like a gunshot in its intensity, and the sound echoed around the large space.

"You'd do well not to start these matters with threats, Englishman!"

"I do not, Premier. I am here to state the position of my superiors, and simply ask that you give it full and serious consideration."

Stalin rummaged for a match and made a dramatic sweep across the wooden top before bringing it to the bowl of his pipe.

The wait seemed to last a dozen lifetimes.

"Then state the position of your masters."

"Premier Stalin, as all of us are aware, the loss of life and destruction wrought upon Vilnius, Kiev, and Odessa were not the result of any action on the Allied part. The three atomic explosions were brought about by circumstances as yet unclear to us, but most certainly by actions commenced and authored within your own borders."

Stalin's eyes narrowed and Beria started furiously polishing his glasses again.

Nazarbayeva examined both men equally, her eyes betraying nothing of the turmoil inside.

"What the reasoning behind this incredible act of self-mutilation is, we cannot understand or begin to comprehend. But the fact that you use this cover to launch an attack upon the United States of America is perfidy and deceit of an extreme and pure form unprecedented in the history of the world, and it cannot... it will not go unanswered."

"Again, you threaten me? You bomb us and expect nothing in return? Expect us to turn... how do you say... the other cheek? Mudaks!"

Stalin's false rage was impressive but fooled no one.

"We did not bomb you, Premier."

"That's not what history will record, General Horrocks!"

Horrocks, suddenly off script, thought on his feet.

"Those who write our histories will have much to record once this day is done, Premier Stalin."

Beria stopped polishing his glasses and spat out a reply.

"Choose your words carefully, Englishman. Our understanding with Sweden only goes so far and you hold no favour here."

Stalin nodded at his henchman.

"Quite so, Lavrentiy. So, spit it out and then get out."

"As you wish. As you will already know, our land, air, and naval forces started occupying your eastern provinces as of yesterday morning. You denuded your forces there, so will know you will not be able to prevent us expanding the bridgeheads and eliminating your military. That is just the start of our operations. Today, the Allies will strike the Soviet Union with two devices, the equivalent of the damaging attacks upon the United States of America. You will not be able to prevent us from doing so, not

244

now, today, tomorrow, or any other day, should these matters not end on this day."

The puffing of the pipe increased, but the General Secretary stayed silent.

"There will be no further attacks, unless you continue with your own aggressions in this regard. Further use of atomic or biological weapons, or nerve gas, will result in a swift and overwhelming display of force in kind... and beyond."

Stalin laughed.

"You threaten us with what? You hold precious little by way of nerve gas... no biological weapons except the puny British stocks... and we know you are reduced to a handful of atomic weapons. What wonder weapon do you propose to throw at us now, eh?"

The two men laughed, not sensing that Horrocks was unphased.

The British general held out his hand and Ramsey slid the required papers into it.

"According to your intelligence, you presently assess that we hold six atomic devices."

It was not a question; it was a statement of fact, something not lost on Beria, who suddenly heard alarm bells in his head.

"Allow me to enlighten you, Premier."

Horrocks made great play of skim reading parts of the papers in his hand, speaking sufficiently loud enough for both of his enemies to hear and comprehend what was coming long before he arrived at the point.

"Priority code..."

"Agent Alkonost..."

"A-alpha-A..."

"Ah yes... here... from your agent Emilia Perlo, or Alkonost as you call her, confirmed intelligence places stocks at six devices. A+. Can-sun."

Beria snapped his glasses with a sound like a pistol shot, as Horrocks read the last Alkonost report word for word.

"Perlo is our agent. What you think you know is not the truth, simply the truth that we chose to present to you. I am instructed to inform you that our capacity to wage war at the new awful levels is infinitely greater than you believed... and infinitely more than you can endure."

Beria's mouth was wide open but unable to work properly, the only sound being a low bubbling as the moisture rose in his throat.

Stalin was more forthcoming.

245

"So you think you fooled us, eh? We always take such reports lightly, and set no store by them. We're not so foolish as you think, Englishman.

Horrocks moved forward gently and dropped the supposedly secret reports from agents Gamayun, Kalibr, and Alkonost on the desk, their names in bold print, designed to catch the eye.

The sound was slight, but still made Stalin start.

"My superiors will need an answer from you today. What happens today is brought upon your people by acts from within, from people within your own borders... if not you, then those who answer to you. By the end of the day, we will both have suffered grievous losses, but there is no need for any more."

Horrocks' Russian was up to the task of the confrontation, whereas Ramsey was struggling with many of the words. However, the tone was unmistakable.

Stalin was in no doubt as to the strength of his enemies' words.

Stalin was also in no doubt what to do about it.

He lifted the receiver and requested a specific coded exchange number.

He was quickly connected, but not before he had extracted a piece of card from his pocket.

"This is the General Secretary. Get the 901st Special Regiment's commander immediately... get him on the phone now!"

Horrocks and Stalin locked eyes, the latter in an attempt to project force of will, the former in an attempt to divine the veracity of what was taking place.

The General Secretary spoke unhurriedly and with great precision.

"Ah, Comrade Polkovnik. You recognise my voice? Good. Standby for orders."

The silent exchange continued as the two men mentally battered each other through steely eyes.

"Ready? Authorisation code is..." Stalin read the card aloud, selecting the appropriate line, "...Zoloto-dva-gusya-pyat'-kop'ye-tri-devyat'. Confirm authorisation."

The shocked man on the other end of the line did just that.

"Good. I am issuing you with a direct order. You will prepare to enact special orders sixty-three and sixty-four immediately, in full, within the necessities of the operational plan of the day. I order you to take-off as soon as is possible, if not immediately. Once you are in the air, you will not deflect from this mission, no matter what. I and only I will recall you, using the authorised recall code, and you will not accept any such order from another party. You will ensure that special orders sixty-three and sixty-four are completed before you return and report your success directly to me. Repeat your orders."

On the other end of the line at Stakhnovo Airfield, Colonel Sacha Istomin repeated the orders, word for word.

"Excellent. How long before you can fly the missions?"

As the latest standing order had two of Istomin's aircraft held in the new bunkers, both already loaded with atomic devices, the answer was more than satisfactory.

"Comrade Polkovnik. The Motherland stands threatened again. In the event that you become aware of any atomic attack on the soil of the Rodina, I authorise you to execute the missions without further orders but on my full and direct authority, just in case I myself am the target of one of these enemy attacks. If you do not hear directly from me with a return order, initiate your attacks at 1430 hrs precisely. Is that fully clear?"

Again, Istomin understood his orders completely.

"I wish you every success, and your Motherland thanks you."

Stalin replaced the receiver without breaking eye contact with Horrocks.

"You have my reply, Englishman."

"So it would appear, Premier. I will inform my superiors."

Both he and Ramsey saluted and were ushered to the door by Nazarbayeva.

"Comrade Nazarbayeva, remain please. There are urgent matters for us to discuss."

The door closed on the departing delegation.

Nazarbayeva took a look at the clock on the mantelpiece.

'Sixteen minutes... and then revenge is mine!'

She took up a position at the attention on the other side of the huge map table and braced herself.

"Now, woman, tell me what you know of this present treachery... and I warn you. Leave out nothing. Tell us all, and understand that we already know a very great deal."

In a room one floor below, Kaganovich slid off the headset and swallowed nervously as their plan... his plan... entered the final dangerous stages.

Two telephone calls later, he replaced the receiver and shared a quiet but decidedly strained look with Khrushchev.

There was no going back.

Both men concentrated on listening to the exchange in the map room above them.

Even though Kaganovich had briefed her, as best as he could in the short time available, she was still knocked off her stride by the questions.

She eased her damaged foot in the boot, somehow drawing comfort from the familiar manoeuvre.

"Yes, Comrade General Secretary."

"Willingly?"

"At first, I was drawn in, despite the circumstances that prevailed. I have always been loyal to the Motherland. That loyalty remains, but the needs of the Motherland changed."

"The needs changed? What the fuck do you mean by that, woman?"

"It became clear that the Motherland was best served by a new leadership, one that valued lives and freedoms more than the one that was responsible for the deaths of millions, including my sons."

"That was regrettabl…"

"No! That was you… and you!"

Stalin's eyes widened as he saw the woman in a new light.

She had to know that her life was forfeit already, but still she stood haughty and proud.

'Balls of steel!'

He made himself smile with the thought.

"Sit down, Nazarbayeva."

She sat down, bringing her more to Stalin's level and reducing her tension, the more relaxed position often promoting increased calm and reason.

Standard interrogation stuff.

"So, you, Kaganovich, Khrushchev, Gurundov, Gorbachev… anyone we've missed?"

"Marshal Vasilevsky, Comrade General Secretary."

"Ah yes, of course, how could I forget that treacherous rat."

There was something missing from the woman's demeanour, or possibly, something unexpectedly present.

Both Stalin and Beria, the latter more so, could sense its presence but not its meaning.

Outside of the map room, the last elements of the plan slid into place.

Orlov and Rufin strolled openly past the new door guards and into a side room, wherein two pistols had been concealed.

In silence, they waited, nothing but their laboured breathing to mark the tension of the moment.

In the courtyard, Zhukov and his aides continued their conversation, the timing of their walk having been practised a number of times.

Khrushchev took his leave of Kaganovich and went to be with Molotov, by prior appointment, for which he was already running late.

Kaganovich himself checked his pistol and slid it into his belt, counting down the last few seconds before he took his own measured walk, timed to coincide to the second with Zhukov's arrival.

Now, it all depended on the woman.

In the room above him, the conversation continued.

"Why?"

"Each will have had their own reasons... but we had a common goal... to replace you... to save the Rodina."

Beria leant forward, his words almost a hiss, his face carrying a sneer that Nazarbayeva just wanted to wipe off with as much pain as possible.

"No... you... why you?"

She imagined smashing him in the face with a rifle butt, and it felt good.

"You ask me why? You, of all people, ask me why, you Chekist bastard!"

Beria had expected vitriol, but the naked fury in the woman's eyes was beyond his experience, and in that moment he understood what the something was that he had recognised absent in her demeanour.

She had no fear of what was to come.

There was no reservation in her, no hint of a controlled approach to lessen her crimes against the state.

Simply a reassurance that she would be revenged.

249

Suddenly, he felt afraid.

He exchanged looks with Stalin, the confused looks of men for whom the conversation was not proceeding quite as expected.

Beria decided to tackle matters head on.

"So, you know."

"Yes... I know. I've endured that which should not be endured, in order to bring myself to this moment with you... and you."

She looked away from Beria and brought Stalin under her cold eye.

"Even with the death of my son, I was loyal. Loyal beyond measure, loyal beyond your worth and your capacity to understand. And still, you heaped misery upon my family! My sons! You killed my sons! You tried to kill my husband... oh yes... I know about that too! And then... you humiliate me... rape... that wasn't rape... that was a desecration and humiliation! I should rip your miniature cock off, you fucking excuse for a man!"

Even though the mood, indeed the balance, in the room had changed, Stalin could not help but find amusement in her words as he knew they would find fertile ground in Beria's heart.

"I've seen the film you took... the things you did, your men did... that monster did... all in the name of what? Of the Motherland? You fucking pair of shits are not worthy of a peasant's cloak, let alone leadership of the Rodina!"

She eased her boot off as the increase in blood pressure made her stump throb.

Plus...

"You ask me why? My reasons are clear, both personal and as a patriotic citizen. My reasons are to rid my country of the stain that you bring! The bombs! For fuck's sake... Comrade..." she didn't know what else to call him, "... you bomb our own... kill our own... in their thousands!"

'How does the bitch know that?'

They both thought it.

She hesitated, trying to find the words to describe her feelings.

"This is not new for you, either of you... but in this way... for this purpose... it's fucking monstrous!"

"Enough, woman. I'll hear no more. Lavrentiy, summon the guards and have the witch removed. You'll be tried for your crimes against the state!"

Beria rose but stopped, cut short by a sharp voice that could not be ignored.

"I've not yet finished, you Chekist fuck."

She moved uncomfortably in her seat, arranging her feet in the right position.

"What happens now is for my sons… for the Motherland… my Motherland… for my husband… and for myself. I've no regrets except one perhaps… simply that you'll not suffer as you should."

"You've talked yourself out of a clean death, Tatiana."

She stared Stalin down with a contemptuous look, leaving Beria to take up the challenge.

"So be it… the film of your activities will be shown to all, including your surviving son, if he still lives, right before I execute him personally."

"Oh he lives, Chekist, and he knows everything. In fact, he knows more than you do."

She moved almost imperceptibly, but not quite.

Both men's sense of self-preservation lit off in an instant and were reinforced by her words, and by the slightest metallic sound.

"And so you die, by my hand, you fucking bastards!"

Something touched Stalin's foot.

He looked down and knew his death was upon him.

It had once belonged to Corporal Liam D. O'Malley of the 82nd US Airborne Division, until his death at Heiligenthal on 7th August 1945.

It had lain unnoticed in the grass for five days until the then Lieutenant Colonel Nazarbayeva had taken a stroll through the battle site and stumbled upon it, thinking it nothing more than a stone until her soldier's instinct made her exercise more care. Then she discovered it was a US-made Mk II Fragmentation grenade that its dead owner had placed beside his foxhole, to be ready for instant use during the desperate fight for the Curau River.

That same grenade now lay gently but malevolently against Stalin's right foot.

"You bitch!"

Despite her half foot, she reacted quicker than either man and jumped onto the table top, just in time.

The room trembled to the sound of the grenade's detonation.

The explosion was the signal a number of people had been waiting for.

Orlov stepped outside of the room and shot the first guard down, the man halfway through the turn towards the doors of the map room.

Rufin fumbled for a good aim, but Orlov, experienced veteran that he was, was still quicker and dispatched the second guard with a head shot.

The secretary simply sat and waited for death to take him.

Switching his aim, Orlov blew the man's chest open with two shots.

He turned to Rufin in order to tease his co-conspirator, only to take a round full in the face.

His body dropped instantly.

Rufin swiftly picked up the dead man's pistol and gritted his teeth, firing it into his thigh at close range, carefully trying to miss everything vital.

He knocked himself to the floor with the hammer blow, but still had enough composure to throw Orlov's weapon towards the dead body, where reinforcements would find it, and find his story of heroic defiance all the more acceptable.

In his office, Fedor Kuznetsov, head of the GRU, was enjoying her mouth but the dull thud drew him back from the precipice of orgasm.

"What was that?"

Sonia Laberova hastily took her mouth off his erect cock and stood, whilst her twin sister, Ludmilla, pulled her breasts back into her bra.

"I believe that was the sound of your guilt being established."

"Pardon?"

The girls had drawn lots to decide who did what, and it fell to Sonia to do the dirty deeds.

She shot the commander of the GRU in the throat and chest, and then scrambled for his weapon, a stylish German PPK pistol, which she took hold of and aimed with great reluctance.

"Sorry, sister."

"Hurry yourself!"

She shot Ludmilla in the arm, the small bullet tearing through flesh and into an expensive vase on a stand, one of an identical quartet that graced the GRU commander's office.

The PPK was carefully inserted into the dying man's hand and Sonia helped him further on his way with a punch to the throat wound.

He gurgled his last few seconds away, trousers by his ankles, unable to comprehend the reasons behind his death or the treachery of which he would yet stand accused.

By the time help arrived, the scene looked very different, and wholly in line with their story of an arrest gone wrong.

Zhukov and his party were at the metal detector when Kaganovich arrived.

There was an awkward moment when the necessary call to action was absent, but the sound of the explosion soon reached all ears and set their part of the plan in motion.

"The Secretary General!"

Kaganovich shouted, drawing attention back to himself.

"Secure these men! They're not to move! If they do, shoot them all!"

He indicated Zhukov's party, and the NKVD guards immediately aimed their weapons menacingly, with clear orders from a senior officer to guide them.

"You, Comrade Marshal, come with me! Give him your weapon, Comrade Kapitan."

The guard commander immediately handed over his AK to the Army's senior Marshal.

Had he not, Zhukov still had his pistol in his holster, as he had stepped around the detector in the confusion.

The two rushed off up the stairs.

She had no idea how much time had passed, even though the heavy table had shielded her from most of the blast.

Its weight had prevented it from shifting too much, but still she had been displaced and thrown to the floor. The effect upon the two men was more defined.

Stalin was dead, his right leg still there, but damaged beyond description and attached in name only, the majority of it decorating various parts of the walls, ceiling, and furniture.

He had been penetrated by a number of pieces of shrapnel, but none had killed him, neither had the blood loss from his appalling leg wound.

His end had come in more bizarre fashion, swiftly and with undue mercy, as contact with the fireplace behind him had broken his neck as cleanly as an executioner's axe.

Unsteadily rising to her feet, Nazarbayeva sought her balance, the single boot unable to properly support her.

The other boot, which she had slipped off to release the grenade, had disappeared in the blast.

Conscious that she probably had little time, she moved around the table to where Beria lay, parts of his intestines spilt from the gaping wound in his side, and his left leg bent with bone laid bare, where the blast had opened the limb from knee to hip with all the precision and enthusiasm of a blind trainee butcher.

Through the pain, he spat blood and phlegm at her.

She looked around for something fit for her purposes, even as he was trying to form words of insult and threat.

"You bitch! ...You fucking bitch! ...You've failed!"

She turned with the foot long splinter of table in her hand.

With all the strength she could muster, she kicked out with her right foot, driving the steel toecap into Beria's genitalia, bursting one of his testicles with the force of the blow.

The injury moved Beria into new realms of agony, and his scream was like nothing on earth.

She lost her balance as the damaged foot slipped on some blood.

Dropping to her knees, she grasped the splinter in both hands like a sacrificial dagger.

"Yes, I failed... but only in not saving my country the pain of your presence months ago! For my sons... die, you fuck!"

The sharp splinter journeyed into his chest, once, twice, three times, seeming to miss everything vital except that which brought excruciating pain.

Beria screamed like an animal at slaughter.

"And this is from me, and then I shall think of you no more!"

The thrust was with every ounce of power she could muster, and she ensured she maintained the forward progress of the wooden blade as she slammed it home hard, parallel to the floor and upwards into his crotch.

Her strength drove the wooden blade deeper, inspired as it was by memories of loved ones lost, or of her decency despoiled.

It penetrated his already ruined scrotum, passaged his bladder, and ripped open part of the bowel.

Still Beria clung to life, the pain excruciating.

It was not enough for the woman.

She struggled to her feet and, in one simple but powerful movement, kicked the splinter hard, driving it and her toecap into the soft flesh, falling to her knees with the effort.

The other testicle exploded as the splinter did its work, destroying the intersection of his abdominal aorta and the femoral arteries.

His scream was high-pitched and trembling, as pain embraced his every being and then became the last of his earthly memories.

"Bastard!"

She pulled the splinter from the cadaver and stood erect, the wicked piece of wood dripping with the vital fluids of her enemy.

The door flew open and in burst Zhukov and Kaganovich, who froze in their tracks.

Nazarbayeva hawked and sent a gobbet of phlegm at the glassy-eyed corpse.

Suddenly unsteady on her feet, the shock of the minute catching up with her, Nazarbayeva supported herself on the table edge.

"It's done, Comrades."

"What fucking great tits… really, what fucking great tits she's got!"

"You ain't wrong there, tovarich."

The two men relaxed into the huge bath and enjoyed the high-quality vodka that the woman had supplied.

"We've hit the jackpot here, Sard, the fucking jackpot."

They had received orders from Marshal Beria's office to get close to and establish the affiliations of a member of Moscow's society… actually, from Kaganovich's office via a loyal man.

The woman had turned out to be a widow with a taste for the finer things in life and the means to enjoy them, and who had already talked them out of their clothes and into the huge bath. Their uniforms, along with her own stunning dress and underwear, lay on a chaise-longues, the contrast between the two sets of items as stark as the contrast between their rough soldier's bodies and her perfect china-doll curves.

"Hurry up with the booze, Elizaveta. We're dying of thirst here!"

The two burst into laughter and were joined by the naked Elizaveta Voluzdieva, bearing two full bottles of the prime vodka.

One found its way to each man and they drank as they admired the woman's curves.

She moved around the huge bathroom, busying herself with laying out towels and robes, applying perfume, and rummaging in a drawer.

Both men's attention was firmly on her curvaceous backside until they switched, in a frightening instant, to the silenced automatic in her right hand.

"Keep quiet, and you may just live."

"What the…"

The pistol spat a bullet and it missed Rafael Sarkisov by the smallest of margins.

"Quiet. I've a message for you, one you would do well to heed, you fucking scum."

Nadaraia spoke carefully.

"We're listening."

"My message is from a woman, much like me, but one who had no choice about the company she kept. She asked me to say hello and to remind you both that, eventually, your sins catch up with you. I bring greetings from Comrade Tatiana Nazarbayeva."

They both knew real fear in that instant, but had little chance to further react.

The woman fired twice in succession, half happy to be done with the killing, half wishing she could have prolonged the agony for the two rapists.

Both men took a single round in the forehead and sank under the reddening water.

The woman quickly dressed in slightly less formal clothing, wrapped up her expensive dress in a newspaper and secreted it in her shoulder bag, extracting the man's clothing she had 'liberated' from the Hotel National's laundry room earlier that day.

She dressed the scene to look like a gay tryst gone wrong and then checked that all traces of her presence had been removed and, once satisfied that all was as it should be, Hana Rikardova slipped quietly away.

Orders were orders and he didn't particularly mind either way, although his preference tended to be for women.

Today his target was a proper soldier, no less than a highly decorated Guards major, a man of great interest to his master.

As ever, an interest he could not really understand, but his job was simple and the benefits were outstanding, if for no other reason than he never had to serve in the frontline, unlike his intended victim.

For extra support, just in case, another officer, a burned colonel of tanks troops, was staying in the dacha, ostensibly because there was no other available space within the complex but actually to provide Stranov with back-up should the situation turn nasty.

He was assured that the combat hero's proclivities extended to homosexual sex, but the extra presence was reassuring for a man who had never seen any form of combat except that undertaken beneath the bed sheets for state purposes.

He checked with the other officer and moved off, taking a few deep breaths on his way.

Stranov knocked on the door after checking his appearance in the mirror. Casual, smart, and as alluring to the male of the species as he could be and still be properly dressed in mess uniform.

"Come in."

"Comrade Mayor, You've had a long journey so I expect you're intending to retire for a few hours before your appointment, so unless there is anything else I can do for you. Anything at all?"

The combat veteran had already loosened his tunic but the decorations of a real soldier were well displayed still and Stranov could not help but admire them, and the man, for what they represented.

"Yes, Comrade Stranov. Will you share a drink with me?"

"It's against the rules, Comrade Mayor."

"Fuck the rules, eh? Come, drink with me. It's no great fun drinking alone."

Stranov relaxed as he sensed certain keywords being exchanged, words that would guarantee his work would progress easily.

He accepted the vodka and relaxed into a chair, having turned down the two gaslights that gave the room a homely and welcoming feeling.

"Your health, Comrade Mayor."

They drank, and poured another.

"What else shall we drink to, Comrade Mayor?"

"Your wife, Comrade Stranov?"

Inside he laughed, as yet another sign of an approach slid easily from the Major's lips.

"I'm unmarried, Comrade Mayor."

"Oh. Well, in that case, let's drink to my wife then."

He raised a glass as Stranov's confusion got the better of him.

"To Tatiana!"

"To Tatiana," Stranov echoed, unsure why he suddenly felt strange...

"To Tatiana... Sergievna... Nazarbayeva... my wife... the mother of my children... and the woman you raped!"

The glass had disappeared and had transformed into a service automatic, held in the hands of a man with merciless eyes.

"Yes, Stranov... I've seen the film... seen the bestial things you did... in the name of those fucking shit holes, Beria and Stalin! I'm here to exact the price of my wife's revenge!"

"Comrade Polkovnik! Help! Help!"

"Sit down... he won't help you."

The door opened slowly and the burned colonel, Leonid Ferovan, Zhukov's right-hand man, strode purposefully in, a Nagant revolver firmly in his grip.

Yuri Nazarbayev wanted to extract the maximum amount of pain from his revenge but he had been told forcefully that he should not dally.

"From my wife, my sons, and me!"

He shot Stranov twice, the first simply to inflict pain, the round ripping through the man's lower abdomen and shattering his spine on its passage in the woodwork beyond.

The second struck the heart and stopped the organ in an instant.

He stood up and grabbed for his bag and greatcoat.

"Truly, I am sorry, Comrade."

"Thank you, Comrade Polkovnik, but she's now been revenged and..."

Nazarbayev turned to see the muzzle of Ferovan's revolver aimed at his face.

"You're bastards... all of you... you're all bast..."

Yuri Nazarbayev was propelled back over the chair and crashed onto the floor as the back of his head opened and blood and brain matter decorated the two ornate gas lamps and the wall beyond.

Ferovan quickly slipped the revolver into Stranov's lifeless hand and then checked to ensure that there was nothing that could possibly reveal that he had been present.

He slipped outside and into the waiting car.

Bogdan Atalin pulled away in a deliberately unhurried fashion, heading towards the dacha that had been set aside for the two Army colonels.

When they were inside their own sanctuary, they shared a large vodka.

"Any problems, Comrade?"

Atalin shook his head and poured a second glass.

"None at all. Vovsi accepted the gift and poured a drink straight away. He drank, I didn't. I left the note and other stuff. Nice and simple. You?"

"I shot a good man today... a good man who'd no fucking idea he'd been dead since he agreed to the plan. Life's a bastard and then you die."

"We do the Marshal's bidding, for the good of the Motherland."

"Apparently so, Comrade. Another glass."

It was not a question, and Atalin poured a third one.

"Za zdorovje!"

They drank and waited for the call.

Nazarbayeva both smiled and frowned.

The relief of removing the sources of her own personal torment, accompanied by the freeing of her Motherland, had given her a headache of monumental proportions.

Their eyes locked for the briefest of moments, and both saw horror reflected back at them.

Zhukov was unskilled with the AK-47, so only the first two bullets struck her, the impacts enough to knock Nazarbayeva off her feet and onto the wooden floor.

"Quickly, Georgy... no time for sentimentality!"

Kaganovich strode to Beria, and then Stalin, ready to finish the work the woman had started. He found nothing to test his own weapon skills.

Zhukov stood over the crying GRU officer, the tears of pain and betrayal mixing on her cheeks, her whimpers of agony sharing her last seconds with the hisses of a woman betrayed.

"Why... Yuri, oh no... Yuri... why... I did everything you asked... you bastards..."

"Do it, for fuck's sake, man!"

Zhukov shot Kaganovich a look but saved his words for Nazarbayeva.

"I'm sorry, Tatiana. We had no choice... but the Motherland will survive and prosper... goodbye..."

He aimed carefully, conscious of the hate and fear in her eyes.

Again the weapon wandered off target, but the four bullets that hit her robbed her of life as sure as if the whole clip had been on target.

The sound of running feet echoed through the halls of the Kremlin, and both men moved to their leaders, feigning concern and an attempt at rescue, all for the benefit of those who would be first through the doors.

Three officers from the Kremlin Guard burst in, pistols at the ready, and halted in a mix of terror and shock.

Kaganovich slipped into his pre-planned routine.

"The GRU! The fucking GRU did this! No one leaves the Kremlin! Arrest all GRU personnel... get a doctor... get all the doctors... the General Secretary's badly wounded... move!"

The room emptied and filled again in a second, as more men arrived.

A military doctor ran in, chivvied by two NKVD guards, a fellow conspirator who was 'found' close at hand; a man who was prepared to administer the coup de grace had either Stalin or Beria only been wounded.

He simply played the game of saviour, trying, not too hard, to bring the General Secretary back to life.

More bodies were located, the guards and secretary slain by Orlov and Rufin, the latter of which nursed his wound and spoke of his attempt to stop the assassinations, the former of which lay dead, testifying to the veracity of Rufin's account.

None the less, the NKVD and Kremlin guards handled him roughly, and he was bundled into the meeting room with two fewer teeth and a split lip for supposed resistance.

Kaganovich vouched for the man, but still the senior Guard officer insisted on placing Rufin under arrest.

The doctor loudly pronounced both Stalin and Beria dead.

Khrushchev arrived immediately after, accompanied by Malinin, who made a beeline for Zhukov.

"Comrade Marshal, you are unhurt?"

"I'm fine, Mikhail. I need you to pass a message to Vasilevsky immediately. Mikhail!"

Malinin's eyes and attention were wholly fixed on the three uncovered bodies.

"Mikhail!"

He started, such was his concentration on absorbing the sights on offer.

"Comrade Marshal?"

"Concentrate man! I need you to speak to Vasilevsky immediately. Tell him what's happened and that he is to take firm control of the Army whilst I sort it all out. Make sure he knows of the GRU's treachery."

Malinin, with firm orders, wrenched himself away from the scene and disappeared to tell Vasilevsky, who already knew what was going to happen and simply waited on word from Zhukov, which the uninvolved Malinin unwittingly provided.

Meanwhile, the troika made their play, shouting orders and sending men in all directions.

All too briefly they had a moment alone, the only other man present being the doctor of whose integrity they were assured, him being Kaganovich's son in law.

"The Allies are going to strike... and these two idiots have sent our bombers out with yet more bombs! It'll never end!"

"Call the bombers back, Comrade Marshal."

All too quickly the moment passed as the room filled again, this time with stretchers and medical personnel to remove the bodies.

The senior men moved aside to let them work and exchanged urgent whispers.

"You must call the bombers back or there'll be nothing but pawn for pawn, knight for knight... exchange after exchange... the Amerikanski have misled us... fed us lies... they have many more bombs than us! You must stop our bombers!"

Zhukov had not heard Khrushchev's previous words and was just starting into delayed shock from the necessity of killing Nazarbayeva.

"Eh?"

"Listen, for fuck's sake, Georgy! You must call the bombers back. You.... We have our roles and must carry them out. Call them back, or this will go on and on."

Zhukov started to comprehend.

"Right... yes, right. Stakhnovo... what's the secret exchange code?"

"Mudaks! I don't fucking know!"

"Get me that code!"

The raised voices drew attention from those loading the corpse of the woman general onto a stretcher, but they quickly looked away as the senior men's eyes cut through them like daggers.

"Where are you taking that?"

Zhukov's angst suddenly had a focal point and the stretcher party shrank before his eyes.

"To the infirmary, Comrade Marshal."

"Good... and quickly about it. You're both responsible for that body! Remain with it at all times until relieved by me personally. Now get her out of here!"

The two men almost ran from the room, such was their confusion and fright.

Zhukov stared at the bloody spot that marked where she had fallen, almost hypnotised by the shimmering red puddle.

"Georgy!"

He came out of his sudden reverie.

"Here... this is it."

Kaganovich's notebook slipped into his hand.

"Right... blyad! I'll stop the bombers, you get on top of this mess."

"There's a complication."

He explained about Stalin's additional orders.

Zhukov absorbed the implications and made a swift decision.

"So be it. You need to speak to those Allied officers quickly. Tell them everything... leave out nothing... they need to know we'll try to stop this happening. I'll do my best."

The telephone lay where it had fallen, and the Marshal half wondered if it would work.

As the other two conspirators started to shout more orders, he sought connection to the Stakhnovo base with the secret exchange code.

"This is Marshal Zhukov. Connect me to the commander of the special bomber squadron immediately!"

His knuckles went white with impotent fury.

"When?"

'Mudaks!'

He clicked the connection off and was back through to the switchboard in an instant.

"Get me Marshal Novikov immediately!"

The wait seemed interminable.

263

"Office of Chief Marshal of Aviation Novikov. Mayor Touraschkin speaking. How m…"

"This is Zhukov, Connect me to Marshal Novikov immediately."

"I'm afraid the Marshal is away inspecting bases in the Crimea, Comrade Marshal."

"Who's there in authority? Buiansky?"

"Yes, Com…"

"Put me through to him immediately!"

The connection was made in a heartbeat.

"Buiansky."

"Nikolay Nikolayevich, it's Georgy Zhukov."

The introduction and lack of titles was unusual and Novikov's deputy sat upright in an instant.

"What's wrong, Comrade?"

"Everything! The General Secretary has been attacked and killed in the Kremlin… and it appears that your special bomber force has been sent on a mission against the Allies by someone impersonating him. We're trying to get control here, but the bombers must be stopped. It's vital."

"Comrade Stalin dead?"

"Yes, dead… the GRU tried to stage a coup but it's been stopped. It cost the General Secretary his life, but the GRU have been stopped."

"Yob tvoyu mat! What? How? Why do you need to stop the bombers?"

"There's no time now, Nikolay. I can only say that if we bomb, the Rodina will be in great peril from vastly more capable and equipped enemies than we had understood them to be. Just have any GRU detained immediately, as we need to stop the rot. We'll sort out everything quickly, but you concentrate on stopping your bombers."

"I'll have them radioed immediately."

"There's a complication, Nikolay. They've been told not to respond to any return order."

"I'll radio them directly mysel…"

"No, that won't be enough."

Buiansky worked it out.

"I understand perfectly, Comrade Marshal. I'll see to it personally. They will not complete their mission."

"See that they don't, Nikolay, or the Motherland will suffer as she's never suffered before!"

Buiansky skim read the file of the senior officer of the 901st Regiment whilst his aides scurried around, threatening and cajoling in equal measure, establishing every fact possible about the missions on which the heavy bombers were engaged.

Time was of the essence, which meant that threats outweighed all other approaches.

"Comrade Polkovnik General."

He had only been promoted recently and failed to realise that the colonel was speaking to him.

"General Buiansky!"

"What!"

He jumped, drawn from his examination by the shout and hand on his arm.

"Apologies... this is the flight plan for both forces."

The simple map revealed the routes to be taken, and was also marked with time dated locations.

"So the lead group is about... here?"

"Yes, Comrade Polkovnik General."

"Right... make contact immediately. Have the mission commander... this... Istomin on the radio."

The two moved to the alpha radio position, whose operator had already been warned and was ready with his radio set to the correct frequency.

"Albatros-obucheniye-adin, "Albatros-obucheniye-adin, this is Komandovaniye-dva, over."

The hail was repeated twice more before eliciting a response.

"Komandovaniye-dva, go ahead, Albatros-obucheniye-adin over."

The operator passed the handset to his commander and settled back in his chair, content to be a bit-part player in what was happening.

"Albatros-adin, this is Komando-dva Buiansky speaking. Abort your mission... I say again abort your mission. Acknowledge your order. Over."

There was a long silence, broken only by distant coughing.

"Komandovaniye-dva. I do not acknowledge your order, over."

Radio procedures rapidly disappeared as the tension ramped up on both ends of the exchange.

"Albatros-adin, this is a direct order from Polkovnik General Buiansky of Air Force command. You will abort your mission, I repeat, abort your mission. Acknowledge this order immediately. Over."

The silence that followed allowed them to imagine a number of different scenarios aboard the former American B-29 bomber carrying one of the Soviet Union's atomic devices.

"Komandovaniye-dva. This is the mission commander speaking. I cannot accept your order, over."

Buiansky took a more direct approach, examining the front sheet of the man's file as he spoke.

"Comrade Istomin, listen to me closely. You've been tricked into launching a mission that threatens the Motherland. There has been an attempted coup, and you are an unwitting part of it. I'm ordering you to return to your base immediately, over."

"Comrade Polkovnik General. I regret that I cannot comply. My orders come from the highest source, are very specific, and cannot be rescinded at any cost, over."

One of Buiansky's aides had been tasked with a different agenda, and he stood close at hand waiting for the signal.

The Colonel General made one last effort.

"Comrade Istomin… I admire your loyalty and devotion to the Motherland, but understand this. If you do not return to base immediately, I will be forced to prevent you from flying this mission by any and all means available to me. For the Rodina's sake, boy, listen to me. Listen to me! Abort and return."

The static seemed to be screaming its own objections to all that was happening and all that was to come.

Istomin broke the silence.

"Kommando-dva. With regret, my orders are very specific. I cannot return to base without completing my mission. Out."

"Istomin!... Istomin!... Albatros!… answer me!…"

Nothing but static.

"Get him back! Get him back on the radio now!"

Even as he screamed at the operator, he gave the nod to the waiting officer, who leapt across another communications station, where the telephone was live to a number of senior officers across Europe.

The order they received was simple, if not bewildering, and not a little worrying.

266

Rumours of the events in Moscow had already started to circulate, and nothing really seemed out of the ordinary in the whirl of arrests and accusations that were already gathering momentum.

Not one refused the order.

Back in Moscow, a great deal had changed in the short time since the assassinations.

More and more evidence of the GRU's treachery had been uncovered; the wounded Rufin, and the Laberova twins, all of whom trumpeted long and loud about the culpability of their intelligence colleagues.

Reports of other deaths in Moscow, some even in the dacha district set aside for the Vlasti, the cream of Soviet society.

Khrushchev had slipped into position by stealth, issuing orders to one and all, organising the GKO meeting, appearing to be the man to come to for answers and orders, which inevitably made him the man to come to for answers and orders.

Kaganovich had spoken with Horrocks, who was on his way to the Swedish Embassy with a strong contingent of NKVD guards to ensure no interference in his passage.

His priority was to inform the Allies of the events in the Kremlin, assure them of good intentions, understanding of what was to come, and denials of responsibility for the potential strike of Soviet bombers, accompanied by oaths that all would be done to prevent the strikes.

For a few hours, the telephones and radios of Europe were crammed with more open talk and uncoded messages than the intelligence agencies could readily cope with.

And no one cared, for there were more important things at stake.

"No."

"But General… sir… you could give that order."

"Yes, Colonel Hood, I could give that order. I just happen to be choosing not give that goddamned order!"

Actually, neither of them were certain sure that Patton could give the order to stop the atomic missions as they were Presidential orders, but George Patton had already made his mind up that he would not do so in any case.

Hood pleaded his case again.

"Sir, everything's changed. With Stalin dea…"

"You've said it all already. Enough, Colonel! I will not cancel the missions. They were sent to avenge our people on the east coast, and I'll be damned if I'll stop them. Nothing's changed, except there's a new set of bastards in the Kremlin whose names we don't yet know… they'll still be communists, and still be the enemy. Nothing's changed, Colonel!"

The door opened, admitting a white-faced major.

"Sir, General, sir. Field Marshal McCreery on the line for you. Most urgent."

Patton went to pick up the receiver but stopped short, turning his gaze fully on Thomas Bell Hood.

"Confirm that the President has been informed… yes, I know… do it again. If he orders it, we'll have them stopped."

"Yes, Sir."

Hood doubled away, keen to afford Truman every opportunity to escalate the war.

"Field Marshal."

Patton listened with growing excitement.

"Where exactly?"

He clicked a finger at the major and mouthed the words 'map and 'Lithuania'.

The rustle of papers ended quickly as a large-scale map was slid onto Patton's desk.

"Right… right… I see… yep… what have you got for exploiting this?"

Patton made some notes on the side of the map, nodding more and more with each extra mark he made.

"Excellent. Go for it, and go for it hard. Experts have advised giving Vilnius a wide berth for a while… say twenty miles… but give your boys their head and see where this leads. I'll make sure the Krauts play their part… oh yes…eh?... what alternative?"

He sat down with a bump as the possibility McCreery laid out became a reality in his mind.

"If the Germans can do it… no, they'll do it… scrub the coast, forget that. I'll make sure you both get the supplies you need, and air force priority. Get your initial planning to me within two hours. I'll speak to Guderian, but he'll be on board with this or sacked, whichever is quickest."

He took his leave and went back to the switchboard.

"Field Marshal Guderian's office."

Patton looked at the waiting major.

"Son, go find General von Vietinghoff and get him in my office an hour ago."

Whilst he waited for the connection, Patton looked back at the map.

'Minsk... encirclement at Minsk... history has a way of repea...'

"Ah, Field Marshal Guderian. Patton here, Field Marshal, we have an opportunity."

Meanwhile, many hundreds of incursions were being mounted into Soviet airspace, in the main to mask the two that mattered.

The aircraft of Mission 2116 from Karup, and 2285 from Shaibah, flew inexorably on.

In Moscow, order started to establish itself, or what counted for order in the wake of the assassinations of two of the State's leading figures and the rounding up and summary executions of the majority of the senior officers of the State's military intelligence unit.

Khrushchev had assumed the reins by common assent, backed up by the sudden appearance of a few thousand men of the Moscow Military District under the command of fellow conspirator Gorbachev, who controlled his anger and disappointment at the death of Beria, a death he had claimed for himself.

Kaganovich seized full control of the NKVD with ease, and his backing went a long way to ensuring a relatively calm transfer of power into his comrades' hands.

1530 hrs, Tuesday, 15th April 1947, Missions 2116 and 2285, USSR.

Despite a glitch over permission to fly through Swedish airspace, as the Swedes baulked at allowing such a thing to fly over their territory, both missions went to schedule and the two atomic missions arrived over their targets.

The coordination was exceptional and the release of both weapons occurred within two minutes of each other.

Both targets had been selected for their symbolism to the Soviet people, and to the world at large.

The US bombers from Karup flew directly over Kotin Island, but at an increased altitude.

Using the unique horseshoe shape of the Institute of Finance and Economics as the aiming point, the lead B-29, 'Casey Jones III', placed its bomb on the money, as befitted a highly trained crew and top bombardier. The airburst occurred at roughly fifteen hundred feet above sea level and obliterated vast areas of the already damaged city of Leningrad.

The USAAF group based at RAF Shaibah used the large watercourse to bring themselves to the target, a notable and significant landmark and, importantly, one easily recognisable from the air.

Set to one side of the southern railway station, the grain elevator stood tall and proud, a symbol of the Soviet people's resilience and resistance.

The bomb exploded at an altitude of just under sixteen hundred feet and completed much of the destruction commenced by the German Sixth Army over six of the bloodiest months in mankind's military history.

Reports soon started to filter back to a Moscow already teetering under the hammer blows of the double assassination.

Leningrad and Stalingrad, icons of the Patriotic War and symbols of the resistance of the Soviet people, were ravaged beyond imagination.

One of the consequences of the reports from the two cities was a sea change in the minds of those who had ordered their fighters to intercept and destroy the Soviet bombers.

Most of the commanders decided, without consultation, that circumstances had now changed and called off their regiments.

Some sought further guidance, but getting through to someone in authority was difficult, as the lines to Moscow were clogged and confusion still reigned supreme.

Orders were modified to intercept but not attack, pending further instructions.

Only five fighter regiments kept their initial orders.

One of them found the northern group of the 901st over Lithuania, on its way to the prime target of Berlin.

Historians on both sides would debate long and hard as to whether what happened next made any great difference in the greater run of things.

Allied fighter squadrons would most probably have hacked the Soviet aircraft of the Northern Group from the sky long before they reached their target.

Certainly, the aircraft of the Southern group, targeted against Warsaw, were quickly destroyed by a concentrated Allied response. Their wreckage, including the unexploded carcass of Obiekt 901, the Soviet atomic bomb intended to lay waste to the Polish capital, littered the Polish countryside.

To the north, Obiekt 902 would claim many lives.

1610 hrs, Tuesday, 15th April 1947, Albatros-obucheniye-adin, over Lithuania.

"They're ours!"

"Proper reports, Alexey!"

"Sorry... Soviet fighters approaching, two o'clock low. Seven... no eight, Comrade Polkovnik."

Istomin moved his head, but could not see the approaching aircraft.

'Fighter cover or something sinister?'

Since the radio exchange with Buiansky, his mind had been doing cartwheels.

"Albatros-obucheniye-adin, Albatros-obucheniye-adin, this is Yaguar-krasny-adin. Respond, over."

"Comrade Polkovnik. The fighters are calling us. Should I respond?"

"No. Leave it to me."

Istomin nodded to Leonid Bolkovsky, who took a firmer grip on the co-pilot's controls.

"Yaguar-krasny-adin, Albatros-obucheniye-adin, receiving, over."

"Albatros-obucheniye-adin, you are ordered by Air Force High Command to abort your mission. I repeat, abort your mission. If you do not, I'm authorised to shoot you down. Over."

The last words were partially obscured by the whoosh of eight Klimov turbojets, as the brand new Yak-17 fighters of the 2nd Guards

271

Special Red Banner Order of Suvorov Fighter Aviation Regiment buzzed the bomber.

"Yaguar, Albatros, too close, far too close!"

He instinctively grabbed the controls as the jet wash caused the B-29 to buck and tremble.

The army officer returned to the flight deck, his face red and flustered for more reasons than the efforts he had just been making.

"Comrade Polkovnik, the bomb is armed. What the fuck's going on?"

Unlike the USAAF procedures, Istomin was the mission commander and the army officer was a pure functionary, who had just discharged his sole duty.

"Thank you, Comrade Mayor. Small difficulties with our escort. I suggest you find a seat and hang on tightly."

The co-pilot waited until the new man was safely out of earshot.

"What are we going to do, Sacha?"

"Our duty, Leonid... we've no choice. The Motherland is depending on us."

In the lead Yak-17, the regimental commander switched to his unit's frequency.

"Attention Yaguar, this is Yaguar-krasny-adin. Do not attack, repeat, do not attack. I'll try one last time, but if they don't turn, we shoot them all down. The Motherland is depending on us. Out."

He switched back and spoke again.

"Albatros, this is Yaguar. You know me, Sacha. You know I'll do this thing. You have to turn away. You've been given illegal orders. Please... I'm begging you. Turn away."

"Yaguar... you know I can't do that. You wouldn't do it either."

"I'll shoot you down, Sacha!"

"I **will** defend myself, Konstantin!"

"I know... but I'll still shoot you down, my friend."

The fighter pilot reached the depths of despair.

"Last chance... Yob tvoyu mat! I don't want to do this, Sacha! You leave me no choice!"

The Yaks turned away and broke up into groups, one group for each of the huge aircraft.

"Attack!"

The three supporting bombers opened fire, their crews having been silent witnesses to the radio conversation between the two friends.

As the Yaks closed in, the turret mounted 23mm cannons, installed in place of the original .50cal machine-guns, demonstrated the bomber crews' desire to remain airborne at all costs and protect their leader.

The first fighters aborted, easily dissuaded from their paths by tracer rounds, as their doubts were fertilised by the prospect of death or injury at the hands of comrades.

"Attention all Yaguar. Press home the attack. Shoot them down immediately!"

Answers came from some, silence from others, but the attack was renewed.

The trailing B-29 took numerous hits from the attacking fighter's own NS23 cannons, the experienced pilot walking his strikes up the fuselage, chewing apart metal and flesh as they went.

The bomber pilots died and the aircraft rolled over gently, prescribing a gentle arc on its way to the Lithuanian earth.

A six-aircraft flight of RAF Hornets showed up but decided to observe the spectacle of Soviet aircraft fighting each other whilst waiting on confirmation of the non-engagement policy and seeking clarification on how to respond to any perceived aggression.

A second B-29 burst into flames as a wing yielded to heavy hammer blows and its fuel tank caught fire.

One of the Yaks took some hits as Istomin's rear gunner saw an opportunity.

The brand new fighter wheeled away like a bird with a damaged wing, which was in essence correct. Beyond proper control, the pilot chose to eject as the airframe shuddered and started to disintegrate around him.

Two minutes later, Istomin's B-29 was alone, save for the circling Soviet fighter aircraft and the increasingly inquisitive Hornets of 65 Squadron RAF, whose orders were very specific but decidedly curious.

"Attention all Yaguars. Form up and shadow the Allied fighter aircraft. Do not intercept unless they interfere. Out."

The regimental commander lined up on Istomin's aircraft, choosing a rear quarter and lower angle to minimise the risk to himself.

Tracers flashed past his cockpit, showing the worth of his adversary.

He pulled the Yak away on a tight port turn and lined himself back up again, this time angling his approach even more.

His target dropped its left wing in a gentle turn, unmasking the upper turrets, which immediately brought him under fire.

'Mudaks... you're everything they say you are, Sacha.'

He rolled his aircraft away, feigning a retreat and then rolled back again, coming in under the turning B-29.

His cannon shells struck home, but the time did not permit a sustained burst and he flashed up and by the wounded bomber before he could cause mortal damage.

The gunners saw their opportunity and two shells struck the Yak as he turned away, deciding to cross past and under the nose of his adversary.

A piece of shrapnel stung his left calf and the rudder suddenly felt spongy and unresponsive.

'Yob tvoyu mat. You're a top crew... bastards...'

"Well done, Vanya, well done!"

The obvious hits on the attacker caused a round of noisy celebrations amongst the bomber's crew.

Istomin congratulated his gunner, although inside he felt confused and angry.

"He's coming in again, eight o'clock low... same plan?"

"No... he'll be ready... wait on my order... wait..."

Istomin snatched glances out of the window but couldn't see the attacking aircraft, so relied on the words of his fire controller.

"Wait..."

The controller gave distances and angles, all of which built a picture in Istomin's mind.

"Ready, Leonid?"

Bolkovsky hummed his response and grabbed the levers with both hands, tensed and waiting for the order.

The mental picture came together and Istomin shouted.

"Now!"

Bolkovsky pulled back on the throttles, and the bomber lost speed instantly.

In the Yak, Djorov, ready for another wing drop, miscalculated and overshot.

Three cannon shells struck his aircraft and he had less than a second to make the decision.

His reactions did not let him down and he rose into the cold air as the ejector seat did its job, pushing him up and out of the disintegrating aircraft.

Three seconds later, the Yak exploded dramatically, its wings seemingly flying independently for a few more seconds, almost as if they hadn't realised that the main fuselage had shredded into a hundred pieces.

The chair fell away and Djorov found himself dangling beneath white silk as the bomber flew inexorably on.

He also had a ringside seat as his regiment, angered by his loss and now devoid of any qualms, set about Istomin's B-29.

Istomin had reapplied power and somehow prevented the aircraft from stalling, but now had to cut two of the four engines as damage rendered them useless.

More reports assaulted his ears, as men died in the fuselage behind him, and the aircraft started to suffer fatal damage.

Many thoughts whirled through Istomin's mind.

'Bombs armed... if I drop it... can't bail out now... need distance... can we survive... bail out... yes, bail out now...'

"Commander to navigator... confirm we're over enemy territory."

"Confirmed, Comrade Polkovnik."

"Commander to crew. Abandon aircraft... abandon aircraft."

He turned to Bolkovsky who looked at him with mouth wide open.

"You too, Leonid... go on... we knew it was impossible... but we tried... now go..."

"No."

"I order you to go. Do not disobey me or I'll have you shot."

The weary smile on Istomin's face was greeted by a toothy grin from his co-pilot and friend.

"One final order. Make sure the people know what happened here today. Now... quickly... go..."

Bolkovsky saluted and moved away, following the flight engineer out of the hatch and into the air.

Istomin felt the aircraft shudder as another attack came in, more cannon shells striking home around the tail.

The top gunner's body was further desecrated as fire took hold in the rear compartment.

He increased the dive of his aircraft, picking up more speed, trying to put distance between himself and his crew.

Perhaps it was inevitable that it was Oligrevin that fired that fatal burst.

The shells ploughed into the port inner engine, wrecking it in the briefest of moments, and then chewed their way into the fuselage.

Istomin grunted as one shell struck him in the hip.

Had it exploded his life would have ended instantly, but it failed and, having struck the chair at the same time, simply expended its remaining energy burrowing its way into his flesh.

He screamed with pain but no one heard, the aircraft now deserted.

The B-29 fell away, lacking power enough to hold its own.

He tried everything, but nothing worked.

The fall from the sky accelerated and Istomin simply tried to stop the plane from disintegrating as best he could.

Regaining a modicum of control, he reached into his tunic pocket and slid out a cigarette, following it with the lighter.

He drew in the rich smoke and did his best to keep the wrecked B-29 under what counted for control.

Every now and then, his eyes flicked to the altimeter with little more than professional interest.

One thousand metres rapidly became nine hundred... became eight hundred...

"Yob tvoyu mat! Stop the plane, I want to get off!"

Istomin laughed as the altimeter passed six hundred metres.

He drew down on the cigarette, savouring the moment.

Five hundred metres...

"What a shitty way to go! Not a drink in sight! Goodbye, comrad..."

At four hundred and eighty-one metres, the barometric detonator informed Obiekt-902 that its moment of destiny had arrived.

Many miles behind the lines, the maintenance routine had been interrupted by the overhead display.

Two of the crew stayed in the tank to finish up some minor tasks, but commander and driver were outside and decidedly curious.

They had their binoculars firmly on the action above.

"So what the fuck's going on?"

Lazarus Wild considered his response for a nano-second.

"Fucked if I know, boss."

"Me either."

Silverside stuck his head out of the hatch.

"What's happening then?"

"Fucks knows, beefy."

Major Heywood arrived, drawn by the spectacle and seeing the two men perched on top of their tank.

"I say, Charles. What's happening then?"

Wild gave Lieutenant Charles an innocent look.

"There's a fucking parrot in here."

Charles giggled.

"What's that you say, Lieutenant?"

Glaring at Lazarus Wild, Charles decided on an informative approach.

"As best as we can make out, Sir… some American bombers on the way back from a mission got hit by some Russians brylcreems. Hit hard too, all four of them are down… that's the last coming to earth over there. What I don't get is that those other aircraft look like RAF Mosquitoes to me … or possibly the new Hornets to my driver…," he conceded to Wild, who had first spotted the twin-engine late-comers.

"Damn poor show if they didn't interfere though."

"Pardon, Sir?"

"I said it's a damn poor show if our boys didn't get stuck in."

Wild whispered out of the corner of his mouth.

"Told you there's a fucking parrot in here."

Lieutenant Andrew Charles cuffed his driver round the ear in mock punishment and laughed in spite of himself.

And then there was a flash of light…

… and they laughed no more.

He was sat alone, unusually withdrawn and quiet, the draft report covering the attacks on American soil in front of him, its pages covered with stark words about submarines, missiles, and death on an unprecedented level.

The reports of the successful dropping of bombs on Leningrad and Stalingrad had also reached him.

There had been no expectation of any problems, and the report was both delivered and received in a very matter-of-fact fashion.

Master Sergeant William George Meekes, his valet, poured the drink and placed it before his commander.

He sipped on his Calvados, a taste he had acquired since his time in Normandy. It was earlier than normal, but he felt the need for its calming influence in his veins.

Unusually for George S. Patton, he felt nervous, doubts gnawing away at his confidence.

The orders to push forward had flowed from his headquarters, and his commanders were doing an excellent job, thus far.

The phone rang.

"Patton."

Guderian's strident tones assaulted his ear, the excited voice revealing success in the downing of one of the Soviet atomic attacks.

"Thank you, Field Marshal. Good day."

'One down...'

He sipped the calvados again, drawing strength from the burn in his throat.

"General?"

"Yes, George?"

"You ok, Sir?"

Patton examined the amber liquid as he considered his response.

Meekes had been with him since Noah parked his boat on Ararat, or so it seemed, so already knew his commander was troubled.

He decided to come clean.

"George... I'm a cavalry general... my sort of war was fought against the Krauts... and is being fought now. Until this moment... from this moment I believe war has changed... we've changed it... the commies have changed it."

278

He took a healthy sip of the Norman apple brandy.

"War in the future will not be on the battlefield, not as we know it... yes, the bombers laid waste to the cities of our enemies... and London took some heavy hits... but there was a chance... a possibility that the bomber wouldn't get through... and what it brought was a bomb... yes, yes... I know the bombs got bigger... but now..."

Patton looked up, engaging his valet with a mournful eye.

"What I know is that war will now be brought to the heartland of every nation in a most horrible fashion, and there'll be no defence against it... and the front line soldier will become an anachronism... a throwback to another time... there'll be no place for dinosaurs like me in times to come."

Meekes remained quiet, unsure how to deal with the unusually melancholy Patton.

He drained his glass and refused the top up Meekes offered.

"Shit... least I had my time, eh George?"

"Yes sir, General, sir."

A knock interrupted the pity party, and the door opened on a white-faced Colonel Hood.

"General."

He handed the report to his commander and shared eye contact with Meekes, silently seeking understanding of the strange atmosphere in the room.

"Goddamnit!"

Patton skim read it and then once more, but slower taking in the details of McCreery's horrendous initial assessment.

A Soviet device had detonated just to the southwest of Alytus in Lithuania.

Civilian casualties seemed to be extreme, particularly as a refugee camp had been established almost directly underneath the explosion.

The nearby British Guards Armoured and much of the 55th Division had simply disappeared whilst resting and refitting near the Lithuanian town.

An ammunition store had exploded, adding to the wholesale destruction wrought by the Soviet device.

A footnote recorded that a flight of RAF Hornet aircraft had simply disappeared after reporting Soviet fighters and bombers in close quarter combat with each other.

279

"Colonel... I need more information before I speak to the President. Get this firmed up a-sap. Get Arthur Tedder to find out the air story. Get back to the Field Marshal and get me more information."

Hood virtually flew out of the room.

Leaning back in his chair, Patton breathed out, long and hard.

"Guess I'll have that refill now, George."

Truman replaced the receiver and breathed out, long and hard.

"Well, gentlemen... it seems that the Soviets were good to their word and stopped...or at least tried to stop their bombers."

He moved around the Resolute Desk and sat on a chair placed at the head of the two sofas.

"Seems that the Lithuanian explosion was caused when a bomber they shot down exploded as it was coming down."

There were more sighs of relief from the assembled grandees.

"Thank God for that, Mister President!"

"Amen to that, Henry."

Stimson wiped his brow and continued.

"So, we'll not be retaliating to this attack?"

Truman steepled his fingers before answering.

"Well... we've batted this around for some while now... and with the confirmation, I believe the next step lies firmly with those in charge in Moscow... whoever they may now be."

The nods and hums of agreement stopped as Truman continued.

"But... it would be imprudent of us not to take steps to protect ourselves and our Allies. I will be ordering our atomic forces to prepare for further action. Failure to do so could leave us open. None of us wishes for this exchange to continue, but we must not allow ourselves to be found wanting here."

The rollercoaster of decision-making carried them back down into a dip from the peak of Patton's confirmation.

"Do you agree, gentlemen?"

There were no dissenters, and the order went out and the politicians went their separate ways.

Their plans quickly changed and they were ordered to return with all speed.

Twenty minutes later, they were back in the Oval Office, listening to a broadcast from the other side of the world.

"Socialist Comrades! Citizens of the Union of Soviet Socialist Republics! Soldiers! Sailors! Airmen! Workers! And to you in other countries who are listening to my words! By now you will have heard rumours and stories."

"You will understand that if I, Nikita Sergeyevich Khrushchev, am addressing you that, sadly, there is truth in what you have heard."

"I must report to you all that our leader, Iosef Vissarionovich Stalin, is dead."

"The General Secretary and Generalissimus was killed in a plot devised by, and carried out with great efficiency by, members of the Glavnoye Razvedyvatel'noye Upravleniye... the GRU... an organisation that has clearly gone rotten from its very foundations to the very top of its structure!"

Khrushchev spoke with deliberate slowness, but he still knew how to milk a crowd, so his voice could not help but emphasise certain words and come to the sort of climax designed to incite feelings among his audience.

"The full details of this heinous crime will be revealed to you in due course... and I promise you, on my sacred oath to the Motherland, that there will be nothing hidden. We will strip bare this conspiracy and ensure that you are all informed as to who is responsible for this madness... this... this... atrocity against the Rodina!"

His voice became hardened, conspiratorial, and yet almost embracing of the listener, as if he was speaking to each individual in their own home.

"I already know... no ... we already know many of those who devised this abomination... and the decay goes deeper than you could begin to imagine, Comrades."

Khrushchev exchanged looks with the men sat to one side of him, looks that betrayed nothing and gave no indication of the depth of betrayal the three were responsible for, both of their leadership and subsequently those who they suborned to their plan and sacrificed to shift blame from themselves.

Zhukov and Kaganovich just sat silently, listening to words they had already heard. More accurately, had a hand in writing.

"For the moment we must look to the Motherland and set aside our grief and anger. We are a country at war, and that war does not stop because a faction within us decided to act in gross fashion, against the figurehead of our country and party."

"I have taken charge until a new leader can be properly decided upon. That is with the assent of our leadership in the Council of Ministers and other senior political officials."

"My immediate decision, following the arrest of Comrade Bulganin, is to replace him as Minister of the Armed Forces with someone familiar to you all; Comrade Marshal Zhukov."

"With the death of Marshal Beria, his deputy, Polkovnik General Kaganovich, is placed in temporary but full command of the NKVD, and he will be responsible to me... and to you, for a full and thorough investigation of these events."

Across the world, the new appointments were already being analysed, although the listeners in certain places, namely OSS and MI6 offices in Washington and London, heard no great surprises, save for the arrest of Bulganin.

"The GKO has met and I can tell you that we intend to seek an armistice on favourable terms as soon as is practicable, and from a position of strength."

"There are matters here which cannot yet be discussed with you, but they will, I assure you... and the recent exchanges of atomic weapons between the two sides have proven that both sides possess the capacity to inflict huge damage and casualties on the other."

"We, the USSR and her people, are a peace loving country, and undoubted victims of this latest aggression."

He could not hear the howls of derision in the cities on the other side of No Man's Land.

"But that must not prevent us from acting to end the bloodshed, in the best interests of all mankind!"

In Whitehall, a fit of complete pique saw fine crystal and cognac smash into the wall adjacent to the radio, which was very un-Winston like behaviour.

"There is no order that will inhibit the Red Army and all its forces... nothing will tie the hands of our soldiers until an armistice is agreed. There is no other way, or our enemies could choose to exploit our genuine quest for world peace."

In Whitehall, Churchill's valet, Frank Sawyers, withheld the replacement cognac until he was sure Churchill's rant was over.

"I know you will all have questions, but I hope you understand that there is much work to do before the Motherland can feel settled and safe again. Arrangements for a fitting funeral for our leader will be announced in due course."

Again, he caught their eye. It was a regrettable need that they would have to afford Stalin a state funeral, rather than throw his body on some stinking midden and piss all over it, which had been Gurundov's contribution to the discussion on a proper and fitting disposal.

"I ask you, the people... my comrades... and our allies too, stay strong and resilient in the face of this shocking news... stay strong whilst your party leadership brings about calm and understanding... stay strong whilst we ensure that the Rodina is unthreatened and can soon return to peace and prosperity."

The radio broke into the national anthem, and those who did not immediately start singing might have caught the sound of Nikita Khrushchev himself joining in.

'United forever in friendship and labour,
Our mighty republics will ever endure.
The Great Soviet Union will live through the ages.
The dream of a people their fortress secure.
Long live our Soviet motherland,
Built by the people's mighty hand.
Long live our people, united and free.
Strong in our friendship tried by fire.
Long may our crimson flag inspire,
Shining in glory for all men to see. '

The net effect on the world was one of shock and relief, mainly the latter, as the new administration, no matter how temporary it might be, committed the USSR and her allies on a path to peace.

Although, in one German city, the effect of Khrushchev's words had more of a galvanising effect upon a man who commanded millions of soldiers and had the will to use them.

With the tears a land hath shed,
Their graves should forever be green.

Thomas Bailey Aldrich.

CHAPTER 206 - THE ARMISTICE

Europe

Patton pushed his forces hard, determined to make the greatest possible advances in the days ahead, encouraged by Khrushchev's unprecedented radio broadcast and by the stunning progress of the Pacific forces.

The weakened Red Army resisted valiantly, but the effect of a potential end to the fighting encouraged even courageous men to think more of the years to come than the immediate hours ahead and fighting for something no longer attainable.

In truth, many of the Allies also saw little point in risking life and limb for a few kilometres of foreign soil, all save the Germans and Poles, for whom matters were fresh and personal.

In particular, the German resilience and desire to wage the war to its fullest extent was incredible given the suffering the nation had already endured, or inflicted upon itself, depending on how the beholder saw matters or, indeed, what they actually knew.

The British had certainly had enough, the immolation of two divisions in Lithuania to nothing more than happenstance being the final straw.

The Allied drive petered out, despite Patton's threats and bluster, and even those were stilled once Truman flew to Amsterdam, where a hastily convened summit of Allied leaders reeled the American warrior in on a short leash, virtually ending the fighting without a proper agreement in place.

No little part was played by Allied intelligence services, who played the middleman in communications between them and the new hierarchy in the Soviet Union.

In Camp Vär, again the site of the negotiations, the weariness of both sides was only equalled by the genuine willingness to search for a swift, long-lasting, and peaceful solution.

Truman and Churchill had only been in the Netherlands for two days before the call came from Sweden.

Peace... on terms that had been on the table many weeks previously... and which would have settled matters then to everyone's satisfaction... without the hundreds of thousands, possibly millions, who had died in the interim.

The other leaders were consulted and the agreement was unanimous, although muted from Polish and German quarters.

Amongst the relief there was genuine anger, either openly expressed or kept hidden within, often tempered by direct knowledge of what actually occurred on those days in the middle of March.

Whilst most of the world gave thanks for their deliverance, some made oaths... promises to friends both living and dead.

The war would claim more lives, well past the date that the signatures dried.

1511 hrs, Thursday, 17th April 1947, Röszke, Hungary.

16th/5th Lancers had experienced a decidedly mixed sort of war.

Caught up in the Soviet advance into Northern Italy during the early days of the war, they had suffered heavy casualties as they battled to stop the Red Army's momentum.

Withdrawn from the front line for rest and refit, 6th Armoured Division found itself only engaged piecemeal, and the Lancers avoided much of the heavy combat as the forces edged towards the ceasefire and the fighting that followed the renewed combat.

It was only in the last three days of fighting that 16th/5th suffered again, and that was precious little compared to what had gone before.

Two of their tanks had been knocked out by tenacious Soviet anti-tank gunners, and another had lost a track to Yugoslavian forces keen to enforce their borders.

Five men were killed or wounded in the two incidents, and they proved to be almost the last casualties that the 16th/5th, indeed the 6th Armoured Division, suffered in the war.

Only one more man was lost before the division returned home.

Following the burial service, the Lancers' commanding officer decided to visit the unit nearest the Yugoslavian border.

286

Their casualty was in the hospital, so none had attended the funeral for the three men from B Squadron's 3rd Troop.

Lieutenant Colonel 'Biffo' Haines decided to go and surprise his old crew, so jumped into his armoured scout car.

Regimental command had consigned him to the small vehicle and removed him from the protection of his tank.

Biffo's Bus, or the third version of it since Majano, was sat in laager by the Madarász-tó, a lake some two hundred metres from the Yugoslavian border.

His arrival brought the military norms of salutes and shouting NCOs which, as was Biffo's unconventional style, rapidly gave way to the joy and handshakes of the momentous times they had survived to experience.

In turn, that gave way to the more raucous pleasures enjoyed by men who had shared hardships and perils together, as the Colonel met with his former crew.

Something unpronounceable appeared and was spilt into their mugs, and the reunited team raised their drinks to many things, proposed in turn and drunk to heartily.

Clair, now a CSM and commanding the tank, encouraged the new boy to drink more readily.

Lawrence Gage was seventeen and ten months, but looked much younger.

"You sure he's old enough, Sarnt Major?"

"I begin to wonder, Sir."

Another voice interjected.

"I swear I found a fucking rattle in the tool box the other day, boss."

Cooke kept his face straight as Gage howled.

"It's not mine!"

The old timers laughed and drank some more.

"Well, we survived… thank fuck. 'Spect the Generals won't be letting us go home yet… not anytime soon… not after the last balls up."

Cooke wiped his hand across his mouth.

"Any chance of it kicking off again, Boss?"

Haines considered his answer, assisted by another swig of the colourless liquid.

"My money's on not. Mind you, thought it was over last time… but this time we've fucked them up real bad. I don't think it'll kick off again, least not for years… until some bastard further up the food chain forgets the cost of his decisions and we all do it again."

The low murmurs of agreement showed what they thought of those who made such choices.

"Anyway, I'm off to see our young friend. Got promoted, he did."

"What to? Private?"

Haines cocked an eyebrow at Cooke.

"I can send you to that exalted position in an instant if you like?"

"Nah. I think I'll keep the extra couple of bob, if it's all the same to you, boss."

"Sergeant then, is he?"

"Actually, he bumped straight up to CSM, Sarnt Major."

Clair tried to imagine the man that had fought alongside them in the Gail Valley as an equal rank.

He failed, despite rehearsing the title in his mind.

'Company Sergeant Major Powell… no fucking way!'

"Well, pass on our congratulations and find out whose ass he kissed to get that."

"Not mine… but they think very highly of him over in A Squadron."

Clair laughed, ready for more banter at Powell's expense.

"He's doing well. To be honest, I think they bumped him up to keep him out of my claws."

"Like you want that wanker back, eh Boss?"

"Not a chance!"

Banter aside, they would have welcomed Powell back in an instant.

Haines came to his feet, and his former tank crew rose with him.

"Fuck formalities! Give me your hand, Gary… Malcolm… yes even you, young Larry. We've seen it through. We'll make it home. Good luck and let's make sure we meet up for a bonzo when we're back in Blighty, eh?"

"Too true, Boss!"

Haines slapped the two old timers on the shoulders and took his leave.

Twenty minutes later, he arrived at 'A Squadron's headquarters.

He missed CSM Gary Powell's death by six minutes.

288

Although the mortar shell had not killed the NCO outright, the shredding of his legs and severe lower body injuries meant he dwelt in the land of the living just long enough for a medic to fill his collapsing system with morphine to ease him over the last few difficult moments.

Gary Powell was the last but one Allied soldier to die to enemy action, albeit a round fired accidentally by a sixteen-year-old Yugoslavian recruit practising with his mortar platoon; the last man to die still had five more months to live.

The Yugoslavian CO crossed the divide to apologise and display the culprit's body.

A few minutes after the ambulance took Powell's body away, the unofficial truce declared by commanding officers along the frontline became an official reality, and the guns were silenced once more.

Those who experienced the growing quiet hoped it would be forever.

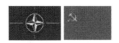

The venue had been easy to agree upon, the purpose-built facility at Camp Vár more than suitable for the ceremony, and also considered a fair tribute to the Swedes who had always made their land available to give negotiations for peace a chance.

For the Allies, the main signatories were Patton and McCreery, backed up by delegations from all the Allied nations.

On the opposite side of the table sat Zhukov and Malinin, reunited for the task of putting their signatures to a document that would return Europe almost precisely to the political borders of 1st September 1939.

There were a few differences, of course.

The Polish access to the Baltic was now set in stone, and there was some tinkering along the thousands of miles south to the Caspian Sea, but to all intents and purposes, millions more people had died for nothing more than the whims of their masters and the honour of their country, such as honour is claimed in times of conflict.

The copies circulated and were signed in turn.

The last was signed and blotted dry at 1518 hrs precisely.

According to the stated terms, the war was officially ended at 1800 hrs on Thursday, 17th April 1947.

According to the soldiers in the trenches and armoured vehicles, it already had.

Applause broke out, some enthusiastic, some muted by the memories of those lost en route to this memorable point.

The two delegations stood and moved around the table.

Malinin and McCreery shook hands first.

Patton and Zhukov engaged cautiously, the little engagement between them in the time running up to the ceremony having been unimpressive to either man.

"General Patton."

"Field Marshal Zhukov. I hope you get your country sorted out so this thing sticks."

Patton found himself half-meaning it.

Zhukov waited whilst the interpreter gave meaning to the American's words.

"This will stick, as you put it, General. We have no wish for further bloodshed."

Patton nodded, not wholly convinced by the interpreter's monotone delivery.

"You know, Field Marshal... you were lucky."

Zhukov frowned at the tone, and his brow furrowed more when the words were translated.

He spoke rapidly to the interpreter and came to attention, reeling Patton off an immaculate salute before moving on to McCreery.

The interpreter looked uncomfortable.

"Shoot then, son."

"Err..."

"Word for word."

"Comrade Marshal Zhukov said... err... we were all fucking lucky, Comrade General."

Later on, when the tensions had mainly departed, the delegations mixed together, or what counted for mixing between disparate military groups that had recently been trying to kill each other.

A Soviet officer accosted Ramsey and took him off to one side.

"Comrade Polkovnik."

"Mayor... err?"

"Rikardova in this uniform if you please."

290

"Mayor Rikardova. We meet under less trying circumstances."

"Yes, Your Russian really is excellent."

"Hardly, but it is improving."

"I have someone who wishes to speak with you. Please come with me."

She grabbed him by the waist and they moved off.

One or two noticed their departure, assuming from their demeanour and closeness, that the armistice was to be approved in a more comradely and sweaty fashion.

Rikardova, feigning sexual interest in Ramsey, used her closeness to keep her eyes moving in all directions.

Satisfied that there was no undue attention, she steered him towards a side room.

The door opened when she knocked and Ramsey found himself in the presence of Marshal Georgy Zhukov.

"Comrade Polkovnik Ramsey."

The Englishman was caught in two minds, whether to throw up a salute or accept the offered hand.

His arm movement adapted and made the salute into a move forward to take Zhukov's hand in his.

It was firm, the sort of handshake that indicates sincerity and honour.

"I've little time or I'll be missed. I wanted to meet you as you were Nazarbayeva's contact. Without you... and she... much of this would not have been possible."

"Thank you, Marshal Zhukov. It's such a shame that she could not enjoy the fruits of your efforts... her efforts. She was a very fine woman."

"Yes, she was."

For a moment, Ramsey suspected he saw moisture in Zhukov's eyes.

"What happened, Sir?"

"She blew the bastards up, but was shot immediately afterwards."

Ramsey decided to ask the question that had been burning him the moment he saw Zhukov.

"Yes... the reports I heard stated that you shot her yourself, Marshal."

Zhukov shrugged.

"A lie… a simple necessity for the people. It made me look good publically and helped our move into power. Actually, a guard killed her, but died in the process. Unfortunately, she cannot be honoured openly for her sacrifice."

Handshakes can lie.

"I understand, Sir."

"She lies in an unmarked grave, away from the sights and sounds of men. The best I could do for now."

"I understand, Sir. We hear that you've destroyed the GRU? Purged as conspirators?"

Again, Zhukov shrugged.

"Our people have need of people to blame. The GRU provided that… and that's strengthened our position more. This can only be good for the prospects of peace between us."

"I sincerely hope that is true, Sir."

"As do I, Polkovnik Ramsey. Your Russian is excellent by the way."

"Thank you, Sir."

"Now, I must go before I'm missed."

This time they saluted formally and Zhukov swept out of the room.

Ramsey stood staring at the wall.

"We shall have to wait for a while."

"Of course, Mayor Rikardova."

They sat down opposite each other and their eyes locked.

"Tell me… did he just lie to me?"

"About what?"

"About Nazarbayeva?"

Rikardova pursed her lips as she considered her reply very carefully.

"No."

The word was spoken in a tone and wrapped in a facial expression that revealed her thoughts on the matter.

Patton had long since taken his leave for reasons that everyone present interpreted with differing degrees of accuracy, although almost all started with the probability that Patton was decidedly pissed that the war had ended before he had covered himself with enough glory.

The evening wore on and the celebrations grew more muted as the Swedish hosts' liquid provisions were consumed at an alarming rate, consigning many a hardened drinker to a corner chair or sometimes the floor, worse the wear at best, insensible at worst.

Horrocks and Zhukov, more controlled as befitted their senior status, had gravitated towards each other, more by dint of a shared language than anything else.

Of all things, they were discussing the Market-Garden operation, and both of them were being less than complimentary about Montgomery and his master plan to end the war by Christmas.

Ramsey drew close to take his leave but Horrocks reeled him in.

"Comrade Marshal, may I introduce my aide, Polkovnik John Arthurevich Ramsey, twice holder of the Victoria Cross."

Zhukov rose to his feet and extended a hand.

"Polkovnik Ramsey, your fame proceeds you."

"I'm flattered, Marshal. Thank you."

"Not at all. Know your enemy. I read of your actions in Northern Germany. Your leg?"

"Legs, Sir."

He rapped each in turn.

Zhukov nearly gave the game away in his surprise.

"I had no idea. You move so... err... naturally."

"Practice, Marshal Zhukov. It comes with practice... plus... your own specialists have made the prosthetics so much better, I owe them a debt of thanks."

"Excellent, Please... sit."

Zhukov then proceeded to switch to full military mode, and talked the Battle of Barnstorf through with Ramsey, using details that made the Englishman wonder if the Russian had been there on the field, walking the same German grass as he all those months ago.

They debated points, talked around the 'what ifs' until Zhukov sat back.

"The aircraft... always the aircraft."

"Yes, Marshal. And he was a very brave man."

Zhukov nodded.

"It was a time for brave men, was it not?"

"Yes, sir."

"And our Polkovnik earned his cross there, did he not, General?"

Horrocks nodded as Zhukov brought him into the conversation.

"I believe he did, Marshal... and in unusual circumstances, too."

"Oh?"

Horrocks moved forward in his seat.

"Very unusual. The recommendation came from one of your officers."

"Mudaks! Really? Tell me more, Polkovnik Ramsey."

And he did, telling the story of Arkady Yarishlov down to the finest detail, starting with the first meeting at the US divisional exercise before hostilities started, all the way through to their meetings in Moscow.

"That is some story, General."

Horrocks could only agree.

"I've not heard it all until today either, Marshal."

Ramsey considered he had earned the right, so spoke again.

"Sir, if I may. I would love to know how he's doing. I know he was promoted and heading off to a warmer climate. That's all. It would be good to see him again sometime."

"I'll see what I can find out."

Which from the man who commanded the Red Army most certainly meant 'the information will be with you shortly'.

Not wishing to outstay his welcome, Ramsey rose and offered a salute to both officers, which Zhukov returned from the sitting position, not wholly trusting his legs for the task.

Again, he offered his hand.

"Thank you, Comrade Polkovnik Ramsey. We will meet again, I've no doubt."

The aching British Colonel was just finishing his breakfast when an orderly disturbed him.

A messenger had arrived with a letter addressed to Ramsey.

It was from Zhukov.

True to his promise, it contained news of Yarishlov.

The words slowly came to life as his reading skills were challenged, but they revealed some details of the attempted NKVD arrest, and of Yarishlov's resistance.

After rereading the message, Ramsey returned to the Embassy foyer, where the messenger was waiting.

He was surprised to find it was a full Colonel of the Red Army.

"Polkovnik. I apologise. I did not know the messenger was an officer."

"There's no issue, Polkovnik Ramsey."

"Will you please thank the Marshal from me? Tell him I will mourn the loss of this fine man and friend, a soldier who was a credit to your country."

"I will do so immediately, Polkovnik Ramsey."

"Thank you."

1902 hrs, Thursday, 17th April 1947, Friedrich-Ebert-Strasse, temporary government building #1, Magdeburg, Germany.

"Our venture has failed."

"Yes and no, Herr Kanzler."

"How not?"

"They've taken huge hits. Through the use of the new atomic weapons, upon their capacity to manufacture, financially, manpower, and, perhaps more importantly, their psychological perception of their own invincibility."

"But we have not expanded... the Czech lands aren't ours... you have not secured the Baltic States... how..."

"That was the best we could hope for. Our Allies would have made us concede it all back... surely you knew they would?"

Władysław Raczkiewicz, his health failing but still mentally sharp, pressed home his views.

"Our nations have set aside our recent differences and we have secured our joint future. Our mutual enemy is crippled. Our mutual Allies equally so, from what I can see. Yes, as are we… our countries have sustained great losses, but we are also probably best placed to recover from them."

A bout of coughing ended his speech temporarily, and Speer pushed a carafe of water towards the Polish president.

"Thank you. Our allies will use us as a buffer between East and West, and they will build us strong… you mark my words now. They will rebuild our nations as a priority… to act as a bulwark… a version of the Great Wall pointing the other way. I think you need to remember, Herr Kanzler, where your country was two years ago, eh? Defeated and in ruins, with no place conceivable in Europe for a generation, if not longer. And now, your army is restored, and it's almost like all is forgiven and forgotten in the rush to stop the Communists."

"Yes… yes… I know… but they're not defeated."

"I think they are, in everything but marking our own victory with a parade through the Red Square."

"They're cowed, that's all."

"Cowed is a victory as well, is it not?"

"Possibly, but it's not enough… it's not what we risked so much for."

"So what do you want? The original goals are unattainable… were probably always unattainable. What is it that you want now, Herr Kanzler?"

Speer told him.

The old Pole closed his eyes and a quote from Berthold Brecht popped into his mind

'Don't rejoice in his defeat, you men. For though the world stood up and stopped the bastard, the bitch that bore him is in heat again.'

"No."

"No?"

"No, Herr Kanzler. Enough."

And with those simple words, the biggest risk to a continued peace evaporated.

It took precious little time for the soldiers to start flooding home and the sea-lanes were full of vessels taking weary men back to their loved ones.

Of course, the hunt for the submarines responsible for the attacks on mainland USA continued, but none were ever located until long after the war had ended, save for 'Soviet Initsiativa'.

After an incredible one hundred and twenty day voyage from the Black Sea to the United States and home, the Type XXI arrived in Murmansk on 30th June 1947.

Kalinin was arrested but subsequently released, as the need for further reprisals against the dissident factions that had brought the Motherland to the brink of oblivion receded as the conspirators tightened their control.

Khrushchev and his band of plotters had played every card possible to sully the reputation of the GRU and certain old school politicians, even revealing to the Soviet people that the destruction at Vilnius, Kiev, and Odessa was home grown, initiated by men long dead and beyond further punishment, although the blame was not placed on the heads of those truly accountable. As ever, the political needs overwhelmed the truth of the matter.

The border between the two armies was dormant, with no more than the occasional understandable excursion or exchange to ruffle local feathers.

Casualties were more often than not civilian, shot or blown up on mines, often for nothing more than trying to see loved ones on the other side of the divide.

Patton returned home to his ticker tape parade, accompanied by men of the armies that he had commanded in the field.

The 2nd Rangers formed part of that parade, without Lukas Barkmann, whose soldiering days were long over.

Men of the 12th US Armored Division, led by their indomitable general, John L. Pierce, marched with heads held high, their division having been awarded the most Presidential Unit Citations in the European theatre during the new war.

At the end of the parade came the soldiers that had so recently caught the imagination of the American public.

The mission to Uspenka and Camp 1001 had become known, and the authorities had decided to milk everything they could from its heroic success, or failure, depending on how it was represented in the press.

Hughes, Odekirk, and Petrali accompanied the parade, each pushed in their wheelchairs by a man of the 1st SSF.

Leading the parade of the survivors of the 1st Special Service Force was America's latest hero, a soldier who was being spoken of as the best of the best and the most fightingest soldier of the war.

Colonel Marion J. Crisp marched with pride, surrounded by his officers and followed by his NCOs and men, all stepping out with military precision, but yet somehow still managing that special gait belonging to men who had seen and done that which most could not imagine.

Perhaps the only exception was Ferdinand Sunday, who was incapable of anything but a precise parade ground march of the most impeccable kind.

Two rows behind Crisp marched the lofty figure of Charley Bluebear. Each step provoked the memory of the wounds sustained on the banks of the Volga, but he marched with purpose and pride none the less.

1st SSF later paraded at the White House, where a considerable number of its soldiers received awards directly from the hands of President Truman himself.

Perhaps, finally, justice was done when the Medal of Honor was slipped over Crisp's head for his actions at Uspenka, when many had thought it should have been placed there a number of times before.

The day marked the final official act of the force and it was disbanded the following morning, following a fine and emotional speech by the latest recipient of the MoH.

Rewards were distributed across the spectrum of combatant nations, some deserving, some less so and more of a sop to political pressure, or as a result of 'old boys' influences.

Rossiter was bumped up the rankings and found himself in command of OSS as a Major General.

Megan Jenkins and her team received recognition for their superb contributions throughout the hostilities, and she again visited the palace, this time to receive a well-earned DSC from the hands of the King.

In the Soviet Union, the taste for military matters waned considerably and, although the warriors were still feted, the rhetoric faded and political priorities turned to rebuilding the nation, both physically and mentally, and to repairing relationships abroad.

The Czechoslovakian troubles rumbled on, killing and maiming in the name of one political cause or another, or in some cases, purely for local rivalry and paying off old scores.

With the full agreement of Allied governments, who sought no further casualties among their own forces, and who also employed the concession as a tool to secure no further mention of the rumours regarding the renewal of the war, the Soviet Union was permitted to intercede militarily.

The USSR's forces brought peace the region, restoring some of its prestige in the process and, much to the later chagrin of other nations, restoring Soviet influence and strengthening the communist's hand in the country.

2359 hrs, Sunday, 4th May 1947, House of Madame Fleriot, La Vigie, Nogent L'Abbesse, near Reims, France.

The bullet fired on the 13th March that year finally completed its work.

Despite the feelings of pain and nausea, Armande Fleriot soldiered on without complaint.

The stiffness restricted her movement but still she dressed herself and continued with her daily routine, and never did a word of complaint or a stifled moan escape her lips.

Perhaps, had she done so, she might have lived.

The previous day the latent infection in her wound had burst forth into her system and taken her from her feet to her bed in less than an hour.

She refused to be moved to hospital and the infection raged through her body until she conceded the unequal struggle.

She found comfort in the fact that she died holding Jerome's hand, her last breath passing a few seconds before the hall clock struck the midnight hour although, in truth, Armande Valerie Capucine Fleriot died alone.

299

1356 hrs, Tuesday, 20th May 1947, Église de Saint-Martin, Berru, France.

The ceremony was formal, high church, and seemed interminable to some present, mostly those nursing some wound or other as a token of the recent conflict.

The organ struck up her favourite piece of music, the finale from Saint-Säens Organ Symphony, a piece of music as inspiring to the listeners as the former Deux agent had been in life.

Men of the Legion and SDECE had carried her coffin into the old stone church, and now carried it back out into the cobbled forecourt.

With studied care they returned it to the horse-drawn hearse for the journey back to her home, where she would be laid to rest, according to her wishes.

The attendees watched as the horses pulled their treasured load away for the one and half kilometre journey to Armande Fleriot's home.

On some unheard order, they moved off towards their own vehicles, ready to follow on.

Over the murmur of voices keeping a respectful tone and volume, the sound of an infant in need of food rose loud and strong.

"This one needs feeding. You'll have to start without me."

"Yes, Cherie."

Anne-Marie Knocke comforted the child by tutting and rocking gently as the staff car pulled away.

"Not the way I imagined."

"Sorry, Cherie?"

"Not the way I imagined... this... Armande..."

She reached out a comforting hand and laid it on his leg.

"I know, Cherie. But at least you're home... home in time for her... for little Jürgen ... the girls... and for me."

He squeezed his woman's hand and leant to one side, ignoring the sudden pain, and planted a tender kiss on her cheek.

"Yes. I'm home... and home to stay."

Ernst-August Knocke even meant it, except for the one final mission that he, and he alone, would undertake.

300

"To Armande!"

The specially assembled guests raised their glasses to the memory of the indefatigable old lady.

The other mourners had long since departed, but those who remained had done so at Knocke's bidding and were already set to the purpose to which he was now dedicated.

Knocke nodded and they all sat, their chairs arranged in a tight group, all the better to hear the low voices with which they intended to conduct their business.

"Thank you all for coming today. She would have loved seeing all of you here."

They nodded courteously to Anne-Marie, who immediately ceded prime position to her husband.

"I echo those words, and also thank you for attending this meeting. I think Armande would understand the necessary subterfuge and probably encourage it!"

There was no doubt she would have joined the conspiracy in an instant.

"You all know why I've asked you to be here... sorry... we've asked you to be here."

He senses rather than saw Anne-Marie's involuntary bristling.

"When we spoke previously, or you spoke with my wife, you were agreed. Is anyone feeling differently now?"

He looked from face to face for any sign that the owner doubted the undertaking ahead.

Haefali's face burned brightly, as bright as it had done those weeks ago in Poland.

Braun and Durand, thick as thieves, nodded formally at the enquiring eyes.

Lavalle, his old friend, sat alongside the poker-faced Ribiere, his new one, simply smiled.

Hässelbach, not feeling out of his depth in the high-ranked company, was the only one to speak.

"They have it coming, Oberführer."

Knocke shared a look of satisfaction with Anne-Marie before deferring to Ribiere.

301

"Mes Amis. What you propose to undertake will take careful planning, and is not without pitfalls and dangers, as you will all know. However, I can help... will help. This is what I know now. I will find out everything else we need soon enough."

He moved to the blackboard and started to record names and information.

"No notes, please. Memorise what you need... only what you need."

Each notation also had the name of one of those present, save Lavalle and de Montgomerie.

Braun moaned loudly.

"Nothing for me at all, Herr Ribiere?"

"Nor for me?"

Anne-Marie sounded both hurt and angered by the lack of information in her zone and shared a look with Braun, who was in a similar predicament.

"It will come, mes braves! Intelligence takes time to develop. Look at what we have already, eh?"

It was a fair point.

He turned to face Knocke.

"For you, the situation is a lot more complicated... but I have a possible solution. I need time to explore the possibilities. Are you all still intent on this symbolic timing?"

The Swiss Legion officer's exasperation was laid bare in his words and tone.

"Monsieur Ribiere, we've manufactured the circumstances where we're all free for this task around that date. If you can get the information we need, why wait?"

Haefali made a fair point.

"Fine. Anyway, we still lack assets for this problem."

He circled a notation on the board.

A voice piped up from near the fireplace.

"Maybe we will let that one go?"

Lavalle immediately wished he had said nothing, as all eyes swivelled in his direction in a group challenge.

"Perhaps not then."

Ribiere chuckled, lightening the uncomfortable moment.

"There may be someone. Leave this one to me for a moment."

They deferred to Knocke, who nodded his agreement.

302

"Thank you. Now, planning."

The meeting went on long into the smallest hours and was interrupted solely for a modest evening meal, and feed times for baby Jürgen.

It ended with a plan and a date.

[Author's note - On the matter of the submarines and the relative ease of their approach to the US mainland, a great deal has been written and the actions, or lack of them, by the defensive forces charged with US safety have been examined at length.

Without a doubt, there were errors, although the wave of sackings that followed caught many good and innocent men who did not deserve to forever stand responsible for the deaths of so many Americans.

It is beyond argument that the blame can be spread in many directions. From the Turks who were so riddled with agents and sympathisers that their own sacred waterway became an easy thoroughfare for the Soviet and Japanese submarines.

The failures to locate any sign of them in the notoriously 'unfriendly to submarine' Mediterranean has never been fully explained, by any of the navies that plied their trade in those clear waters.

The Royal Navy's enquiry into the Gibraltar debacle was reconvened once the passage of the enemy group was revealed. More jobs were lost as the circumstances that allowed the enemy to escape into the Atlantic were assessed and those responsible found wanting.

Contact reports from aircraft and shipping revealed other opportunities lost or misinterpreted.

The US had developed a plan called Operation Teardrop, to counter just such a mission after intelligence taken after WW2 indicated that the Germans were developing the technology.

Questions remain to this day why they neither shared the existence of such technology with their allies, nor implemented the defensive plan, given their own understanding of what the Soviets could now possess.

Apologists explain that there was no warning of such a mission inbound to the Eastern Seaboard.

Others will say that the warnings were consistently missed.

It has been estimated that there were no less than seventeen possible encounters or confirmed contacts with something unknown between Turkey and their final destination that could have resulted in discovery or, at least, some sort of warning being given.

What is unequivocal is that the mission experienced a huge amount of luck, and events contrived to bring the majority of the missile boats into a position where they fired upon their targets.

Had they all managed to fire and had all the missiles worked, then the loss and destruction would have been so much more.

Apart from 'Soviet Initisativa', no other submarine returned.

'Soviet Vozmezdiye' disappeared without a trace and there is nothing recorded to suggest that she ever made any contact, human or land, ever again.

In 1964, I-402 was discovered off the coast of the Bahamas, roughly forty-five miles due south of her firing point.

The US Navy undertook underwater demolition of the wreck without internal examination.

In 2014, the NOAA ship Okeanos Explorer was off Cape Hatteras, searching for wrecks from WW2, expanding on work commenced in 2011.

By August, teams had identified the locations of the sunken U-576 and SS Bluefields, vessels both lost in 1942 during the battle surrounding Convoy KS-520.

That is public knowledge.

What is not known outside of intelligence circles and the very highest political office is the fact that another vessel was also identified, lying a few hundred yards off the wreck of the Bluefields, a vessel that showed signs of huge damage to the engine room and pressure hull.

I-353 lies at a depth of 612 feet and, as agreed by both the American and Japanese governments, will never be disturbed.

The mysteries of her voyage and subsequent disappearance will never be solved.

Probably.]

As she has planted, so does she harvest; such is the field of karma.

Sri Guru Granth Sahib

<u>CHECKMATE</u>

CHAPTER 207 - THE HASHSHASHIN

There were deaths all over Europe, even in the developing peace.

People died of disease, of hunger, of neglect, and by direct action.

Deaths amongst the men and women of the HIAG were numerous, and the organisation started to fracture as its members sought security by moving to safe places that were unknown to their comrades and, more specifically, unmentioned in the HIAG files that were being used to track former SS members down and eliminate them.

The Jewish avengers did not have everything their own way, and Kumm organised a subtle trap that accounted for five members of the Irgun in bloody fashion.

None the less, the revenge killings continued.

1256 hrs, Monday, 2nd June 1947, Magdeburg, Germany.

He rose to greet the bemedalled Army officer.

"Thank you for coming, Herr Oberstleutnant."

Gesturing towards a seat with one hand, the man without his uniform used the other to attract the waiter.

"Coffee?"

"Danke."

"Two coffees, please."

The waiter retreated, leaving them alone.

The Lieutenant Colonel, resplendent in the uniform of the newly formed Chancellor's Guard, listened intently as the former officer spoke at length, his eyes occasionally widening in surprise, or narrowing in disgust.

A file appeared and von Scharf examined it at length, occasionally seeking a clarification here or expressing disbelief there.

Lunch came and went and a third coffee was served before a silence descended upon the pair.

Cigarettes appeared and were lit. Strangely, neither had smoked during their entire meeting to that point, so earnestly were they engaged.

"I understand fully… but what you ask is too much. Too much by far."

"Without you, there's no guarantee of success, Herr Oberstleutnant. With your assistance… rather lack of obstruction, success is guaranteed."

"I'm not a fool, mein Herr. I understand this."

Sipping the last of his coffee, Baron Werner von Scharf-Falkenburg struggled with his duty, conscience, honour, and desire.

None of them won, but desire gained a slight advantage.

"I will discuss it with my men."

"Thank you. When?"

"As soon as possible, mein Herr."

"When? You understand the urgency here."

Von Scharf bit back his first ill-considered response.

"Forty-eight hours. Here?"

The man in the impeccable suit nodded his acceptance.

"I need not remind you that my life is in your hands, Herr Oberstleutnant."

"Whatever my answer, I'll not betray you. You have my word as a German officer."

"Danke. Please, Herr Oberstleutnant… understand that whatever you say, we **will** do this thing. With or without you, it will happen. With you… well…"

"I'll put it to my men, Herr Knocke."

Knocke's heart missed a beat as the four immaculately uniformed men strode in. His hand automatically twitched towards his hidden weapon, but something made him check his movement.

Von Scharf clicked his heels and nodded, by way of salute and greeting combined.

"May I introduce some of my men, Herr Knocke?"

In turn, Knocke shook hands with the two officers, noting the array of medals each wore, a mark of their worth in combat.

He wondered if it was a mark of their honour too.

"Hauptmann Jankowski."

The handshake was firm and told Knocke a great deal.

"Hauptmann Horstbeck."

Again, the grip was that of a man's man, but Horstbeck's eyes were not as welcoming or relaxed as his fellow Captain.

"And finally, der Speiss, Stabsfeldwebel Keller."

The man's decorations almost shouted in Knocke's face, marking the man as a consummate combat soldier, and yet his hand was the lightest and most relaxed of them all.

They made small talk until lunch was before them and the private room's curtains were drawn.

"So, have you decided, Herr Oberstleutnant?"

"No. Not yet."

"Oh."

Keller spoke freely.

"We want to see the file, Herr General."

"But of course."

Knocke watched on, sipping his coffee, a twinkle of amusement in his eye as the folder did the rounds and ended up in front of Keller, the NCO.

Each of the officers seemed to be waiting on his say-so, almost like the NCO, above the others, had the last word.

The wait was interminable and Keller seemed to digest every word, occasionally flicking back to reference some point again.

Keller looked up from reading, his face furrowed with disgust.

"And this is true, Oberführer?"

"I have absolute faith in it, Stabsfeldwebel. One of my artillery officers noticed it, developed the data, and then it was brought to me. It's accurate."

"Schwein… grosse schwein."

Von Scharf extended a cigarette packet to the NCO, who accepted it and lit it without exhibiting any pause in his reading.

He finished it at the same time as he read the last words in the secret Legion report.

Keller pushed the file back towards Knocke with an air of finality.

The others waited, almost stopping breathing in an effort to hear the man's words.

"If that's true, I can understand why you're acting."

Knocke leant forward and held eye contact with Keller.

"Every word of it, Stabsfeldwebel. It's all true… every single word of it."

"Verdamnt normal!"

Keller sat back in his seat and took a deep breath.

"I'm in."

The three officers breathed out, having held their collective breath for what seemed like two lifetimes.

"Then we're in."

"Excellent. Truly!"

Knocke ordered more coffee and waited until they were alone again.

"This is what I need you to do."

Approaching the 2200 hrs deadline, Friday, 13th June 1947, Europe.

Anne-Marie and her accomplice, Khlóe-Simone, rechecked their weapons.

The presence of the SDECE agent was a sop to her husband, who insisted that she did not tackle her target alone.

Whichever of them was the most surprised when she agreed to his request was unclear.

Khlóe carefully set down her weapon of choice, a Sauer 38H, one of the rare examples chambered to take the .380 ACP cartridge.

She turned to her back-up weapon, the smaller and more easily concealed Walther PPK.

Anne-Marie slotted home the magazine in her Browning Hi-power and nodded to herself, satisfied with her work.

Both of the women knew of the other by reputation alone, a reputation for efficiency in the cold art of killing, in which both considered themselves better than the other.

With a professional hand, Anne-Marie assessed another tool of her trade; a short but deadly knife given to her by a member of Marseilles underground many years before.

In many ways, Anne-Marie's mission had been the hardest to plan, given the nature of the target and the constant movement that marked a tendency towards safety and a desire towards longevity.

One of Ribiere's contacts in the Abwehr had eventually come good, so the pair had quickly travelled across country and found rooms in the Schloss Ort, a hotel on the spit of land that graced the junction of the Danube and the Inn and Ilz rivers.

The view from their room was spectacular, the Danube idling by on its way to the Black Sea almost immediately below their window.

The sound of laughter rose from the terrace below and it had the effect of focussing them both back on their work.

The mantle clock ticked gently on towards the deadline.

The man that Ribiere had felt would help them had jumped at the chance.

Whilst he was a loyal Pole, he was also the brother of two boys lost off the Baltic coast when Soviet aircraft attacked their ship.

He was also the brother of a sister raped and murdered by the Soviets in 1939.

He was also the commander and comrade of a lot of men who had been consumed in the latest conflict; one that was brought about with the active help of the man he intended to kill.

Romaniuk checked the clock, noting with disgust that it had hardly moved since his last glance.

After the debacle with Gruppe Storch, he had returned to the Polish Army and seen action at the end of the war and in the renewed conflict.

Promotion and the recommendation of his superiors, combined with glowing reports of his conduct, had brought him to the command of the Presidential Guard.

He had an established reputation for checking on security matters at any time, day or night, so although off-duty, his presence would not arouse suspicion, only concern in the mind of those who guarded his target.

He picked up his czapka and adjusted it on his head.

310

Satisfied with his military bearing, Romaniuk checked the time once more and quickly decided to take a slow walk to his destiny.

The meeting had been arranged a week beforehand, but still preparations had been rushed, especially when the location had been unexpectedly switched, at the request of the other side.

Perhaps it was a security measure, or perhaps it was some sixth sense on the part of the target.

Whatever it was, the man now seemed relaxed, as Ribiere and he enjoyed a fine meal together, discussing the matters of state intelligence, within the boundaries of their own needs and issues.

The SDECE owned a well-appointed house on the shores of Lake Geneva at Bourg-en-Lavaux, and although the nearby train line occasionally brought interruption to the conversation, it was well suited to the needs of the higher members of international intelligence organisations, who saw it as a neutral ground on which to relax and exchange gossip, or sometimes conspire.

As he listened to talk of greater cooperation between the two intelligence agencies, Ribiere kept glancing towards the longcase clock.

With part of his brain focussed on his counterpart, he used the rest to will time to fly so he could end the misery of listening to the evil bastard's voice.

Time, in its turn, simply took its time.

The scene in the Alsace was completely different.

Haefali hovered in a shadowy arched doorway across the street from la Vieille Tour, one of the oldest restaurants in Selestat, waiting for his target to exit the premises with a woman, or even two, on his arm.

This one had been the easiest to locate as rumours of his love for the two sisters had quickly been established as fact.

Unusually for a man in his position, he kept a schedule that made him vulnerable to those who loitered in shadowed doorways and did not have his best interests at heart.

For the last of many times that evening, Haefali felt the reassuring chill of the silenced pistol in his pocket.

To him, the deadline was a guide, the opportunity would dictate when he would act.

He tensed as the front door swung open and the Maître D'Hôtel emerged, ready to receive some important guest.

Haefali shrunk back into the shadows and tried to relax, his heart racing and rising further and further as his tension grew.

Situated on a track that ran along the river bank, the residence was relatively modest in size, but its position on the east side of the Elbe, its seclusion, and its luxurious interior meant it had been an easy choice as the private residence of a great man.

Herr Uhlmann presented himself at the guard post at the allotted hour, dressed in a nondescript civilian coat.

The guard commander was summoned as the 'civilian' did not appear on the official list.

Keller accepted the clipboard and made great play of examining it and the ID of the visitor.

"Herr Uhlmann, there must have been some mistake. You're not listed here."

"So your gefreiter says, Herr Stabsfeldwebel. None the less, I'm here for an important meeting. Perhaps the mix up is yours?"

Keller, playing his part to perfection, bristled.

"Perhaps not mine, Herr Uhlmann. Wait here. Gefreiter... search this man thoroughly."

Keller turned on his heel and made his way to the guard hut.

The telephone connected immediately.

"Herr Oberstleutnant, I have an unlisted visitor called Uhlmann here. Apparently, he's expected?"

The two men in the hut listened half-heartedly, their attention more on the paperwork that Keller would shortly be inspecting.

"Jawohl, Herr Oberstleutnant."

He strode back out to where 'Uhlmann' waited patiently.

"Just this and a wallet, Herr Stabsfeldwebel."

Keller passed his eyes over the leather pouch and the small bottle of Ansbach.

"Give them back to the man, Finze."

He waited whilst the visitor accepted the returned items.

"Herr Uhlmann. It would appear to be clerical error. You may proceed. Do you know the way?"

"No. I'm afraid this is my first visit."

Keller seemed about to decide which of his guard he would assign when one of his seniors strode up to the checkpoint.

He saluted the Hauptmann, who saluted back with great style and aplomb.

"Herr Hauptmann, I wonder if I could ask you to show this gentleman to the secretary's office?"

Jankowski shot the visitor a look and then nodded curtly.

"It's on my way. Come, mein Herr. Follow me. Good night, Keller."

"Good night, Herr Hauptmann."

The two moved off and any casual observer would have spotted the military gait of the civilian, as the two unconsciously strode off in step across the yard to the main entrance.

Once inside the building, the presence of Jankowski ensured no interference from any of the guards as they moved towards the secretary's office.

"In here."

'Uhlmann' followed the captain's lead and found himself in a small room with von Scharf.

"There's a problem, Herr General."

"What?"

"Ten minutes. That's all you have. Ten minutes. Senior officers of the Fallschirm-Sturm-Regiment will be arriving for a quick medal presentation. Needless to say. All hell will break loose then, and I can offer no guarantees. You must be finished and gone."

Knocke set his jaw, his rehearsed speech, the act of nemesis, the pleasure of watching the bastard squirm, all disappearing in the new reality.

"So be it. The weapon?"

A CZ1927 and a silencer changed hands.

Von Scharf appreciated how Knocke checked the weapon and squirrelled it away in his trouser pocket, all in one easy movement.

"I'm ready."

"Fine. Follow me, Herr General."

As they walked, Knocke divested himself of the overcoat, creating a whole new image, one that caused von Scharf to hesitate as he got to the door of the secretary's office.

He saw Knocke for the first time as others saw him; a superb soldier, resplendent in his French uniform, complete with the medals of Imperial Germany, the Third Reich, and France…clearly a…

"Herr Oberstleutnant?"

He had been struck dumb and hadn't realised it.

"Is this it?"

"Yes, Herr General."

They both looked at their watches.

Time had marched on relentlessly.

"Seven minutes, Herr General, Not a second more."

"Seven minutes it is."

"Good luck, Herr General."

Knocke disappeared into the secretary's office.

2200 hrs, Friday, 13th June 1947, Europe.

Elsewhere in Magdeburg, Hässelbach had been the first to fulfil his task, for no other reason than his target burst into the gasthaus toilet as the Legion NCO was preparing himself.

Strauch, his bladder bursting and distracting, failed to see the warning signs in Hässelbach's eyes and turned towards the porcelain, fumbling with his flies.

The blade flashed once, twice, and a third time, his screams stifled by the firm hand over his mouth.

"For Germany and my comrades, you fucking bastard!"

The dying man was allowed to collapse in a controlled fashion and Hässelbach steered the body to the ground, ensuring that the head came to rest in the urinal's channel, steeped in blood and urine.

Just to make sure, the blade was wiped across Strauch's throat, sufficiently deep to open the jugular and hasten the man's death.

Shortly afterwards, Durand discharged his mission, blowing the back of Krankel's head off with a single shot, the act cutting short the man's pleading for mercy, a plea that had heightened in urgency once Durand had told him why he was about to die.

Also in Magdeburg, Braun interrupted Pflug-Hartnung's slumbers long enough for the man to understand why death was visiting him that night.

Braun's chosen method of execution proved singularly effective.

He struck with all the strength he could muster, in memory of his comrades, and the blow silenced the screams instantly.

A single sweep of the sharpened Soviet entrenching tool was enough to split the Abwehr officer's head in two and integrate parts of the nasal bone into the pillow beyond.

In Bourg-en-Lavaux, Rudolf Diels took his leave of Ribiere, not knowing that he carried with him a substance that would end his life as he slept.

It had been introduced into his after-dinner coffee, a drink poured by Ribiere himself, the waiters dismissed under the guise of a need for intimacy.

Despite his own wishes, the French spymaster had chosen a less triumphant approach to the killing, and Diels went to his maker without knowing that he had been discovered and that retribution for the deaths of thousands was the reason.

He developed a limited understanding of what was happening a little way into the final stages of his death, as his system closed down, and he slipped away with more dignity and peace than his actions had afforded so many others.

In Selestat, Haefali was behind time, his target as yet engaged within the old restaurant.

Again the door opened and the Maître D'Hôtel emerged, but this time he was followed out by a threesome, two stunning women either side of the man he had come to kill.

A generous tip changed hands and the senior man waved as his clients walked away.

Haefali waited until the man had gone back inside and hurried after his target.

Catching up was easy and, sparing a moment to look round for others out for a stroll or hurrying home, he acted.

"Stand still! Hands up! Move away, ladies!"

315

The two women did so with incredible speed, understanding the tone of the robber, as well as the message of the weapon he was holding.

They started running and Haefali doubted they would stop before the sun came up.

"Give me your wallet, you bastard."

The target turned.

"Do you have any fucking idea of how much you've just fucked up?"

"Your wallet."

A hand extracted it from a jacket pocket.

"Do you know who I am, you fucking street maggot?"

Haefali snatched the wallet away.

He could not resist the moment.

"Yes. You're Hans-Lothar Vögel. The man who brought about the war, and killed our alli…"

Vögel surged at the gun but an evening enjoying some fine wine and brandy robbed him of his speed.

Two shots put him onto the pavement, gasping for air, his lungs already filling with blood.

Conscious of the sound of running feet, Haefali assessed the wounded man and decided there was still work to be done.

A single bullet struck his heart, but still the organ still struggled to maintain its work rate.

Haefali turned and ran.

By the time help had arrived, Vogel was dead and his assassin was safely back in his rented accommodation and already removing his false moustache.

███████

Romaniuk inspected the four guards and found severe fault with two, fault that would have needed a microscope and years of searching to locate, but that suited his purpose that evening.

"Go and get cleaned up immediately, Return here, ready for full night guard duty. You have ten minutes."

The two luckless guards doubled away, keen to get their uniforms in order and avoid further punishment.

The two remaining guards listened to their instructions.

"Guard this door. Forget the other door... no one can get to that without passing you. I'm going to complete my rounds. Stay alert."

The two clicked their heels and assumed a position of rigid attention, all the more to impress their commander.

Romaniuk moved off, around the corner.

Within two minutes, he was within the President's private chambers by way of the now unguarded door and stood over the slumbering old man.

With time against him, he simply picked up a spare pillow and pressed it over Raczkiewicz's face.

There was no resistance and death claimed his life comfortably, certainly more comfortably than Romaniuk considered the bastard deserved.

He let himself back out of the chambers, ensuring that all was as he had found it, and walked back past the two rigid guards, not seeing either of them in his concentration on the minutiae of his inspection.

He ensured that he was back in position on the dot of ten minutes and the two breathless guards received another full inspection, during which he struggled to find anything that was less than 100% perfect.

Detailing them to further duty at the other door to the presidential quarters, Romaniuk returned to his quarters, his hands trembling with the release of tension.

In Passau, the pick-up had proved to be much easier than they had expected, although that probably had a great deal to do with the keenness of Khlóe-Simone's tongue and the receptiveness of their target's mouth.

The three had giggled and groped their way up to the room overlooking the Danube, where Anne-Marie had made her excuses and gone to powder her nose, leaving the other two to get better acquainted.

As she looked in the mirror, she saw not only herself reflected, but also the faces of the people who were about to be avenged.

In that instance, she determined the manner of the execution.

Returning to the bedroom, the two bodies were naked and wrapped around each other, but not so entwined that Anne-Marie could not make eye contact with her partner, who held the target closer to her in a display of passion that also meant the chance of escape evaporated totally.

Anne-Marie slid across the bed and took hold of an arm and, in an instant of extreme surprise and pain, wrenched it back and round behind the target's back, causing damage to the tendons and sinews.

The scream was of genuine pain and the struggle commenced.

A blade at the throat stopped all movement and focussed the target's mind on matters.

"Do you know what's about to happen?"

Irma Mallman shook her head, although she knew very well what the two intended. Despite her damaged arm, she was assessing how to get to the weapon in her evening bag.

The tip of the knife pricked her neck, and blood trickled down it and onto the sheet.

"We're here for some other people. They send their regards, Irma... or von Fahlon... or Obermann... or Friese... or is it Radzinski today, eh?"

"I don't know what you me..."

"Shut your fucking mouth, you piece of shit."

Khlóe had slipped away and was now sat holding her pistol, covering the pair on the bed, just in case.

"Gag."

Anne-Marie's voice commanded attention and Khlóe quickly looked for something appropriate to use.

With a grin, she selected the most inappropriate appropriate thing she could easily find to hand and tossed her selection to her senior.

With the blade point firmly lodged in Mallman's neck, her free hand caught the knickers and stuffed them into her victim's mouth without the slightest hint of delicacy.

The knife relaxed from her throat and moved away, but the grip of the other hand returned, as did the binding of the legs.

Anne-Marie flicked her wrist and skimmed the top off Mallman's left nipple.

The knickers did their work, but the squeal was still apparent and decidedly satisfying.

"Would that I had the time to make you suffer, you fucking bitch."

Another movement of the blade brought more pain as it opened a flesh wound across her belly.

Again, the scream died in the material stuffed in Mallman's mouth.

She wriggled but her struggles quickly stopped because of another movement of Anne-Marie's wrist.

The sensation of torturing Georges de Walle's killer was rewarding.

"Time."

"I do fucking know!"

Anne-Marie bit Khlóe's head off, her anger at the presence of the hated enemy only matched by her anger at having so little opportunity to take a full revenge.

She nodded her apology to her partner and concentrated on Mallman.

"You killed a lot of my friends… you've killed a lot of people… so this is their message to you."

The words hissed into Mallman's ear and she knew genuine fear.

And then genuine pain, as Anne-Marie slid the double-edged blade into her stomach, working it slowly from side to side, and then turning it over in her hand, ravaging the vessels and intestines in its path.

The damage was immense and irrevocable, and the pain was extreme, the dying woman's screams overcoming the mouthful of cloth.

"Shut up and die with dignity, you piece of shit!"

She scrambled the blade once more, bringing a fresh wave of pain.

Khlóe hissed a warning and Anne-Marie released the blade to use that hand on Mallman's mouth.

On the terrace below, a group of happy diners gathered to take in the evening air.

Anne-Marie grabbed the knife and rolled Mallman onto her front, no resistance offered by the hideously wounded woman.

"For Georges!"

With her surprisingly considerable strength, she drove the blade into the right ear of her victim, deep enough to ravage brain and blood vessels.

Death was quick, far too quick for Anne-Marie's tastes.

They wrapped Mallman up in sheets and towels and waited into the small hours, before lowering the bundle down on to the deserted terrace below and then consigning the 'bitch' to the flowing river.

319

The body was discovered two days later in Obernzell, and considered to be yet another victim of nocturnal criminal activities.

Knocke straightened his uniform, took a single clearing breath, and entered the room beyond.

"What is the meaning of this?"

He closed the door behind him, ignoring the question.

"Who are you?"

"My name is Knocke, Herr Kanzler. Ernst-August Knocke of la Légion Étrangère, and formerly a member of the Waffen-SS."

"What do you want? You just can't walk in... how did you get in here?"

"What matters is that I'm here, Herr Kanzler. Here with you."

Speer took in the vast array of medals that covered the intruder's uniform and could not help but be impressed, despite the concern that was growing in the pit of his stomach.

"What do you want?"

The tremble in Speer's voice was unmistakable and Knocke drew some small comfort from it.

"I am here to find out why."

"Why what?"

Knocke produced a small bottle and placed it on the desk.

"Why you took us all back to war again... why you killed Eisenhower... why you provoked another conflict... why my comrades died in their hundreds... that's why I'm here, Herr Kanzler."

Speer ripped his eyes away from the bottle of Ansbach and composed himself as best he could, trying to assume an air of studied indifference.

"I don't know what you're talking about, Herr Knocke. The whole idea is preposterous."

Knocke produced the weapon from behind his back and Speer's eyes went wide in an instant.

"That is exactly how you expected to get away with it, I assume. Because it is so preposterous... no one would believe that you would do such a thing."

Speer made a casual move for the phone, which Knocke allowed.

"Won't do you any good. No one will answer."

Speer pressed the button anyway.

Taking a quick glance at the clock, Knocke realised he was wasting too much time.

Speer held the telephone, the call to the security detail unanswered.

"Men who fought for Germany from 1939 fell in your little private war."

"It was for Germany!"

"It was for you and your lust for power! Don't you dare claim that you acted for Germany!"

Knocke slid the silencer into place, an act that made Speer tremble with fear.

"You have betrayed Germany... betrayed her people... her soldiers... everything of value!"

"What are you going to do? You can't shoot me. There are guards everywhere."

"How do you think I got in here, Herr Kanzler? Why do you think the phone is still ringing in your hand?"

It was, which Speer hadn't even realised.

As Knocke anticipated, the lack of response demoralised the Chancellor.

He replaced the receiver and held his hands apart, palms towards the judge and jury opposite him.

"So... let's talk. What now? We both know you won't shoot me. You took an oath."

Knocke smiled, an act that brought no comfort to Speer's eyes.

"I took an oath to the German people and Adolf Hitler. I also took one to the Legion. I've no recollection of taking one to you and your pack."

Knocke checked again.

'Verdamnt! Time... time...'

He opened the bottle and poured some brandy into Speer's glass.

"Drink, Herr Kanzler."

The nervous Speer welcomed the fiery liquid, drawing on its burn to give him some courage.

Knocke's mind worked overtime...

…The pistol chugged four times in rapid succession, and blood spouted from holes in Speer's clothing.

Still he stood, rocking unsteadily on his feet as his lifeblood ebbed away.

'Enough. Just kill the bastard.'

Knocke shifted his aim and put the fifth shot neatly into Speer's face, where it smashed through his upper teeth on its way through his mouth.

He fell back into the chair moaning in pain.

The sixth shot entered Speer's left eye and the moaning stopped instantly.

Except none of it happened, and Speer still sat there, and the gun was silent and unused in his hand.

How he wished he had the time.

"Drink, Herr Kanzler, drink."

Knocke poured more brandy, which disappeared as quickly as the first.

"Another."

"I lost some of my best soldiers in Poland… comrades… friends! Why could you not let the peace continue, eh? Why scheme and plot? Why's power such a drug for you bastards, eh?"

"If you have to ask, then you'd never understand, Knocke. You're just a simple soldier. You take orders and that's your life. A life without imagination, purposed solely to the wishes of others. But to give the orders… to rule over other's destiny… to rule over the destiny of nations… that is power and it tastes good!"

The brandy was taking its effect.

Knocke checked the bottle and the clock, estimating that enough time had elapsed.

"Albert Speer, Kanzler of Germany. You've been found guilty of bringing war to our country, betraying the nation and people, betraying the trust of your soldiers, all at the cost of thousands upon thousands of lives."

"Now, enough of this nonsense!"

Speer stood up in a show of bravado.

"You are sentenced to death. Sentence is to be carried out immediately."

"No! No… listennn…"

He sat down heavily, his face suddenly drained of colour and his limbs weak.

"Would that I could stay and watch you suffer, you evil bastard. It must be enough to know that you'll die, painfully, alone, and afraid."

Speer's eyes bulged from his head as his attempts to breathe grew increasingly more difficult.

Knocke slipped a small empty phial out of his wallet, removed the top, and placed it on the table in front of the dying Speer, who followed the movement all the way.

His eyes asked the burning question, mainly because his mouth no longer responded to his commands.

"Aconitum and Conium cocktail, from our French allies. Highly refined version that acts much quicker than normal. Painful, so I'm told. You'll be gone soon, but it will not be without suffering."

Strained sounds emerged from Speer's lips, but nothing recognisable, not that Knocke tried.

Gathering himself for a moment, Ernst-August Knocke nodded to the spirits of those he had just avenged and left the room.

On his way down the hall, he passed the two Fallschirmjager officers on their way to see Speer, escorted by Horstbeck and two of his men.

The exchange of salutes was tremendous, and the two paratroopers gorged themselves on the display of medals carried by the French officer, both inwardly speculating on the origins and circumstances behind the plethora of German awards he wore.

"Wait here, please."

Horstbeck entered the secretary's office, leaving the visitors alone with his guards.

"I think I know who that fellow is, Kurt."

Schuster pursed his lips as he looked down the hall, the figure long since gone from sight.

"The SS general...Knocke?"

Perlmann, the new commander of the Fallschirm-Sturm-Regiment nodded his agreement.

"Looks the part, doesn't he?"

"Hell of a soldier, so they say, Herr Oberst."

Horstbeck emerged from the office.

"Herr Oberst, my apologies. The Kanzler is unwell and will not be able to perform the ceremony this evening. He has instructed that we find you rooms here and proceed tomorrow. Obergefreiter, take these officers to the guest quarters immediately. Follow this man please."

Von Scharf had quickly come up with the idea, to try and keep Speer's death a secret for as long as possible.

They exchanged salutes and Horstbeck quickly disappeared back into the office.

Horstbeck gathered up the discarded coat and hid it in plain sight on a coat rack.

He left, turning out the last light, and leaving a dead man to grow cold and stiffen in the night.

Meanwhile, as he walked away from the building, Knocke was cursing his stupidity. The civilian coat still lay in the secretary's office where he had discarded it. For a man not given to making errors, it was a mistake that could carry some huge implications, especially now that the Luftwaffe officers had seen him.

He allowed the remaining poisoned Ansbach to flow from the bottle and tossed the empty vessel into the bushes before climbing into the waiting car.

"Oberführer?"

"It is done, Riedler. Now. Let's get away from here."

Riedler dropped the Kdf-wagen into gear and headed back towards Flugplatz Magdeburg-Ost, where an aircraft of the Armee de L'Air waited to take Knocke and others back to Marseilles.

The following morning brought news that rocked two nations.

The Polish President and the German Chancellor had both passed away in the night.

Raczkiewicz taken by nothing more sinister than his advancing years, whereas Speer, by initial reports, might have ended his own life.

By the time that the deaths of others associated with the regimes were noted the transfer of power was already complete, and the new incumbents moved swiftly to disentangle themselves from all elements of the old administrations, given the rumours that were circulating, provided by whisperers who owed their allegiance to French intelligence.

In the interests of future solid relations between the Allies, the matter of the German-Polish renewal of the war simply disappeared.

324

Those who had brought war back and caused the deaths of millions had already paid for their crimes, so across Europe the different forces in pursuit of the murderers were called off.

In September, the great and the good assembled in Stockholm to sign the full and official documentation marking the end of the war.

Heads of state made speeches about the futility of war and how the last conflict would be the final conflict of note in the history of man.

Perhaps Herbert Morrison, the newly elected British Prime Minister, best summed up the hopes of a ravaged continent.

He spoke passionately about a Europe coming together to heal and rebuild in a newfound spirit of brotherhood and understanding.

Morrison almost shed a tear as he spoke of the generations of young men their countries had condemned to die for causes that now seemed wholly foolish and more easily resolved by the discussions of politicians.

Perhaps it was the military men who, better than anyone else, understood that such talk is always present at the end of any great conflict.

The damned politicians who send the young men to die will always beat their breasts at the cost of their decisions, and that the words of contrition and promises for the future lose their brightness from the moment they fall upon the listeners' ear.

Across the room, Zhukov and Patton locked eyes, both understanding that there was an inevitability about the future... that one day, maybe not in their lifetimes, the game would start again.

Anyone who has ever looked into the glazed eyes of a soldier dying on the battlefield will think hard before starting a war.

Otto von Bismarck

CHAPTER 208 - THE SHOT

1357 hrs, Sunday, 5th October 1947, Route 167, the Vosges, Alsace.

The staff car made its way steadily down the 167, its occupants relaxed and taking in the wonderful scenery on their way to a reunion dinner at the Chateau du Haut-Kœnigsbourg.

As the prolonged summer reluctantly gave way to autumn, the High Vosges was a special place, more so than ever.

The colours and the smells were marvellous and the two senior officers enjoyed the relative silence in comfort.

A comfort that was disturbed by barking and shouting.

The Legion major in the front passenger's seat turned round to offer an explanation to the senior man.

"Mon Général, there are still parties out searching the area... the talk of ghosts in the night keeps the population nervous, so we make our own noises to let them know we are here. Maybe they have the trail of the man we have heard so many stories about. Perhaps we should wait?"

Lavalle exchanged looks with Knocke.

"Yes. That's a good idea, Commandant. I need to stretch my legs anyway, and there's plenty of time."

"It may not be safe, mon Général."

"Never mind, I have needs, and you'll keep watch... but not on me I add!"

"As you wish, mon Général. Pull over, Caporal."

The driver, probably the smallest legionnaire either of the officers had ever seen, brought the Bentley Vanden Plas tourer to a slow halt, the 4.5-litre engine purring with apparent delight against the backdrop of increased shouting.

The Legion major stepped out and eased the CEAM assault rifle strap over his shoulder.

Behind them the escort, housed in a less stylish Citroen lorry, stopped and the legionnaires fanned out, more than one enjoying the same comfort break as Lavalle intended.

He was joined by Knocke and the two generals absorbed the breathtaking view as they relieved their bladders.

"If he is still evading the searchers, then he's a brave man and to be admired, eh Ernst?"

"Ja. Incredible scenery but he's spent two winters in it. Impressive, even for a Russian. Personally, I'd like to hear his story."

Lavalle did what men do and buttoned himself back up.

"So would I. If they capture him alive, we'll do it, eh?"

There was no noise, save the sounds of the woods that he had been hearing for as long as he could remember; trees creaking and swaying in the modest breeze, the low chatter of birds and other creatures, and the howling of the pursuing dogs and shouting of men.

He was tired; so tired.

With not an ounce of fat on his body, the man had dragged himself around the High Vosges, ever in pursuit of something to eat and a safe hiding place, forever trying to avoid those who continued to pursue him, long after others had given up.

A diet of fresh meat and woodland fruits had sustained him, unless a visit to some small piece of civilisation yielded a bonus like a loaf or cake.

He was healthy but exhausted.

His exhaustion dragged him down bit by bit, but the resilience he had displayed was incredible, given the time he had been alone.

But now he knew his long game of hide and seek was at an end.

The bone poking through his skin where he had snapped his leg above the ankle testament to the fact that he could no longer evade or do his normal trick of pulling himself up a tree to escape the hounds.

'Always the fucking hounds…'

Looking through the sights, the target loomed large, its eyes betraying no great awareness and alertness.

The uniform was one he knew only too well.

He had seen it many times.

327

He had seen it in the courtyard the day his comrades were slaughtered.

'So... it's come to this...'

The target was in conversation with his companion, and wholly unaware that death was at hand.

'One last blow for my comrades and for the Motherland!'

Gritting his teeth against the pain, Nikitin took careful aim.

The sound arrived with the pursuers and the stationary Legion group both at the same time.

It had opposite effects.

The dog handlers let their hounds go, sensing that their quarry was exposed.

The Legion detachment went to ground and sought the position of the enemy rifleman.

Only two men reacted differently.

One because he had been hit by a bullet, the other because his friend's blood had splashed across his face.

"A moi la Legion!"

"Alive... take hi... take him... alive..."

The words terminated in a bloody wave of spluttering and coughing.

"Lie still, damn you... help here!"

The wounded man's lips moved but now no sound emerged, only red bubbles, the bullet having smashed through the upper chest and respiratory tract, allowing blood to fill the lungs.

"No! Stay awake, man! Stay awake! Help me!"

The lips tried to form a word but failed, and then stopped moving as life came to a bloody and violent end.

The commandant dropped beside the two men.

"Mon Dieu!"

"Commandant, his final order was to take the man alive. Carry out that order. Now!"

The Major leapt to his feet and called his men to him, determined to follow the dogs and act just late enough to ensure they had completed their work before he could obey the order.

Behind him and his men, Knocke closed Lavalle's pained eyes and rose to his feet, shocked and stunned that death had visited them that day.

He slipped his Walther from his holster and followed quickly after the pursuers.

The sniper was easily found, his ability to evade nil.

By some miracle, Nikitin was taken alive, not by the Legionnaires, but by the Moroccan troops who had been pursuing him for weeks.

Knocke, out of deference to Lavalle's last words, kept out of the capture, not trusting himself to be able to observe his dead friend's wishes.

He could never bring himself to visit the prisoner who was, as suspected, a Soviet paratrooper from the group that had attacked the chateau over two years previously.

The man was eventually returned to the USSR, where he was feted as a hero, which he undoubtedly was.

Général de Division Christophe Pierre Lavalle was the final casualty to enemy action in whatever history would call the war following the war that followed the war to end all wars.

*We come into this world and we give and we take. It is my fondest hope
that, when I am gone, I will have been a net contributor.*

Chris Coling

CHAPTER 209 - THE ENDS

1957

Weekend of the 25th - 27th October 1957, Barnstorf, Germany.

The annual reunion of those who fought at Barnstorf had
become an established event, and more and more veterans attended each
year.

Men wore part or whole uniforms, depending on availability or,
quite often, their increasing girth, but the soldiers mixed and told stories,
drank and remembered those who were still missing or buried in the
Nagelskamp Cemetery, just to the west of the German town.

They camped under canvas in a field north of the Schötte,
adjacent to Osnabrücker Strasse, and enjoyed the food and beer heaped
upon them by the owners of the nearby Rasthaus Barnstorf, as well as
numerous gifts that appeared in the hands of the local populace who could
remember the sacrifices the men had made.

Most of those present enjoyed the return to a semi-military
lifestyle, some were still in service, and those that didn't simply accepted
the regimentation as a necessary evil to endure in order to spend time with
old comrades.

The weekend meeting had two huge highlights. Firstly, the
veterans walked the battlefields together, hundreds of ageing men who
minds took them back to those bloody days over ten years beforehand,
shooting a line, or reminding each other of a comrade who fell here or there.

Every time, the men stopped to pay special tribute to the young
RAF pilot who had given his life to bring the bridge down. That, and the
walk over the Black Watch mound were always special moments of higher
tribute and loss, when many a hard man's eye was moistened by a memory.

After one such moment on the east side of the river, Ramsey and
his men moved off to the west side where they met up with Neville Griffiths
and the survivors of his crew, Driver Droves and Butler the gunner. The

Comet that he had brought to the battlefield had played a key part in the defence of Barnstorf.

They talked through the events of Yarishlov's attack and the subsequent napalm strike that halted the infantry surge.

Whenever that moment was recalled, the memory always went hand in hand with another attack, one that claimed Allied lives.

They fell into an uncomfortable silence.

Robertson broke it as he arrived bearing news.

"Sah... yonder's a gentleman waiting to see ye. Strange one, Sah. Won't give his name, just says he's to see ye... and only ye. Says he's come a long way and all. Have a couple of the boys keeping a careful eye on 'im. He's up at the gasthaus, Sah. Something not right, ye ken?"

"I'll bow to your instincts, Sergeant Major. I'll catch up with you three later over a pint, Neville."

"Sir."

As happened so often, the retired men found themselves instinctively throwing up salutes.

"Lead on, Sergeant Major."

The man rose to his feet as Robertson opened the door of the small private room in which he had asked him to wait, accompanied by two men who spoke a language foreign to the little English he had acquired over the years.

Ramsey strode in with purpose, expecting to recognise the newcomer, but finding nothing familiar about him, except for the bearing that marked him as a military man.

"You are Ramsey?"

Robertson reacted.

"General Ramsey to you, whatever your name is."

"Steady, Sergeant Major. Yes, I'm John Ramsey... and you are?"

"Stefan... Stefan Kriks, General Ramsey."

"Do I know you?"

"No... I do not thinking so. But you knows my General, Arkady Yarishlov."

Ramsey suddenly felt his legs go weak and, to cover himself, offered Kriks towards a seat and took up one himself.

"What do you know of General Yarishlov?"

"I was with him in all the war, all way to when he was kill."

"I heard that he was dead. I was very sorry."

"Kill by the bastard NKVD."

"I heard he resisted arrest."

"Yes... he did... they intend to have him kill himself... responsibility for the raid on Uspenka Camp was placed on he. NKVD arrested him... my General did not shoot himself... shoot bastard Skryabin instead... but he die, along with some of Chekists."

Ramsey relaxed, something that communicated itself to those present, and the atmosphere eased considerably.

"Tell me more... excuse me... my manners... a drink, Mister Kriks?"

"I was Praporshchik for my General."

"So be it, Praporshchik Kriks. Drink?"

"One of cold German beer please."

One of Robertson's men disappeared on cue. The other, a scoundrel called McKweon, stayed focussed and alert.

The drinks arrived and were sampled before Kriks moved into the full story of Yarishlov's last days.

It was all new to Ramsey, who consumed every detail without question.

Robertson, a former inmate of the Camp concerned, had listened with studied interest and recognised Skryabin's name.

"So, Skryabin's dead?"

He hadn't realised he had spoken aloud.

"Ach! My apologies to ye both."

"You knew Skryabin?"

"Aye, that I did, Prapychick, that I did. A fucking evil man with nae right tae walk the planet's fine earth."

Kriks nodded gravely and grabbed his glass, understanding more the tone than the words.

"I drink to this!"

Robertson leant over and clinked his tankard against that of his former enemy, the men united in their continuing hatred for one long gone.

"Aye, sorry Sah."

Ramsey grinned and turned back to the waiting Russian.

Kriks finished and took some more of the cold pils on board.

"An amazing story. The man was a great soldier. Praporshchik. Did you serve here too? During the battle?"

"Yes, I fight here with my General. It was bad battle, was it not?"

"Yes... very much so."

Another drink arrived, the gasthaus owner selecting the lull in conversation to push open the door.

"So... thank you for bringing this story to me. I appreciate that the journey cannot have been easy."

"I had no choice, General Ramsey. My General gave me orders."

"Well, you have fulfilled them, Praporshchik. You will, of course, stay wi..."

"Not all are done, General. I have something for to give you."

Kriks removed the precious package from his pocket and placed it on the table in front of Ramsey.

"Do you know what's in it?"

Kriks nodded as he spoke.

"I know what in it, but not what is write, General."

Ramsey broke open the envelope and the Hero Award fell easily into the palm of his hand.

He read the words penned by a man about to die.

Words too brief to say everything he wanted to say, but none the less, words that brought a lump to Ramsey's throat.

"I thank you, Praporshchik Kriks. It seems he thought very highly of you. You are, at his request, and with my agreement... and grateful thanks... most welcome here."

Taking a deep breath, Ramsey composed himself.

"Sergeant Major. Will you take our guest and get him acquainted with the rest of our boys. Look after him well and I'll be down for poet's corner later."

"Aye, Sah. That I will. Come on the noo, Prapychick. Let's see how ye fare on uisge-beatha. I'm sensing ye's a natural."

A date with a serious amount of Scotch whisky was on the cards.

"Don't go overboard now, Murdo."

The old NCO laughed a laugh that failed to conceal his plan.

Ramsey raised an admonishing eyebrow.

"Sergeant Major... if you please?"

"Och Sah, just some fine hostin' for our honoured guest."

Robertson ushered Kriks out in friendly fashion, followed by McKweon, who seemed less inclined to accept the former enemy as a new friend.

"Mac... cut him some slack now."

"Aye, if ye say so, Sah."

Ramsey settled down alone to reread the few words.

Beer in one hand, paper in the other, he momentarily closed his eyes, summoning his range of mental images of the man he had come to see as a friend.

His Russian was up to the task and he translated the words easily, almost speaking them to himself in the voice he could easily recall.

'John Ramsey VC, my friend,

> *You will know that I am now no more.*
> *The man who gave you this is called Stefan, and he is my friend.*
> *A trusted soldier who I ask you to care for.*
> *You and I are not so different, despite our uniforms. I have enjoyed our friendship and regret that we will not meet again, and never again share the stories of our youth and the comrades who journeyed with us.*
> *I give you the medal I earned when the fire ended my days as a proper soldier. Accept it as a gesture of friendship between two old enemies, and as a token of a true friendship forged by the comradeship of war.*
> *I would have wished to have served with you, for the Motherland of course.*
> *My time comes and I am now going to kill the Chekist bastard who is stood grinning at me.*
> *He has no idea.*
> *Live a long and good life, John Ramsey.*
>> *Your friend,*
>> *Arkady.*

From that day forward, Kriks attended the reunion event and over the years, at his behest, more of the veterans of Yarishlov's and

Deniken's force came too, the old enmities set aside, if not always forgotten.

Even the rising political star that was Vladimir Stelmakh attended on three occasions, before fame and status prevented him from crossing over into the West, no matter what his choice might have been.

The walks around the battlefield became more of a voyage of discovery, as each group revealed to the other the facts and feelings that had been concealed by distance and the smoke of battle.

Men developed an understanding of the soldiers who had been on the opposite side, and reconciliation was a constant companion, although it was often hindered by the barrier of language.

However, there was one location on the battlefield where reconciliation found little encouragement, and those that fought there stood apart, divided by experiences of true horror.

Despite his best efforts, Ramsey could never bring the two groups together on the top of the mound where so many had died in such a bestial fashion.

There was no real active hostility, more an unspoken agreement that the two sides could not come together in a place where they had exercised the lowest and basest callings of the military arts.

The annual event drew greater numbers and then, as the participants succumbed to ill health and the passage of time, started to diminish.

The final official meeting of the veterans is planned for 27th to 29th October 2017, marking the seventieth anniversary of the battle.

Of course, it may well be that some will continue to go to that bloody place in the years to come, if body and soul allow.

1963

Camerone Day.

The one-hundredth anniversary of the battle that the Legion held so dear, a defeat for sure, but one steeped in glory and honour.

The Aubagne headquarters was less than a year old, and this was the first year that the ceremony was to be held there.

On site was the new Legion museum, which contained the treasured historical artefacts, including that which was held the most dear; Captain Danjou's wooden hand.

The Legionnaires on parade were mainly a new generation, but there were still old lags amongst them, men who had bled and sweated in Russia, France, and Indo-China.

Taking the review was Général de Brigade Jacques 'Toto' Lefort, General-Inspector of the Legion, who shared the podium jointly with a guest of honour.

To the familiar tones of 'Le Boudin', the soldiers marched past at the Legion's own eighty-eight steps per minute, a slower speed that always saw them bringing up the rear in military parades such as that on Bastille Day.

The pioneers strode by, their leather bibs and polished axes outdone by the tremendous display of facial hair, a prerequisite for membership of the elite force.

The Legion band switched to the march of the 1st REI and the proud soldiers acknowledged the salutes of the two generals on the podium, the melody of their regimental march 'Nous sommes tous des volontaires'.

The band fell silent as the last in line, the colour party, moved past the podium, leaving only the steady pace of the marching feet to break the heavy silence of expectation growing in the audience, civilian as well as military.

The Legion spectacle always attracted a crowd, but today was special for more than simply the date and the centenary.

The sound of the departing parade was suddenly lost in a throaty mechanical roar of unexpected loudness, and heads craned to see the source.

They all knew what it was, but to see it here, on this day, was a privilege they would savour for the rest of their lives.

On cue, orders were shouted and the band struck up 'J'avais un camarade'.

Without orders or pre-planning, the marchers burst into song, singing in either French, German, English, or whatever language their version of the famous march required.

Veterans of the Legion, many of whom had served with the Legion Corps D'Assaut, strode forward in a steady march, impeccably in step, impeccably in formation, the unarmed veterans brought together for a fitting tribute to the memory of comrades, and in celebration of the Legion's ideals and values.

Marching with them were men who now formed part of the living history of the Legion, and who commanded the utmost respect from those who followed behind them.

Leading the line were the former officers.

Spontaneous applause greeted the parade of veterans, causing them, if it was at all possible, to stiffen their poise and thrust their chests out even further.

Behind the line of officers, pushed by Riedler, came the wheelchair-bound Albrecht von and zu Mecklenburg, keen to participate in the march past despite being struck down by polio in the early fifties.

Returning to the parade ground, the soldiers of the 1st REI took up positions around specific markings and waited for the veterans to do the same.

The retired legionnaires marched around and returned to face the podium, split equally to either side, and leaving a space roughly six metres wide between the two columns.

In truth, it only needed to be just over 3.56 metres wide, such was the precision with which the centrepiece of the parade was manoeuvred.

Lohengrin.

Resplendent in a new paint scheme, or more precisely, an old paint scheme reapplied, the one she had first borne during the fighting in France, the old tank rattled onto the parade ground, her Maybach engines sounding as sweet as ever.

The mesh skirts had been removed and the side fenders straightened or replaced, giving the venerable tank a look that belied her years.

Inside her, Meier handled the familiar controls with ease, heeding the instructions from above and bringing the old warhorse to a halt in the precise position required.

The turret swung under Jarome's command and he dipped the mighty 88mm for the last time.

Standing proud in the turret, Köster gave the podium an immaculate salute, which was returned with equal style and aplomb by Toto Lefort and Ernst-August Knocke.

The applause echoed around the parade ground once more, as the rest of the veterans saluted their old commander.

Lohengrin then made her way around the back of the assembly and took up station almost to millimetre perfection in the centre of the parade.

The procession of Danjou's wooden hand then took place, the escort party stepping away from their position by the white stone monument bearing the Legion motto 'Honneur et Fidélité', and striding purposefully down the length of the parade ground to the memorial for the dead where the party took proper station.

Then followed the recitation of events from one hundred years previously, undertaken by a young lieutenant.

Knocke shared eye contact with a few old comrades during those moments.

Haefali, who was now a firm friend of the Knocke family, and Durand, who had gone on to a successful career in politics.

Fiedler, who had worked miracles to keep the vehicles of Camerone on the road.

Leroy-Bessette, Desmarais, and Beveren, all now enjoying the fruits of retirement, serious soldiers whom Knocke had come to respect and rely on.

He caught the eye of the senior former NCO on parade, Johannes Braun, and shared a special moment with him, one in which they both felt the absence of one who had gone before.

'Uhlmann.'

There were others missing too.

Delacroix, lost in a plane crash in Indo-China, and D'Estlain, drowned whilst on holiday in Corsica.

And Hässelbach, whose final battle was against an invisible and inexorable internal enemy that the indomitable rogue could not defeat.

338

Knocke's mind wandered and he saw the old times again, experienced the smell of smoke and explosives, heard the sounds of battle and the voices of those he commanded.

He was so lost in his own world he hardly heard a word of Lefort's speech and was jolted from his reverie when the General touched his arm and opened the way to the microphone.

The weighty silence of great expectation greeted him.

He had no notes and simply spoke from the heart.

"Legionnaires! Volunteers! Comrades, old and new! We gather here today, this centenary day, to celebrate and remember our comrades who fell at Camerone, and indeed all of those who have fallen since, faithfully and with honour."

His brief was to be just that, and the well of emotion he felt decided Knocke on a shorter version than that he had rehearsed.

"I would thank the authorities for inviting us here to take part in this wonderful and honourable ceremony, and to allow us this opportunity to march with old brothers-at-arms once more."

"The code of honour that we adhered to runs as strong today as it has done across the years. That is plain. Plain in the men who wear the uniform of the Legion today, and those who have since set it aside, their duty discharged."

"I am proud to have served with such men; men who honoured their every mission to the best of their ability and often at all costs..."

He paused, trying to find the right words.

"And what a cost is sometimes paid to honour the pledge that we all took."

He nodded to himself, and to the men whose eyes he engaged, soldiers both old and new.

"That pledge is as important today as it has always been, and we should never forget that in honouring it, we also honour those who observed it, even unto death."

"One hundred years ago, Captain Danjou and his men provided us with an example... one that La Legion has consistently followed. It is by examples such as this, and by the spirit of comradeship that binds us across all boundaries of birth... binds us in the extremes of danger... and binds us in the shared hardships of our calling... that La Legion has emerged victorious and with honour, from all the tasks placed upon it."

Tugging his tunic into place in trademark fashion, Knocke came to his conclusion.

"When this parade is done, move around this assembly and meet new comrades, present and past, who are as bound to you by their oath as any man with whom you have shared sand or mud."

"My last act as an officer of La Legion is to bring this ceremony to a close, after which that famous old tank will become a permanent memorial outside the museum here at Aubagne."

"She and I will gracefully retire together, although she will remain here to inspire you all."

"I wish you all bon chance… and I know you will never forget the words that bind us."

Knocke brought himself to the attention and his words rose high into the sky and penetrated the inner self of everyone present.

"Legio Patria Nostra!"

The entire parade echoed the words in their loudest voices, leaving some civilians stunned and with ears ringing.

Knocke nodded to the parade commander and stepped back, the moisture in his eyes apparent and left in place as a mark of his real affection for both the Legion and the men in front of him.

The assembled men returned to the parade ground to escort the old tank to her final resting place, causing no little problems for Köster, who was forever warning Meier about some well-wisher or other who might get squashed.

Lohengrin, intent on having the last word, shuddered to a halt, earning her crew more than their fair share of ribbing.

It had been a risk allowing the old lady to move under her own steam, but it was one that a surprising number of people had insisted upon, some of whom had an awful lot of braid on their shoulders.

The crowd took advantage of the delay to engage with each other and Lohengrin was surrounded by relaxed men, exchanging stories of old comrades and other less savoury encounters in the back streets of Marseilles and the like.

Some Legion mechanics arrived but were given short shrift by Köster, who refused to let them anywhere near the Tiger.

Meier climbed up on the rear and pulled up one of the grilles, suspecting her knew the cause of the problems.

He grabbed the tool kit and sat it on the hull, selecting a roll of tape fit for the purpose of rebinding the electrical cables that were disintegrating with every passing hour.

Meier leant in and removed the old tape, breaking a wire in the process.

"Well, that was fucking bright."

"What was bright?"

"Just broke the wire. Pass me the pliers, kamerad."

The tool arrived and was got to work.

"There's a razor in the box. Need that too."

The man rummaged around and came up with a non-standard issue cutthroat razor.

"Here."

"Danke."

The blade moved around, slicing the old tape off and then was returned, allowing Meier to renew the protection.

He added extra tape, just to make sure that the venerable tank would make it the last few hundred metres.

"That should do it."

"I expect you said that last time you taped it up, didn't you?"

"You cheeky bastard. What do you know about panzers, eh?"

"Sure it's not the bolts?"

Meier nearly choked as he came up for air, Knocke's words reminding him of another time and another place, a time of great hardship on a battlefield far away.

"By all the whores, Oberführer, you've done me again."

Knocke grinned from ear to ear, in which he was joined by Köster, who had silently gesticulated to his old general that the opportunity for a repeat existed.

"She'll get us to where we need to go, Rudi."

Köster deliberately echoed Knocke's words, but affected more sternness.

"You said that last time."

"Yeah, well, the wire was too close to the manifold and melted the tape. I'm brilliant, but not a fucking miracle worker... begging your pardon, Oberführer."

Knocke grinned from ear to ear but did not interfere in the banter.

341

"You'll be a number of things if she doesn't make it this time, Driver Meier!"

"Threats… that's all I get, Oberführer. Threats… and me a senior member of the Legion… and a Ritterzkreuzträger too. No respect, these young officers."

Köster, his Capitaine rank markings as new as new could be, simply raised an eyebrow to his former commander.

"What can you do, Oberführer? Age has dulled his wit and senses. I simply just try to remember him as he once was, a half-competent driver who got lucky. He was moderately funny then too."

The rolled-up ball of used tape sailed past Köster's ear and the two descended into childish laughter.

Meier locked eyes with his friend and made an unspoken suggestion, which Köster immediately approved of.

"Oberführer, would you join me in the turret for the last few metres?"

The smile alone made the day complete for the two old tankers.

"I'd be honoured. Thank you."

Meier slipped around the turret of Lohengrin and dropped into his position, as Köster and Knocke clambered onto the turret and down the two hatches, with Köster offering the commander's hatch, an offer respectfully declined.

"She's your tank, Rudi. I'm just along for the final ride."

"As you wish, Oberführer… but, you'll give the orders please?"

Jarome passed up a headset and throat mic, which Knocke accepted with a smile and a pat on the gunner's shoulder.

The Maybach roared into life, Meier's repair good enough for the job.

"Ready when you are, Oberführer."

Knocke checked around the old tank, noticing that everyone had drawn back a respectful distance.

"Driver, ready?"

"À vos ordres, mon General!"

The two officers shared a nod and a grin, and Knocke imagined himself back with his old unit on the steppes of Russia, and could not resist.

"Panzer marche!"

342

Lohengrin was installed on a concrete pedestal outside the Legion Museum at Aubagne, to serve as a permanent reminder of what was both a glorious and disastrously bloody period in the Legion's history.

The old tank made the final three hundred metres without further incident, save the thoroughly understandable tears shed by her crew.

The final act was to fire the 88mm one last time, a specially prepared blank round ready in the breach.

With moist eyes, Köster gave the order and Jarome discharged the final round of the old tank's life.

Those outside were reminded of the power she could still wield, the crack of her cannon loud and all consuming.

Köster pulled off his headset and hung it up for the last time.

"Oberführer, if I may?"

He whispered in Knocke's ear and received a nod.

"Crew dismount and form up!"

The crew emerged from every hatch and formed a line in front of the silent tank, Knocke being the last to climb down, slowed by age and wounds.

He moved to the front of the line to honour Köster's request.

"Stillgestanden!"

The crew braced at attention, their backs to the legend that was Lohengrin, and faces to the legend that was Knocke.

"Kameraden. Your journey has come to an end, along with this fine old lady. Across thousands of miles, alongside thousands of comrades, against thousands of enemies... you have travelled, fought, and survived."

"You have done so under more than one banner. That of Germany, and that of France, but always with respect and comradeship beyond measure. You have honoured your oaths and done your duty, no matter what the hardships."

He nodded at each man in turn, a special acknowledgement for Wildenauer, who had saved his life at Sulisławice, a few months beforehand.

"Your skill at arms has made you and your tank a legend... an object of both respect and fear... not only within the Allied armies, but within the forces of your enemy... praise indeed, Kameraden."

"For my part, it's been a privilege to command you, and just the once… and what seems like a lifetime ago… to fight with you."

For just a moment, those who had been there were back at the awfulness of Brumath, and the memories were bittersweet indeed.

"The Fatherland thanks you."

"France thanks you."

He took a single step forward and came to parade attention.

"And I thank you."

He threw up the most immaculate salute, which the humbled tank crew returned with equal precision.

"Crew… crew… dismissed!"

1965

Crisp was delighted to find an old soldier from his days with the 187th RCT in the rain and snow of Korea in the mugginess and heat of the Republic of Vietnam.

The old sergeant had hugged the same mud around the Han and Imjin Rivers, north of Seoul, and shot a great line about the Chinese bugging out quicker than the GIs could advance and then, more sorrowfully, talked about good boys that had been lost on the mines and booby traps left behind.

The co-pilot announced his presence with a gentle cough.

"Well, Sergeant, those were the days for sure. I gotta go now. Look after yourself and that ankle, and don't rush back."

Crisp indicated the cast on the man's left leg, the product of nothing more complicated than a stumble.

"Sir, yes, sir! Look after yourself too, General."

They exchanged casual salutes and Crisp moved off, keen to get forward to the main 101st base at An Khe, where he was due to assume command of his old division that very day.

"Problem sorted, Lieutenant?"

"Sure is, General. Simple oil leak. The Chief fixed it up, so it's all dandy. We're good to go, Sir."

"Outstanding."

Crisp checked the clock on the tower and decided that it had long since tired of reflecting the right time.

His watch was more accurate.

'Damn it... two fucking hours.'

"Let's get this show on the road then."

He clambered into the back of the Iroquois and selected the two-man flank seat behind the co-pilot, facing out of the pinned-open doorway.

Reaching out, he caressed the M-60, wondering if the enemy might make themselves known and give him a chance to fire a weapon in anger for the last time.

Divisional commanders did not get their hands dirty with such work, not even paratrooper generals, unlike the days of Market Garden,

345

when Gavin carried a rifle alongside his 82nd boys and Urquhart shot Germans up close and personal with his pistol.

A member of the crew checked his belt and gave a thumbs-up to the pilot.

The helicopter's engine increased in pitch and the Huey rose swiftly into the air, heading towards the 101st's headquarters in the Central Highlands.

It didn't take long before the hurried meal Crisp had grabbed started to agitate and remind him of his recently acquired stomach problem, as yet undiagnosed by any of the physicians he had consulted.

Friday, 22nd October 1965, 1200 metres southeast of Ea Riêng, Republic of Vietnam

The pilot made a slightly exaggerated manoeuvre, turning to the left sharper than necessary, hoping to gee up the two-star who, despite the Medal of Honor and array of other awards, had looked decidedly windy from the moment they hit free air.

The turn was the death of him and his co-pilot.

The pitch control mechanism shifted and started to come loose, resulting in an immediate loss of control over the tail rotor.

In a sense, the deaths were caused by a VC mortar attack on the air base the day beforehand, which resulted in the technicians servicing the aircraft running for cover.

They returned and, quite inexplicably, omitted to fix the cotter pins thru the rotor assembly bolts.

The pilot struggled to maintain control as the tail rotor moved freely on the bolts until the assembly separated from the aircraft and fell away.

The Iroquois flipped over and ploughed into the edge of a small lake, crushing the front enough to hold both crew in position under the water.

Despite their struggles, both drowned.

The sole gunner struggled in the water, desperate to drag his body out of the water, but without the benefit of leverage from his broken legs.

Crisp, his face smashed and bleeding by contact with something hard and unyielding, grabbed the struggling airman, screaming in pain as his fingers protested.

The webbing between two, the index and middle fingers on his left hand, had ripped well into the palm, causing excruciating pain as he tried to get a handhold.

Dragging the screaming man up and out of the water, Crisp looked around to assess where to move to next.

Fig #253 - Vietnam 1965

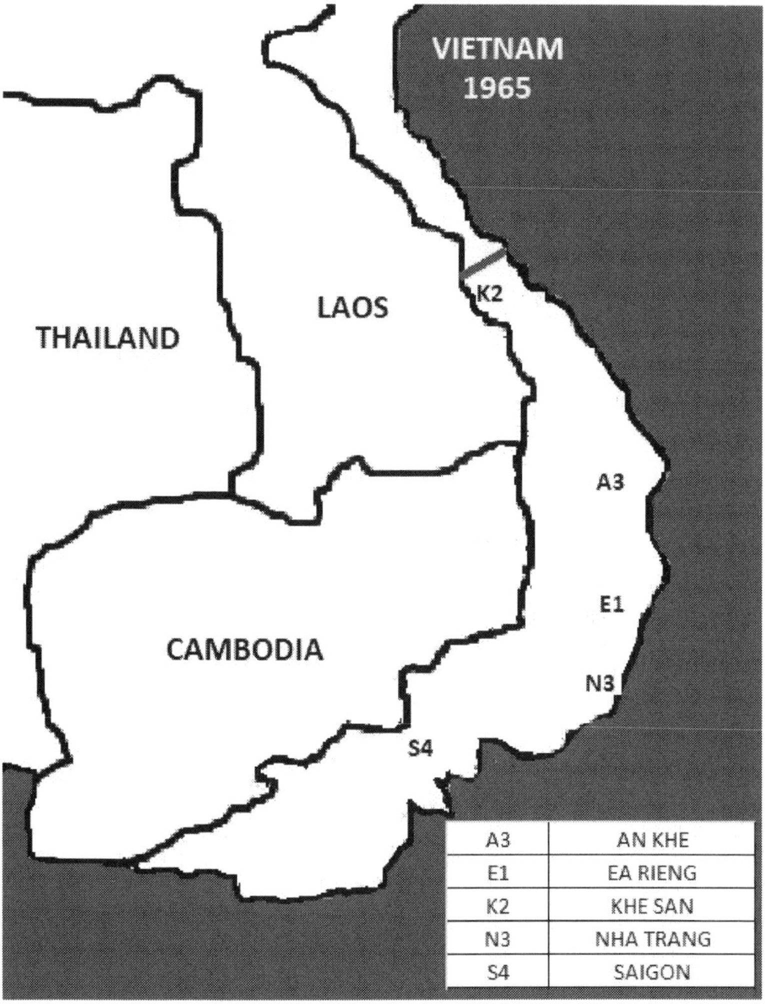
VIETNAM
1965
LAOS
THAILAND
K2
A3
E1
N3
S4
CAMBODIA
A3 AN KHE
E1 EA RIENG
K2 KHE SAN
N3 NHA TRANG
S4 SAIGON

Standing on the back of the co-pilot's seat, he hooked his foot into the dead man's personal weapon strap, bent down and wrapped his arms around the waist of the injured airman and dragged him towards the open hatch.

The man's legs fouled on the bench, causing him incredible pain, something Crisp was immediately aware of as the screams rammed into his brain, overcoming the squealing sound of the engine that was still running, although the rotors had long since fractured and broken away.

Another quick look informed Crisp that he could step out onto a piece of fallen tree, almost without getting his feet back into the water.

Another effort… Crisp wasn't sure who screamed the loudest as the manoeuvre wrought havoc on hand and legs.

The airman, his name tag indicated 'Reece', passed out, much to Crisp's relief.

Getting a good position, one foot on the trunk and the other on the Huey's doorframe, he dragged the unconscious man out of the fuselage and into the bright afternoon sun.

Two more heavy efforts and he collapsed on the lakeside and instantly brought up the contents of his stomach, contents heavily coloured with blood from an internal injury he wasn't even aware of, let alone understood how he'd sustained.

Shouts reached Crisp's ears and his soldier's senses lit up.

'Where the fuck are we? Theirs or ours?'

He released the 1911A from his holster and chambered a round.

Sneaking a look over the tall grass, he noted at least six civilians running like sprinters, directly at the wrecked helicopter.

He quickly assessed his options and decided they were limited to stand and fight, there being no way he could outstrip pursuit with the encumbrance of the insensible airman.

Another look revealed the presence of an AK, in the hands of one of the women.

'Sonofabitch!'

A howl sprang from one of the leading runners.

He had been spotted.

'Shit!'

A burst of fire pattered against the downed helicopter.

Crisp grunted as a round caught him on the end of his elbow, grazing the skin but not creating any damage.

He leaned in and released the crew's M-14, and then suddenly remembered the co-pilot's weapon.

Crisp holstered his 1911 and dropped back into the fuselage to release it.

Acting quickly, he used his knife to cut the AK-47's strap, the co-pilot's chosen weapon. The pilot had stowed an Ithaca 37 shotgun by choice, but that was beyond reach.

Crisp returned to the unconscious airman as more bullets struck the Huey.

He rose up with the AK-47 and put a controlled burst on target, sending the female gunner flying off her feet with the impact of two bullets.

The shouting intensified as the attackers realised their woman was down. More bullets flew and Crisp took a graze on the left shoulder.

He rose again but the intended target had ducked into cover.

The AK spoke briefly but there was no reward of an enemy in distress.

He switched to the right, where the long grass was moving with more than the encouragement of the wind and heard the gasp and squeal as he struck flesh.

A blur caught his eye and two charging VC came into view.

The AK stuttered but he managed to miss both of them.

'Empty! Shit!'

He dropped the AK-47, swept up the M-14 and was immediately rewarded with a burst of crimson as he put a round into the throat of the right-hand man.

Crisp wanted to move, sitting in one place being against all he held dear as a combat soldier, but knew if he did he was abandoning the airman.

Instead, he took a couple of steps to the left and rose up again.

The VC was waiting for him and Crisp felt the impact of bullets.

The body of the helicopter prevented him from falling into the water, and also helped him steady himself for a precision shot.

The bullet took the boy in the face and spread the contents of his head over the long grass behind him.

The other two VC had disappeared, giving Crisp time to reconsider his options.

"How you doing, son?"

The now conscious airman grimaced.

"Just fucking swell, sir," which was spoken in an 'anything but swell' sort of way.

"You hurt too, General?"

"I'm a little too busy to worry about that at the moment. You got morphine?"

"No, sir."

The aircraft's first aid kit was nowhere to be seen.

Crisp held up a finger, as some out of place sound reached his ears.

The tension was unbearable.

He leant down to whisper, keeping his eyes on the long grass around them.

"I'm going to drag you a'ways, son. Gonna hurt."

"Do it."

Crisp got hold of the airman's clothing and was immediately reminded of his damaged hand.

None the less, he pulled the man a few yards into the grass before he had to rest and take stock.

Unslinging the M-14 again, he readied himself but detected no sounds to concern him.

He repeated the cycle twice more before the helicopter was nearly thirty yards away and the two of them were concealed under a lychee tree.

The airman had passed out again, although, in a show of defiance, he had managed to get his pistol out to cover them as Crisp dragged him.

"Best thing for you, son."

Crisp tapped the unconscious man on the chest and wondered where the fresh blood had come from.

A quick check revealed no wound, which meant that it was his own.

Combat can often stimulate a man to such a degree that he loses awareness of himself, but the sight of the blood brought Crisp back down and he felt the pain more keenly.

His stomach was bleeding heavily now, so he pressed a dressing to the wound, trying to recall when he had been hit.

His elbow hurt, his shoulder ached, and he felt sick.

'Shit.'

A piece of wood snapped and instinct took over.

350

The M-14 sent bullets into the grass as he rolled to one side.

The leading VC charged forward, missed by Crisp's hasty burst, but the second in line disintegrated spectacularly as the powerful rounds struck him in numerous places.

The man's weapon, an old PPSh, something Crisp instantly identified, refused to fire and the man ground to a halt, shocked, confused, but knowing he was about to die.

Granted a new lease of life, the paratrooper general aimed and fired, sending the petrified Vietnamese flying back towards his dead comrade.

'Six!'

Crisp sat heavily, misjudging the distance to the ground as his wounds started to affect his functions.

He set the empty M-14 to one side and got his handgun out again.

"That was the most goddamned fucking piece of luck I ever did see, General."

Crisp laughed and brought on a cough, which was accompanied by a bloody discharge from his mouth.

"Yeah, well. Poorly trained, I guess. See the magazine?"

The weapon sported a stick magazine, rather than the more renowned drum version. It was improperly inserted

"Yeah. Don't tell me you saw that before the fucker charged?"

Crisp laughed again.

"Wish I had, soldier. I wouldn't have shat myself then!"

They laughed, not too loudly, given their predicament, but loudly enough to mask the sounds of imminent danger.

The airman took a round in the chest and screamed in extreme pain and fright.

Crisp took yet another wound, the other side of his stomach taking the hammer blow of a pistol round.

He fell over backwards as the force of the heavy bullet overbalanced him and also saved his life.

A second bullet missed him by a fraction of an inch.

His eyes misted with pain and tears, Crisp brought up the M1911A and let rip, unable to aim properly, so concentrating on trying to get something on the darker blob in front of him.

He did, and both attackers went down.

Neither were killed, but they were both out of the fight and with a half a foot across the line between life and death.

'Shit... there were eight.'

He dropped the empty magazine out and slipped a new one home, sending a killing bullet into each of the wounded VC without a second thought.

The sound of an approaching engine helped clear his head, and he looked up just in time to see a Skyraider sweep over the crashed helicopter.

'Go, sandy, go!'

Crisp dragged himself back to his knees and worked to get the airman's dressing out and onto the bleeding wound.

When he was done, he relieved the unconscious man of his sidearm and added it to his ever-increasing collection.

The Skyraider had buzzed around a little, and there had been sounds of it engaging some target a fair distance off.

A second one arrived to relieve the first, which meant that they were probably going to sit top cover until a rescue could be mounted.

Crisp coughed and felt the warm blood fill his mouth.

He suddenly felt incredibly weary and settled himself against the trunk of the Lychee.

He slapped a fly off his face and relaxed.

'I'll let the air force take the strain for a while.'

He was passed out within seconds.

Two more Skyraiders staged their top cover before the rescue mission arrived.

Four choppers from 1st Cav landed in a nearby clearing and the troopers, 3 slicks in total, deployed at speed.

Two slicks spread out to secure the LZ, whilst one group immediately made a beeline for the downed Huey.

The Medevac touched down last, its door gunners primed and ready should things kick off around them.

It took the troopers a little while to recover the bodies of the two pilots, and a little while longer to find Crisp and the other airman, Reece.

The two were carried across to the clearing and loaded into the medevac, alongside the unfortunate pilots.

"Angry Skipper-six, Dustoff-one-niner-two, departing with three KIA, one WIA, inbound your location in two-five, repeat, two-five minutes, over."

"Roger that, Dustoff-one-niner-two, Angry Skipper-six out."

As soon as the Medevac chopper was away from the LZ, the three Hueys filled up with the troopers from 3rd Platoon, D Company, 2nd of the 8th, and the area was left to the VC dead and the now steadily burning Iroquois.

"Angry Skipper-six, Wildcat-three-two-eight actual. Mission accomplished and returning to base. Wildcat-three-two-eight, over."

"Roger. Angry Skipper-six, out."

In the Medevac, the wounded man came round and looked straight up into the medic's face, not the Vietnamese features he had anticipated, but those of a farm boy from Illinois who had done more growing up in his two months in country than the previous twenty years of his life.

"Where am I?"

"Medevac, man, inbound to base and clean sheets. You'll be going home soon, bro. You're one lucky mother-fucker, Reece… one lucky mother-fucker."

At that time, Major General Marion John Crisp was the highest rank to be killed in action during the Vietnamese War, although he was tragically joined by MG John Dillard, who also died when his UH-1 helicopter was shot down over the Central Highlands, ten miles southwest of Pleiku.

Crisp was killed on his first day in the Republic of Vietnam.

He was interred in Arlington Cemetery at a ceremony attended by hundreds of his former soldiers, men who had served with him across WW2, the renewed war, and Korea.

There were others there, men whose presence reflected how the man had been seen by other eyes.

Friedrich August Freiherr von der Heydte, the German paratrooper who had stood alongside Crisp at Sittard-Geleen, supported by an honour guard of survivors from the 6th Fallschirmjager Regiment, who had both fought against and with Crisp over the space of two years.

Lionel Bathwick, the Lord Winsey, who had once brought down fire from HMS Nelson to save Crisp's command at Wollin in Poland.

Sir Roger Marais Dalziel, the First Sea Lord, led the military dignitaries from the United Kingdom, although his involvement with the Viking and Kingsbury missions was still not a matter of public record.

Major General John Ramsey VC was there, recalling the man who should have been called Ryan and one day of fighting by his side against hopeless odds.

Ferdinand Sunday, splendid in his dress uniform and kilt, despite his chronic arthritis, stood side by side with men from the 1st SSF. Charley Bluebear, Rosenberg, Hässler, and Kuibida, the Ukrainian having taken up the offer of US citizenship.

Galkin and Montgomery Hawkes were both there, the former acting as the latter's guarantor for the day release from his psychiatric unit.

Jocelyn Presley, once the highest-ranking female nurse in the US Army, was brought by her grandsons who now cared for her as her body grew weak from respiratory disease and osteoporosis.

Howard Hughes, his eccentricity now the stuff of legend, did not attend but sent flowers by the ton, and a personal message to Eileen Crisp, along with a financial pledge for scholarships in her husband's name.

President Lyndon B. Johnson spoke for some sixteen minutes, praising the efforts of the man who would one day be acknowledged as one of America's finest ever soldiers.

At his own request, it was former President Harry S. Truman who presented Crisp's widow with the flag, on behalf of a grateful nation.

1967

It was a wholly solemn occasion, as it had every right to be.

The moment of the public opening of the Tomb of the Unknown Soldier had come, and the Russian hierarchy and people prepared to pay homage to the millions who had lost their lives in the defence of the Motherland.

The focus was on the Great Patriotic War, in which Nazism was defeated, although the many who died in the subsequent hostilities were also commemorated, in their own way.

The simple star set into a solid base of labradorite, its centre open to allow a gas flame to burn constantly.

It bore a simple inscription…

> **'Your name is unknown,**
> **Your deed is immortal.'**

Behind it was a simple display of an olive branch and soldier's helmet set upon a banner.

In a time of excess and garish memorials across the Soviet Union, the monument was modest and understated and yet, in the estimation of those of high rank and status gathered to witness its public unveiling, perfect.

Guests from around the world, former allies and those who had also been or even still were enemies, found themselves stood side by side in the snow and cold, invited by a Soviet Government that was trying to put an era behind it whilst staking claim to the one ahead.

Heroes, old and new, were on parade.

Marina Yurlova, who emigrated to the USA, was invited back, with full written assurances, a three-time winner of the Cross of St George in the Great War.

She stood two places away from Yuri Gagarin, the first man in space and a Hero of the Soviet Union, soon to be interred within the walls of the Kremlin following a suspicious air crash.

Amongst the crowd of dignitaries were those many military men who had previously eyed each other across the divide, a deliberate act of reconciliation made by those who staged the ceremony, or more accurately, as directed by those who directed those who staged the ceremony.

Work parties had been hard at work, but still the clingy wet snow fell and covered everything.

The band struck up solemn music as the main party arrived.

Leading the way was the General Secretary of the Communist Party, the de facto driver of everything the USSR did and was.

Leonid Ilyich Brezhnev was accompanied by Alexei Kosygin, who together were the new holders of executive power.

Marshal Semichastny and Marshal Zhukov marched side by side, the head of the NKVD and the Defence Minister exchanging quiet, respectful words as they moved into position.

Gromyko, Minister of Foreign Affairs, walked alone, his intended partner, Dmitriy Ustinov, absent with a severe fever.

The procession of the Council of Ministers was followed by a phalanx of military men, and finally, an unexpected guest.

Nikita Khrushchev had aged well, in as much as he was still bald but could easily have looked like the man who stood on the Volga dockside in Stalingrad all those years ago. Ousted from power in a bloodless coup... the public story was a resignation... he had not suffered the fate of those normally removed from power but had been pensioned off and awarded a decent flat in Moscow.

His presence at the ceremony, at the behest of Brezhnev, marked a reconciliation of sorts.

There was no religious invocation, simply a speech made by the General Secretary, one that spoke of honour and glory, the rigours of combat, and the glorious dead.

More than one eye was moist as men who had served recalled comrades long since set beneath the soil, and more than one hardened as they heard a man who had real no idea of combat's rigours wax lyrical about the same.

The gathering held its collective breath as Brezhnev finished and invited forward the man selected over all others.

Bearing the torch on the final stage of its journey from what was left of Leningrad was Major General of Infantry T.N Artem'yev, thrice Hero of the Soviet Union.

On cue, the snow stopped.

Artem'yev marched smartly, not in parade fashion, but as a combat soldier would. He leant forward and the gas ignited, a flame that would burn forever as a memorial to the millions who fell.

The Soviet Union's national anthem was hammered out by the military band and those who could sing did so with incredible gusto, even those who barely knew the language or simply knew the tune, regardless of nationality.

It was that sort of occasion.

The full version echoed off the old walls and it was a moment of great passion for every person there.

There followed a slight shifting of the observers, and then the first ever formal posting of the Kremlin Guard Regiment took place, the highly impressive soldiers immaculately turned out.

Again, the national anthem rang around the Alexander Gardens, before the dignitaries filed away and back towards the warmth of their rooms and offices.

The civilians took the opportunity to more closely inspect the memorial and then drifted away, only to be attracted back as the first change of the guard took place.

At 1800 hours, as requested, Major General John Ramsey attended the site, along with his ever-present NKVD minder.

The man who set the rendezvous place and time was late.

"Mayor General Ramsey. I'm sorry. Business, otherwise I would not leave you waiting in the snow."

In truth, the snow had been shovelled and swept away and no more had fallen, but Ramsey understood that Zhukov was trying to be apologetic.

They exchanged salutes.

"Come. Walk with me."

Without command, the men with Zhukov stepped off to one side and the NKVD minder found something else to do.

It did not go unnoticed by Ramsey, who immediately tensed.

That did not go unnoticed by the Soviet Marshal.

"Relax, tovarich. You have my personal guarantee that you will be returned home after this ceremony. I said that in the invitation, did I not?"

"Yes, Marshal Zhukov, you did…"

"But it never pays to trust anyone eh?"

"Not quite what I meant, Sir."

357

"No, not quite."

They reached the memorial and, without a word, both offered up a salute to the fallen.

"What do you think of it then, General?"

"I actually love its simplicity. Not complicated, Marshal Zhukov. It doesn't... err... detract... is that the right word?"

His Russian was excellent but he was always conscious of the possibility of bad word selection.

"No. Perfectly spoken, General."

"It doesn't detract from the purpose, that of marking the passing of so many."

"No, I agree. There were some who wanted a monument... gold leaf... statues... pah!"

"This is perfect, I think."

"Good. A soldier's memorial, for soldiers, to be understood by soldiers."

Ramsey nodded his understanding and experienced a moment that only a soldier could understand.

Twenty years had passed, but he could still remember some things as if it was yesterday.

"Sir, if I may?"

"You may, General Ramsey."

"Sir, Nazarbayeva... I've heard other rumours..."

"Rumours, General Ramsey?"

Zhukov laughed quietly.

"What rumours have reached your ears, my friend?"

That nearly threw Ramsey... it was probably supposed to do so... but he soldiered on.

"That all was not how it was painted, Sir?"

"How so?"

"That she was an unwitting part of something much greater and became a scapegoat, along with the larger part of the GRU, allowing those who truly plotted the downfall of Comrade Stalin to move forward unimpeded by the stigma of their association with the assassinations. That she was always to be killed in the name of expediency."

"That's a very precise rumour, General Ramsey."

"Yes, Sir, it is."

"How would you like me to respond, General?"

"Is it true, Sir? Was Nazarbayeva the plotter and main force behind the assassination of Stalin and you followed on her coat tails? Was she truly so unhinged by events? Or was she set up, over a period of months, years, to be the sacrificial lamb for your plans?"

"All I will say to you is this. General Ramsey. Lieutenant General Tatiana Nazarbayeva was a patriotic woman who served the Rodina to the best of her ability, right up to the moment she was killed before my eyes. If I had possessed a division like her, I would have been in Berlin in 44. She deserved, and deserves, every honour afforded her before those events, and anything that it is possible to do since. However, she cannot be overtly treasured... she was the scapegoat of a plan that had to succeed in replacing the man of steel and his henchman and therefore she is somehow dishonoured, so we must keep alive her memory in the best ways possible."

"I see, but..."

"That's all I will say. General. I hope you will come to understand my position."

Ramsey considered pushing harder but decided to move on.

"Yes, indeed, Sir. Is it true that there are five bodies interred under the star?"

Zhukov's eyes sparkled.

"Yes. That's true."

"Brought from battlefields all over the Soviet Union, much like the selection for our own unknown soldier."

"Yes, it seemed like an excellent idea, so we copied it. We lost our people far and wide, so we had them brought from all over. Allow me to introduce you to those who were responsible."

Zhukov turned and beckoned towards two men who had been waiting for the signal.

Their feet smashed down on the slabs as they marched in perfect synchronicity, until coming to a halt in front of the Marshal and throwing up tremendous salutes.

"These are the two officers who oversaw the selection of the five bodies. Mayor General Bogdan Pyotrevich Atalin and Mayor General Leonid Vissarionevich Ferovan," the latter of which bore all the hallmarks of someone who had experienced a close brush with a burning tank.

The former was familiar, for a brief encounter in the foyer of the Swedish Embassy half a lifetime ago.

"Under my orders, these two officers brought together a number of remains and then selected five to be permanently installed underneath the star, one at each point."

Zhukov exchanged a look with the two men who were his most trusted aides, men he would entrust with the most important of mission...

...Had entrusted with the most important of missions.

...And the most important of important missions.

"General Ramsey, I understand it's wholly possible that your unknown warrior could be a German... or even worse, a Frenchman!"

Zhukov understood the European enmities extremely well.

"You will understand, that as overseer of this project, I could not take that chance."

"Ah... not so unknown then, Marshal?"

"Not at all unknown, General Ramsey. Come... for your ears only..."

He moved closer to the memorial and pointed at each point of the star in turn.

"An infantryman, a naval marine, a tankie, a paratrooper, and a senior officer... all Russian... all from the very best blood and families that Mother Russia offered to the fighting."

Ramsey nodded, wondering why he was being made privy to such a huge secret.

"The marine was courtesy of your government actually. Took a lot of behind the scenes negotiations."

A light went off in Ramsey's brain, as something he had caught a whiff of some years beforehand came to the fore.

"You know his name, don't you, Sir?"

"Yes, as do you, General Ramsey."

But he didn't...

...did he?

"Fine, then this man, his body brought from France, a paratrooper killed in the earliest hours of the fighting... this man, an older infantry officer killed in 1947. The man you don't know, killed in your own county of Essex, I believe... probably by no lesser person than Comrade Philby."

Zhukov stopped.

Ramsey's face was a picture as he pieced it all together.

"Shall I continue, General, or will you?"

360

Ramsey moved even closer to the monument and indicated the first point that Zhukov had spoken of.

'The infantryman.'

"Yuri?"

He moved again.

'The marine.'

"Ilya?"

"Yes, indeed... well done, John Ramsey."

He moved a fraction.

'The tanker.'

"But Ivan survived, didn't he?"

"Yes."

"Another tanker?"

"Move on for the moment."

He did and pondered the issue, finding a little more in his memory.

"The paratrooper... Vladimir was it? "

"Yes."

The next star point was the prime point, at the head of the star and pointing towards the memorial sculpture.

His mind went into a frenzy.

'No! It can't be?'

"Good grief. I mean... oh Lord."

Zhukov looked sad, and yet happy, his achievement at least known to one other.

"Yes, John Ramsey. I could not do anything to openly honour her, but in death, she lies in the place of highest honour, for ever."

'Tatiana Nazarbayeva!'

"You have the whole fami... the tanker... Ivan survived so... her other son wasn't a tanker... he was NKVD if the file is right?"

"Yes, he was. Unfortunately, his recovery was beyond even I. General Franco was uncooperative."

He declined to say that the Nazarbayev in question was also the bad apple in the bunch and deserved to rot in hell... not that he believed in hell.

"So this one is not a member of the family?"

"No, he's not, General Ramsey."

The sound of striding feet broke the moment, as an aide came rushing in.

361

"I must go, General. I must rely on your discretion, of course."

It was not a question.

"Yes, you may, Marshal… and thank you for sharing this with me. I appreciate the honour."

"How could I not, General Ramsey. And now I must go."

"Sir… the tanker… not a Nazarbayev?"

"No."

Zhukov came to the attention and saluted the memorial, and then turned to Ramsey and offered him the same, which was returned with a mixture of pride and confusion.

"Sir?"

Zhukov smiled and said nothing.

He simply extended his hand and lightly touched the VC on Ramsey's chest.

The Englishman's eyes went wide in an instant, an understanding that Zhukov saw and that motivated him to say more than he intended.

"A true hero… a wonderful soldier… a great leader of men… a warrior… and a fantastic human being."

"That's him to a tee, Sir."

Zhukov laughed.

"So it may be, but I quote from his diary… words he wrote of you. Good day, General Ramsey."

Within seconds, Ramsey was alone with the monument.

Alone with Ilya, Vladimir, Yuri, and Tatiana.

And with Arkady Arkadyevich Yarishlov, his friend.

The tears came, despite his best efforts, the moment so overwhelming that he even sobbed aloud, his tears falling where snow had fallen a few scant hours beforehand.

On the spur of the moment, he decided on a gesture, one of great significance to him and, he was sure, one that would have been appreciated for what it was by the man who was both his enemy and his friend.

He saluted and then unpinned the VC from his chest and gently placed it on the point under which Yarishlov's remains were laid to rest.

Stepping back, he came smartly to attention, saluted again, and took a few minutes to compose himself and say his final farewells, knowing instinctively he would never return.

Ramsey marched proudly away, leaving the simple bronze medal lying on top of the memorial star, a tribute to the man interred beneath.

It lies there to this day.

When the time of reckoning comes, it is not what you said or aspired to be, but what you did and achieved that will count, and that alone will decide how you will be judged by those who come after.

Ernst-August Knocke

1975

Monday, 14th July 1975, Hôtel du Palais, Biarritz, France.

Bastille Day.

The day of military parades throughout the main cities in France.

Though not a garrison town as such, Biarritz had staged its own affair and the modest procession of the local infantry and cavalry units had been cheered all the way along its route.

The parade long since over, the onlookers had returned to their daily business or their celebrations, depending on their plans, and the visitors to one of France's favourite seaside locations had taken station by the beaches and bars to soak up the sun and consume all that the cafes and restaurants could offer.

One such group of visitors had drawn attention from the very moment that they had emerged from the Hôtel du Palais, and still did, despite being quietly sat outside the old hotel, talking softly and watching the world go by.

More than one old veteran made himself known or young child pushed forward to ask questions of those who looked so resplendent in their uniforms.

Ernst-August Knocke, long since retired, still looked every inch the ultimate soldier in his uniform, greatly assisted by the medals and awards that seemingly hung from every point.

His wife, the indomitable Anne-Marie, looked equally as good, her colonel's uniform laden with the rewards her government had bestowed upon a woman who had served bravely and faithfully for all her adult life.

The third also wore a general's uniform.

Haefali had become a great friend to the Knockes.

He had also become their son-in-law and father of their only grandchild, a son born to Knocke's eldest daughter, Greta.

Despite their twenty-five year age difference, they were devoted to each other, and the relationship had received the full blessing of both her proud parents.

Magda had never married, being more harnessed to her work than any one person, the mysteries of her Thermodynamic Physics post with EDF holding sway over all other matters, save for her love of family.

She sat explaining some work matter to Greta's son, Jules, who had also developed a bent for learning, and was studying physics at the Sorbonne.

Anne-Marie was chatting with a woman who proudly wore her resistance medal, exchanging pleasantries and reflecting on less savoury times.

Knocke, now in his seventy-seventh year, had as keen a mind and sharp an eye as ever and shared quiet observations on the passers-by with his friend and son-in-law Albrecht Haefali, and his son Jürgen , clad in the uniform of the Academy of Saint-Cyr, to which he would soon travel to undergo three years training as a French officer.

He was considered too young for the academy by the powers-that-be, until 'powers' with more clout advised them otherwise and Jürgen Knocke became the second youngest officer cadet to wear the proud uniform of the École Spéciale Militaire de Saint-Cyr.

The day was hot, uncomfortably so without shade, but a steady supply of cold beer helped ease the men's burdens.

Serge Gallet, an old legionnaire who had served at Sulisławice, had been visiting the town and identified himself to his former commander.

They had all shared a beer until Gallet's wife had started to feel unwell.

Taking his leave, Gallet faithfully promised to attend the Legion Corps D'Assaut reunion at Sassy the following October.

Both officers relaxed in their seats and enjoyed the gentle sea breeze, occasionally sparing an amused eye at Jürgen and his attempts to remain poised and officer-like at all times.

"Relax, son. Just relax."

"Yes, papa."

The old resistance fighter took her leave and Anne-Marie looked around the table, enjoying the sight of the three men in her life fully at ease, as she was herself.

A man in his forties was stood to one side, taking furtive glances at them, in between consulting an old newspaper cutting and well-thumbed letters.

His mind wrestled with the problems the evidence of his eyes posed before he reached a decision and chose to act.

Reuben Mandl tucked the precious letters back into his inside jacket pocket and checked his trouser pocket, finding reassurance in the cold metal.

He walked forward but deflected away from the table at the last moment, his movement drawing an enquiring look from Greta Haefali.

Instinctively, she followed the man's movements until he disappeared from sight, not having looked back once.

She relaxed again and accepted the offer of a cigarette from her husband.

More cold beers arrived and they settled back into quiet conversation, mainly about Albrecht Haefali's impending posting to Chad.

What happened next took place in the space of a handful of seconds.

Reuben Mandl came back into sight on the edge of Greta's peripheral vision, but it was the reappearance of his yellow shirt set her alarm bells ringing.

Jules finished his scribbling and offered the result to his auntie, who cautiously agreed with his results.

Anne-Marie noticed the look on her other step-daughter's face and automatically reached to her holster.

Knocke threw his head back in laughter as Haefali finished his joke about Chadian cuisine.

A waiter moved in front of Mandl, who was intent on his target.

Jürgen Knocke spilled his beer in a fit of giggles.

The waiter went flying and, unluckily, careened into Magda, who was on her way to her feet.

The rest of the party turned their attention towards the floundering waiter and the attacker lunged over the table, even as Anne-Marie brought her pistol up.

The blade went home as the automatic sent the first of three shots into Reuben Mandl.

Greta recovered her balance and launched herself into the assailant, who, in turn, smashed into Magda's lap, his blood decorating both sisters.

366

Anne-Marie was instinctively on her feet, weapon ready to finish the job she had started.

Greta Haefali, a fully-fledged agent of the SDECE, held Mandl in a vice-like grip, ready to extinguish any signs of resistance.

There were none forthcoming.

Even though he was alive, he had already begun his journey to a darker place.

She checked for the weapon he had been holding, but could not find it.

The knife in question was firmly lodged in the chest of Ernst-August Knocke.

"Ernst! Cherie! Doctor! We need a doctor!"

Anne-Marie, her eyes wide open, took one look at the weapon sticking out of her husband's chest and understood with awful clarity that the attacker would not be dying alone.

Haefali lowered the grievously wounded Knocke to the ground, grabbing seat cushions to put under his friend's head.

Magda's constant metronomic screaming punctuated the whole scene.

"Shut up, Magda!"

Anne-Marie dropped by her husband's side, her face already showing the tracks of tears as she tenderly ran her hand over him.

"Oh my darling, my love."

Magda's screams grew louder.

Knocke's lips moved but no sound could be heard.

Magda's screaming stopped as Greta slapped her hard across the face.

She grabbed her head in her hands and spoke softly but firmly.

"Shut up, Magda. Our father is dying. Do you want the last thing he hears to be your racket? Now shut up."

Haefali moved away from Knocke's still form to allow his wife to be with her father.

He focussed on the man whose blood was running in rivulets across the pavement.

"Why? You bastard, why?"

Mandl turned his head wearily, taking in the uniform before he took in the man.

"SS... his men..."

367

A huge gobbet of blood and phlegm accompanied a brace of coughs.

"His men... his orders... killed my... father...Ahron ..."

More blood came, not just from the mouth, but from the nostrils and open throat wound too. Bubbling and bright red, signifying mortal wounds.

"Killed your father? Where did he kill your father?"

"Mezi..."

Mandl choked on blood, but pushed on, keen for his enemies to know why.

"Meziroli... Cze... Czechoslova..."

Haefali searched his memory and remembered a conversation with Hässelbach and Jorgensen.

He remembered it only too well, as the details leapt into place in an instant.

"The journalist... the man from Theresienstadt?"

"Ye... yes... my father was in... the camp... a journalist... yes."

Mandl groaned as the pain almost overcame his will to speak.

Almost.

"That bast... bastard... killed him... SS bastard!"

Haefali shot a quick look at his friend, whose face was screwed up in his efforts to resist screaming at the pain.

He turned back to the dying Mandl.

"You fucking idiot! He didn't kill your father, he saved him... fed him... had him tended to... and sent him on his way with documents... everything... you stupid, stupid idiot!"

"No!"

The coughing went deeper in tone and action, sending a spurt of blood over Haefali's face.

"Yes! He saved your father! What have you done, you fucking fool?"

Mandl pawed for the documents and held them aloft in a bloody hand.

"I have th... have the proof!"

"You've nothing... nothing at all... except guilt to take to your fucking grave! You've killed a good man!"

People gathered around the tableau, keeping a distance at first, partially because guns were on display, partially because of desire not to intrude.

Greta knelt beside her husband.

With a quiet voice that held all the menace he had ever thought existed, she asked a simple question.

"Have you finished asking questions, Albrecht?"

"Err..."

"Good."

With a single movement, Greta took the table knife from her other hand and swept it in an arc, using every essence of her being.

With tremendous force, she brought the rounded blade down into Mandl's eye socket and ploughed into the brain beyond.

His body and mind resisted for a few seconds before both gave up the struggle and death embraced him.

The sound of crying reached Haefali through the fog of the shock at what he had just witnessed.

Anne-Marie sobbed uncontrollably, her stepdaughter Magda holding both her and the dead body of her father in the tightest of embraces.

Jules held them both.

Jürgen was on his knees, bloody hands on his thighs, his face drained of colour, his eyes leaking liquid grief.

A gendarme, summoned by the commotion and crowd, pushed his way to the front of the throng and opened his mouth to speak.

Wisely, he decided against the idea, as both Haefali and his wife gave him a look that advised him to leave matters be for the moment, if he knew what was good for him.

He did, and used the moment to instruct a civilian to summon more assistance.

The man was dispatched and the gendarme assessed the scene before him.

Four uniformed officers of the French Army, one of whom was clearly dead.

A dead man in civilian clothing who he reasonably concluded was the assailant.

A young man, clearly not military, grieving for the man in uniform.

One civilian, a woman, covered with the blood of one or both of the dead, his keen eye noting the different colours of blood on her clothing, and then the spreading bruise across the left side of her face.

A police sergeant arrived, closely followed by an officer with more men, and the scene was brought under control.

A civilian photographer was persuaded to expend his film stock on recording the evidence on camera, which he did with great gusto and feigned professional precision.

Witnesses were chivvied to one side where statements were taken.

Other gendarmes surrounded the scene, where a man in the uniform of a general of France lay surrounded by people weeping, a scene that the senior officer was reluctant to disturb.

He already sensed that this whole episode could make or break him.

In actuality, things were much worse than the police officer could ever have imagined and he had no comprehension of what lay ahead, given the identity of the bloodied man and the organisation to which two of the women belonged.

He ventured forward and addressed Haefali directly, selecting the senior officer present for two reasons. Firstly, he was slightly detached from the group and secondly, that he looked slight less murderous than the three women cradling the dead officer.

"Général. I'm Capitaine Rousseau. What happened here?"

Haefali told the story in even terms and with great control.

"Why?"

"Because he made a mistake."

"A mistake? Explain, please, mon Général."

Haefali transferred the blood-stained letters to the Gendarme officer.

"He misunderstood these... apparently."

The photographer placed himself in great peril as he tried too hard to get the best possible shot of the deceased officer.

Anne-Marie's voice sent a chill down Haefali and the gendarme at distance, so what it did to the tourist cameraman was anyone's guess.

"Any closer and you will die."

The man wisely retreated and took his photos from a position where Haefali and the capitaine were between him and the grieving Amazon.

"We'll need statements from all of your party, mon Général."

"We're staying here, at the Hôtel du Palais, Capitaine Rousseau."

"Thank you, mon Général... err... the deceased... the dead officer. Who is he?"

370

"Général de Division Ernst-August Knocke."

"Ah... I see... the SS Général. That might explain things."

Rousseau said it without thinking, remembering some of the press coverage that related to the disbanding of the German elements of the Legion, the subsequent promotion of Knocke to the highest ranks of the French Army, and the protests that went hand in hand with the kudos and awards heaped upon him and his men.

Haefali stiffened up.

"Yes, he was once a soldier on the Waffen-SS. But he died as a legionnaire and a soldier of France."

In accordance with Knocke's last expressed wishes, his remains were cremated and then taken on a journey to rest with his men.

Not with Von Arnesen and the early legionnaires who died in and around the Vosges, nor with the men of the 2nd SS who died in the final days in Austria in 1945.

In life, he had spoken on the matter with Haefali, with his son, and with the veterans who came to visit the family home in Nogent L'Abbesse, or whom he encountered at the numerous military reunions and parades to which the old soldier was constantly drawn.

Anne-Marie headed up the family group that travelled the hundreds of miles to a place that would become special to them, as it had become to their lost one.

Nietuja, Poland.

The Legion Cemetary that contained the many fallen from the battles on the Koprzywianka River and specifically, Sulisławice.

There, in a quiet and private ceremony, or as quiet and private a ceremony can be when attended by thousands of old soldiers drawn there to honour a man who had inspired them through the worst times imaginable, the remains of Ernst-August Knocke were laid to rest.

He was in good company, surrounded as he was by those who had gone before.

Those who attended walked between the headstones and spoke to comrades long departed, hearing their voices as if they were casually discussing current events over a cigarette and a glass of schnapps.

The grave of the mad anti-tank gunner, Wagner was next to that of Emmercy the brave.

Felix Jorgensen, the commander of the 1ᵉʳ Régiment Blindé lay surrounded by the men of his command who perished in the defence of the insignificant Polish town.

Maillard the gendarme, who had injured Knocke during Molyneux's attempted arrest, and who redeemed himself so completely in his final battle, lay close to Renat-Challes.

Surrounded by the gentiles who had long been his comrades lay Yitzhak Rubenstein, the old Jewish legionnaire who had worked with Knocke and Haefali at the Chateau du Haut-Koenigsbourg.

On the memorial wall was the plaque to commemorate the passing of Rolf Peters, the rocket gunner, whose remains were not yet identified.

In total agreement with Haefali's recommendation, the family had approved that the old soldier should be laid to rest in a grave that completed a rectangular plot of four.

And so it was that Ernst-August Knocke was finally reunited with his old crewman, Lutz, the indomitable Celestin St.Clair, and a man he had admired as a consummate soldier; Rolf Uhlmann.

The rain started to fall more heavily and the mourners drifted away, resolving to return the following day before starting the long journey back to wherever they now called home.

The Knocke family, tired by the mental exertions of saying goodbye to their figurehead and by dealing with the steady stream of well-wishers and story tellers, made their way back to the waiting cars, leaving only Haefali and a few others in possession of the field of remembrance.

"Mon Général?"

"In a moment… wait for me in the car please."

Haefali's driver returned to usher the family into the waiting limousine, as Haefali strode deeper into the cemetery, resolved to pay one final tribute to the man he had admired and loved.

Alone, beaten by the rain and lashed by the increasing wind, he spoke softly to those who could no longer hear him.

"May his great name be exalted,
And sanctified in the world which he created,
According to his will.
May he establish his kingdom,

And may his Salvation blossom and His anointed be near,
During your lifetime, and during your days,
and during the lifetimes of all the House of Israel,
Speedily and very soon, and say Amen."

Haefali waited but no response came, for he was quite alone.

"May his great name be blessed forever, and to all eternity.
Blessed and praised, glorified and exalted,
extolled and honoured, adored and lauded be the name of the Holy one.
Blessed be he above and beyond all the blessings.
Hymns, praises, and consolations that are uttered in the world.
And say amen."

He swore to his dying day that the growing wind carried the sound of familiar voices raised in unison.
"Amen."

Haefali wept.
"Amen."

THE VERY END.

[If you have borrowed this work on Kindle, please can you log back into Kindle at your earliest convenience to ensure Amazon receive an update on the pages you have read. Thank you.]

Glossary.

1st SSF

1st Special Service Force. Once a unit that served in the Italian campaign, I reconstituted it for the purpose of Operation Kingsbury/Viking.

Avro York

British four-engine transport aircraft derived from the Lancaster bomber.

Banya

Simply put, a sauna. To the Russian, a meeting place for gossip as well, and the buildings are often large and hold a number of other facilities, such as massage and bathing areas.

C-46 Curtiss Commando

Twin-engine US transport aircraft with a range of 3150 miles.

CEAM

Actually produced as a prototype around 1950, I brought forward this French weapon, a development of the ST-44. 7.92mm Kurz in a 30 round magazine.

CZ1927

Czech designed semi-automatic pistol carrying 8 .32ACP cartridges.

De Havilland Hornet

The DH103 Hornet was a twin-engine fighter developed privately by De Havilland and using many of the successful techniques used in the Mosquito, to which aircraft it bore more than a passing resemblance. It had a top speed of 475 mph and carried 4 x 20mm Hispano V cannon, with the additional capability to carry 2 x 1000 lb bombs and 8 x RP-3 rockets.

EDF

Électricité de France, France's main provider of energy.

FL-282	The Flettner Hummingbird [Kolibri] was a single-seat rotor helicopter which is rated as the first production series helicopter in the world. There was a B2 version that included an observer as its primary use by that time was for artillery support.
FUBAR	Fucked up beyond all recognition.
Gaz-61	Soviet four-wheel drive car popular with senior Red Army officers. 3.5-litre engine.
Glühwürmchen	See FL-282. The Glühwürmchen exists only in my mind.
Grumman G-44 Widgeon	US designed twin-engine amphibian that served with the USN, USAAF, Royal Navy, US Coastguard, and CAP. Capable of carrying five persons, it was mainly used for short range patrolling and communications.
Hercules H-4	The Spruce Goose, Howard Hughes' immense amphibian. It had but one brief flight, and was then mothballed.
Iroquois	Nicknamed 'The Huey' the Bell UH-1 Iroquois was an all-purpose helicopter produced in the fifties, and which famously saw great service during the Vietnam War.
Ithaca 37	A pump-action shotgun first produced in 1937, and that remains in production to this day [2017]. It could carry 4, 5, or 7 shells internally, of 12, 16, 20, or 28 gauge.

Jasper	The Jasper is a figment of my imagination. It is suggested to be a rehash of Barnes-Wallis' designs on earth penetrating bombs [such as grand slam and tallboy]. The concept is to allow the bomb to go deep into the ground before exploding an atomic warhead, specifically designed to deal with underground installations such as the VNIIEF facility as Uspenka.
Li-2	Lisunov-2, a license-built Soviet copy of the Douglas DC-3.
L-pill	Developed by British and American agencies to give to agents working in dangerous areas. It was an oval capsule filled with Potassium Cyanide and covered with rubber to prevent accidental breakage, and was often kept in a false tooth.
M-14	US produced automatic rifle that replaced the Garand as the general issue US rifle. It fires the 7.62mm bullet, contained in a detachable 20-round magazine.
M20 Super Bazooka	US designed 88.9mm calibre rocket launcher that had the capacity to penetrate roughly 280mm of steel at a range of 300 metres using a HEAT warhead. [Info differs greatly!]
M-60	US manufactured general-purpose machine gun firing 7.62mm, first introduced in 1957.
Mosquito FB-20 Cranefly	A figment of my imagination, the FB-20 Cranefly [a play on Daddy long-legs] is intended to be very long-range development of the Mosquito.
NS23 cannon	Nudelmann-Suranov 23mm aircraft cannon mounted a numerous Soviet aircraft from 1944 onwards.

Operation Kingsbury	The 1st SSF ground operation against Camp 1001 and the VNIIEF facility at Uspenka, Russia.
Operation Teardrop	A USN operation that would mobilise four carrier groups to prosecute any likely missile submarine approach to the Eastern Seaboard of the USA.
Operation Viking	The overall operation that combined the airborne, land, and diversionary elements against Camp 1001 and the secret VNIIEF facility at Uspenka, Russia.
Paukenschlag	The second happy time, from roughly 1/1942-8/1942, when U-Boats roamed the east coast of the USA and destroyed over 600 ships, many within sight of land.
Prüfstand XII	In English, Test stand 12. By the war's end, there was one completed version, and two over half-finished. They operated exactly as described in the book.
Rakija	Fruit brandy.
Saint-Cyr	École Spéciale Militaire de Saint-Cyr is located in Coëtquidan, France, and is the premier French military academy.
North American F-82 Twin Mustang	Last piston engine fighter ordered for use by the USAF. Based on the original Mustang, it was conceived as a very long-range fighter escort. It looked precisely like its name; a twin fuselage version of the original war horse. It could be manned by one or two personnel, and original versions had dual controls. It had 6 x .50cal M3 Brownings, and could also carry 25 x 5" rockets or 4 x 1000 lb bombs.
UBDA	Yugoslavian State Security.

V2	Also known as the A-4, the V2 was a liquid fuelled long-range rocket that could deliver a warhead approaching 1000 kilogrammes to nearly two hundred miles distance.
Wren torpedo	The G7es [T5] 'Zaunkönig' [Wren], or Gnat as it was known to the Royal Navy, was an electric torpedo that had passive and active sonar detection.

The Red Queen

An ever-present on the covers of the series, the Red Queen symbolises the major player, the one who held the most sway over events.

The Queen is damaged, the representations on the chess piece equivalent to the wounds sustained by Tatiana Nazarbayeva.

Bibliography

Rosignoli, Guido
The Allied Forces in Italy 1943-45
ISBN 0-7153-92123

Kleinfeld & Tambs, Gerald R & Lewis A
Hitler's Spanish Legion - The Blue Division in Russia
ISBN 0-9767380-8-2

Delaforce, Patrick
The Black Bull - From Normandy to the Baltic with the 11th
Armoured Division
ISBN 0-75370-350-5

Taprell-Dorling, H
Ribbons and Medals
SBN 0-540-07120-X

Pettibone, Charles D
The Organisation and Order of Battle of Militaries in World War
II
Volume V - Book B, Union of Soviet Socialist Republics
ISBN 978-1-4269-0281-9

Pettibone, Charles D
The Organisation and Order of Battle of Militaries in World War
II
Volume V - Book A, Union of Soviet Socialist Republics
ISBN 978-1-4269-2551-0

Pettibone, Charles D
The Organisation and Order of Battle of Militaries in World War
II
Volume VI - Italy and France, Including the Neutral Countries of
San Marino, Vatican City [Holy See], Andorra and Monaco
ISBN 978-1-4269-4633-2

Pettibone, Charles D
The Organisation and Order of Battle of Militaries in World War II
Volume II - The British Commonwealth
ISBN 978-1-4120-8567-5

Chamberlain & Doyle, Peter & Hilary L
Encyclopaedia of German Tanks in World War Two
ISBN 0-85368-202-X

Chamberlain & Ellis, Peter & Chris
British and American Tanks of World War Two
ISBN 0-85368-033-7

Dollinger, Hans
The Decline and fall of Nazi Germany and Imperial Japan
ISBN 0-517-013134

Zaloga & Grandsen, Steven J & James
Soviet Tanks and Combat Vehicles of World War Two
ISBN 0-85368-606-8

Hogg, Ian V
The Encyclopaedia of Infantry Weapons of World War II
ISBN 0-85368-281-X

Hogg, Ian V
British & American Artillery of World War 2
ISBN 0-85368-242-9

Hogg, Ian V
German Artillery of World War Two
ISBN 0-88254-311-3

Bellis, Malcolm A
Divisions of the British Army 1939-45
ISBN 0-9512126-0-5

Bellis, Malcolm A
Brigades of the British Army 1939-45
ISBN 0-9512126-1-3

Rottman, Gordon L
FUBAR, Soldier Slang of World War II
ISBN 978-1-84908-137-5

Schneider, Wolfgang
Tigers in Combat 1
ISBN 978-0-81173-171-3

Stanton, Shelby L.
Order of Battle – U.S. Army World War II.
ISBN 0-89141-195-X

Forczyk, Robert
Georgy Zhukov
ISBN 978-1-84908-556-4

Kopenhagen, Wilfried
Armoured Trains of the Soviet Union 1917 - 1945
ISBN 978-0887409172

Korpalski, Edward
Das Fuhrerhauptquartier [FHQu], Wolfschanze im bild.
ISBN 83-902108-0-0

Nebolsin, Igor
Translated by Stuart Britton.
Stalin's Favourite - The Combat History of the 2nd Guards Tank
Army from Kursk to Berlin. Volume 1: January 1943-June 1944.
ISBN 978-1-909982-15-4

The war approaches its end.
On each side, the soldiers, sailors,
and airmen steel themselves for the final efforts.
In Russia, the conspirators continue to plot
the overthrow of the regime
that has crippled their country.
In the Allied nations, particularly America,
the pressures to use atomic bombs
to end the war mount.
Around the peace table in Sweden,
the pursuit of a negotiated armistice
appears to continue unchecked, despite
both alliances' continued readiness
to wreak unspeakable acts of violence upon the other.
In the cold waters of the North Atlantic,
on the tiny island of Cyprus,
and airbases in Iran and Russia, men
whose actions will change the world
prepare to do their duty to the land of their fathers.

The original pic, the fallen leaves being particularly poignant.

Read the opening section of the new series by Colin Gee now...

THE CHANCELLOR CHRONICLES

1800 hrs, 20th July 1916, the Sugarloaf, Fromelles, France.

They came on and on, the young Australians unaware of the horrendous test that awaited them.

5th Australian Division had not served at Gallipoli, nor anywhere of note for that matter, save the transit through Egypt like all their brothers in arms from the ANZACs.

This was their initiation in the great game, and their generals had thrown them forward in an attempt to eliminate the bulge in the line centred around Fromelles.

"Feuer!"

The order was shouted up and down the trench line, leaping from a score of lips as it was repeated by officers and NCOs along the defensive German line.

A subterfuge used by the attackers had worked, at least in part.

The mock show of an assault force using dummies and flashing bayonets having lured the defenders back into position on two occasions, only for more offensive artillery to plaster the trenches where the infantry of 6th Bavarian Reserve Infantry Division stood ready to repulse the assault.

Numerous MG08/15s and a handful of captured Vickers sent streams of bullets into the advancing colonial infantry.

The bolt-action Mauser 98 rifles added their own kind of grief.

Counter-artillery and mortars pitched in causing whole groups of men to disappear in a flash.

But still they came on, shrugging off the casualties as if not even one man even noticed the gaps that were torn in their ranks.

A feldwebel struggled through a smashed section of trench, studiously ignoring the pieces of ravaged flesh that had once been comrades.

"Herr Hauptmann! Machine gun ammunition's low in First Kompagnie. We've lost two caches to their fucking artillery. Need more sent up immediately."

"Scheisse, Schmidt! The phone cable's been cut by the Tommy guns. I've men out fixing it."

He pointed to the rear as, on cue, three shells landed in the direction of the battalion headquarters.

Although neither man spoke of the sight, both felt that they had seen living men tossed into the air by the force of the collective blasts.

'The wire party?'

"Send another repair team, Herr Hauptmann?"

They had shared the same awful thought.

Wiedemann looked around him, and then to the enemy.

"No time...Runner!"

A gefreiter arrived in the blink of an eye.

Wiedemann quickly scribbled out an order for the messenger.

The three men ducked as a trench mortar got a round extremely close, eliciting screams from some unfortunates.

"Get back to the reserve line and get work parties organised. We need machine-gun ammunition brought up immediately. Everything they've got. Here's your orders. For Yahweh's sake, keep your head down and run like the very devil is at your heels, Adi!"

"Jawohl, Herr Hauptmann."

The man leapt away as fast as his feet could carry him, moving in the distinctive crouching run that marked a veteran, and a survivor.

A young leutnant, barely out of school, arrived as the runner departed.

"Herr Hauptmann, we're low on machine gun ammunition!"

"Relax, Heinrich, relax. I've sent a runner for more."

The young man wiped a stream of blood from his eyes, his forehead opened by a piece of something unknown that had travelled at high speed and nearly claimed his life.

"I hope he gets through, Sir."

"Adi always gets through!"

The two saluted their company commander and returned to their men.

Wiedemann turned back to examine the advancing men, clad in khaki and wearing the distinctive pudding bowl helmets.

A whistle sounded to his left, indicating an order to fix bayonets.

He promised himself to reprimand Leutnant Heinrich Obermeyer... if the boy survived the action.

A huge explosion to the rear turned his thoughts back to the runner.

'He'll get through. Adi Hitler always does... always...'

Part One of the Chancellor Chronicles series will be released in 2018.

31113295R00212

Printed in Great Britain
by Amazon